Durra Durra

Dual Fortunes

Book Three of
The Durra Durra Trilogy

J.A.Wells

Dedication

How I came about imagining the world of my ancestor, James Baker Waldon, and telling his tale, was due to the meticulous research carried out by genealogist. Marcia McIntyre. Therefore, it is to her I wish to dedicate *The Durra Durra Trilogy*. Thank you Marcia for inspiring me to bring life to a man from the past, to the present.

Acknowledgments

The manifestation and writing of *Durra Durra*, book three of *The Durra Durra Trilogy*, would not have been possible without the kind support and inspiration of my dear friend, Diane Challenor, who has been a stalwart believer in the project from the very beginning. In addition, had it not been for the revelations regarding my heritage, provided by Marcia McIntyre, this novel would never have come into existence. I would also like to extend my sincere thanks to G.A. Mawer for providing me with his vivid description of life on a transport ship, in his book *"Most Perfectly Safe - The Convict Shipwreck Disasters of 1832-42"*.

Hitherto, I am highly indebted to The State Library of New South Wales, and especially The Mitchell Library, for its extensive research resources, which were invaluable in the creation of *The Durra Durra Trilogy*.

My gratitude also extends to Google, Wikipedia, and Ancestry.com, because without their in-depth databases none of the attempts to create accurate detail would have been possible.

Finally, I would like to express my special gratitude and thanks to my group of willing first-readers for giving this novel such attention and time, and in so doing, making publication possible.

J.A.Wells
2019

About the book

The adventures of James Baker Waldon continue in *Durra Durra*, the third book of *The Durra Durra Trilogy*.

In the previous book, **Mutt Mutt Billy,** two eventful voyages took place, ten years apart; the first bringing young Luke Reddall to the colony of New South Wales where he eventually becomes a gentleman pastoralist. The second brought James Waldon, a convict, serving a fourteen-year sentence for a crime of which he was innocent. Once in the colony, James began his new life as an assigned servant to his master, Luke Reddall. *Durra Durra* continues their story.

In England, a young Victoria has ascended the throne; while, at the home of Lady Edwina Soame, in the fashionable City of Bath, she confides to the blacksmith, John Baker, a secret she has guarded with her life, requesting he journey to the far side of the world, in order to reveal to a young man his true identity.

Meanwhile, away in the colony of New South Wales, James Baker Waldon is establishing a new farm for his master, Luke Reddall, many miles to the south of Luke's previous farm, Mutt Mutt Billy. Here James meets someone who will fill an empty place in his heart.

Tragedy strikes; land is razed; natives attack; bushrangers strike a disastrous blow, parting friends and loved ones forever. Except for Luke and James the story is far from over; both discovering that good-fortune can sometimes prevail over sadness.

About the author

The idea of a Renaissance man may be regarded as old fashioned these days, and rather a cliché. However, the phrase can be forgiven when applied to J.A.Wells. After a twenty-year career as a professional actor on the British stage, then a further twenty years as an artist, J.A.Wells has added storyteller to his list of talents.

Since capturing the world of decadence, laughter and gaiety of the Jazz Age, in his debut novels *The Merry Millionaire*, and its sequel *Pomp and Circumstance*, in his latest narrative, *The Durra Durra Trilogy*, J.A.Wells transports us through a sweeping, panoramic saga, to the far side of the world, to the time of Australia's pioneering past.

The colourful cast of characters J.A. Wells conjures in his stories, stem from actual people from his family's past. Thus, in this way he succeeds to put flesh on their bones, at the same time breathing life into the hearts of souls, long since departed.

J.A.Wells leaves no stone unturned, and is currently immersed in his next narrative that delves into yet another aspect of Australia's exciting and colourful past.

Part One
Searching for the Lost

Chapter One

"Isn't Bath beautiful, even when it's raining. Until the day I die, I'll never tire of seeing it."

In her mind, Emma Baker heard Edwina's words, as if her friend had spoken them that very second. But now the once cosy sitting room, its windows commanding a glorious vista of Bath, felt desolate and void without Edwina's presence.

Emma folded the letter and gazed out at the city, although she saw little of it through the rain drenched windowpane, and her own tears. Her mistress was dead. Emma hardly dare think it, the idea so dreadful to contemplate. Suddenly, she needed to sit down, and with difficulty, she crossed the drawing room, and sat on the sofa. Smoothing her black satin mourning dress, and wiping her eyes, Emma stared at her mistress' chair beside the fireplace. How often had she watched Edwina working at her embroidery or reading the latest novel?

For a long while, Emma knew her friend was unwell, Edwina appearing tired and listless, often falling asleep in her chair, in the middle of the day. However, when the decline finally came, it was rapid, causing everyone distress, quickly turning a house once full of joy and merriment, into one of sorrow.

It was ten years almost to the day, since they moved into Oakwood, Emma remembering the early heady days, as they established the school. How marvellous it had been to see Lady

Soame's rheumatism cured by the assistance of Bath's remarkable remedial waters. Everything was running so well, until that dreadful day in March. A day when all sense of order and justice disappeared from the world.

***

"He's gone!" Lizzie screamed. "We'll never see him again."

"Please, my dear," Henry implored. "You'll be ill if you carry on so."

Lizzie held him, her hands gripping his arms, as if she were clinging to her own sanity.

"But what happened?" she wailed. "James would never do such a thing. Never."

Henry Waldon took his wife in his arms.

"I've told you Lizzie. It was Soame. He set it up. He admitted the whole thing on the bridge."

"If that's the case, Her Ladyship should know. She must help us. What about her rich friends? People with influence. They'll step in. Her Ladyship will see my boy's free."

"I can't say anything. She's grief stricken. Lady Soame's also lost a son."

"But she has to know, before it's too late. Where is she?"

Lizzie tried to break loose from his hold.

"Upstairs in her room. Mary and Emma are with her. It is no matter anyhow. I'll not allow you to see her. It wouldn't do any good anyway. She's so shocked; we've not been able to tell her about James. Who's to know she'd believe us anyway. It's Soame's word against mine, and now he's dead."

"But Her Ladyship knows her son, and how evil he was. Wouldn't she realise our boy could never do such a thing?"

"I've been to the court again, and appealed to the registrar. But he told me, James has been found guilty and sentenced, and there's nothing more to be said. He has been convicted, and already on his way to Ilchester, where he'll wait to be transported.

"Don't!" Lizzie cried. "I can't bear it. It's a nightmare."

The curtains were partially open, spring sunshine streaming into the bedroom, a beam of light crossing the room to the sofa, where Mary was sitting.

She had been in attendance all night, listening to her mistress breathing, and then weeping. How she must feel, Mary wondered. All alone. No husband and now no son.

An angler found Soame's body, grotesque and twisted around a fallen tree, his eyes fixed in a stare of terror. In those last moments, Mary wondered what he had seen. The gates of hell perhaps? He would surely be there. She was convinced. Soame was a devil, and Mary was pleased he was dead. It gladdened her heart to think she would never see his sneering face again, and hear his smarmy voice making fun of her pockmarked face, or reminding her of the night of Lady Soame's midsummer ball at Thurlow Hall.

Mary knew there was little love between them, so was surprised by Her Ladyship's reaction to the news of Soame's death, her mistress weeping bitterly the whole day, neither speaking nor eating.

There was a knock on the door, and opening it, Mary saw Alice Jesshope, holding a breakfast tray, her bloodshot eyes betraying her grief.

"Mrs Denton wonders whether Her Ladyship would like some breakfast." Alice whispered.

"Maybe," Mary said softly. "Bring it in anyway."

"Don't go Alice," she said, once Alice had put the tray on the table. "Keep me company for a while."

Together, they sat down on the sofa.

"Oh Mary!" Alice said quietly. "I feel wretched. I miss him terribly. What's to become of me?"

Mary held Alice's hand. "It's been a terrible shock for all of us."

"Who would believe my dear James would do such a thing?"

"Alice! He didn't," Mary said, under her breath. "Haven't you heard? It was Soame. He made up the whole thing. He told Henry before he fell."

Lady Soame stirred.

"Shush!" said Mary. "She mustn't hear."

"She mustn't hear what?" Lady Soame said, from behind the bed curtains.

"Nothing, My Lady," Mary answered. "It's nothing. You know us girls. Gossiping. Always gossiping."

"Well I'd rather know what's being said that I'm not supposed to hear, than not hear it at all."

Aghast, Mary looked at Alice.

Mary got up, and drew back the bed curtains, while Lady Edwina sat up in bed, adjusting her pillows.

"I smell toast!"

"Yes, My Lady," Alice said. "Mrs Denton wonders whether you would care to take breakfast this morning."

"I know I should, otherwise I'll make myself ill. I'll try a little toast, and some tea. Pour me a cup, Alice dear."

Alice did so, carrying it carefully to the bed.

"You've been crying." Edwina said, as Alice passed her the cup and saucer.

"Yes My Lady. Sorry, My Lady."

"Did you care so much for my son, you would weep for him?"

"No My Lady!" Alice exclaimed. "Certainly not! Oh, I'm sorry, My Lady. I didn't mean it like that."

"I know Alice. And you don't need to be sorry. All of us knew full well my son's character."

Suddenly, Alice wanted to tell Her Ladyship everything. How her son was about to blackmail her and James, after seeing them together in the greenhouse. And how, to satisfy his wicked designs, Soame wished for James to become his valet, and whatever else the wicked man had planned for her sweetheart.

Mary saw the look on Alice's face, and knew she was about to speak.

"I'll get up today," Edwina said. "There are things I must do. Arrangements to be made. I've to bury my son. Lay out my black mourning, Mary, if you please. I'll visit the abbey this morning, so please ask Mr Ives to have the carriage ready."

Alice opened her mouth, but Mary shook her head. Now would not be the time to tell Her Ladyship. Nevertheless, the knot of anxiety in Alice's stomach, told her it was crucial they act soon, because the longer Lady Soame was unaware of the truth, the further away James would be.

George Jesshope helped Lady Soame out of the carriage, a March wind blowing across Abbey Churchyard, catching her veil, and ensnaring it in the feathers in her bonnet.

While adjusting it, Lady Soame looked up at Ives. "It's cold Mr Ives, so I'll try not to be long."

Mr Ives and George watched her walk towards the west door, a black figure, crossing the flagstone square, appearing diminutive against the vast chiselled frontage of the abbey.

Once Lady Soame had disappeared inside, George retracted the steps, and climbing back into the postilion seat, joined Mr Ives, both sitting in silence, muffled in their winter uniforms, endeavouring to keep out the bitter wind. Nevertheless, each was engrossed in thought.

It was only two days ago, Mr Ives realised. The carriage was in the exact same place. He chastised himself. None of this would have happened, had he remembered to post the letter himself. Unquestionably, James was innocent. He had no reason to do such a thing. Steal a silly handkerchief! He had plenty of handkerchiefs of his own. The boy need only go to the linen press, or ask Mrs Ives. She would gladly have given him one. Young James had employment. Money in his pocket, and a father, mother, brother, and sisters who loved him.

It was too bewildering. Whatever could be happening to the lad? The thought made Ives shiver.

A cold north wind cut through George's tunic and gnawed at his bones, but as he pulled his hat down over his ears and tucked his chin inside his scarf, nothing could dispel the chill in his heart. It was strange being there without James sitting beside him. James was his chum. The mate he teased and taunted. The lad his sister was sweet on, also the man who would have surely become his brother in law.

One day James was there, the next gone. As if he had died, or been killed. Shutting his eyes against the wind, George sensed a weight in his chest, a tear trickling down his cheek. And even the daffodils, dancing gaily in the breeze in the flowerbeds, failed to cheer him, as he wept for his lost friend.

Back at Oakwood Girls School in Bath, Emma had to deal with her own emotions, as sitting at her desk, writing remarks in the end of term reports, she found it hard to concentrate, Soame's evil face filling her mind, his smirking mouth, and lustful eyes, burning into her brain.

He was dead, Emma told herself repeatedly. Dead! She would never see him again. No longer to feel the shame of bearing his child. She was free!

Nevertheless, she felt empty and drained. Maybe because there was now no reason to endure the hate, missing the feeling of vengeance she harboured in her heart all the years.

Emma was determined to cast emotion aside, and carry on with her life. Her Ladyship would need her now, more than ever, and Emma would be there to care for her. Emma began writing once more, in an attempt to dispel morbid thoughts. Yet the sound of Lizzie's screams reverberated in her mind.

Soame's last treacherous act had been appalling. The most evil of all his depraved deeds, although a deed that Emma hoped, would dispatch him straight to hell.

The day after the trial was worse than the day before, Emma remembered. However, Edwina had been kind and understanding to the Waldon family.

Henry Waldon and Mary Bennet, butler and parlour maid to Lady Soame, heard the wheels and horse's hooves on the cobblestones outside, so quickly opened the front door to allow Lady Soame inside. Removing her bonnet and gloves, she gave them to Mary, and then crossing the hall, began climbing the stairs, but suddenly stopped.

"Will you please accompany me, Henry?"

"Certainly, My Lady."

Henry looked askance at Mary, and closed the front door, following Lady Soame up the stairs, and along the corridor, until they reached the drawing room.

Once inside, Edwina gazed out of the window, wondering how

often she had marvelled at Bath's beauty. Today, however, it appeared despondent, a fine mist of rain obliterating the houses, and bell tower of the abbey. In its forlorn guise, Bath seemed as unhappy as herself.

"Henry, I've noticed the girls whispering," she said, turning from the window. "There seems a strange atmosphere about the house."

"Yes, My Lady. Everyone's in mourning for your son."

"Nonsense!" Lady Soame retorted. "It's more than that. I am quite aware of the staff's opinion of Sir Humphrey. There's no need to hide it from me. Is there anything I should know?"

Henry hesitated for a moment, unable to think of where to begin.

"We thought it best not to bother Your Ladyship," he said finally. "We feel you'd enough to endure, as it is."

"Henry! You know me well enough by now. I'm a tough old woman. I can take it."

He smiled.

"What is it then?"

Henry took a deep breath.

"My son, My Lady."

"Yes. Where is he? I looked for him this morning on the carriage. I've not seen him for a few days. Is he ill?"

"No, My Lady. He's been arrested."

"How dreadful! It can't be true?"

"I'm afraid it is, My Lady. We've no idea where he is. Except, he's not in the city."

"For heaven's sake. What's the boy done?"

Suddenly, feeling the blood drain from his face, the gaping features of Soame engulfed Henry's mind,

"Please, My Lady. May I sit down?" he said. "I feel rather unwell."

"Of course. Would you like me to call someone?"

"No thank you, My Lady. I'll be all right. I'm just a little tired. We've had no sleep, you see."

Lady Soame helped Henry to the sofa, and he sat down.

"But what on earth caused him to be arrested?" she said, sitting beside him.

"We were at the trial, Lizzie and I. It was very quick. It seems he

7

was caught picking a pocket."

"What! Why on earth would he do that?"

"I know My Lady. That's what his mother and I wondered, until we saw the witness."

"Who was it?"

"Your son, My Lady."

"My son! I can't believe it. How or why was my son involved in this?"

"After they took the boy down, My Lady, I followed Sir Humphrey, to ask him the same question. Once I'd caught up with him on the bridge, he turned on me. He was angry, and wondered why I was following him. I asked why he testified against my son, and it was then he came out with it."

Henry faltered. After all, Her Ladyship might not believe him, his story sounding like the ravings of a mad man.

"Well what did he say?" Lady Soame said, impatiently.

Henry took another breath.

"Sir Humphrey said he planted the handkerchief in the boys' hand. He said my son needed to be taught a lesson, for speaking to him out of turn. In so doing, My Lady, he said he was finally reaping revenge on me, my family, and Emma Baker's brother, for all the hurt we caused him in the past."

Edwina was silent, her eyes wide in astonishment.

"That's nonsense," she said finally. "What could you or John Baker have done to Humphrey for him to do such a wicked thing?"

Henry sighed with relief.

"You may not like what I'm going to say, My Lady, but I feel the story has to be told."

"I knew my son better than anyone, Henry. I'm well aware of what he could do. There are things he's done of which even you are unaware, and I pray you never will. Now, what is it I should know?"

Swallowing hard, Henry began.

"From our first day at school, Soame, I mean Sir Humphrey, My Lady, had his sights set on John Baker. If you understand my meaning."

Edwina lowered her eyes.

"Of course." Henry continued. "John dismissed him out of hand. Nevertheless, one day he saved your son's life. When we were older, there was an argument at the forge. Sir Humphrey challenged John's father to a duel. But John took it up instead. When your son saw that he was losing a fair fight of fisticuffs, he produced a knife. He and I got into a scuffle on the frozen river, falling through the ice. But John Baker saved us. You would presume Sir Humphrey would have held John in his debt. But no, the obligation seemed to deepen his hatred of John and me."

"My son was completely irrational, Henry," Edwina said. "I despair of knowing what reason he had for all the dreadful things he did."

"Forgive me for saying so, My Lady; because Sir Humphrey hankered after John, he became jealous of his and my friendship. I believe this could be the reason he sought reprisal. It seems he was developing similar feelings toward my son. But when young James refused to comply with Sir Humphrey's wish for him to become his valet, this seems to be the point which drove him over the edge into madness."

Once again, Edwina's attention went to the window, but the pelting rain was obliterating the view.

"I'm so sorry," she whispered. "You must be devastated. Poor Lizzie. I can't imagine how she must feel."

Henry watched her pull a handkerchief from her sleeve, and dab her eyes.

"There's something else My Lady. Something more you should know."

Edwina looked at him, her eyes full of tears.

"I watched him fall."

The handkerchief dropped to her lap.

"He lost his footing on the cobblestones, and toppled over the parapet. I saw him fall. I saw his face. I'll never forget it, as long as I live, My Lady."

"Did he say anything?"

"No My Lady. For a moment, he looked puzzled. Then he was gone."

Edwina shuddered, then seemed to shake herself free of the thoughts, and getting up, crossed the room, pulling the satin sash hanging beside the fireplace.

"I think we both need tea."

"Thank you, My Lady. You're very kind."

"I must stop this," Edwina said, once more sitting down beside him.

I'm afraid it's too late, My Lady. The law's the law. There were witnesses, statements, and a judgment. He's been sentenced to fourteen years transportation."

"How terrible. But I must do something to stop it."

Lady Soame made numerous attempts to bring about a change in the verdict, but to no avail, since there was no proof the story she told was true.

As Edwina, Emma and the staff, sought to put the events of that day behind them, life at Oakwood gradually returned to normal. Subsequently, as the years passed, there was never again a mention of Humphrey Soame, or young James Baker Waldon. Soame was hardly missed, his mother being the only mourner at his funeral. However, everyone who knew James grieved for him silently.

Meanwhile, young girls arrived at the school, and left young ladies, and as year followed year, the memory of the day in March eventually became a simple flicker of sadness in the mind, the years showing themselves in other ways.

Older now, and with his wife Lizzie having returned to Great Wratting, caring for Edward Myson, her aged father and Prudence Bailey, her step mother, Henry went about his work less briskly, except the image of his son, and the sound of his voice, remained imprinted in his mind, emerging now and again. The golden haired boy, standing beside the table, singing for all his worth.

Chapter Two

In the subsequent months after James' disappearance, Alice's life also changed, the horror of the dreadful day in spring, turning to dread by summer. It was August. Five months since the afternoon in the greenhouse, Alice now certain she was pregnant, and it was James' baby. Obviously, Soame's sudden appearance on the other side of the glass caused James to forget to be careful. Anyway, such events were hardly important, she was having a baby, and nothing was going to alter the fact, what to do, the most important question on her mind.

Despite the corset she wore, soon Alice was unable to conceal her secret from Mary, and one day, while they were washing sheets in the laundry, the older woman challenged her on the subject.

"Come on my girl! Own up! I've seen it before. You're glowing. Look at your chubby face! You can't stop eating either. I've had my eye on you."

"Hush! Keep your voice down!" Alice whispered, looking over her shoulder, towards the kitchen. "Mrs Denton will hear. And you know what'll happen then, she'll tell Mrs Ives, and then Her Ladyship will know."

"We're all going to find out, sooner or later," scoffed Mary. "You can't wear a corset forever. What are you going to do with the baby anyway? Poor little bastard!"

Flinging down the wet sheet angrily, Alice turned on Mary.

"Don't call my baby a bastard!" she said through her teeth. "James and I were getting married."

"So it's James'. I guessed as much."

"Why not. We loved..." Alice checked herself. "We love each other! And he's coming back to me one day. I know he will. You mark my words."

"Grow up Alice. His sentence was fourteen years. Don't you see? He's gone for good. They don't come back. Get used to it! You'll never see him again."

"Stop it!" Alice screeched. "Why say such a dreadful thing? You're wicked Mary! It's all the hope I have. The thought he's somewhere waiting for me."

Alice began to cry, tears welling in her eyes.

"You're jealous! That's what it is," she sobbed. "Who'll ever fall for you? Look at you."

"Alright!" Mary said. "I'm sorry. I know I can say nasty things sometimes. But who's going to look after you and the baby, until James does come back. Her Ladyship won't let you remain here."

"She let Lizzie Waldon stay, when my James was a baby."

"But she and Henry were married, and they lived in a cottage at Thurlow."

"Well times have changed. She might keep me on."

"With a baby screaming the place down," Mary said laughing.

"Shut up Mary! You're frightening me. I don't know what to do."

By now, Mary could see Alice was becoming hysterical.

"Sorry. I'm sorry. Look! Just let's get on with the washing."

They began to scrub the sheets on the washboards, steam once more filling the laundry. Nevertheless, after a long pause, Alice spoke.

"What shall I do, Mary? Help me please."

"If it was me, I'd tell Her Ladyship. She'll know what to do. She did before."

"What do you mean?"

"Nothing. Something that happened a long time ago. When you were just a baby. I've kept the secret all this time. No one but me knows, and no one ever will."

Alice looked at Mary, and seeing her expression, knew she spoke the truth.

"What will Her Ladyship do?" Alice asked, as they lifted the sheet, and carried it to the ringer.

"She'll be kind. She's always kind."

While Alice fed the sheet through the rollers, Mary turned the handle, water running into a tin bath beneath.

"She was kind to me once," Mary said, distantly. "Something happened. I was desperate. She was the only one I could turn to."

"Mary! You've never said anything before."

"Of course I haven't. A girl doesn't go blurting things out. I tell you. What happened to me was horrible. Vile. It's ruined my life. Just make sure this baby will never do that. If anything else, for my sake at least."

Alice regarded Mary differently after that day, and consequently, one morning, several weeks later, she searched for Henry Waldon, finding him in the butler's pantry, preparing luncheon.

"Excuse me, Mr Waldon," she said, standing in the doorway.

"Yes Alice."

"Mr Waldon. May I speak with Her Ladyship?"

"Can I ask why?"

"I can't say," Alice said, blushing, and looking away. "It's private."

"Very well. Lady Soame's in the garden. Come with me, and we'll see."

Henry led her through the house, into the dining room, then out of the French windows. From the steps of the patio, he led her down a gravel path leading to the highest lake. It was a beautiful August morning, the sun shining from a radiant sky, its reflection turning the surface of the water to gold. Rounding a large rhododendron bush, adjoining the path, they discovered Lady Soame sitting in the shade of an old oak tree, beside her, a cane table, set for coffee.

Alice considered the picture, the prettiest she had ever seen, noticing the dappled sunshine, dancing over Her Ladyship's pale blue dress, and across the book, she was reading.

Henry Waldon coughed, and Lady Soame looked up.

"Yes Henry?"

"It's Alice Jesshope, My Lady. She wonders if she could speak with you."

"Of course. You may leave us, Henry."

Watching him walk away, Edwina smiled. He was becoming quite the stately gentleman, she thought. Most likely in his late middle years, although it seemed to Edwina only yesterday that he was a stable boy, and she a young woman, just married.

Looking up through the canopy of oak leaves, she sighed. How old was the tree, she mused? One hundred years, maybe? If it were, then it was planted twenty years before she was born, and here it is still standing, tall and strong, ready for perhaps another hundred. Not for her, however. Her life was drawing to a close. How rapidly the days go by, now that she is old. Why? Edwina wondered. One would imagine they would pass slowly as one aged, when a person no longer has the energy to do all the things that once filled their life.

Edwina turned, and gazed at the girl standing in the shade of the tree, her freckled face shining, copper coloured hair falling in tousled ringlets; her skin as smooth as a peach, eyes bright blue, sparkling in the reflection from the lake.

To be young again, Edwina thought. To know life was before her. To feel the excitement of not knowing what the future held, or of whom she would marry, and how many children she would bear. Never the thought of death. No realisation that one day she might be old and die. She was immortal. A goddess. The vast expanse of an eternal life, stretching ahead.

Alice could see Her Ladyship staring at her, and bowed her head, Edwina failing to notice a small tear trickling down her cheek.

"Alice dear," Edwina said, "over the past months I've often wanted to talk to you. But sometimes I felt you would hardly wish to be reminded."

"Thank you, My Lady. It's been difficult."

Alice took her handkerchief from her sleeve.

"I'm sorry," Edwina said. "I know you and James were close."

"We were My Lady. We loved each other. We were to be married. That's why…"

Alice hesitated, for a moment unable to say the words. Then courage overwhelmed her.

"That's why I'm going to have his baby."

"Alice dear! You poor unfortunate child."

Edwina put down her book, and stood up.

"Come here."

Powerless to hold back the tears, Alice ran into Edwina's open arms.

"My Lady," she sobbed. "I'm so sorry. It'd be all right if he were here. I'm alone. What am I to do?"

"You're going to have the baby, and we'll be here to support you."

"But what's to become of it?"

"Don't worry about such things. Everything will be alright."

"Thank you, My Lady. I don't know what I'd have done if you'd abandoned me."

"You know that would never happen. Now dear, dry your eyes. You've a very important job to do. You've to tell Mr Waldon. Somehow, I think he'll be extremely pleased to hear the news."

Eight months after James' arrest, with the November winds turning icy, frost covering the lawns; Lizzie Waldon received a letter from her brother, containing troubling news. Her father, Edward Myson, was gravely ill, the doctors unable to discover any cause. And, with the widow Bailey beside herself with worry, and incapable of caring for him, Lizzie's brother begged his sister to return to Wratting, to care for their father.

There was no alternative, Lizzie aware no one else could fit the task. Her daughters were still young, and had finished their schooling, and were working, Rebecca in a bakery, Mary in a flower shop, on Pulteney Bridge. It was hardly fair for Lizzie to disrupt their lives by sending either of them to their grandfather. As a result, and after much deliberation, she and Henry came to a decision. Lizzie must return to Wratting.

As usual, Her Ladyship was supportive, and understanding the predicament, gave Lizzie money for the two coach rides, plus the bed and board necessary for the journey.

Therefore, it was a sad morning when Lizzie said goodbye, and with the coach waiting outside Oakwood House, ready to take Lizzie and Henry into the city, they visited Alice in her room.

"You look after yourself," Lizzie said, kissing Alice on the forehead, "And take good care of that little grandchild of ours."

Alice tried not to cry.

"I will. And take care Lizzie. I'll miss you."

"Now don't upset yourself," said Lizzie, fighting back the tears. "It's not good for the baby. I'll be back in no time, you'll see."

For Lizzie, seeing they had never been apart in all the years they had known each other, parting from Henry was even more painful. After saying goodbye to everyone, Mr Ives drove them to the White Horse, where the London Mail Coach was due to leave.

"I'll write every day," Henry said, helping Lizzie out of the carriage.

"Don't be silly dear. You know what a slow reader I am. I'll never have time to read seven letters a week."

Henry laughed. Lizzie could always make him laugh. She was the sunshine in his life. It would be dreadful to be separated from her.

After loading her trunk, Henry settled Lizzie into a corner seat of the coach, covering her knees with a blanket. Seeing Lizzie's face framed by her best bonnet, Henry thought she looked sad. Sadder than he had ever seen her. But she smiled, took hold of his hand, and kissed him.

"It won't be long," she said. "You'll see. Then everything will be alright again."

"I'll miss you," Henry said, kissing her.

"All aboard for London!" the coach driver bellowed, the guard blowing a blast on the post horn.

For a while, Henry could see her face at the window, then the coach disappeared around the corner, and Lizzie was gone.

With autumn turned to winter, Mary and Jane Baker found they were doing all of the housework, since by now, Alice was too large to climb the stairs, or even perform the lightest task. Instead, she stayed in her attic room, which the girls made cheerful with coloured quilts, and watercolours donated by Her Ladyship. Despite the steep stairs, Edwina made a point of visiting Alice at least twice a week, bringing her chocolates, or candied fruit.

One morning in mid-December, Alice woke earlier than usual, wind whistling around the eaves, and the soft patter of snowflakes brushing her casement window, causing her to wake. She was cold. So she pulled the blankets close around her, and shut her eyes.

With the snow outside getting deeper, Alice dozed, and finally fell into a deep slumber.

The corn was high, the sun so hot she could hear the grain cracking. Here and there, amongst a sea of gold, bobbed flame red poppies, their paper-thin petals fluttering in the breeze. Alice waded through the corn, letting one hand brush the tops of the wheat-ears, feeling them tickle her palm. In her other arm, she held her baby, his hair shining in the sun, as if made of spun gold, his cornflower blue eyes sparkling. Alice could see James waiting at the gate, looking tall and handsome, his chest bare and tanned.

Alice loved him. What will he say when he sees the baby? Will he be pleased, Alice wondered. She waded on towards him. But strangely, he remained far off, never getting nearer.

"James! Come here!" Alice shouted. "Don't go away."

He smiled, and shook his head.

"But look!" she yelled, holding up the baby. "It's a boy. A little boy."

James put his hand to his lips; blew a kiss; then vanished.

"James!" she screamed.

Alice woke with a start, and clutched her side, pain causing her to scream. Intense, searing, grasping, convulsive.

As the pain subsided, she looked at the clock on the bedside table. It was half past nine.

"I must call someone," she said aloud. "But they'll be working."

Throwing back the blankets, tipping her legs over the side of the bed, using the bedstead for support, she stood up, and began staggering to the top of the stairs.

"Is anyone there?" she yelled. "Can anyone hear me?"

The pain returned, Alice gritting her teeth, gripping the balusters until it passed.

"Help!" she screamed. "Help! Is anyone there?"

All of a sudden, Alice felt a strange pounding in her chest, along with a sharp pain in her jaw.

"My heart! It's racing so fast!" she gasped.

Breathing hard, she sat on the top step.

"Help me someone! Please!"

The door at the bottom of the stairs opened, and Mary appeared.

"My God! You've started," she shrieked.

"I think I have," Alice panted. "There's something else though. I don't feel right. I've a pain in my chest."

"No dear," Mary said, hurrying up the stairs. "The pain's in your tummy. You're having a baby."

"No Mary. It's my heart. It fluttering."

"Come on!"

Mary put an arm around her friend.

"Let's get you back to bed."

Once Alice was under the blankets, Mary tucked her up.

"Just you lie there quietly while I tell Henry to get the doctor."

By now, the snow lay thick on Bathwick Hill; Mr Ives knowing the coach would be unable to make the trip. So saddling the late Duke of Thurlow's stallion, he prepared to ride to Doctor Hughes' house.

As soon as Ives left, Henry went to Her Ladyship's bedroom to tell her the news. Subsequently, as if hit by a bolt of lightning, everyone in the house moved quicker, jobs usually completed slowly and laboriously, finished in a trice, everyone making ready for Alice's baby.

An hour later, Henry was relieved to hear Mr Ives returning with Doctor Hughes.

"We very nearly didn't make it," the doctor said, standing on the doorstep, shaking snow from his cloak and hat. "It's drifted four foot deep on the corner of Edward Road."

Henry stood aside to let him in.

"I'll show you the way, doctor," he said.

Doctor Hughes climbed the last flight of stairs, and reached the bedroom.

"Hello Mary. How's the young lady?" he asked, breathlessly.

"Doing well, doctor. The pains are getting closer together. I've been watching the clock, and timing them."

"Good. Now we'll need towels, and hot water."

Mary hurried away to collect everything requested, and when she returned Alice was closer to having the baby than ever, the doctor having drawn back her blankets, leaving only a sheet draped over her knees.

"The pain!" Alice cried. "I can't bear it."

"Push girl!" the doctor shouted. "We're nearly there."

Alice screamed, straining with all the strength she possessed.

"Here it comes!" Mary shouted, peering between Alice's legs. "I can see the head. Go on Alice. Push!"

"Good girl!" encouraged the doctor. "The shoulders are through."

Doctor Hughes took hold of the slimy wet infant, and pulled it into the world.

"It's a girl," he said, holding the baby upside down, and smacking her soundly across the bottom.

"Did you hear, Alice?" Mary shouted over the baby's screams, while the doctor dealt with the placenta and cord. "It's a girl."

Wrapping the baby in a towel, Mary held her up, so Alice could see.

"A lovely little girl."

Alice smiled at the baby in Mary's arms, and then closed her eyes, her head falling back onto the pillow.

"What's the matter, doctor?" Mary said. "She's fainted? What's wrong?"

Doctor Hughes took Alice's hand to feel her pulse. Then put his fingers on the girl's neck, under her ear.

"I'm afraid she's dead," he said, turning to Mary, his face drained of colour.

"She can't be!" Mary bawled, rushing to the bedside, the baby wailing in her arms. "She's young. She can't be dead. Alice! Alice! Wake up. Come on! Look at your lovely baby girl."

"It's no use, Mary," whispered Doctor Hughes. "She's dead."

Mary clutched the baby tight, and sobbing, sank into a chair.

"She tried to tell me. When the pains started, Alice said she didn't feel well. She said she had pains in her chest, and I didn't listen. I didn't take notice."

"Then it was her heart," the doctor said. "Sometimes it's just not strong enough."

Mary hugged the baby girl close.

"What's going to happen to you now, you poor little thing?" she said through her tears. "Your mummy's dead. Your mummy's dead."

***

Ostrich feathers on the horses' heads, fluttering in the cold north wind, the shining hearse and cortege wound its way down the hill into the city, the oak coffin, covered with dark green ivy, and white lilies, appearing sad, behind the etched glass windows.

Lady Soame, together with the staff of Oakwood, attended Alice's funeral at Walcot Cemetery, each man in Lady Soame's household taking a side of the coffin, and carrying it into the chapel. After a short service, during which Henry read the eulogy, and George Jesshope, Alice's brother, the reading, they carried Alice into the churchyard, to the plot Her Ladyship purchased, the freshly dug grave situated close to the wall, underneath a willow tree, a short distance from the road. A peaceful place for Alice to take her final rest.

Sadly, everyone returned to the house, to continue their daily duties, the sound of a baby crying somewhere upstairs, filling them with sorrow.

Later that afternoon, endeavouring to keep busy in the pantry, Henry attempted to push aside his melancholy. Suddenly he heard a bell jingling merrily, and looking up, saw the summons came from the drawing room.

Knocking softly, he entered.

Lady Soame was still wearing her black satin gown, and sitting in her favourite chair beside the window.

"Thank you, Henry," she said.

"Is there anything I can do for you, My Lady?"

"Yes Henry. Please sit down and relax."

Edwina gestured to the sofa.

What was this, Henry wondered? Whenever Lady Soame requested him to sit, a bombshell was likely to land nearby.

"I have a great deal to reimburse you for Henry," she said, looking at him closely. "Indirectly, I've caused your family much unhappiness, which I mean to rectify."

"But My Lady."

"No Henry. Please! Let me finish. I know you're her grandfather, but the little child needs a mother. Mary has her work. She can't be expected to look after the baby forever."

Henry felt awkward sitting in her presence. Nonetheless, he waited for what she was about to say.

"I require some joy in my life. The past months have been sorrowful and difficult, to say the least. Something, such as this would give me much pleasure in my old age. If you agree, I would like to adopt your son's child. However, I don't want to change her surname, although, I understand her Christian name is still undecided."

Shocked and amazed, Henry sat stiff and upright.

"If it's your wish, My Lady," he stuttered. "Sorry My Lady. Yes, My Lady. You're correct. I've written to my wife regarding a name, but have yet to receive a reply. But if I know my Lizzie, she would prefer the baby to be named after Susan, Lizzie's late mother."

"Then Susan she shall be. Darling little Susan. But I would like to know your feelings on the matter. Or am I being presuming, and too audacious? Please tell me?"

"Certainly not, My Lady! Quite the opposite. It would be the greatest honour you could bestow on our family. And I know Lizzie would feel the same. In fact, it will be a huge weight off our minds to know the poor little one will be looked after for the rest of her life."

"Thank you," Edwina said. "I want both you and Lizzie to see it as my way of saying sorry for the grief my son has caused."

"Yes, My Lady. Thank you, My Lady."

"Very well Henry. I'll have Mr Perkins draw up the appropriate documents."

Henry closed the door quietly, but his heart was beating hard. Up until now, it had been a difficult and sorrowful day. Only half an hour earlier, he felt he was about to burst into tears, his emotions so close to the surface; nonetheless, how quickly one's feelings can change, since his heart felt like it might burst with joy. The granddaughter of Henry Waldon, butler of Bath, to be the ward of the Duchess of Thurlow. Who would have believed it? He could hardly wait to dash off a letter to Lizzie. She would be overjoyed by the news.

However, when Henry reached the top of the stairs, another notion struck him, causing him to stop and stare into space.

Not only will his granddaughter be the ward, Henry suddenly realised; she'll be the heir. The beneficiary of the estates, and the Soame fortune. With a spring in his step he had not known for years, Henry made his way back to the pantry.

Chapter Three

Lady Soame was true to her word, as the following week, her solicitor drew up the adoption papers, which Henry, as Susan's next of kin, duly signed. With the formalities over, Mary carried baby Susan out of Alice's room, and down the stairs, into a brand new nursery. Where a smart young nanny, Emily, took over the job of caring for her.

There seemed no indication to Henry, or the household, that Lizzie would ever return, her father remaining alive, although debilitated by the mystery illness that was slowly killing him.

Lizzie's brother, George, still lived in Great Wratting and was now married with children. He was lucky to be the only son of Edward and Susan Myson, so had the privilege to attend The Soame School, and could subsequently read and write. As a result, Lizzie turned to her brother often to read Henry's letters aloud. Then George would reply to them, as Lizzie dictated. The letters arrived infrequently and although Henry was pleased to receive them, he found them difficult to decipher, as George's handwriting was scribbly, with strange spellings, and many mistakes, and crossing's out.

Lizzie told of her life at the cottage with the red roof, her father's decrepitude, and Prudence Bailey's flights of fancy. Henry could detect that Lizzie was depressed and lonely, although her mood changed to joy by a visit from their dear friend John Baker, who she said looked well but was still unmarried, much to her amazement, and apprehension.

In a letter to his wife, Henry asked whether she visited the hall at any time. He received a letter two weeks later.

Great Wratting, January 1832

My darling,

I hope this sees you well, as it does me. Thank you most kindly for your last letter, which I read with interest. I'm so pleased to hear John James, Rebecca and Mary, are keeping well, and my darling granddaughter is being good to her nanny, and Her Ladyship. Isn't it nice to see the flowers again, and feel the sun on our faces? I hope the weather is nice in Bath.

I do miss you, and everyone terribly, but I have my duty, and must remain here. Dear father continues frail.

He eats, but is very weak. I feel so sorry for Prudence. The poor dear is becoming so confused, and calls Edward by the name of her first husband. I don't think he minds. He still has his sense of humour. God bless him! The twins have grown. You would hardly recognise them, they've grown so. Joshua's on Manor Farm, and Ruth's with the Cullam's, at the Vicarage. They're both happy, and have sweethearts. How is my darling Susan? I hope she's not getting ways, just because she's the ward of a Duchess. She's only one of us after all. Just a Waldon.

Now my dear, you ask if I've been to the hall. Well strangely, John came over last week, and he and I rode over there. He went so fast; it was all I could do to hang on. I'm sure he did it on purpose. Thurlow Hall is just as we left it, all those years ago. The windows are shuttered, and boarded up, and it doesn't seem like anyone has tried to break in. Although, we did notice a broken window by the kitchen door, which John said he would board over?

The garden's looking rundown, and terribly overgrown, with nettles up to your shoulders, and the stable yard is full of weeds. Mr Denton and Mr Ives would not be pleased.

I was sad to see the hall again. I remember when it was a happy and busy place. People always coming and going, and lots of parties and balls. It seems to be waiting for something to bring it back to life. I was glad to leave.

Afterwards, John and I rode over to the forge, to call on his dear mother and father. They were keen to hear any news of Emma and Jane, and I was glad I could tell them everything was well. They have heard of our good fortune, and are full of happiness for us. But sorry about dear Alice, of course.

Well, I think this is all I can write my love. Thank you darling for writing to me as often as you do. I just don't know what I would do without your letters and wonderful John Baker for a friend. I think I would go quite mad. Give all my love to John James, and dear little Susan, and Rebecca and Mary. Tell them Mama loves, and misses them.

Please send my love to all my friends. My fondest regards to Her Ladyship, of course, and a big hug especially for you my darling husband.

Your loving wife, Lizzie."

Taking off his spectacles, Henry rubbed his aching eyes. He leaned back in his chair, and smiled wistfully. He was pleased to hear his beloved Thurlow Hall was still standing, but sorry it looked forlorn and lost, remembering how it appeared when he used to return from Wratting, after visiting Lizzie, all the windows ablaze with light, as if a great beacon was guiding him home through the darkness. Would they ever be lit again, he wondered? Will his granddaughter order some other butler to light the lantern over the great door? Henry hoped with all his heart, she would.

***

"Happy Birthday to you. Happy Birthday to you. Happy Birthday dear Susan. Happy Birthday to you."

The chorus rang around the dining room, as the sun streamed through the crystal chandelier, sending cascades of rainbows over the damask walls. Lady Soame and Emma, and the servants, were gathered around the table.

"Blow out the candles, Susan," Edwina said.

"Do I have too, Grandmamma? They look so pretty."

"Of course, my dear. And don't forget to make a wish."

The little girl shut her eyes, and took a deep breath, then opening them, blew out the eight candles.

"Hoorah!" everyone cheered.

"Granddad!" Susan called to Henry. "Light them granddad. I want to do it again."

While everyone laughed, Mrs Denton came forward, holding a cake knife, handing it to Susan.

"Now my dear, you've to cut the cake."

Looking suddenly serious, holding the knife over the centre of the huge cake, Susan brought it down gradually, until it sliced through the thick pink icing.

"I'll finish it, if you like my dear," Mrs Denton said. "I've to cut a piece for everyone."

"Here's your slice," Mary said, passing Henry a plate. "You must be very proud."

He was indeed proud, watching the little girl laughing and giggling with Lady Soame and the younger servant girls. Proud to be the grandfather of such a beautiful child. If only his son could see her. What would he think to know his daughter was the granddaughter of a duchess? With her golden hair, fair skin, and eyes the colour of cornflowers, Susan was the image of her father.

Also, Lizzie would be pleased to see her granddaughter grown into such a clever, well-mannered young girl, educated, graceful, and already accomplished in singing and playing the pianoforte. However, Henry knew Her Ladyship should take the credit for turning the daughter of a footman and a scullery maid, into a lady.

Gazing out of the window, tasting the sweet sponge cake, Henry mused. The last eight years had flown by. One minute Susan was a baby, the next a toddler, Henry holding her hand, as they stood beside the lake, feeding the ducks. Then, in the next minute, Susan was trotting around the lawn on her pony, a birthday present from Her Ladyship.

During the eight years, Lizzie's father, Edward Myson, finally succumbed to illness and died. Yet, Lizzie felt unable to return, now worried about leaving the very old, and senile Prudence. Sometimes, Henry despaired of ever seeing his wife again.

Overall, life at Oakwood ran much as always. Lady Soame entertained the doctor and the vicar, twice a month, giving an 'at home' or a ball every once in a while, this serving to keep the servants on their toes, and up to scratch.

Although, nowadays, everyone began to see changes in their mistress, which Emma was first to notice, one day speaking to Henry on the subject?

"She seems tired all the time," Emma said, frowning. "Not her usual self. Maybe we should ask the doctor to see her."

"Over the years, Her Ladyship's injury has caused her much pain," Henry said. "It's little wonder she's slowing down. She's over eighty, after all."

"Indeed Henry. None of us is getting any younger. But the change is quite dramatic."

Several weeks later, Edwina called Henry to her bedroom.

"I'll not get up this morning," she said, raising herself on the pillow. "I'm feeling a little tired. And I've a tiny headache."

"But you haven't touched your breakfast, My Lady."

"No. I'm sorry. I'm not hungry. Take it away."

Henry shut the door quietly.

The following days saw a rapid decline, as Lady Soame drifted in and out of consciousness, occasionally, speaking, but the words unintelligible. Baffled, the doctors were unable to discover a cause. However, one morning, while Henry was in the room, Lady Soame opened her eyes, and raising her head, spoke weakly, but coherently.

"Henry," she whispered. "Come close. I need you to do something for me. The most important task you've ever done in your life."

"Yes, My Lady," Henry said. "Of course."

"I wish you to get a message to John Baker. I must see him. However much it costs, I have to see him before I die."

As he hurried from the room, Henry almost ran into Emma.

"Her Ladyship wants to see your brother."

"For heaven's sake, why?"

"I've no idea. I've to get him here as quick as I can. But how?"

Then a thought struck him. George must ride to London, then on to Thurlow.

Consequently, later that morning, his pockets full of money, his horse saddled, and the instructions ringing in his head, George Jesshope took off down the hill, and straight on, until he reached the London Road.

At Oakwood, the end was near, curtains drawn and blinds pulled, as each member of the household embraced their memories and grief, since the woman who had been the mainstay of their existence, for as long as they could remember, was about to die.

On the last day, the priest was called, and Doctor Hughes was in attendance. It would not be long.

The evening of the same day, at almost six o'clock, Mr Ives heard loud knocking on the gates, hurrying down from his quarters over the coach house.

"Mr Baker!" he cried, seeing John and George standing on the doorstep. "You're here. I pray you're not too late."

"Thank you, Mr Ives. I hope so too. We've ridden nonstop the whole way."

Henry was at the bottom of the stairs to greet his old friend.

"John," he whispered, clasping his hand. "It's good to see you."

"You too," John said.

"Her Ladyship's waiting."

Giving his cloak and hat to George, John followed Henry up the stairs and along the corridor to the bedroom.

Inside, John saw a melancholy scene, his sister standing beside the bed, Mrs Ives near the curtained window, a nanny, and young girl sitting beside the fireplace, and the doctor and priest, a little aside from the others.

John's attention turned to the bed, and Lady Soame. He remembered how lovely she once was, although, staring at her wrinkled face, he still could see a semblance of that beauty, despite the years. Still beautiful. Yet changed, but no less lovely.

"I knew you'd come," she whispered. "I dreamt it, and now it's true."

Opening her eyes, John fell under their spell once more, as he had so many years ago. Brilliant discs of pale green, sparkling like crystal. They were unaltered. How could he have forgotten them?

"Henry," Edwina whispered. "Please ask everyone to leave. Mr

Baker and I need to speak in confidence."

"Certainly, My Lady."

Henry held the door, while they filed out of the room, then closing it behind him.

When they were alone, Edwina lifted her hand, and gestured to John.

"Come nearer," she said.

John moved closer to the bed, bending in order to hear her.

"Mr Baker," Edwina continued, "I'm about to tell you something I've kept secret for almost thirty years. It will be wicked of me if I don't tell the story, and I'm pleased to say, I've never done a wicked thing in my life."

"Very well, My Lady," John said, kneeling beside the bed.

"The reason I'm telling you is because you're the man who can do something about it."

"My Lady. I don't understand."

"It concerns your sister. But she must never know. Not yet, anyway."

Mystified, John leaned closer.

"Nearly thirty years ago, and unbeknown to you and your family, your sister had a baby."

John froze, feeling the pulse in his temple begin to throb. What was he was hearing? His darling Emma, deceiving them all.

"Don't think ill of her though, Mr Baker. Emma's a good woman. However, a devious scoundrel who was out for revenge seduced her. Revenge on you and Henry Waldon's family.

"Do you mean, who I think you mean, My Lady?"

"Yes Mr Baker. My son."

Edwina paused, endeavouring to catch her breath.

"Your sister told me she was going to have a baby," she continued, after regaining some strength. "That's why I sent her away."

"What happened to the child?"

"It was adopted by my friends, Mr and Mrs Reddall."

"Yes. I remember. They visited the hall once. Emma told us you were giving her to Mrs Reddall, as her maid."

"That's correct. But Emma returned."

"She told us Mr and Mrs Reddall took pity on her, and let her return home."

"While the baby remained with the Reddalls, who raised him as their own."

"Then it was a boy?"

"Yes. A boy. Isabella wrote to me often, telling me her news, and about her little son. However, I estranged myself from her, since hearing about him made me feel awkward and uncomfortable. Isabella had no idea he was Soame's son. I told her the baby's father was a village lad. The little boy she nursed on her lap, and kissed goodnight was my only grandchild. I found it increasingly difficult to read her letters, without becoming angry. After all, it was I who arranged to give him away. However, at the time Soame was still alive. What he would have done if he'd known he had a son, I dread to think."

"What became of the boy?"

"The Reddalls emigrated to the colonies, over twenty years ago. The child would have been six or seven when they made the voyage. The family settled in New South Wales. Thomas became a chaplain, and a teacher, as I remember. I received letters from Isabella, but never replied. We were good friends once. She must have thought me a horrible woman."

Edwina closed her eyes, appearing suddenly exhausted, so John let her rest, sitting in a chair beside the bed.

"Do you know his Christian name?" he said, after a while.

"Luke," Edwina murmured. "Luke William. The Reddalls named him after his paternal grandfather."

John could see she was growing weaker, the effort of raising the past taking a toll on her poor frail body. Nevertheless, she summoned the strength to continue.

"In her letters, Isabella spoke of her son a great deal. It was clear he was the light of her and Thomas' lives. He was good, kind, happy and cheerful, with no sign of spite or malice. An angel in fact. How unlike his father, I thought. And reading on, I also began to love the child. Maybe my grandson would fail to turn into the evil monster, like his father. For this reason, I'm revealing the secret I've been keeping for almost thirty years. Mr Baker, I ask a great favour of you. Please. Would you go to the colonies, find Luke, and tell him who he really is? He needs to know that he's the rightful Duke of Thurlow."

"But what about the little girl? Lizzie tells me she's your ward. Won't she, one day, inherit Thurlow?"

"Susan's a sensible girl. She'll understand. If this Luke William is as good as his mother says, then he'll make a fine head of the House of Soame."

"It'll be quite a shock. He may not believe it. I'll have to convince him? That's if I ever find him."

"Don't worry. I've entrusted a letter to my solicitor, Mr Perkins, or his successor. It cannot be opened until someone claims the dukedom. In the left hand drawer of my dressing table, you'll find two letters. One is addressed to Luke, the other to Perkins."

John went to the dressing table, and pulling open the drawer; sure enough, there were two sealed envelopes, emblazoned with the Soame crest, lying inside. Turning, he saw Lady Soame had raised herself in the bed, and was looking at him keenly.

"Keep them safe. It's very important that Luke open his in your presence. When you and he finally see my solicitors, once you've brought him home, your testimony of this meeting, plus the letters will be his proof. Not a soul must know. This is our secret. Promise me."

"I promise," John said.

Edwina lay back on the pillows, exhausted.

"Thank you. "

After a pause, she seemed to rally.

"You're a strange one, John Baker," she said, smiling. "I believe you had feelings for me once. I've known it in my heart, since the day you rescued me from the flood. I saw it in your eyes.'

John hung his head, his eyes filling with tears.

"You've loved me from afar," Edwina whispered. "My only sorrow is that I was too proud to show you that I felt the same. A blacksmith's son and a duchess. Wouldn't that have caused a stir?"

She laughed feebly, John suddenly seeing her face become

beautiful once more.

"Now, however," she said, as their eyes met, "you can make a dying woman happier than she has ever been in her life. You can kiss me."

John bent over the bed, and as they kissed, the thought of her beauty and loveliness filled his soul, and all the years of longing, melted away in a moment.

"Thank you," Edwina murmured, as their lips parted. "Could you ask the others to come in, please?"

John opened the door, standing aside as Susan, Emma, Henry and nanny filed in, followed by the staff, the doctor, and the priest.

"If you could see yourselves," Edwina said smiling. "You look so sad. But please don't be. You've been my family, all these years. And how lucky I've been. I've loved every one of you. I truly have. Please don't grieve. All I pray is that one day we meet one another again in heaven. What memories we'll share. What fun. What laughter..." and slowly, as her voice drifted away, until it was the faintest breath, Lady Edwina Soame died.

Chapter Four

A day or so after Lady Soame's funeral in Bath Abbey, Emma was sitting in the drawing room at Oakwood, still grieving deeply for her lost mistress. However, wiping her eyes with her handkerchief, she unfolded the letter, and read the contents over again. Then crossing to the mantelpiece, pulled the sash on the wall. In moments, there was a knock on the door.

"Come in, Henry."

"Can I help you, Miss Baker?" he said, entering the room.

"For heaven's sake, Henry. Lady Soame may no longer be with us, but in all the years we've known each other, I've always been Emma."

"I'm sorry, Emma. But now you're head of the household, it becomes rather awkward, particularly with the other members of staff."

"If that's the case, then let it be Miss Emma, at least."

Henry smiled and bowed.

"Henry, we have a visitor this morning. Mr Perkins, Her Ladyship's solicitor. It seems he wishes to see the staff. Would you ask everyone to assemble in the dining room? Also, can my brother John also be in attendance."

"Very well, Miss Emma," Henry said, bowing and leaving the room.

Mr Perkins of Perkins, Perkins, and Perkins, stood on the doorstep, a large black document case under his arm.

"Good morning," he said, as Henry opened the door.

"Good morning, Mr Perkins. Please come in."

Ever since Lady Soame's arrival in Bath, Henry remembered Mr Perkins being her solicitor. But strangely, his memories of him were never as a young man, which of course he must have been. Now, here he was, old and shrivelled, the skin on his gaunt face, so thin, it was possible to see the blue veins creeping within it, his hair, white and wispy, hanging in untidy tufts from the yellowing skin on his head. In fact, Mr Perkins had the general appearance of dishevelment. As if, he no longer cared about his appearance.

"I've gathered Miss Baker and her brother, together with the servants, in the dining room, as requested Mr Perkins," Henry said, ushering him inside the hall.

"Thank you. I've several words to say to them. In addition, I wish particularly to see Mr Baker."

Under the watchful eyes of the sixteenth century portrait of the first Sir Stephen Soame, Lord Mayor of London, benefactor and wealthy merchant, hanging over the fireplace, everyone stood in silence, grouped around the dining table, as Mr Perkins entered the room.

"Please be seated," he said. "I'm sure Lady Soame would have wished it."

Feeling embarrassed, and unaccustomed to such informality, tentatively each person drew out a chair, and sat down.

"Ladies and gentlemen," Perkins said, sitting in the chair at the head of the table; the chair that once belonged to Her Ladyship, "the reason I've called you together, is because Lady Soame has made bequests to each of you in her will."

His words caused astonishment. Nevertheless, the staff remained silent, and respectful.

"Her Ladyship held you in high esteem," Perkins went on. "Lady Soame regarded you as her family, and refers to you as such in her will. In her bountiful goodness she has made provision for you all."

His crooked old fingers opened the document case, from which he took a large rolled parchment, breaking the wax seal. Then, spreading it out on the table, he anchored the corners with his fists.

"Her chief concern is of course the house, and the continuance of the school. Therefore, the majority of her bequest goes towards the maintenance and upkeep of Oakwood Ladies College. Her Ladyship urges everyone to continue the hard work that has been the cause of its success, and hopes that it will remain the finest educational establishment for young women in the country."

Emma smiled. It had been difficult in the beginning. However, the early labours were finally reaping fruition.

"Miss Baker and Mr Waldon. I'll begin with you, if I may. Lady Soame has bequeathed you an annuity of five hundred pounds, given annually, monthly or quarterly, as you so wish. This will be for the term of your natural life. If, and when you retire, you may remain in the house, and the annuity will continue."

Everyone gasped, since such a sum was a fortune. Yet, ignoring the atmosphere of astonishment, Perkins carried on.

"For the rest of you, and you'll forgive me if I don't mention you individually, Her Ladyship wishes you also remain in the house, still holding your positions, and paid at your usual rates. If, however, in the future, should the need arise, then a review will be conducted, and the wages adjusted. On your retirement, you will receive the sum of two thousand pounds."

Perkins said this so casually that no one reacted at first. But as each person realised the enormity of his words, all they could do was stare at each other in amazement.

"You mean she's giving us two thousand pounds?" Mr Ives broke in. "Just tell me I'm hearing right, Mr Perkins."

"That's correct, Mr Ives. I believe it's a fair sum on which to retire. Do you not think so?"

"Yes sir. To be sure."

Suddenly there was a babble of excited conversation, as in their wildest dreams the servants never imagined such a thing as inheriting wealth.

Perkins' thin voice interrupted their enthusiasm.

"Mr Baker!"

John stood up, as if in church, and about to sing a hymn, his massive frame seeming to dwarf everything, and everybody in the room.

"In your case things are rather different," continued Perkins, peering at John over his spectacles, "as you are not technically a member of the staff. Nevertheless, several months before she died, Lady Soame added a codicil to her will, naming you particularly."

All eyes turned to John, in anticipation of his bequest.

"Lady Soame bequeaths you the sum of five thousand pounds sterling, as a mark of her esteem, and as a reward for the service you have provided the Soame family."

Henry stared in astonishment at John, standing motionless, his huge hands by his side.

In the shocked silence, Mr Perkins began rolling up the parchment.

"Should any of you care to call at number twelve Belgrave Terrace, the firm of Perkins, Perkins and Perkins will be happy to supply you with details of your inheritance. In the meantime, let me be the first to offer my congratulations on your good fortune. Your mistress was a very special woman. The finest lady I personally have had the pleasure of knowing, throughout my long life."

Mr Perkins returned the parchment to the case, locked it with a small key, he took from his pocket, and then stood up to leave.

"No Henry," he said. "Don't worry. I know my way. I'll see myself out."

Once the door closed, everyone began talking at once, Henry going up to John and shaking his hand, although John seemed otherwise distracted.

"I reckon a celebration is called for, don't you think my friend. Her Ladyship would have wished it."

"Yes." John said, suddenly returning to reality. "Of course. I'm sorry Henry. I was thinking."

"What are you going to do with the money?" Henry asked, as he and John walked along the corridor.

"I'll give something to mother and father of course. I'd have to be sure they're provided for."

"But you'll be with them at Thurlow?"

"No," John answered. "I won't be able to run the forge."

"Why ever not?" Henry asked.

"I'm going to Australia."

"Why on earth are you going to Australia?"

"To find my godson."

Henry stared at him.

"Is that why Her Ladyship wished to see you?"

John smiled.

"I knew there was something going on, as soon as she sent for you. That's wonderful news. But it should be me. I should be the one to find him."

"It was Lady Soame's dying wish. I'll not go against it. But you're the only one to know. I promised her I'd keep it a secret. Anyway. You can't go. You're needed here, to help Emma."

"If you really think so. I can't believe it. Can I tell Lizzie?"

"No. Not even her."

"You'll need to see Perkins, Perkins, and Perkins, before you leave. You'll need your inheritance."

"And then I'll return to Thurlow. Once mother and father are cared for, I'll book passage."

"Well this really does call for a drink." Henry said, clapping John on the back, "As soon as I finish my duty, we'll take a stroll down to The Crown."

"That sounds good to me." John said, as the friends shook hands.

After Mrs Denton's excellent dinner, Henry watched George and John James return the silver to the safe. It felt strange using it, because, with Her Ladyship gone, there was little need for formality. Nowadays, the dining room was only used for special occasions, since Emma preferred to eat with her friends below stairs.

With their figurehead and mainstay no longer at the helm, the servants went about their daily work as usual, but with less sense of station or rank. Even so, everyone endeavoured to cling to the old ways, behaving politely to those they felt above them.

Since there was no Lady Soame to dress or care for, Mary and

Jane had time on their hands, which they used by taking walks in the garden, or helping in the kitchen. Whereas, Mrs Denton and Mrs Ives, both now in their seventies, felt Lady Soame's loss terribly, since each had served the family for most of their lives, missing the hustle and bustle of life in the home of a titled family. Consequently, with no house parties or banquets to arrange and cater for, like Jane and Mary, both had time to spare. However, as they were hardly young, and less able to do anything as vigorous as walking in the garden, the old ladies filled the time crocheting, or in needlecraft.

On the other hand, their husbands, with the prospect of inheriting money, had plenty to occupy them. Too old to do much work in the extensive gardens, Mr Denton employed two young garden lads, therefore partially easing his burden. But this also gave him time to follow his new passion, having become a devotee of the turf, and a frequenter of Bath Races. At first, his wife tried to ignore his occasional flutter. Even so, beneath her feigned indifference, she worried to see him gambling his weekly wages.

Alternatively, Mrs Ives had more reason to be concerned, as she began to see her husband's health endangered. Daniel had always been partial to a drop of the drink. But with the promise of wealth, plus the thought of a secure old age, he was fast becoming quite the 'Bon viveur', and was found most evenings, carousing at The Crown Inn in Bathwick Street.

It was to The Crown then, that Henry and John were heading that evening, and as they strolled down the cobbled street, approaching the inn, they began to hear the sound of singing.

"I know that voice," Henry said, as he ushered John through the door.

It was bright and cheerful inside the public house, with golden light from a dozen gas lamps, as well as a fire burning merrily in the hearth. The taproom was crowded, men packed against the bar, all of them smoking clay pipes, talking, laughing, while gulping tankards of ale or cider.

Outside, opulent terraced houses faced each other along Bathwick Street, the homes of rich and titled families. The street was also popular for lodging houses, where the less well off, or invalided, boarded while taking the cure. Consequently, a large population of servants lived in the vicinity, the men frequent customers of Tom Vincent's establishment, The Crown. From boot boys, stable lads, grooms and gardeners, to coachmen, footmen, and butlers, when they had a few hours off, after supper, the men and lads could be found at The Crown, enjoying a drink and a 'chin wag'. Rarely were women present, except those of a profession where it was necessary to be in the company of men.

To the dulcet refrain of a man singing, John and Henry edged their way through the crowd towards the counter.

"That's Mr Ives," Henry shouted over the din, having paid for the drinks. "Since we heard the news, he's here every night. I don't think Mrs Ives is very pleased."

"I shouldn't think so," John said, picking up his tankard of ale. "Shall we sit over there?"

He pointed to a vacant settle near the fire. So the friends pushed their way towards it, and sat down, taking a gulp of strong ale, while relaxing, their sense of friendship needing few words.

"Will you retire?" John asked, as they stared into the glowing embers.

"Not yet," chuckled Henry. "I'll wait till my bones tell me to."

"But why not? You don't need to work. You've an annuity."

"As you say John, I'm needed here to help run the school. But when I do retire, I'll return to Wratting, and my Lizzie. We'll settle into life there, and grow old together."

Gazing into the fire, Henry wondered what marvels his friend would see on his travels. Over the years, since losing his son to the colonies, he had deliberately erased Australia from his mind. Refusing to see pictures, or even read books about the colony, for fear of opening up the past, and reliving bitter memories. But he could hardly help overhearing stories told by people who had been there.

"Why are you smiling?" John said, lighting his pipe.

"I was thinking. I wonder how you'll find Australia."

"We should talk about young James," John said. "What shall I say to him, when I find him?"

Henry found John's question difficult to answer, since he had not even spoken his son's name in many years.

"I don't know, to be honest. I've tried forgetting James even exists, just so I can remain sane."

"Let's have another drink," John said, picking up the tankards. "It's my turn."

Henry watched John return to the bar, his huge frame carving a swathe through the crowd, so he took time to ponder on John's question. If he were travelling to the far side of the world, what indeed would he say to his son, should he find him?

"If it was me," he said, once John was sitting down again, and two brimming tankards faced them on the table. "I would shake his hand, and say, sorry lad."

"Sorry for what."

"I would want to apologise for not doing more to stop it happening."

"But you couldn't. You told me you did your best. And Her Ladyship tried for nearly a year."

"But I feel guilty."

"Then what shall I say?"

Henry had begun to feel the effects of the ale.

"You can put your arms around him, and say you're safe now son. Nothing's going to harm you ever again."

"That's all very well. But he'll be a grown man. He might think that a bit strange. Who knows what he's become, or what's become of him."

"Alright then." Henry said. "Just say his mother and father send their love. We hope he's well, and that we'll see him again one day."

John smiled.

"Do you reckon you'll find him?" Henry asked, taking another drink. "They say Australia's a huge country."

"There'll be records. I understand the government records everything.

"You'll let us know?"

It was beyond Henry's comprehension to think John might discover James was dead.

"If I'm able."

The fire was dying, so John Baker reached for a log in the pile, stacked against the wall, tossing it on to the glowing embers, sending sparks up the chimney.

"Do you remember us both going to the Cock Inn, that night?" Henry said, refilling his pipe. "The night I first arrived in Thurlow, to attend the Soame School."

"You were certainly a green horn. You'd never been inside an inn before."

"I had."

"You hadn't. You were petrified."

"Alright!" Henry chuckled. "I admit it. I was scared. But I was only nine. You weren't such a big man then either. Your father gave your game away, as I remember."

They laughed, the ale finally taking effect.

"Come on!" Henry said. "Let's go and see old Ives. I reckon the man needs some support."

Entering the snug, a great 'hoorah' greeted them, for sitting beside Dan Ives, swaying along to his song, was old Mr Denton.

"Come in men," he cried. "Come and join us. Dan's beginning to flag."

The friends joined the merry making, both of them trying to forget, that on the morrow they would say farewell, and perhaps for the last time.

After breakfast, the following day, everyone made a point to be at the front door.

Despite feeling the worse for wear, Mr Ives had risen early, in order to prepare John's horse for the long ride, and was waiting at the animal's head, while John said goodbye.

"We haven't had much time to talk," John said, taking his sister aside from the others.

"I know," Emma, said, "I've been so busy in the school. Miss Newcomb became ill, the day after the funeral, and I needed to take her classes."

John looked into Emma's eyes, wondering what she would say, if she knew what he was about to do? How would Emma feel knowing he was aware of her secret? She was now a respectable school headmistress, and must have striven hard to banish the shame of bearing Soame's child. John hated lying to her. But he could hear Her Ladyship's voice in his head. Now was not the time to tell his sister of his purpose, of that he was certain.

"I need to tell you what I'm about to do," John said instead.

For a moment, he saw a flicker of worry appear on her face.

"What's that?"

"I'm going to the colonies."

"Why?"

"I fancy I'll seek my fortune. Others have. So I thought I'd have a go."

"John! Have you told mother and father?"

"No. I've only just decided. I'll tell them when I get home. They'll understand."

"But you'll put yourself in danger. Who knows what will happen to you. I've heard terrible things. You'll go, and I'll never see you again."

John took Emma in his arms, and held her close.

"Don't be silly. I'm a big strong man. I can look after myself."

As he held her, Emma could feel her brother's strength envelope her.

"But John," she said, looking into his eyes, "you're my brother, and I love you. I don't know what I'd do without you."

"Don't you think I feel the same about you? You'll see me again. Never fear. I'll make sure of that."

"Well you better had," she said, brushing away a tear.

Kissing her forehead, they held each other close. Then John returned to the forlorn group gathered beneath the portico, shaking their hands, each person urging him to return soon, completely unaware of John's plans. Everyone, of course, except Henry.

"Goodbye my friend," John whispered, gripping Henry's hand. "This time it's me who's going on a journey. I promise to find your boy, and bring him home."

Henry watched John mount his horse.

What a figure he made, he thought. Romantic. Like a character from a novel by Walter Scott, or a knight from King Arthur's Camelot. John was off on a quest for a soul long thought lost. But of the other soul John was to rescue, Henry had no idea.

The women and girls waving their handkerchiefs, whilst the men cheered, John rode out of the gate, and looking back just once, waved, then galloped down the hill, and out of sight.

Chapter Five

As always, at shearing time, work at Mutt Mutt Billy began before sunrise, with Luke and the men gathering the flocks from the surrounding pastures, driving them to the holding pen beside the creek. However, before shearing, it was necessary to wash the sheep.

Lately, the price of wool had been low. In his letters from England, John Reddall, Luke's uncle, and wool broker, complained continually about the quality, and condition of the fleeces. Therefore, by ensuring the fleeces were clean, and to raise a good price, Luke endeavoured to provide him with the best possible product.

Firstly, the men drove a batch of ewes into the creek, the air in their thick fleeces causing them to float, the men following. Standing in water up to their chests, they dunked each animal, until they were saturated, afterward, washing the fleeces vigorously using paste made from wood ash, at the same time, removing any dried droppings, grass seeds, or sticks. Soaking the ewe once more to rinse her, she would swim to the opposite bank, where she would dry in the sun. Obviously, with a flock of over five hundred, this activity took most of the day. Until finally, all the sheep stood dripping in the yard adjoining the shearing shed.

Next day, the sheep were dry enough to shear; the shining fleeces eventually piled high on the sorting table, and inside the bales, pressed ready for shipment.

The shears clattered, resembling scythes cutting dry meadow grass, the sound carrying all the way to the kitchen, where Martha was busy baking pies and pasties, to feed the hungry men. Looking through the window it amused Martha to see the scrawny white sheep in the pens, no longer, carrying their huge burden of wool, their long ears drooping comically, beside narrow, bony faces.

By the end of the third day, with shearing complete, it was time to rest, Luke putting on his shirt, and wiping his hands on the knees of his pants, already thick with grease.

"Well done, you blokes," he said. "You deserve extra grog tonight. Tell Martha I said to tap a fresh barrel of beer."

"Good on ya! Master Luke," everyone cheered.

Seeing the men run across the yard to the washhouse, Luke knew he was not quite ready to go inside. He needed air. Fresh air. Since all he had inhaled for the past days was the hot breath of sheep.

Therefore, he turned towards the Bald Hill behind the farm, and with the sun sinking below the distant ranges, traversed the creek, kneeling beside the pebbly ford, to splash his face. Feeling the cool water on the back of his neck, and his hot tired eyes, he began to wade through the long grass, making his way up the hill. At the top, Luke sat down, hugging his knees to his chest, and facing the setting sun.

By now, Luke had lived at Mutt Mutt Billy for twelve years, having seen a day like today a dozen times. Nevertheless, to him it always seemed like the first. The day he sheared his first sheep.

Dick Spittle laughed.

"The poor critter!" he shouted across the shed. "She'll bleed to death, if you don't watch out Master Luke."

It was a funny moment. Luke clearly remembering the other men laughing.

All right! She was his first sheep. It was obvious he was going to make a mess of her. But he would learn. And learn he did, each year becoming faster. As a result, nowadays, only Bill Poney, out of all of them, could shear a ewe faster than Luke.

Luke enjoyed shearing time, since, yet again, he could appreciate the fine bunch of men he employed. They were like family to him, each trustworthy, and hardworking fellows. Not a bad one amongst them. Ticket of Leavers now, they chose to remain at Mutt Mutt Billy. As a result, he never needed to apply for other assigned labour. Something he loathed, believing they might bring new influences on to the farm.

Sitting on top of the Bald Hill, watching the red disc of the sun slowly disappear behind the range, and with his mind dwelling on comradeship and family, Luke endeavoured to avoid other thoughts, filtering into his mind. Memories with which he would rather not contend. It was too late, however. He was tired, and too weak to resist, his eyes filling with tears, his chest suddenly feeling heavy with a wealth of sorrow.

It was a day like any other, a bullock was slaughtered, Luke and the men hunting in the morning, catching and killing two old roo bucks, and a wild dog. Yet, when Luke returned to the house, there was a strange horse standing at the rail.

"Who is it Martha?" Luke called, crossing the veranda, and tossing his panama onto a chair.

She was standing at the back door.

"The gentleman's in the parlour," she said. "I'm just getting him a drink."

"Did he tell you his name?"

"Mr Holsworthy, from Glen Alpine."

"Whatever does John want, coming all this way?"

"He didn't say, sir."

Luke opened the parlour door.

"Good to see you, John," he said, seeing him standing in the centre of the room. "You're a long way from home?"

"Good to see you too, Master Luke. Are you well?"

Luke shook John's hand.

"I am sir. And you John?"

"Quite well sir. Thank God."

"You look exhausted. Sit down. Martha's bringing you a glass of beer."

"I'd rather stand sir, if I may."

"Very well, John. But you look so serious."

"Yes sir. I am. I'm here on serious business."

"Don't tell me! My father! What's happened now? He and Mr Terry have had another set to."

"No sir. I'm sorry sir. It's far more serious than that."

Luke was at the cabinet, and about to pour a glass of wine, but the tone in John's voice made him turn.

"What's happened?"

"I've known you since you were a lad, Master Luke, and served your father for nigh on sixteen years. But this is the hardest thing I've ever had to do."

Luke put the crystal glass back on the tray.

"Yes John?" he said quickly. "What are you going to tell me?"

John looked at the floor, not wishing to see the young man's face, when he heard the news.

"Your father, Master Luke. He's dead."

His eyes fixed on the dark red and black pattern of the carpet, in the silence that followed, John heard Luke breathing.

"When?" Luke said faintly.

"Five days ago. Your mother told me to ride here, the day it happened. I should have arrived yesterday, but there were floods cutting off the bottom road. I needed to take the Razor Back."

"What happened?"

Luke dropped onto the sofa, his legs suddenly weak.

"They say its influenza. A dreadful fever. Many are dying in Campbelltown and Liverpool. Poor Mr De Arrieta and his wife were carried off, the week before your father."

"Oh no!" Luke said, his eyes filling with tears. "I don't believe it! Dear Mr Arrieta and Sophia."

"It's a terrible thing, sir. People are dropping like flies. Your father married a couple in the morning, and by nightfall, he was dead. We're all in a dreadful state of shock."

"How's mother?"

"Anne's a tower of strength, of course. We can thank heaven for her. Though I can't say Mrs Reddall's taking it well."

"Does John know?"

"He's in India. And not expected home for several months."

"I'll write a letter. I should be the one to tell him. We'll take it with us, and see it makes the first boat to Calcutta."

"Are you alright, Master Luke?" Holsworthy asked, finally able to look at him.

"I think so. But I don't know that it's quite hit home."

"No sir. I still can't believe it."

There was a knock on the door, and Martha came in, carrying a glass of beer on a tray.

"If you'll excuse me, John," Luke said. "I'll not join you. If I do, I mightn't stop, until this terrible news becomes a bad dream. I need to have my head straight. There's a lot to be done. If you don't mind, I'll go to my room. Martha will see you get some dinner, and a bed for the night."

Luke looked at his reflection in the mirror. Why was it he never saw his father reflected there? Every so often, in his brother John, he had seen almost a mirror image of their papa. His eyes, the shape of his head, even the way his ears were made. But in Luke's case, try as he may, he could never find a resemblance to either his father, or the Spanish semblance of his mother, with her once dark brown curling hair, and deep brown eyes.

"Why?" he said aloud. "My eyes are green, and my hair's straight, and black."

Luke stared at his arched nose. Not at all his father's. Papa's nose was small, and squat. Then his chin was squarer by far than the other Reddall men. And his lips were full, not thin, as in their case. Perhaps he resembled his paternal grandfather, the man after whom Luke took his name. The man he never knew.

He sat down on the bed, a feeling of despair welling inside him, the final realisation dawning. Never again would he see his father's face, or hear his voice urging him to succeed. Praising, never scolding, not once patronising. What would he do, now he was gone? No one from whom to seek approval, or show he had grown into a man. Tears stung Luke's eyes, and he was powerless to control his sorrow, as anguish exploded from deep inside, in waves of silent grief.

"Rather than me ride back alone," said Luke, the following

morning. "I'd like you to come with us Jim."

"Of course, Mister Luke," James said. "I'll saddle Dan."

"And get Clarence ready for me!" Luke shouted after him.

By the time the sun was at its highest, everything was ready. Consequently, as the tiny bell of Luke's pocket watch struck noon, the three men rode out of the yard, the horsemen barely casting a shadow, as they galloped up the track.

Reaching the road, they turned east, heading over the plains towards Goulburn, John Holsworthy, and James respecting Luke's feelings, by remaining silent for most of the way. Luke also hardly spoke, his mind rapt in memories.

Glen Alpine appeared quiet, as the men galloped through the gate, and arriving in the garden, Luke jumped from his horse, passing James the reins.

"Look after him." he shouted, running up the steps, and onto the veranda. "I must see mother."

Inside, Luke stood in the hallway, his ears searching the silence. Then, from somewhere far away, he heard the sound of weeping. Not issuing from the bedroom end of the house, where he would have expected, but from the kitchen. Running down the corridor, Luke reached the back door.

It was partially open, so Luke could see across the yard into the kitchen, and a woman sitting at the table, her head, and arms across it, weeping hysterically. It was Anne Farrell.

"Anne! Anne!" he yelled, rushing into the kitchen. "Whatever's the matter?"

"Master Luke. Thank God you're here."

She leapt up, clinging to him, her arms entwined around his neck.

"It's like evil's come upon this house sir. The angel of the lord has swept over it, and taken everything in its path."

"What do you mean, Anne?" Luke exclaimed angrily, trying to disengage her hold. "Get a grip on yourself."

"Your sister, Master Luke!" she wailed. "My lovely Julia. The little girl I helped into the world. Gone! Gone!"

"Gone?" Luke shouted. "Gone where?"

"Gone sir! Dead! Dead! Yesterday. Not four days after your dear father. And now! I can't bear to think! It's too dreadful."

"What Anne? What? I can't believe this is happening! Please Lord, tell me it's all a dream!"

"Get out of the house, Master Luke. It's cursed. Cursed I tell you. You'll be a dead man. You mark my words."

Luke shook her.

"Anne! For God's sake! My sister's dead?"

"Yes sir. Yes sir. It's true. But sir! I can't bear to say it. Only hours ago."

Anne slumped into the chair, laying her head on the table, weeping uncontrollably.

"What!" Luke screamed.

"Your mother, sir."

Anne looked up into his face.

"Your mother too."

"No!" Luke cried, sinking to the floor. "My God! Tell me Anne it isn't true. Tell me it's one of your dreadful lies. Tell me Anne! Tell me!"

"I can't sir. I wish I could. But I can't. Your darling mother. She's in her room. I can't bear to see her. What to do? What to do?"

Wringing her hands, Anne dragged her fingers through her tangled hair, her old face strained, her eyes stained by days of grief.

All of Luke's strength drained away, and he prostrated himself on the stone floor, and wept helplessly.

Outside in the yard, James heard a sound coming from the kitchen, resembling the noise of wind, moaning in the gum trees. So, seeing the horses had food and water, he ran towards the kitchen yard, the sight greeting him when he reached the door would remain in his mind forever.

His master lay on the floor, overwhelmed with grief, while an old woman at the table was wringing her hands, and wailing. The scene seemed unreal, like something James would see on the stage. Nevertheless, this was no melodrama. This was real.

"What's happening?" John Holsworthy said, appearing beside him. "All the servants have vanished. The place is empty. Everyone's scarpered."

"I don't know," whispered James, as they stared into the kitchen. "Something awful, by the look of things. I've never seen him like this. What'll we do?"

"Nothing. We'll have to wait till he calms down."

"What about the woman," James said. "Can we get any sense out of her?"

"It doesn't look like it. All I hope is there's not murder been done here. We should look around. You take the front. I'll do the back."

Tiptoeing down the corridor, past the dining room, the study, and the library, James found everywhere quiet, and undisturbed. Nothing to give an indication any violence had taken place. Looking into the drawing room, he even saw an embroidery frame, standing beside the fireplace, coloured silk threads, sitting on the top of a walnut workbox.

A corridor ran each side of the drawing room, James presuming it led to the bedrooms, so quietly he opened the first door he reached.

The bed was unmade, the sheets and blankets pulled back, falling onto the polished floorboards, a surplice and cassock across a chair beside a dressing table. A door was across the corridor, facing the back of the house, so James opened it, and peered inside.

A girl lay on the bed, wearing a nightdress, and partially covered by a colourful patchwork quilt. Suddenly James felt embarrassed, worried he might have disturbed her. He was about to close the door, when a feint odour drifted into his nostrils; a scent he had never before experienced. Sweet. Yet acrid and quite revolting. Horrified, James realised it was the smell of death.

By the look of the girl, she had been dead for some days. Had she been murdered? James considered whether to uncover her, to look for a wound, but decided to leave her alone instead. Closing the door, he was about to return to Mr Holsworthy with the news, when something drew his attention to the room next to the chaplain's.

"I may as well check," he whispered, quickly opening the door.

"Mrs Reddall!" he exclaimed aloud. "I'm sorry!"

James began to close the door. However, looking again, he saw her lying on the bed, wearing a black satin dress, a hand across her chest clasping a handkerchief, the other hanging lifelessly towards the floor, the fine fingers tips almost touching the silk carpet.

"She's dead too," he exclaimed aloud. "Both dead."

Covering his mouth and nose with his hand, James recoiled from the door, and ran back to the kitchen.

Holsworthy was at the door.

"Sir," James whispered. "Sir. They're…"

"I know," he said. "Dead. Anne's managed to tell me."

James peered into the gloom of the kitchen, seeing Mister Luke sitting at the table, staring blankly at the wall, while an old woman shuffled about, moving pots and pans.

"Make us some tea, Anne, please," John said.

As if in a trance, Anne reached for the kettle, filling it with water from the pump.

"Certainly, Mr Holsworthy."

"We're all in need of a cup," Holsworthy continued. "I reckon Master Luke could do with one too, I dare say. Don't you Master Luke?"

Luke shook himself; like a dog waking from sleep.

"Yes. Yes, I would Anne. Thank you. Tea would be nice."

While Anne made tea, Holsworthy took James aside, and away from Luke's hearing.

"As soon as Master Luke is feeling better, I'll ride to Parramatta, and bring back Reverend Forrest."

"But we'll need to get the women into somewhere cool," James said. "Got any ideas?"

"The stone walls of the dairy store are good and thick. It's always cold in there."

"Do you reckon we'll manage them on our own?"

"We'll have to. These two are hardly up to it."

When James and Holsworthy finished their tea, John spoke up.

"Don't look for us for a while, Master Luke. We must do something. We'll not be long."

"What?" Luke said, as if in dream.

"Nothing you need bother yourself with, sir. You stay here with Anne."

First, they made space in the dairy store, by clearing the shelves of churns and presses. Then, after moving all edible goods to another storeroom, they returned to the house, and Miss Julia's room.

"Have you a handkerchief?" John asked, as they reached the door. James shook his head.

"Alright. Wait here."

John hurried down the corridor, and opening the chaplain's bedroom door, disappeared inside, emerging shortly with two large handkerchiefs.

"Right! Tie this around your face. We don't know what's killed them. We need to be careful."

It was the first time James had seen, let alone touched, a dead person. However, he surprised himself, because, as he and Holsworthy lifted the dead girl, he had no feeling of horror or revulsion carrying her, realising the body was nothing but a shell, or empty barrel. When life left the child, so did her soul.

After laying her on a shelf in the storeroom, they returned to Mrs Reddall's room to repeat the procedure.

Once the women were in place, James and Holsworthy covered them with large bed sheets, closing and locking the door.

"While I ride to Parramatta, will you be alright here on your own?" Holsworthy asked.

"Don't worry, sir," answered James. "I'll be fine."

"I hope to be back by sunset. Have a scout around, and see if you can find food. Get some into your boss. He's had nothing for days."

As soon as John left, James returned to the kitchen, where he found Anne sitting at the table, quiet now, her eyes staring, and her face vacant. Luke though, was nowhere to be seen.

James returned to the house, where he began searching the rooms, and reaching the door to the library, saw it slightly open, so he quietly peered inside.

On the far side of the room, below a large painting, swung away from the wall, Mister Luke was rotating the dial of a safe. Sensing someone was watching, he turned sharply.

"What are you doing, Jim?" he shouted. "Spying on me?"

"No sir!" James exclaimed. "Of course not! I was worried. I couldn't find you. I wondered where you were."

"I'm sorry James. That was wrong of me. It's just that I don't know the bloody number. Father never told me. I must get it. We mustn't leave the house without the cup."

"What! The Macquarie Cup!" gasped James. "Is it in there?"

"Yes. It's been here all these years. Along with my winnings."

"Everything you won?"

"More or less."

"But there must be thousands of pounds in there?"

"There are. And I need to have them."

Irritably, Luke ran his fingers over the reels, pulling on the handle in frustration.

"Perhaps your father wrote down the combination," James said.

"If he did, where do you think it might be?"

"On his desk?"

"Could be! Come on. Let's go to the study."

They needed to pass through the drawing room, and while doing so; Luke suddenly stopped and stared at the workbox, and the tapestry on the frame.

"What am I thinking?" he said. "Here I am worrying about money, when my mother, father, and sister are dead. What will I do? I've no one. No one in the world."

He slumped onto a sofa, weeping helplessly.

"See the workbox," he sobbed. "I gave it to mother. I found it in a shop in King Street. So pretty! I knew she'd like it. How pleased she'd been that Christmas. She said it was the best present she'd ever had."

Watching his master weeping, James felt helpless, wishing he could find the words, or do something to comfort him.

Finally the sobs subsided.

"Why did everyone leave?" Luke asked, wiping his eyes.

"You mean the servant's, sir?"

Luke nodded.

"They were scared perhaps. Maybe the fever frightened them away."

"But wouldn't you think they would stick by the family, and not run off as soon as their master and mistress were dead?"

James had no answer. Nonetheless, he was sure that he would never do such a thing, certain of his loyalty to Luke. However, Mister Luke was a very congenial person, fair, as well as kind. The best master a man could have. Perhaps things were different at Glen Alpine.

"We'll shut the house," Luke said, taking control of his emotions, while closing the portrait over the safe. "With my brother in India, there's nobody to look after things. John Holsworthy will be too busy handling the stock. Come on! Let's look for those numbers."

The study was dark and stuffy, so Luke opened the windows, letting in fresh warm air. Then, turning his attention to his father's desk, he sat down in the leather chair, and began searching through the layers of papers, the first appearing to be a draft of his father's Christmas sermon. Sadly, it remained unfinished.

While sifting through the documents and letters, Luke's mind began to drift.

Better to die as his father, he thought, with no idea of pending death. One moment in the midst of life, the next, nothing but the vastness of black eternity. However, would it be an eternity of nothing? No! Not according to his father's teachings. 'Heaven is waiting for us all', he had said. That is of course, if we lead a good and true Christian life. In this heaven, might Luke see his mother and father on the great day? Luke doubted it. He was a sceptic when it came to the concept of heaven. Is there such a place? A realm where he will be reunited with his family, living together with them forever, bathed in the glory of God. He wished he could believe it, but Luke had to admit he found the concept difficult to accept. The strong belief held by his father, had never rung true for Luke, the notion of heaven seeming fanciful. A myth created by humanity. To placate its fear of the unknown.

"Can you see anything?" asked James, "Any numbers written down anywhere?"

"If there are," Luke said, going through the papers one by one. "I'd think they'd be in a book."

"How about a bible?"

"Yes! That'll be the place."

The bible was on the desk, and open at the book of Chronicles, obviously, where his father was to draw his text. Closing the heavy book, Luke opened it again; the flyleaf stained, and blotched with small brown marks, appearing to have been subjected to damp air, and seawater. However, the page was blank. Then, turning the next page, Luke saw a scribbled text, in the top left hand corner.

"Seek and ye shall find," he read aloud. "What does that mean? I know it's part of a verse from the bible. But from which book?"

"I'm sure I know it, Mister Luke," James said. "I remember from my time on the ship. I'm almost positive it's from the Sermon on the Mount, in the gospel of Saint Matthew."

Luke flicked through the pages, until he came to the New Testament, and running his fingers along the edge, found Saint Matthew.

"Here it is," he said. "'Seek and ye shall find'. Clever old Jim!"

"What's the verse number?"

"Seven."

"And the line number?"

Luke counted down the text.

"Seven. Although there's usually three numbers in a combination."

"Well Matthew is the first of the gospels, so number one could be the first number. Joining the numbers together, we get one, seven seven. Let's try it."

"But it's too easy. I'm sure it can't be right."

"Too easy perhaps for someone who can read? But how many clever bushrangers, runaways, and thieves do you know?"

"All right. Come on! Let's try it."

Once Luke had scribbled the set of numbers on a scrap of paper, they hurried out of the study.

Back in the library, Isabella Reddall looked down serenely from her portrait, her dark brown hair, touched here and there, with tints of light, her beautiful face glowing with life and health.

A month before the family left England for Australia, Luke's father commissioned the famous portrait painter, Sir Thomas Lawrence, to paint his wife's portrait. The picture had survived the voyage, packed in a straw filled crate, buried deep in the hold of The Morley. Fortunately, it remained untouched by seawater that frequently surged across the decks, and down the hatches.

On their return to the library, Luke stopped, and gazing up at his mother, felt another surge of sorrow. Except, this time he shook himself, and taking the edge of the gilt frame, pulled the picture towards him, revealing the metal door, and the reel of numbers.

"Alright. Turn it to number one."

James stood beside him, reading from the scrap of paper.

Luke twisted the dial to the first figure.

"Now seven."

They heard a click from inside the safe.

"We've done it!" Luke exclaimed, giving the door a tug. However, it stood fast.

"Put in the last number."

Doing so, and hearing another click, Luke pulled on the door again, and this time it swung open.

"Thank heavens!" Luke cried. "We've done it. Well done Jim!"

On the bottom shelf, an object was wrapped in a brown flannel cloth.

"The cup," he whispered.

Lifting it out, and putting it on the table, Luke removed the cloth, revealing the Macquarie Cup, shining as brightly as it did on the day he held it above his head, six years earlier.

"What'll we do with it?" Luke said. "It's too valuable to take to the farm. Though it can't stay here, in the empty house. Anything could happen."

"What about the church?" James said. "You father's church. There must be a place where he kept the chalice and candlesticks?"

"I suppose so. But I wouldn't know where. John Holsworthy says a new reverend's taken father's place. Maybe he'll be able to help."

Luke stared inside the safe once more, seeing a stack of brown paper packets, tied with string. It was his money. Luke's mother had methodical kept everything neat, and in order. Once again, Luke knew the money must not remain at Glen Alpine. He would take it back to Mutt Mutt Billy. But he would need to hide it in a safe place.

Perhaps in a hole under the house.

"Come on Jim," he said, suddenly shutting the safe, and putting back the portrait. "I think we've had enough of this. Let's go to the kitchen. All of a sudden I feel extremely hungry."

John Holsworthy must have ridden hard, because he was back at Glen Alpine by late evening, along with the Reverend Forrest, following in his buggy.

"I can't tell you how sorry I am, Luke," Forrest said, as they stood on the veranda. "Everyone at The Grange is dreadfully shocked. There's nothing to describe our sorrow. Mr Holsworthy tells me, he thinks the funeral may be tomorrow, so I've sent word to the Governor. He'll be as overcome as we are."

"Thank you, sir," said Luke. "I still can't comprehend it myself. Nevertheless, life must go on. Mother's servant, Anne, prepared supper. Shall we go inside?"

Luke and Forrest walked ahead, giving John Holsworthy a moment with James.

"Has he been inside the dairy?" he whispered.

"No. And he's not said a thing. Not even to ask where they are."

"Do you think he's alright?"

"He seems to be getting a hold on himself. But who knows."

Supper was a subdued affair, Forrest doing most of the talking, telling tales about the life of his predecessor at Saint John's, the Reverend Samuel Marsden, making it clear to Luke, John, and James, that he was hardly an admirer. The stories he told of the old chaplain's activities, contained accounts of beating runaways and absconders, hanging bushrangers, and punishing disconsolate factory women. Hardly surprising then, that Marsden was known in the colonies as 'The Flogging Parson'.

Unable to join the conversation, Luke got up from the table.

"If you'll excuse me, gentlemen," he said. "I really must go to bed. I feel quite exhausted."

"What will happen in the morning?" Forrest asked, once Luke had left the room.

"We've a gang wagon, still on the place," John said. "It's completely enclosed, so James and I will put Mrs Reddall and Miss

Julia inside, then drive to Mr Brooker the carpenter and undertaker in Campbelltown. Then you can follow with Anne and Master Luke."

"That sounds a fine arrangement," Forrest said.

"We'll bury them in the afternoon," John said. "That'll give the grave diggers enough time to dig the graves."

"You're a good man, Mr Holsworthy," Forrest said. "Mr Reddall would be pleased to see you handling this so well."

John put down his napkin, and got up from the table.

"It's all I can do for my master. Allow me to show you to your room reverend."

Anne awoke the following morning feeling better. For days since Julia's death, the dreadful nightmare had shocked her awake. Julia was calling. Reaching out to her. Begging. Pleading. The girl's voice so clear; Anne could hear it echoing through the house, as natural as if Julia were alive. Yet now, Anne felt at peace. Maybe the poor child's soul had been released from the world, entering another place of calmness and tranquillity.

Once washed, and her hair brushed, Anne went into the kitchen to light the range. An hour later breakfast was ready.

"How's your master this morning, James?" Holsworthy asked, once the doors of the wagon were shut.

"Mister Luke rose early," James said. "He came to the bunk house, and said he wanted fresh air, asking me to saddle Clarence. When he got back the horse was well lathered. So he must have ridden him hard."

Later that morning, James and John Holsworthy stood outside Mr Brooker's workshop, after carrying the bodies inside.

"He'll take care of things," Holsworthy said. "It'll be well after midday before Mr Brooker's ready. How about the hotel?"

"I've no money, sir," James said.

"Don't worry, mate. I think I can afford to shout you dinner and an ale."

Mr Hurley appeared unusually gloomy.

"Come in, Mr Holsworthy," he said. "Welcome to The King's Arms. It'll be a drink you're after, I'll be bound? And bless my soul! It's Luke's servant. The lad who saved the Macquarie Cup.

"Thank you, Mr Hurley," James said. "It's good to see you again."

The old man filled two tankards with beer from a barrel on the bar.

"I'm sorry to hear about the chaplain," he said. "He'll be sadly missed in the town."

John took his drink, passing the other to James.

"Thanks, Mr Hurley. But you obviously haven't heard."

"What?"

"Young Julia and Mrs Reddall were taken, only yesterday."

Hurley stared in disbelief.

"Does Luke know?"

"Yes sir."

"How is the dear boy? He must be devastated."

"He's handling things rather better today. In fact, he's on his way here. The funeral's this afternoon."

"I'll shut the hotel. They must have a proper send off. I'll let everyone know."

Patrick Hurley did a fine job, because, several hours later, as Mr Brooker's hearse pulled out of the stable, the streets of Campbelltown were crowded, people removing their hats, and bowing their heads as a mark of respect for a family that had been highly regarded in the town, even before it was established.

With the crowd shambling along behind the cortège, when it reached Saint Peter's church, Mr Brooker drove the carriage up to the front doors.

Having buried their beloved chaplain five days previously, the sorrowful congregation watched the coffins make their way up the aisle towards the altar, Luke standing alone in the front pew.

Important dignitaries from Sydney and Parramatta dropped everything when they heard the news, and now crowded the pews behind Luke. Mr Kinchela was there, along with his daughter Mary, also, Archbishop William Broughton, Samuel Terry's widow Rosetta, representing him, since he died earlier in the year. W C Wentworth, and his wife Sarah were also in attendance, as well as Luke's sister in law, Martha, the wife of his bother John. Representing the Governor, Sir George Gipps, was Sir Edward Deas Thomson, the colonial secretary.

With the organ droning sombrely, the bearers lifted the coffins onto trestles, Reverend Forrest stepping out of the shadows to address the gathering.

From the back of the church, James could see his master keeping his emotions in check, now and again, glancing at the coffins.

At the finish of the service, and once Mrs Reddall and Julia were put to rest beside their father and husband, everyone crossed the street to the Kings Arms Hotel. Mr Hurley had produced a lavish buffet, the bar soon crowded with people taking advantage of free food and drink. Huddling in groups, muttering, and shaking their heads, people were keen to maintain the sombre nature of the gathering.

James and John watched Luke approach them across the room, holding a glass brimming with red wine. And by the way he was reeling, it was clearly not his first.

"My men!" he said loudly, throwing his arms around them. "What would I do without you? My stalwarts! My squires! I'll repay you, never fear! You know that, of course!"

"Yes sir," John and James said together.

"Drink lads! Go on! Have a drink! My father would want it. He would have loved all this."

Luke swung an arm around the room.

"Father loved folk enjoying themselves. So did mother. So do I! Drink up everyone!" he shouted. "Be cheerful. Talk. Laugh. Let's not make this a sad affair. Because, who knows, tomorrow we could all be dead."

Everyone laughed uneasily, since it was difficult to be merry. Such a tragedy to strike one family was hard to minimize. All except for Anne Farrell that is, who was well on her way, John and James seeing her stagger and sway towards them through the throng.

"I'm bloody glad you two are here," she said, grabbing their arms, to keep from falling. "You're the only buggers I know. All these bloody toffs. Would you believe it? Swarming round Master Luke like leeches. We know the chaplain left debts. But you'd think these bastards would have a bit of decorum, and choose a better time.

Even Mrs Terry is here to collect."

Anne shouted so loudly, it was obvious everyone could hear, especially Rosetta Terry, who was busy in conversation with Mrs Wentworth.

"Shush Anne!" John said, "Not so loud. You're causing a scene."

"Causing a scene am I?" she said, faking a whisper. "I'll cause a scene alright. If I tell all I know of some of the folk hereabouts, and what they say about my dear master and mistress. How they talked behind their backs. They thought stupid old Anne couldn't hear, or didn't care. Well she could, and she did. But I kept quiet, didn't I, for fear of upsetting my darling mistress, and her dear dead husband."

"Come on Anne!" John said. "Let's go outside. I think we could do with some fresh air."

Left alone, James saw Luke talking to Mr Kinchela, and a young woman. Suddenly they looked his way, and Luke beckoned to James to join them.

"You remember Mr Kinchela, don't you Jim," Luke said.

"Yes sir," said James. "Very well."

"Well this is his daughter, Mary."

"I'm very pleased to meet you again, sir," James said, bowing. "And to make your acquaintance, Miss Kinchela."

"Well my boy!" Kinchela said. "It's good to see you. I've often wondered about you, since we met on the day of the races. Luke says you've been getting along splendidly."

"Yes sir. Very well indeed."

"Eh?" the old man said.

"You'll need to speak up, young man," Mary said. "My father's terribly deaf."

"Very well indeed, sir," James shouted. "I'm a blacksmith on Mister Luke's farm, at Mutt Mutt Billy."

"But that will change very soon, Mr Kinchela," Luke shouted into the old gentlemen's ear.

James glanced at his master.

"I've just spoken to the Colonial Secretary," continued Luke. "I told him I wanted a change. Something new in my life. A challenge."

"Sometimes Luke," said Mary, "that's just what we need, when something like this happens."

"That's right!" he exclaimed, taking another glass of wine from a passing waiter.

"But wait!" Luke shouted, searching the crowded room. "Elliot!"

James saw a fresh faced young man, pop his head above the throng. And smiling, he began easing his way towards them.

"May I introduce, Elliot Herriot everyone," Luke said, when the young man was beside them. "His father, and my uncle John Reddall, were at Eton together. Elliot! May I introduce my friend, Mr Kinchela, his daughter Mary, and my man James?"

Nodding, the young man eagerly shook their hands.

"Elliot's out from England. His father's sent him to the colonies, to learn the ropes. Isn't that right, Elliot?"

Elliot smiled warmly.

"Yes sir. Father seems to think I need some experience of life. So I hope you won't mind me tagging along for a while."

"Of course not, Elliot," Luke said laughing. "The more the merrier. What do you say Jim?"

James nodded.

"But going back to what I was saying," Luke continued, putting his hand on James' shoulder to steady himself. "Sir Edward agreed, allowing me to purchase two and a half thousand acres, in the south west. That's where you'll be going Jim. You. Bill Poney and Elliot here. As soon as I sign the papers, you'll be heading to a place called, Ten Mile Creek. Sir Edward tells me the run is close to the Hume River, and called 'Durra Durra', but for heaven's sake, don't ask me why."

Chapter Six

Fourteen years had passed, since Hume and Hovell, set out to discover a route south to Port Philip.

When Hamilton Hume first saw the river, he was so impressed by its magnitude; he named it after himself, explaining to his fellow explorer, William Hovell, that the name Hovell would hardly be appropriate for such a mighty watercourse. One evening, during their exploration along the river, Hume and Hovell happened upon a bend, where the river was wide, and tumbled over a multitude of pebbles and boulders. Appearing to be a likely place to camp, they pitched their tents for the night. In the morning, Hume woke early, and gathering together his shaving gear, walked to the riverbank in order to wash and shave. He balanced his mirror on a rock, seeing in its reflection a group of aborigines watching him intently.

"Good morning!" he said, at the same time soaping his face with the shaving brush. "Lovely morning!"

They were approaching, appearing to be interested to see him scraping the razor across his chin. Once he finished, he went to the water's edge to splash his face.

"What do they call this place?" he asked, pointing to the water tumbling over the pebbles and rocks.

An old man, appearing to be the chief of the mob came forward.

"Durra, Durra, Durra, Durra," he said repeatedly.

William Hovell was once a ship's captain, and therefore an

excellent navigator and mapmaker. These skills resulted in Governor Brisbane choosing him to join Hume on the expedition. Hume narrated the story of what had just occurred that morning, so when Hovell came to map the location where they camped, he wrote beside it, 'Durra Durra'.

***

Luke remained in Campbelltown for a month after his mother and sister's funeral, since there was business to arrange, and debts to be addressed. Although, there was another task to undertake. Once they were buried, Luke instructed Mr Gibbs the stonemason, to construct a marble vault, in order Thomas, Isabella and Julia might spend the rest of eternity together.

His father's Will caused few surprises. Glen Alpine and the surrounding land was to be divided between Isabella, had she survived Luke's father, then Luke and John, and their sister, had she lived. Luke and John inherited Glen Alpine and Mutt Mutt Billy, respectively. Millbong, the property south of John's run at Breadalbane, belonged to Isabella, and it was bequeathed to Luke. However, John's cattle ran on the land, Luke having hardly a reason to change the arrangement. Luke's father left little money, so Luke settled the debts with his own, dipping into the savings from years of racing. Fortunately, with these paid, and the property Durra Durra on the Hume River finally purchased, Luke retained enough cash to stock his new run with cattle.

Luke made a list of the servants that ran away from his father's house on the day his mother and sister died. Then sent it by coach to Sydney, to be posted in the Gazette, whether or not the runaways were apprehended hardly concerned him. He almost forgave the escapees, believing anyone, given the circumstance, would have fled the scene for fear of their lives. Maybe they had earned their freedom, since they had been loyal to his father for many years. It must have taken a great deal of fear for them to run away. Glen Alpine and his new farm, however, were unable to run themselves, and Luke needed additional servants, for the former, and stock for the latter. Hence, he made an application to the Superintendent of

Convicts, for an assignment of twenty government men.

The convict men arrived a week later, Luke appalled to see them confined inside a clearing gang wagon, the consequence of their journey to Campbell Town, clearly evident inside. Immediately, Luke ordered them to wash themselves. Then supplied each man with new clothing. Afterward, having scrutinized the indents, he chose six men suitable to work with stock, assigning them to his late father's overseer, John Holsworthy, giving the remainder to Mr Hurley, who housed them in sheds behind his hotel, the following day, putting them to work on labouring jobs around the town. Then John Holsworthy and James Waldon, plus six men from the assigned servants, began the long ride to the government herds at Cawdor, where they would purchase three hundred long horn cattle, and then drive them back to Glen Alpine.

With everything arranged, Luke saw no reason to remain in Campbell Town, so returned to his family home to await the arrival of his stock, accompanied by the young and enthusiastic, Elliot Herriot.

***

Galloping through Narellan, James was amazed, recalling how it appeared when first he saw the town, six years previously. What was then a settlement, comprising a few slab huts and a lock up, was now a bustling working community, residing in brick and stone houses, alongside shops, hotels, and even a church. By mid-morning, the riders reached the Nepean River, a wooden gate beside a cottage inhibiting their progress across a stone bridge.

"Ha' penny to pass, sirs," the tollgate keeper said, appearing at the cottage door, clearly having heard their approach.

John Holsworthy tossed a coin, and the man opened the gate.

"On Sunday's Macarthur won't let anyone cross," shouted Holsworthy, as they galloped over the bridge. "He brought in the rule as a mark of respect. The tolls he's collected have already paid for the bridge."

Hearing the name, James remembered the curses Mr Macarthur hurled at his new boss, that evening after the races. Even then, people were witnessing Mr Macarthur's mental condition becoming serious. He was going insane, folk at the time well aware of the fact. Two years later, Macarthur was dead. What a legacy he left behind, nevertheless. A magnificent breed of sheep, unsurpassed throughout the world, their wool clothing the backs of millions. Fine pedigree cattle, together with thriving vineyards. There was also Camden; a complete village built by Macarthur, specifically to house the workforce of his estate, Camden Park. Macarthur gave them the bridge; a church; a courthouse, a hotel, shops, and cottages. Everything built on a geometric grid of roads, similar to the roman towns of old. Macarthur was indeed the cleverest, and the most beneficial man the colony had ever seen.

Beyond the imposing mansion of Camden Park, the horsemen eventually reached the Cawdor Road, beginning the ascent that would ultimately lead to the Razor Back, John Holsworthy's party arriving at a clearing, where the government hut once stood. Several years before Governor Macquarie left the colony, he paid a visit to Cow Pastures, to inspect the herds of wild cattle that grazed the ranges at that time. The superintendent of herds then resided in a small primitive slab hut. However, nowadays the present superintendent lives in a substantial dwelling, constructed of sandstone and wood, located at the end of a wide dusty road.

"You men set to and pitch the tents!" John shouted. "Jim and I'll find Mr Fisher."

Holsworthy and James rode on towards a white paling fence, enclosing a sandy paddock, and surrounding the house. Tethering the horses, James noticed several white nanny goats with kids, grazing in the paddock, a big old Billy goat, with a long beard, and imposing, twisting horns, apparently in charge.

Holsworthy opened the gate, allowing James and himself to enter the paddock, where they began walking towards the house. Except, no sooner had the old Billy heard the click of the latch, he began to make a grumbling sound, issuing from the back of his throat, while he slowly plodded towards them.

"Keep walking," whispered Holsworthy. "I know goats. Don't turn around! If he senses we're afraid, he'll have us."

Although they were almost halfway to the house, the Billy was getting closer. So near, in fact, James could hear his hooves brushing the ground, and the wheezing of his aged lungs.

"Don't worry," John Holsworthy said from up ahead, "he'll soon lose interest."

Disregarding John's earlier warning, and glancing over his shoulder, James saw the old goat had stopped, and was watching them walk away. John was right, he thought. The old boy's not bothering anymore. Holsworthy certainly knew his goats, James continuing to follow John towards the house. Feint at first, like a distant drum roll, echoing off the surrounding hills, when James looked around to see the cause of the noise, he was horrified to see the old Billy charging towards him. Undaunted nonetheless, James waited until the last minute, nimbly stepping aside, leaving the way clear for the beast to head straight for Holsworthy.

"Hey mate!" James shouted.

But it was too late. Two horns cannoned into Holsworthy's backside, sending him careering forward on to the ground.

Checking to see if any marauding nanny goats were preparing to butt him, James saw they were completely undisturbed by the events and happily chewing the grass, their kids scampering around them.

Having floored the first intruder, old Billy now turned his attention to James.

James began to run.

"Come on mate! Quick!" someone shouted, and looking up at the house, James could see a man leaning on the veranda rail.

"And you too!" the man shouted to Holsworthy, who by now was dragging himself out of the dust, "or he'll have you again."

Confused, unable to choose whom to attack next, the Billy stopped in his tracks, looking from one man to the other, allowing them just enough time to reach the house, and the safety of the veranda.

"A good guard dog, you have there sir," panted James.

"Yes mate," the man replied. "Old Marmaduke's been on the station for years. He must be twenty, if he's a day. Although, he's always ready to have a go."

"My name's John Holsworthy," said John, removing his hat, while brushing off the dust. "I'm the overseer of the late Reverend Reddall. And this is James Baker Waldon, his son Luke's man. We're here to purchase cattle, if we may."

"Fisher's the name," the man said. "I'm pleased to make your acquaintance, gentlemen."

"We've camped in the clearing back there," Holsworthy continued. "We'll start out tomorrow, if that's alright with you."

"Perfectly," Mr Fisher said. "But you'll find the beasts a wild bunch. You'll have a high time mustering them."

As they were about to leave, Mr Fisher turned to James.

"Mrs Macarthur was here yesterday," he said. "She told me what happened to your master's family. Although I've never met the lad, please send him my condolences."

"Thank you, Mr Fisher. I will sir," said James.

Returning to the camp, James and John Holsworthy found only three horses tied to the trees.

"Where are the others?" Holsworthy asked the remaining men.

"Gone," one said.

"What do you mean?"

"Scarpered. Taken the horses and saddles; the lot."

Holsworthy turned to James.

"I might have known," he said through his teeth. "The bunch of crooked bastards. I should have been more careful. Obviously they'd do a runner. We're only lucky these three stayed. Do you know their names?"

He directed his question to the men, idly smoking their pipes.

"No," one said. "But your boss has the indents. I'm McGuire."

"Good day, McGuire! And who might you blokes be?" Holsworthy asked, looking at the other two.

"Traynor," one said,

"Blease," said the other.

Holsworthy nodded.

"I see you've not been idle since James and I left."

McGuire, Traynor, and Blease had stretched a canvas awning between the trees, a fire crackled merrily, and a billycan of hot sweet tea steamed in the ashes, and after Holsworthy and James, tethered their horses, and approached the fire, Traynor took out his harmonica, and knocked cold spittle into his palm.

"Any favourites?" he said, looking at each man in turn.

No one spoke.

"Come on!" he said. "There must be one tune you'd like to hear?"

"How about 'Hearts of Oak'? James said.

"I know it," said Traynor, "but I haven't heard it for years. I might be a bit rusty."

While the billy boiled, and a pot of salt pork bubbled over the fire, the strains of the old sea shanty drifted across the paddocks, to where old Marmaduke lay in the dust, surrounded by his harem. He flapped his ears, and chewed the cud, as the dusk fell quickly around them.

***

At first light, the men prepared to leave.

"How much riding have you done, men?" Holsworthy asked, as they kicked out the fire.

"I was a stable hand, and a groom," Blease said. "I rode in the hunt a few times a year."

James was listening, because that was all he had ever done, never having ridden in a cattle muster in his life. Driving sheep on Mutt Mutt Billy was easy. Just sauntering alongside the flock, while the dogs did all the work.

"Then you'd better watch out," continued Holsworthy. "This is a hell of a lot harder than riding to hounds. The cattle are mean and wild. They'll resist being caught. Watch out for a cow with a calf. She'll send her horns into your horse's side, as soon as look at it. She'll protect her calf with her life."

The sky grew lighter, the higher they became, and having left the packhorses at Mr Fishers, and taking the barest supplies, the five men rode into the bush, choosing a well-used track, running beside a creek. Ultimately, they reached a ridge commanding a clear view of the valley below, where beneath the gum trees, hundreds of cattle peacefully grazed in the twilight.

"There you are, mates," Holsworthy said, standing in his stirrups.

"More beef than you'll ever see in a lifetime."

James could only marvel at the scene, thinking it a shame to disturb the beasts, since they appeared so serene and content, although he refrained from saying so aloud.

"We'll need to get around the far side of the herd," whispered Holsworthy. "Then stampede them back this way, and into the gully. James and I will ride out wide, and then come up on them from behind. When we're near, I'll whistle. The second whistle will be the signal for you two blokes to pick them up from here."

John Holsworthy and James rode away in opposite directions, until they were level with the herd. Then turning their horses, they began riding towards the cattle, James senses as keen as the morning air, because the closer he came to the herd, the more he could smell the animals, and hear them snorting. Pulling up his horse, James waited for Holsworthy's whistle, and the signal to gallop, all the while Dan breathing hard, and champing at his bit. After what seemed a lifetime, James suddenly heard a piercing blast, so digging in his spurs, and snapping the reins, he began galloping at full speed towards the herd. A hundred feet away, on the other side of the mass of cattle, Holsworthy was doing the same, all the while whistling and shouting, James also yelling, and cracking his whip.

The beasts on the outer fringes became suddenly alarmed, and realising they were about to be assailed, began hurtling away from the shrieking riders, finally joining the main herd. Almost immediately, James and Holsworthy had a barrage of steers thundering along in front of them, with no idea where they were heading. The further the riders galloped; shouting, whistling, and cracking whips, the more cattle they collected. Until at Holsworthy's next whistle, Traynor, McGuire and Blease, on the extreme left and right, began closing in on the bunch, forcing them together, the riders flanking the stampede, driving them towards the gully.

"Look out, Traynor!" shouted Holsworthy over the din of bellowing cattle and rumbling hooves. "He's trying to get out."

Sure enough, an enormous black bull, with large horns, was making a bid to escape the stampede, rushing at Traynor's horse, lunging with his horns. Traynor deftly reined the horse aside however, thus avoiding the deadly weapons, Blease, then hurtling his mount at the animal's side, forcing it back into the mob.

Onward they charged; the air full of dust, and the sound of cattle bellowing, horses thundering, and men yelling.

"Hold fast, Jim!" Holsworthy yelled, pointing ahead. "See the cliffs?"

James stared into the glare of the rising sun, only to see a sheer escarpment, winding away to the north, the valley five hundred feet below, covered in dense impenetrable forest. Towards this abyss, the cattle were hurtling headlong.

"You blokes!" Holsworthy cried. "Get in front! We've got to turn them! Or we'll lose the lot!"

Traynor, Blease, and McGuire dug in their spurs, and riding hard, they flanked the leading steers.

Common sense told Traynor that their only chance to turn the stampede was for him to pull up in front of it, trusting the beasts' natural instinct not to trample him and his horse. The maneuver might be enough to divert the animals from imminent disaster. It was an enormous risk. Yet, reaching the front of the herd, Traynor reined in his horse; stopped dead, and with the cattle thundering towards him, he waited motionless. Coming within a breath of him, the leaders suddenly wheeled to the right, a great curve of horns and heads, Blease picking them up, and forcing them back, cracking his whip, until they swerved towards the west.

The cattle at the rear, and centre of the charge, seeing the leaders charging towards them, turned and joined the stampede. In this way, the men avoided a catastrophe, eventually moving the entire herd back towards the gully, and into the holding pens.

It was now too late to move the cattle further, so the men collected wood, and made a fire. Soon, with the billy boiled, a damper in the ashes, and salt pork and peas in the pot, supper was ready. Then, once the sky grew dark, and stars appeared, the men rolled out their beds, and prepared to sleep. James was second watch that night, and sitting beside the fire, his thoughts dwelt on home.

How old would Alice be, he wondered. She was older than him by six months, so she would be twenty-seven. Alice would be a woman, although James found it hard to believe. All grown up. As he was a man, grown up. However, here in his new country, he scarcely felt like a grown man, since he remained a lad in the eyes of blokes who had been here far longer. Gazing into the black sky, where a trillion stars sparkled, James pondered upon the vast new land he now called home, having heard tell of mighty mountains, capped with snow, and rivers so wide a man could barely see the other side. Also, apparently there were deserts, where the earth was as red as blood, and flat as a table top. He was keen to see such wonders. Strangers occasionally wandered onto Mutt Mutt Billy, with an odd glint in their eyes. They spoke of places where diamonds simply lay in the dust, ready for anyone to pick up and own. Tales of creeks running with gold, and mountains oozing with nuggets, causing James to yearn for adventure. Maybe, if he found such treasure, it might be his passport to freedom, and a means by which to return to Thurlow.

'What if I find the biggest diamond in the world,' he said to himself. 'Then I could take it home to Alice.'

Was she still waiting for him, he wondered?

Shifting closer to the fire, James hugged his knees. But Alice was an impatient girl. Surely, by now she would have found a man and married him, and almost certainly have children. Recalling her laughter, his insides gave a jolt, as a sick pang of loneliness overcame him.

"Alice," he whispered. "Please wait. You're the only girl for me."

James rolled up his sleeve, seeing by the light of the fire, the four blue black letters etched on his arm.

'JWAJ'.

"That's enough," he whispered aloud. "You'll be crying like a baby in a minute. You're not a kid anymore.

He stood up; stretched, and then, kicking the fire into life, took a walk to the holding pen to check on the cattle.

Next morning, the men prepared for the ride down the gully to the stockyards. So, after breaking through the brush-holding pen, Holsworthy and Traynor urged the cattle forward, while James, Blease, and McGuire opened the far side, joining the leading steers that were surging out of the pen. However, the pace was leisurely compared to the previous day, the beasts seeming resigned to their fate, as if something deep in their wild brains told them that once they had been domesticated. Even so, occasionally a renegade attempted to break ranks. Although it was promptly rounded up, and forced back into the herd, James able to use the rope he carried on his saddle, alongside the leather sheath, housing his gun.

The way down the steep ravine was perilous, but soon the roof of Mr Fisher's house appeared, with the stockyards beyond. Three hundred and fifty six steers, cows, heifers, bulls, and calves were mustered that day, John Holsworthy paying Mr Fisher for each beast. Fifty-six more than the original target.

With the sun high in the December sky, the men, horses, and cattle began the slow trek back to Campbelltown, leaving the homestead at peace. Mr Fisher, old Marmaduke, and his family, to bear witness that the events of the past days had ever happened.

***

Elliot Herriot leaned on the gate, and watched the men washing themselves in the horse trough.

'They're terribly thin,' he thought. 'Straight off the transports. Half-starved most likely.'

Elliot arrived in the colonies on His Majesty's Transport Ship, 'John Barry', and remembered seeing, from the safety of the poop deck, soldiers leading scrawny convicts up on deck for their morning ablutions; Elliot thought at the time that they appeared to be in need of a few hearty meals.

How did Elliot come to be on a convict ship in the first place? A question he had asked himself more than once. His father paid for the voyage, telling his son that it was time he went somewhere to learn to be a man, Elliot never having a notion of being otherwise. He was aware however, that he was a fellow with a delicate disposition, or so his mother believed.

Elliot enjoyed reading, and the plays. Also, he found the company of women more desirable than that of men, whom he considered rough and rascally creatures, like the boys that teased him when at school. His father, however, was a man's man, Lieutenant Colonel,

William John Herriot, of the East India Company, Bengal Division, retired. The colonel had no time for the classics, or theatre, finding women silly creatures, only useful for one thing, and that done as least as possible.

Colonel Herriot was in India for most of Elliot's childhood, and since Elliot had no brothers and sisters, he and his mother, Sophia, became close. From time to time, his mother's sister, Frances, called at the house, Elliot's cousins, Louisa and Maria, accompanying her. Elliot enjoyed playing games with the sisters, even if they involved their pretty porcelain faced dolls. Sometimes at Christmas or Easter, Uncle Oliph, their father, would join them. He was a clergyman, the Reverend Oliph Leigh Spencer, of All Souls College, Oxford, and was a funny man; Elliot liked him.

Uncle Oliph told magical stories, about faraway places, such as Africa and Australia. As a result, when Elliot's father gave him his marching orders, it was Australia Elliot chose, over Africa. The reason being, that black people made him nervous, being aware that there were many on the African continent.

Before Elliot embarked, his father the colonel arranged a contact for him in the colonies, as co-incidentally, Luke Reddall's uncle, John Reddall, and Colonel Herriot were school pals at Eton. Therefore, as soon as Elliot was ashore, he immediately went to the colonial secretary's office to enquire as to the whereabouts of Mr Luke William Reddall, being duly directed to Campbelltown, travelling there by Cobb and Co coach.

"Do you know sir, the town of Sydney surprises me," Elliot said to a weary travelling companion while on the journey south. "It's really much the same as an English country town. Except all the roads are straight and at right angles to each other. I suppose, rather like the way the Romans laid out their towns."

In addition, the great number of inebriated folk Elliot saw in the streets amazed him.

Day or night,' he told his mother in his first letter home, '*it's as if the whole town is drunk.*'

'*Once I reached Campbelltown,*' his letter continued. '*I found I'd arrived at a very unfortunate time, since a funeral was taking place of the mother and sister of my new associate. However, I soon made acquaintance with Mr Reddall at the wake; riding with him to the house, they call Glen Alpine. On the ride, I did most of the talking, since Mr Reddall, seemed to take an interest in my stories of home. During the wake, Mr Reddall appeared to drink a great deal. But was not the only victim of over indulgence. Because a crazy old woman at the hotel, Anne by name, Mr Reddall's servant I believe, carried on like a banshee, swearing and cursing, calling everyone names. Thankfully, Mr Reddall's men, Mr Holsworthy and Mr Waldon, took care of the mad old thing. What a night it was. My first introduction to life in Australia.'*

It certainly had been a night, and here he was overseeing six convicts. What his father would think of him, Elliot had no idea.

"Oi!" shouted one of the men. "Watcha starin' at?"

"I'm not!" Elliot said, suddenly embarrassed. "I was thinking."

"Then do your thinking looking the other way, mate; us gents like our privacy you know?"

When Elliot turned his back, and faced the house, they laughed.

Glen Alpine appeared sad and desolate, with iron fastenings firmly fixed across the shutters. It must have been beautiful once, Elliot decided; elegant and stylish, the Reddall's obviously people with excellent taste. Early on the morning after his arrival, and waking before anyone else, Elliot presumed Mr Reddall to be still asleep, because he noticed his door was closed. So with his curiosity getting the better of him, Elliot wandered from room to room, and was much impressed by the rich fabrics, fine furniture, eminent paintings, and plush carpets.

Elliot found the kitchen, and was relieved to see that there was no trace of the crazy Anne. So he began searching the cupboards and larder, since he was hungry. Mr Hurley's spread the previous evening had been magnificent, but Elliot was too busy talking to eat a thing. Elliot peered inside the larder, but saw nothing fresh, except a lone loaf of flat bread, beside a bowl of eggs.

"Boiled eggs, and soldiers. That's what I'll have," Elliot said aloud. "Just like cook used to do for me."

He found a pitcher, and poured water into it from a pump he

discovered in the yard. Then, taking a saucepan from a cupboard, he filled it with water, next dropping in two eggs. Anticipating a hearty breakfast, Elliot was disappointed to discover the range was stone cold.

"Well that's a shame!" he said, sitting down at the table. "I was looking forward to that."

"Looking forward to what?" a voice said.

"Oh! You startled me, Mr Reddall," Elliot said, turning around. "I thought you were in bed."

"Hardly Elliot. I've been awake for hours. Clarence needed his morning gallop. What are you up to?"

"I'm sorry, Mr Reddall," Elliot stammered. "I was making boiled eggs for myself. But the fires not lit."

"Alright Elliot!" said Luke, patting him on the shoulder. "Now's your chance to do your first job in the colonies. You can light it, dear fellow. You'll find wood in the shed. And put another two eggs in the pot for me."

Without complaint, Elliot followed Luke's instructions, and soon there was a hot fire burning in the stove, and water boiling in the pot.

***

"Thanks Elliot," Luke said, mopping up the last of the egg yolk with a crust of bread. "That was most enjoyable. I can see you're going to be a great asset at Durra Durra."

"I'm a little concerned though, sir," said Elliot, getting up from his chair, and taking their empty plates to the sink. "I hope I'm not going to be a burden to your good self, Mr Poney, and Mr Waldon."

Luke smiled, leaning back in his chair, at the same time, taking a gulp of tea, which Elliot had also brewed while waiting for the eggs to boil.

"Not at all, Elliot," he said. "We know you're a bit of a green horn. But have no fear. We'll show you the way we do things down there."

Elliot was still unsure though, taking the opportunity to ask the question that had been on his mind for a while.

"Are there many of those native chappies where we're going?" he asked, tentatively. "I didn't think there were any in the colonies, until I saw a few black faces in Sydney town. I do find them rather frightening, I must admit."

"Yes Elliot. A few," Luke said, endeavouring not to smile. "Just remember to never turn your back on one. That's all you need to know. Also, never give them grog."

Luke got up from the table.

"I'll wash the plates, Mr Reddall," Elliot said.

"Thank you, Elliot," said Luke. "And when you're ready, can you oversee the government men? I'd like them to tidy the garden. Get them up and washed, while I continue securing the house."

"What's to become of all the lovely things?" Elliot asked.

"They stay here for the time being," answered Luke. "I've to wait for my brother to return from India. He may wish to live here, and until I speak to him, I've no way of knowing his plans."

***

The small town of Narellan was almost deserted that same morning, as John Holsworthy, James and the others, drove the cattle through the town. The men had made good time since leaving Mr Fisher's house, finding little hindrance to their progress away from Cawdor. But driving the steers onto the Campbell Town Road, James drew John's attention to a lone horseman in the distance, horse, and rider approaching at speed.

"Who is it, Mr Holsworthy?" asked James. "A bushranger?"

"He'd be a bloody fool if he was," John said, laughing uneasily. "He's pretty much outnumbered."

Might it be a trap, James wondered, looking about him. Yet the countryside was open, with no place for a gang to hide.

As the rider drew close, James had a clearer view, observing him wearing a cabbage tree hat. Nothing very remarkable in that, seeing they were common attire. Although, James had resisted donning one, since he secretly thought them rather peculiar looking. Then again, the man riding towards them was wearing his perched on his head at a jaunty angle, causing him to resemble a toff, or an actor. In addition, the man's jacket was white. In fact, whiter than white, betraying its lack of use to date.

"Hey!" James shouted. "It's that bloke Elliot. What's he doing here?"

"Master Luke sent him to greet us, most likely," said John. "Get him out of his hair, I shouldn't wonder."

"Look at him!" James said, laughing. "Have you ever seen the like?"

"Good afternoon, Mr Holsworthy and Mr Waldon," said Elliot, riding up beside them. "I remember you both from Mr Hurley's hotel. I trust you've had a pleasant muster."

"Thanks mate. We have," John Holsworthy said, looking askance at James. "And how about you? You seem to be enjoying your ride."

"I am, sir! I am!" said Elliot. "The weather's most pleasant. But the sun's quite strong. I'm glad for my Cabbage Patch Hat, I can tell you."

"I'm sure you are." John Holsworthy said. "I fancy Mr Reddall sent you to meet us."

"Correct, Mr Holsworthy. He did. He also said he'd find me a native scout to keep me on the road, except I declined the offer."

James and John Holsworthy were endeavouring not to laugh.

"What fine beasts you have, gentlemen," Elliot said, surveying the herd. "They look fat and healthy."

"They are, Elliot," James said. "They've been feeding on good long grass, up in the highlands."

Elliot was having difficulty holding his horse, while riding beside John and James, revealing his lack of experience as a rider

"How interesting, Mr Waldon," he said. "I'm looking forward to joining you, when Mr Poney, you and me start for Durra Durra. I hope you'll give me some lessons in mustering and whip cracking. I'm more than ready to learn."

"We will, Mr Herriot," Holsworthy said smiling. "We will."

***

In order to prove to his brother John that he had not removed anything from Glen Alpine without permission, Luke systematically worked through the house with a notebook, itemising the contents of each room, knowing John would want to see everything in its place. The letter Luke received from John that morning, gave Luke clear instructions that he must catalogue every item. Also, it conveyed an odd coldness regarding the receipt of Luke's sad news. John's lack of emotion hardly came as a surprise to Luke, since his brother had altered from the kind and caring person he remembered.

In his letter, John stated that he would book passage on the first ship bound for Sydney. Meaning, that even if John found a vessel on the same day that he wrote it, considering it took six weeks for the letter to arrive, John was still at least two months away. This was far too long for Luke to wait. He wished to be gone, sooner rather than later, partly to leave behind painful memories, but principally, to discourage squatters taking over his new run at Durra Durra.

Luke moved from room to room, old Anne Farrell following, draping the furniture and pictures with sheets. Before long, the entire house took on a shrouded, sombre mood. Endeavouring to shake off a sensation of melancholy, Luke snapped shut the notebook at the last entry. Fresh air! That was what he needed. So opening the front door, he walked onto the veranda, and taking out his pipe, sat in his mother's favourite wicker chair. He gazed across the lawn at her rose garden, seeing it sparking a memory. It was the morning Anne Farrell woke him with the news his oxen had broken free of the yard, and were running amuck amongst his mother's roses. When was that, Luke wondered? It seemed a lifetime ago. A time when he was swathed by the love of his mother and father, as well as, having a little sister to cherish. Now they were no more. Interned in the vault in Campbell Town graveyard. Luke had no one. His family decimated in a moment. He was alone in the world.

Forbidding morbid thoughts to overwhelm him once more, Luke knocked the dry spent ashes from his pipe into his palm; afterwards throwing them over the rail, as a faraway sound pervaded the cool evening air. He listened, while thumbing tobacco into the bowl. Then, finally lighting the pipe, the curling smoke appeared to catch and highlight the distant sounds. Men shouting. Whistling. Together with the unmistakable resonance of a cracking whip. Jumping out of the chair, Luke stared down the track, seeing a great cloud of dust in the distance.

"It's the herd!" he shouted. "At last! I'm free! We can go!"

"They're back, Anne!" he called, running inside the house. "Stoke the range! The men will be hungry."

Anne turned on him sullenly.

"Yes sir," she said. "Does that mean you'll be leaving?"

"It does Anne," Luke exclaimed, laughing. "And the sooner the better."

"And what will happen to me, Master Luke?" she said, her eyes filling with tears.

"Anne! I'm so sorry," Luke said, taking her hands in his. "With all the work as well as everything else, I've not had a chance to talk to you."

"Yes, Master Luke," whispered Anne. "I've been worrying. What's to become of me? Yer old Anne's not getting any younger. I ain't many years left, I shouldn't wonder."

"Don't be silly!" Luke said, hugging her. "You're as strong as an ox. You'll out live us all."

Anne pushed Luke away, her old eyes gazing into his.

"Get on with you, Master Luke," she said, smiling at last. "You've always been a smooth talker; even when you were a littlun."

"Alright Anne!" said Luke. "You can make a choice. You can stay here, and cook for the men, or come with me to help Martha at Mutt Mutt Billy."

"I'll come with you, Master Luke, if I may," she answered. "This house gives me the creeps. There's too many memories here for me."

Luke put his arm around her.

"Mother would be pleased you're with me," he said. "She would have wanted me to look after you."

"Thank you, sir," Anne said, hugging him. "You're an angel."

By the time they walked back through the house, the cattle were so near, Anne and Luke could hear them bellowing.

***

The herd shut inside the holding pens, the men washed, and crowding into the eating-house, Anne having put two haunches of mutton, bowls of steaming turnips and peas on the table. Luke opened a barrel of the best wine, and everyone feasted well into the night.

Before leaving the following morning, Luke wrote a letter to Mr Hurley, begging his pardon, and asking if he might take Luke's quota of government men, to employ them on projects in Campbell Town. Then he emptied his father's safe, locking the paper money inside a strong box, the Macquarie Cup now secure in the vaults of Saint Peter's Church, much to Luke's relief. Then, making sure not to be seen by anyone, Luke hid the strong box deep inside a half-empty crate on the dray, concealing it by piling sacks of salt on top.

James' final task was to harness Dan to the late reverend's sulky, Mister Luke having asked James if he would drive it, in order old Anne Farrell might have a comfortable ride to Mutt Mutt Billy. Thus, by the middle of the morning everything was ready for yet another exodus.

It was with mixed emotions, Luke said farewell to Glen Alpine. He could recall many happy times occurring in the house. Cheerful days. Merry Christmas'. Joyous birthdays. Memorable parties. Even so, his wonderful mother and father were responsible for such happiness, not the house. Without them it was merely a shell, with the heart vanished. Luke resisted a final look back. James however, did, recalling the previous time he took leave of Glen Alpine, Mrs Reddall asking him questions about his home in England. Why had she been so curious? It had puzzled him ever since, recalling Mrs Reddall's sudden reaction, when he told her he came from Thurlow.

Suddenly, as the name sounded in his mind, James saw a picture of a different house, on a frosty morning, long ago, and one more parting, on another journey, when he also looked back.

***

With the veil of remembrance clearing from his mind, Luke returned to the present, noticing the sun had disappeared behind the ranges, and with it, the memory of that sad time in his life, which still remained difficult to endure. Although, thankfully, as well as sad, the times were exciting. After all, he had been about to begin a new phase in his life. A life far away to the south, on a new property, called Durra Durra. All in all, Luke was able to appreciate at last, the amount he altered during that month in Campbelltown. He was no longer a child, the younger son, or baby brother. Luke was his own man; grasping life with strength and courage. No one to care for him or to see him safe. He was on his own, and by rights, the thought should have filled him with anticipation, as well as fear. Except, Luke felt challenged, and eager to face whatever life would have in store for him.

Walking back to the house, he gazed at the farm. The shadow of The Bald Hill, slowly creeping across the paddocks, immersing the shorn sheep in a deep violet dusk.

Shearing was always heavy, exhausting work, and Luke was looking forward to his bath. He did his best thinking while relaxing in the warm water. Tonight he would make plans. Plans for Durra Durra. Now shearing was over, it was time for another visit. It was such a pleasant place, nestled in the lee of a huge escarpment. Already, James Baker Waldon, Bill Poney, and Elliot, had been there for many months. It would be good to see his men once more.

"Yes," Luke said aloud. "I'll see Durra Durra again. And this time I'll stay awhile."

After bathing, and changing his clothes, Luke wandered into the kitchen, where Martha was busy cooking.

"What's for supper, Martha?"

"A roasted fowl, Mister Luke," she said. "With garden vegetables."

"That sounds good. I bet you didn't kill the chicken," Luke said, chuckling.

"I couldn't, Master Luke," Martha replied, shyly. "The poor darling thing! Anne did it for me, like she always does."

Luke laughed. "I'll be on the veranda. Call me when it's ready."

From his chair, Luke watched the huge bogong moths beating against the lampshade. They were so large; it still amazed him how blackfellas gorged on them at this time of year, always wondering how they might taste.

Lighting his pipe, frogs croaking in the creek, and crickets causing the air to ring, Luke heard another sound, and listening hard, discerned through the clamour insects, the sound of horse's hooves. A rider was approaching down the hill.

Luke stood to greet the visitor, and staring into the darkness, saw a horse and rider suddenly appear in the light from the house.

"Good evening, sir," said the stranger, having seen Luke silhouetted in the lamplight.

"Would this be Mutt Mutt Billy?"

"It is sir. Can I help you?"

The rider dismounted, Luke suddenly astounded by the stature of the man walking towards him.

"To whom am I addressing, sir?" the man asked.

"Luke William Reddall, sir,"

Luke walked down the veranda steps into the yard.

"Very pleased to meet you, Mr Reddall," the man said, holding out his hand. "John Baker, at your service."

Chapter Seven

"Come inside, sir," Luke said, as they shook hands, "I'll have someone see to your horse. I'm about to have supper. I'd be honoured if you'd join me."

"Thank you, Mr Reddall. I'm much obliged. It's been a hard ride from Goulburn. I've not had a bite since breakfast."

John Baker unstrapped his saddlebag, slinging it over his shoulder.

Standing aside to allow him on to the veranda, and into the house, Luke took a moment to assess his guest, his first impression being that Mr Baker was extremely tall. Taller than himself by far. Possessing broad shoulders, and strong limbs, by the way his physique filled his smart tweed suit, Luke concluded his guest to be almost certainly an athlete.

After taking his coat and hat, Luke showed John into the parlour.

"Please sit down, Mr Baker," Luke said. "Would you care for a drink?" He indicated the sideboard. "I've a reasonable Madeira?"

"Do you have ale, Mr Reddall?" John said, sitting in a chair. "I'm partial to a drop of ale, being the countryman that I am."

"I certainly do, sir. My servant Martha brews excellent beer. If you'll excuse me, I'll go to the kitchen, and fetch a bottle."

Left alone, John looked around the large, well-furnished room, at the deep sofas, and comfortable armchairs, everything displaying the owner's obvious good taste. Opposite him, between two French windows, stood an elegant walnut table, on it a Chinese vase, the pale blue and white pattern glinting in the lamp light. To his left, a deeply carved oak sideboard glistened with age, while watercolours, hanging on the green damask walls, depicted rolling English countryside. In addition, above a black marble fireplace, hung a large oil painting, in a gilt frame. A portrait of a woman. An extremely beautiful woman, with dark brown hair, John fancying she appeared foreign. Spanish, or maybe Italian, by her deep mystifying eyes, and olive toned skin.

Luke returned almost immediately, carrying two stone jugs, and going to the sideboard, poured the contents of one into a tall glass, putting it down on the table.

"There you are, Mr Baker! Mutt Mutt Billy's own special brew."

Returning to the sideboard, he poured himself a glass of red wine.

"Dinner won't be too long," he said, sitting down on the sofa.

"I hope I've not put you to any trouble, Mr Reddall."

"Not at all sir. It's my pleasure."

In the ensuing silence, both men enjoyed the drinks initial taste, John eventually speaking first.

"Since my arrival from England,' he said, "I've been impressed by the excellent quality of the food and wine in your country, Mr Reddall."

"Thank you, sir. Yes. Things have certainly improved since my mother and father arrived, twenty years ago. In those days, folk purchased provisions from the government stores. Except of course, for fresh meat and bread, which were obtained in town. Vegetables they grew themselves. The remainder of the groceries, like sugar, tea, salt, and tobacco, were imported."

As they conversed, Luke realised it had been a while since he had entertained a guest, particularly a person from across the sea. And judging by his expression, Mr Baker seemed keen to listen, Luke surprising himself, at being so eloquent, after a busy and tiring day in the shearing shed.

"Things were very difficult for the remote settlers," continued Luke. "They needed to survive on stores they purchased, and went without when these dwindled, until they were able to get to town, and buy more supplies. Thankfully, nowadays, things are different. We have a good deal more choice, some farms being self-sufficient.

We've excellent beef, pork, and lamb. Abundant fish, both in the sea, and the rivers, and a good amount of game. With our large herds of cattle, fresh milk is available, with butter and cheese made daily. There are bountiful supplies of fruit and vegetables. Also, our wheat stocks are such that we no longer lack bread. Thanks to pioneers such as Mr Macarthur we're fortunate to also have excellent vineyards, and some very good wines."

"And the beer isn't bad either," chuckled John.

"May I enquire the reason for your being in these parts, Mr Baker?" Luke said, sipping his wine.

"Certainly, Mr Reddall. I've a mind to see the country, with a view to buying land. I've come into an inheritance, and wish to invest the money in property."

"Then you won't go far wrong looking in Argyle, Mr Baker. I've six hundred and forty acres of fine grass, and with good soil, and plentiful rainfall, my sheep do well. But then I'm talking fleeces, not meat of course."

"I understand. The sheep grazing on these plains are famous throughout the world, for the fine quality of their wool."

"Thank you, sir. And yes. I do pride myself on having possibly the best sheep in the region. Of late, my wool is reaching a good price in England. Five shillings a pound, last month. And I'm hoping, with the fleeces we've baled recently, they'll reach even higher."

Assisted by strong ale, and heady wine, the men had begun to relax in each other's company; so much so, they hardly noticed Martha standing in the doorway.

"Supper's ready, Mr Luke."

"Thank you, Martha. Shall we adjourn to the dining room, Mr Baker?"

The meal was a jolly affair, the roast chicken proving delicious. And while Martha brought more jugs of beer, Luke opened another bottle of wine, John Baker listening to Luke speak of farming, breeding livestock, and the mysteries of sowing and harvesting crops.

All of this, plus horses and horseracing. He was indeed a charming gentleman, John decided. Intelligent. Good mannered. Well educated, and less like his father, Humphrey Soame, than he could ever be.

While Luke talked, John studied his host's face.

He resembled the Humphrey Soame that John remembered from school days; the open face of a young man, sitting in the classroom, as yet unchanged by years of debauchery. John could also see something of himself. Luke was his nephew after all; John clearly seeing the shape of Luke's face was that of his sister, Emma. But his strong chin and fine nose belonged to his grandmother, Lady Soame.

However, Luke's most striking features were his eyes. Exactly like his grandmothers. The eyes John saw on the day she died, captivating him, urging him to fulfil her dying wish. Here they were again, in this young man. Eyes filled with fire, passion, joy, and wonder. Equally intoxicating and hypnotising.

"But forgive me, I'm being rude," Luke said. "Here am I chattering away about myself. I've not allowed you a word, Mr Baker."

"That's quite all right, Mr Reddall. Farming is not my occupation, so your conversation is very interesting."

"What is your profession, Mr Baker? If you'll forgive me asking."

"Not at all sir. I'm a blacksmith. My father has the best smithy in the county."

"A blacksmith! I used to have an excellent blacksmith here at Mutt Mutt Billy. But he's on my new station. We miss him a great deal."

"Then should you have any jobs need attending, I'd be more than happy to oblige."

"You'd be most welcome, Mr Baker!" said Luke, looking at John in surprise. "But that would mean you staying awhile. Don't let me detain you from your business."

"No harm! Business can wait. I've been travelling for a month. It would be good to settle for a while. But of course, I'd need to be invited."

Leaning back in his chair, the sensation of food and ale had caused John Baker to feel bold.

"Definitely, Mr Baker!" Luke exclaimed, refilling John's glass. "It would give me the greatest pleasure. It gets pretty quiet around her, and I'd be pleased to have your company."

Drinking his ale, John smiled, his thoughts dwelling on the letters, safely tucked away in the strong box, inside his saddlebag. When would be the best time to tell this young man who he really is, John wondered? Only until he has his complete trust. The news will be devastating. Mr Reddall will be angry, and may not believe him. John had no wish to make an enemy of this charming young man.

"Tomorrow," Luke said, "I'll show you around Mutt Mutt Billy."

"Not all six hundred and forty acres, I hope," chuckled John.

Filling his own glass, Luke laughed.

"No sir. But we'll ride onto the plains. It'll give you an idea of the extent of the run."

"It's a curious name."

"I agree! I've tried discovering the origins, learning the blackfellas call the creek hereabouts, by that name."

There was a knock on the door, which was opened by Martha.

"Can I clear the dishes, Mr Luke?"

"You may Martha. And thank you for a splendid meal."

Luke could hardly miss, Martha quickly glance under her eyelashes, in John's direction.

"Of course, Martha, you've yet to meet our guest," he said. "May I introduce, Mr John Baker. He's very kindly agreed to stay a while with us, at Mutt Mutt Billy."

Martha smiled, and curtsied.

"Very pleased to meet you sir, to be sure!" she said.

"And pleased to meet you too, Martha," John said, getting up from the table. "Thank you for a delicious meal."

"Thank you sir," she said, blushing, "I aim to please, sir."

"Well," Luke said, picking up a lamp. "I think we should be getting to bed. We've a busy day tomorrow. I'll show you to your room Mr Baker, if I may."

Forsaking his nightshirt, and lying on the bed, with just a linen sheet covering him, the flickering candle visible through the gauze of the mosquito net, John listened to the noises of the night.

In his bedroom at Forge Cottage, he might occasionally hear the hoot of a lonely owl, the bark of a dog fox, or the howl of a vixen. But here, the night was filled with a cacophony of noises. A symphony of beats, rattles, croaks and whistles, issuing from more creatures than John could ever imagine. Nevertheless, the chorus succeeded in soothing and relaxing him, resulting in a deep and dreamless sleep.

Chapter Eight

Looking at his sore hands, Elliot groaned, since they had never felt as raw, and looked so blistered.

"I know how it feels mate," James said, watching him from across the table. "I had eight months of it, and they never seemed to heal. At least all the hard graft is over now."

"Well I certainly hope so," sighed Elliot.

Bill Poney, James, and Elliot spent the first week at Durra Durra, stripping bark from the surrounding trees. Then, by making a pair of simple axels and wheels, from two stout poles and sliced tree branches, attaching the axels to one-half a hollow tree, Bill Poney constructed a sturdy cart, strong enough to carry a considerable load. Laden with bark, the oxen towed it back to the site, where the intended homestead, huts, and stockyards were to be located.

Close enough to the river, and fresh water, the spot chosen possessed fertile soil, certainly able to sustain vegetables and maize, the surrounding ground, once cleared of trees, free for hogs to forage and turn over.

In no time, the men built three substantial huts. One for Mister Luke, when he visited the station, a smaller dwelling for Bill Poney, the overseer, and another for Elliot and James. Consequently, they were at last able to shelter from the pouring rain, which had been relentless since their arrival.

The journey from Mutt Mutt Billy proved long and arduous. With only three men on the drive, the cattle moved slowly, because preventing the beasts from straying caused James and Bill to repeatedly leave the herd, to retrieve deserters.

Elliot conversely, was proving more of a hindrance than a help, since he was hardly able to stay on a horse, let alone ride alongside a galloping heifer, when the requirement was for the rider to use a whip and rope.

However, Bill and James were patient, realising the young man's weaknesses, at the same time, recognising Elliot's courage and fortitude for even attempting such a venture. As compensation for his ineptitude, Bill gave Elliot the job of bullock driver, which the young man enjoyed, constantly cracking his whip across the backs of the two sorrowful creatures.

All this occurred months ago, however, because by now the men were settled into a daily routine on Durra Durra.

"Have some more tea, Elliot." Bill said, taking the billy from the fire. "It'll take the pain away."

"It's too strong, Mr Poney. I can't get used to it. In England we drink tea much weaker."

"In the colonies lad, we boil tea till it stews. It takes away the taste of the rotten meat."

James and Bill laughed.

"Well I can see the sense in that, I suppose." Elliot said, despondently.

The hut was small, smelling of eucalyptus and earth, at one end, a mound of thick turf, protecting the bark from a small fire burning in a stone hearth. Each man had contributed something to the hut, James constructing a table, from a slice of iron bark tree, then laying it across two wooden crates.

"I reckon we did well." Poney said, swallowing a mouthful of tea. "It's the best hut yet, in my reckoning."

James looked around, remembering how it all began.

It was raining the day they said goodbye to Charlie Blackman, on his station at Yass, and it continued to rain persistently, well beyond the day they finally reached Durra Durra.

Before leaving Mutt Mutt Billy, Mister Luke gave Bill Poney a map, marking the limits of the new property. The northern and eastern boundaries ran along the bank of a small river marked, 'Back Creek', flowing south to meet the Hume River. The Hume served as the southern edge of the property, at a point where it made a right-angled bend in its course west, eventually to join the mighty Murray.

Discovering these features, Bill, James, and Elliot were in no doubt they had arrived.

Leaving the cattle to graze at will, Bill's intention was to begin erecting tents. However, the torrential rain, and high wind hampered their attempts to un-sheet the dray. As a result, the men went hungry, wet, and cold for the first night, sleeping under the dray for protection, until the weather eased, and they were able to unload some of the essential supplies.

Eventually, the rain ceased, giving Poney, James and Elliot time to hunt for firewood. And while exploring the riverbank, they found a cave in a rock face, finding inside a good supply of dry wood.

"We may as well stay here tonight, mates," Poney said. "It's dry, and it doesn't look as if we've seen the end of the rain."

Subsequently, they remained in the cave until the first hut was finished.

Poney decided to group the huts and stockyards in the midst of a natural clearing, amongst the trees, close to the riverbank. Consequently, respecting his experience, James and Elliot followed his instructions to the letter.

Initially, they dug a trench, four feet deep, two feet wide, and fifteen feet square. Then, on each corner, and equally spaced along the trenches, they sunk substantial poles, to a height of six feet. Next, sheets of bark, eight feet long, were placed in the trenches, and then nailed to the poles, reaching along each side of the square, overlapping one another, forming the walls.

The trench was then filled with soil, embedding the poles and bark into the ground. The rooftree and gables were assembled next, and nailed to the poles, a lattice of saplings, over the gables supporting strips of bark used for the roof.

While Elliot and James collected stone and turf for a fireplace and chimney, Poney cut openings in the bark walls for doors and windows. After a day of hard work, the slab hut was finished, meaning the men were able to exchange their bat-infested cave, for a dwelling. Although crude and rudimentary, with James' slab table, slices of tree trunk for seats, bark for beds, and a hot fire burning in the fireplace, the men felt warm, dry, and safe.

The following day, James, Bill, and Elliot erected the second hut, which would be the main house, where Mr Luke would live, Poney designing it to have three rooms, each divided by a bark partition. The front section, served as a living and eating room, including a hearth, plus a chimney leading through the bark roof. This left two back rooms for bedrooms, each section of the house connected by a bark flap door.

Built next, was a lean-to, with a skillion roof on one side of the house, also doubling as a servant room, or store. Finally, and away from the main house, to lessen the risk of fire, the men built a kitchen, with its own fireplace and chimney.

Therefore, by the end of the first week, quite a collection of substantial buildings stood in the clearing.

Being aware the river gum was resistant to ants, and since there was an abundance of red river gums along the Back Creek, the men selected the youngest and easiest to fell, splitting them with wedges and mallets, using the hard wood as fence posts, and railings for the stockyards. With everything almost complete, the last apparatus constructed was a gallows, a stout wooden device, where cattle carcasses hang for gutting, skinning, and quartering.

It was of little wonder then that a young man, lately arrived from England, never having done a days work in his life, found the week exhausting. All the same, Elliot reluctantly accepted Bill Poney's offer of another cup of strong tea.

"If you'll excuse me, gentlemen," Elliot said, wearily, swallowing the last mouthful. "I'll go to bed. What do you think we'll do tomorrow, Mr Poney?"

"We're in need of relaxation, lad. Why don't we catch us some fresh meat. What do you say, Elliot?"

"I say hear, hear! Mr Poney," Elliot said eagerly. "Hear, hear!"

***

At Luke's suggestion the next day, which was John Baker's first on Mutt Mutt Billy, it was with easy care that he and Luke rode around the property, Luke taking pleasure seeing his new friend's reaction, as he realised the extent of the run, together with the number, and quality of the livestock.

"It's certainly different from my homeland," John said, gazing over the plains, from the top of Bald Hill. "There, all the hills and dales seem to be on top of each other."

"Which part of England are you from, Mr Baker?" Luke asked.

"Suffolk. My father and mother still live there."

"That's funny. The name sounds familiar. I think my mother knew people from there. I remember her speaking of it."

John watched as Luke puzzled with the problem.

"How about you, Mr Reddall?" John asked. "Were you born in Australia?"

"No. Father and mother said they lived in Cambridge, when I was born. After that, in London. Lambeth I believe, while father trained to be a teacher. I was six when we made the voyage."

"Can you remember being at sea?"

"Not really. I think mother's recollections assisted my memories. Mother said we came out on a ship called the 'Morley'. It carried a cargo of women convicts. She said there was much 'goings on'. Well you can imagine, can't you."

John smiled, and nodded.

"The Eden brought me here," he said. "We carried two hundred and seventy men. Poor devils! There was a storm, a few days out of Portsmouth. The scene in the prison must have been beyond description."

For a while, John and Luke sat in silence, the breeze drifting over the plain, the rattle of the horses bridles the only sound.

"My parents came from Staffordshire." Luke said, finally. "Is that near Suffolk, Mr Baker?"

"No," John answered. "A fair distance north. More towards the centre of England. Suffolk's east."

"I remember our geography lessons. Father taught us a lot about his country. But I remember being surprised how small it is."

"Indeed, it's small compared to this great land. I'm sure you could fit England into it many times. Would you like to visit one day?"

John studied Luke's face closely.

"Yes. It's good to go back to your roots. It gives one a sense of perspective. I used to like history at school. Father was a good teacher, and knew plenty about his homeland. So I'd enjoy seeing the castles and mansions he and mother used to speak of."

John smiled. Little did this engaging young man know, he thought, that he had a mansion all his own.

When John Reddall finally returned from India, the question of what to do with the contents of Glen Alpine was ultimately raised, Luke hardly minding what his brother decided to keep, as long as he was happy. Lately, by the tone of his brother's correspondence, Luke noticed John becoming increasingly volatile, and irrational, caused no doubt, Luke surmised, by his growing dependency on alcohol.

The night of the annual Turf Club dinner had been the last time Luke and John had met, twelve months previously, Luke was certain then that his brother was far worse than the previous year.

After several exchanges of letters, John Reddall decided Luke should have the furniture, Luke pleased by his decision, having nothing of his own to speak of at Mutt Mutt Billy. It was decided John would examine the books, taking the ones he chose, leaving the remainder for Luke. The paintings were treated similarly. Except Luke requested the portrait of their mother, and was pleased when John made no objection, John choosing the painting of his father instead.

When John and Martha Wentworth married, the couple moved into Molle's Main, in Minto, Martha's father Darcy, having furnished it with all his daughter required to make her life as comfortable as it had been at her previous home at Homebush.

Thus, John had little need for carpets, crockery, or commodes, resulting in Luke acquiring almost the entire contents of his family home. The problem of transporting everything from Glen Alpine to

Mutt Mutt Billy was solved, when, in a moment of generosity, John loaned Luke his dray and bullock team, Mick McMahan travelling to Glen Alpine, conveying the house contents south.

Therefore, once the dray was unloaded, and with everything in place, Luke's house took on a most comfortable appearance, even seen by some to be luxurious. Not that others saw it often.

By this means, Luke was proud to offer his guest John Baker, a comfortable bed, fine crockery from which to eat, and crystal to drink from. Crisp Irish linen tablecloths and napkins dressed the dining table, and cool cotton sheets and pillowslips graced the beds. However, the library Luke acquired was his showpiece. Luke's brother, never having been an avid reader, left almost all his father and mother's books to Luke. And quite an eclectic catalogue they presented. From tawdry penny dreadfuls such as, 'The Newgate Calendar', and Lloyd's 'History of the Pirates of all Nations', to sensational novels such as Cleland's 'Fanny Hill', and Fielding's 'Tom Jones'; romantic tales by Walter Scott, and Robert Louis Stevenson, through to the classics of Homer, Voltaire, Dante, and Shakespeare.

Subsequently, after supper several weeks later, it was to the library the men adjourned, each now deep into his chosen book.

"I hope you'll forgive me asking, John," Luke said as they sat reading. "Is it common in England for a blacksmith's son to read and write?"

"Actually no," John said, looking up from his book. "I was lucky. In my village, there's a school founded many years ago by the squire, Sir Stephen Soame. He made a rule that the eldest son in each family should achieve literacy."

"How extraordinary," Luke said. "There's another name that sounds familiar. I must find mother's journals. She's bound to have mentioned these places. Do the Soame's still live there? Perhaps she mentions them?"

John's stomach reeled. What if Luke delves too deeply, he wondered? Reaching a conclusion before he had time to break the news to him gradually.

"They're somewhere amongst all this," Luke went on, staring at the bookshelves. "Knowing John, he must have thrown everything in tea chests. It'll take months to find anything specific."

As the days went by, Luke resisted asking John if he was contemplating moving on, convinced he would miss his company, should he do so. Besides, being stronger than any other man, John was handy around the farm. Changing the wheels on the dray took less time. Harnessing the bullocks was an easy task. In addition, something as simple as chopping wood was performed more swiftly, when John swung the axe.

However it was in horsemanship where John excelled, having tremendous control, turning a horse on a sovereign, if need be, branding young steers, searching for strays, and the monthly muster, benefitting from having big John Baker lending a hand.

Moreover, Luke was becoming fond of the big man. John had become a friend. In fact, Luke's first true friend. Because, up until then, there had only been the companionship of his servants, and he could hardly find intimacy with ex-convicts, despite them being loyal and true. So attached had Luke become, he realised the place would not be the same if John were to leave.

Chapter Nine

Almost a month had passed since John's arrival, and he and Luke were beside the creek, lazing away a hot afternoon by swimming. John had attempted to give Luke a lesson, as he did for James, his godson, all those years ago. However, John failed to persuade Luke to take his feet off the creek bed. Therefore, after several more failed attempts, laughing, the men waded to the bank, and climbing out, flopped down on the grass, allowing the sun to warm their bodies.

John was dozing, but Luke had more on his mind. Soon he must leave for Durra Durra. He would already have been there, were it not for the arrival of his guest. Luke was certain Bill, James and Elliot were wondering what had become of him.

Gazing through a gum tree, spreading its shimmering branches over them, Luke saw a cicada fly into the tree, settling for a moment amongst the leaves. Then, as if winding up a clockwork toy, it cranked into life, the whirring sound piercing and shrill.

Then turning, Luke noticed a fly had become entangled in John's golden hair.

The son of a blacksmith, and a clergyman's son, he mused. How dissimilar they were, coming as they did from differing social classes, where normally there would be a huge divide. However, Luke could see no dissimilarity between them. John was educated, charming, and good company.

Watching John Baker as he slept, Luke knew he was becoming a close friend.

As a boy, living so remotely, and taught by their father, Luke and his brother John made no friends, simply relying on each other as playmates. Reaching manhood, and obtaining their grants, John became embroiled in romantic affairs, and alcohol, Luke escaping with his servants, to the outskirts of nowhere. As a result, he had never known the depth of companionship that can be achieved between two men. Perhaps, this was the reason he so enjoyed John Baker's company, maybe resurrecting the friendship he might have had with his brother.

John stirred, and opened his eyes.

"Wow! I went right off," he said. "What time is it?"

Luke reached for his jacket, and finding his pocket watch, flipped the lid.

"Quarter past four. Time we were heading back."

"This is too good!" John said, stretching languidly. "The sun! I don't think I've ever enjoyed it as much. It's fantastic. You're a lucky lad to live in such a wonderful country."

"Your country now, old chap," Luke said, pulling on his breeches. "Hey! I've been thinking. You know you've heard me talk of Durra Durra?"

John nodded, dislodging the fly in his hair.

"Well, I'm thinking of travelling there, and remaining for a while. Would you care to join me? But then, you've probably a dozen things to attend to."

"On the contrary, Luke," John said. "I'd be keen to join you. The way you've described the place, it'll be wonderful to experience."

Certainly, he was going, John thought. He was not going to let Luke out of his sight. He needed to watch over this young man, at all costs.

"Good!" Luke said. "We'll start in the morning."

After loading the packhorses with supplies, and saying goodbye to Martha and Anne, Luke and John headed down the track towards the Cullarin Road, the morning air keen and crisp, as it can be on the plains, when autumn turns to winter.

"We'll stop at Mr Coopers, in Gunning," Luke said. "We'll need tobacco, tea, salt pork, and peas. I didn't want to run down the farm stores."

"The vastness is amazing," John remarked, overwhelmed by the expanse and beauty of the scenery. "But you must be accustomed to it."

"Not at all," Luke replied. "The landscape was the reason I decided to take up the grant. I was in two minds whether to come this far south. But when I saw the setting, I fell in love with it."

Once past the hamlet of Cullarin, the men rode on, talking casually for the most part, Luke asking questions about England.

"I didn't tell you John!" he said. "I've found mother's journals," he said, unaware of his friend's sudden apprehension. "Something to read at night. They're in the saddlebags. In a bit of a mess, I'm afraid. But I've managed to find two that should be most revealing. They're the diaries from 1810 to 1820. The years before we came here. I might find some clues to the names you mentioned. What were they again?"

"Sorry Luke?" John said, pretending not to have heard.

"The names you mentioned from your birthplace. What were they?"

"I can't remember. What did I say?"

"The place where you're from."

Despite his reluctance, John had to answer.

"Suffolk. I'm from Suffolk."

"Then you mentioned the school, and the man who founded it."

"Sir Stephen Soame," John replied, unwillingly.

"Yes! That was it. I'll read through them, and see if they crop up."

John fell silent, determined not to mention any more places, or surnames.

How honest had Mrs Reddall been to her diary, he wondered? Had she needed to tell it everything, in order she unburden her conscience? Although, even the truth might have been too much to reveal to a blank piece of paper.

Anyhow, even if they did finally reveal to Luke the secret of his birth, and the identity of his mother, he would still only have half the story. Mrs Reddall never knew the real father. Only John knew. When the time came to tell the lad, he would need to choose his moment carefully.

Very soon, the township of Gunning came into sight, straggling the straight road, simply a jumble of houses, lining the street. There was no mistaking Mr Cooper's store though, as eight bullocks, and a dray stood in front, along with a string of horses tied to the rail.

Luke and John rode up, and tying off the horses, strode onto the veranda, the doorbell ringing merrily as they stepped inside.

"Hold fast!" a voice growled from behind the door. "Or I'll blow your brains out!"

Luke and John froze.

"Throw down your guns."

Luke felt under his coat for his gun belt, dropping his pistol on the floor.

"You too mate," the man said to John, kicking the pistol away.

"I don't wear a gun."

"Well ain't you the brave'un. But then, by the looks of you, I reckon you could certainly take care of yourself."

The barrel of a fowling piece was digging into Luke's back, a pistol into John's.

"Now move inside."

Entering the store, Luke and John quickly realised they had interrupted a hold up.

Tom Cooper was standing behind the counter, his face white as ash, his arms in the air, a man beside him holding Cooper's wife, his hand clasped over her mouth, her terrified eyes staring at Luke. All the while, three men ransacked the shelves and boxes, pulling out drawers and cupboards.

"Come on, you bloody bastard!" one of them shouted. "Where do you keep it?"

"That's all I have," pleaded Cooper. "I've nothing else. I swear!"

"You're a sodding liar," yelled the man behind John and Luke. "Everyone knows you're fucking loaded. If you don't tell us where it is, your wife gets it. We feel ready for a jump this morning, don't we lads. We're randy as roos."

It was then Luke saw a large man, lying on the floor, wearing leather trousers, and a sacking jacket. The bullocky, he thought. Then noticing blood running from beneath him, and across the earth floor, Luke realised he was dead.

"I bet you're sorry you dropped by, gentlemen," the man said in Luke's ear. "But if you're lucky enough to survive this day, you'll be able to tell your grand kids, you were stuck up by the Whitton Gang."

Obviously, Luke knew of Tom Whitton. His gang were lately working the Great South Road. Not only between Goulburn to Yass, but all the way to the border with the Port Phillip District, holding up mail coaches, travellers, homesteads, inns, and supply stores, nothing exempt from their trail of tyranny.

"Have I the pleasure of addressing the man himself?" Luke asked calmly.

"You do sir. Now both of you move over to the counter. Then turn around."

Luke and John did as he was asked, but when Luke faced Tom Whitton, he was surprised to see how young he was. By the look of his fresh face, he and Luke were practically the same age.

"Now gentlemen," said Whitton, "empty your pockets on the counter, and be quick about it."

Both men dug into their breeches, fishing out the contents. Everything John owned was outside in the saddlebags, so the only items he put down were his pipe, and tobacco pouch. Luke, however, possessed a wallet, and his watch. So, as the rest of the gang continued hollering at Cooper, and manhandling his wife, Whitton walked across the store, brandishing the fowling piece and pistol.

"What have we here then?" he snarled, picking up the wallet, and looking inside, at the same time, casting an eye over the watch.

"Not much I see. Except a handsome timepiece. I thank you, sir."

"It has great family sentiment, Mr Whitton," Luke said. "Please don't take it."

Whitton flipped open the lid.

"What's it say here?" he said, squinting at the engraved inscription.

Luke's voice suddenly filled with emotion.

"It says, *'To my son, Luke William Reddall, on reaching twenty. Your loving father, Thomas Reddall, Clergyman, Campbelltown.'* Let me have it back please, Mr Whitton."

"I'm sorry, Mr Reddall. I can't do that. It's a nice piece, and I'll probably get a good price for it, once I've got rid of the words that is. But there again, I might just keep it. I've a need for a new one."

He put Luke's watch into his waistcoat pocket, and then opened the wallet once more.

"Not much in here for the likes of a gentleman such as yourself."

"We only came to buy tobacco."

"With two packhorses and saddlebags outside."

Whitton was quick. Luke had to give him that.

"I just might have a look in them bags, if I may," Whitton continued.

Gesturing to Luke and John to move back to the door, Whitton forced them outside, and keeping the firearms aimed at their chests, went up to the first packhorse, and began unbuckling the leather straps holding down the canvas covers.

"Stick your hands up!" a voice shouted from across the street. "I've got you in my sights Whitton. One move and you're a dead man."

Startled, Whitton turned, attempting to see where the voice was coming from, giving Luke and John an opportunity to run into the shadow of an alley, at the side of the store.

"Where have you gone, you bastards?" Whitton cried, reeling around.

At that moment, a shot rang out, a bullet smacking into the wooden boarding of the storefront, Whitton ducking under the packhorse, attempting to see from where the shot came.

"What do you want?" he shouted.

"You Whitton. You and your gang."

"You'll never take me alive!" Whitton screamed. "You'll have to kill me first."

"Then that will be my pleasure, Mr Whitton."

Peering out from the shadow of the alleyway, Luke searched the houses on the far side of the street, seeing only curtains twitching here and there, as people watched the fight through their windows.

Then suddenly, something inside an open doorway drew his attention. Light flashing off the barrel of a gun. Whitton must have seen it too, because in a split second, a loud report preceded a windowpane shattering.

"Out here you blokes!" shouted Whitton to his men. "But keep your heads down."

John and Luke huddled in the darkness against the wall.

"Come on," John whispered. "Let's get out of here, while we've the chance."

With Luke following, they scurried down the alleyway, and finding the back door of the store was open, they ducked inside.

With all of the gang outside in the street, Luke and John were able to run unchallenged into the rear of the store, finding Mr Cooper consoling his hysterical wife.

"Let's find my pistol," Luke said. "Whitton kicked it over there somewhere."

Together, they hunted amongst the boxes and barrels, all the while shots resounding from the street.

"Who do you think is firing at Whitton?" John asked, turning aside a sack of flour.

"I don't know. Could be the troopers. But to me it appears to be one man."

"If you're right. Whoever he is, he's doing a grand job holding them off."

"Here it is!" John yelled, finding the gun behind the sack.

"Come on!" Luke shouted, as they ran to the front door.

"They've spread out," he continued, partly opening it, and peering into the street. "We'll be clear, if we get to the horses."

Using the animals as a shield, they quickly established the position of the gang.

"I can see one bloke next to the post office," said John, over the clatter of gunfire.

Luke squinted in the glare of the sun.

"There's three ranged along the front of the hotel," he said. "I can see smoke from their guns."

"Where's Whitton?" John shouted, looking around. "There's no sign of him."

What about the man in the doorway? Luke wondered. Was he still there?

Yes. He could see the shadowy shape, and the barrel of the gun, as the man rapidly reloaded between rounds. It was then Luke saw Tom Whitton, creeping along the veranda, hugging the wall, getting nearer every second to the open doorway.

"Whitton!" yelled Luke, letting off a round in his direction. "Hey you inside!" he called again. "You better watch it, or you're a dead man."

Whitton though was young and fast, and with one barrel of the fowling piece, sent a volley of shot over Luke's head. Then rushing into the open doorway, he fired the other barrel into the house. Luke quickly reloaded. But it was too late.

"Come on mates!" Whitton shouted to his gang. "Let's get out of here."

Sprinting across the street, and back to the store, firing his pistol as he ran, Whitton grabbed the reins of Luke's horse.

"Fine bit of horse flesh mate," Whitton shouted. "I'll take him if I may."

"You bloody bastard!" Luke shouted, running into the street, firing at him. "I'll kill you!"

Whitton laughed, and climbed into the saddle.

"No you won't," he shouted. "You'll have to catch me first."

"I'll hunt you down, Whitton!" Luke screamed. "Mark my words! There'll not be a day go by, without you won't look for me over your shoulder. Because one of these days, I'll be there."

"And what makes you think I'll not search you out first, and finish you off," Whitton shouted, joining his men. "I've got your name, Mr Reddall. So look out."

Whitton and his gang galloped away, Luke hearing the scream of a terrified horse.

Once the dust cleared, Luke and John peered into the open doorway.

"Hey you!" Luke shouted. "Are you alright?"

There was no reply.

"Who is it?" John whispered.

"I don't know."

Luke moved slowly though the door.

"We're friendly!" he called. "Whitton's gone,"

Still there was silence.

"I'm coming in!" Luke shouted.

His eyes growing accustomed to the darkness, Luke saw a man lying on the floor, a pistol in his hand. It was obvious he was dead. Who was the mysterious fellow, Luke wondered? Certainly, a brave man, to say the least, since, had it not been for his intervention, they all might be dead.

The man was well dressed, and obviously one of means. So leaning over the corpse, in order to see his face, Luke instantly recognised him. He was Luke's neighbour, his property, Collingwood, bordering the eastern boundary of Mutt Mutt Billy. It was John Kennedy Hume.

"Do you know him?" John asked, from the doorway.

"My God! This'll kill Elizabeth." Luke whispered. "All his children! What was he thinking, putting himself in such danger?"

"He was a courageous man," John said. "He saved our lives."

"We must get him away from here. I'll ride your packhorse, and we'll put Mr Hume over mine."

As Luke and John carried the dead man across the street, people were appearing in their doorways, relieved to see the fight ended.

"Who is he?" Mr Cooper asked.

"Mr Hume," Luke replied. "We're taking him home."

John Kennedy Hume was a clever, prosperous, convivial man, working tirelessly to raise the standard of his livestock and crops. Luke held the greatest admiration for him. Well connected, John Kennedy was the brother of Hamilton Hume, the pastoralist and explorer, who, along with William Hovell, opened up the south, by discovering a route to the shores of Port Phillip, and the great Lake George. Not possessing the thirst for adventure and discovery as did his brother; John Kennedy put all his energy into improving his grant, and siring nine children.

His house, Collingwood, was an example of colonial architecture at its best, displaying Hume's immaculate taste, with its perfect symmetry of style and form. It was here that Luke and John brought Hume's body, on that hot afternoon, after their solemn journey from Gunning.

An old male servant came out of the house when they entered the yard.

"May we see your mistress?" asked Luke.

The man, however, seemed not to hear, his eyes fixed on the body lying across the horse.

"I think it best I see her first, don't you?" Luke continued.

"Yes sir. Sorry sir," the old man said, suddenly realising he was being spoken to. "I'll take you to Mrs Hume."

Luke nodded to John, who dismounted, leading the horses to a water trough, in the shade of trees.

Luke and the old servant found Elizabeth Hume in the parlour, surrounded by five of her nine children, Luke seeing them enjoying a jolly game of blind man's buff. He was confounded. How was he to tell Elizabeth his news? In the next few minutes, her life would end.

"Mama," one of the children said. "There's someone to see you."

"Mr Reddall!" she said, taking off the blindfold. "How delightful. It must be nearly four months since our little party. How time flies. Are you keeping well?"

"Very well," mumbled Luke, "thank you, Mrs Hume."

However, his expression caused Mrs Hume to look keenly into his eyes.

"My husband's not here, Mr Reddall," she said. "He's gone to Gunning, to the stores. You may have seen him on the road. Is your business with him?"

Luke blinked, but no words came.

"Robert dear," she said to her young son, "could you take the others into the garden to play? But not out of the front door, around the back. Am I correct, Mr Reddall?"

Luke nodded, their eyes meeting in mutual understanding.

"What's happened?" she said quietly, once they were alone.

"I think you should sit down, Mrs Hume."

"Then it's that bad."

He nodded.

Elizabeth Hume sat on the sofa, smoothed her white linen dress, and then folded her hands together in her lap.

"It was Tom Whitton," Luke faltered. "He was holding up the store. Your husband bailed him up, plus his gang. John saved our lives. He was a hero."

"Was?" she said.

"Yes Elizabeth. I'm afraid so."

Inhaling sharply, a sob taking hold of her for a moment, she was still again.

"Where is he? Do I have to send anyone into Gunning?"

"No. My friend and I have brought him here. I think your man is seeing to things."

"Yes. Shepherd's very capable. He'll make sure everything's correct. Can I get you some tea?"

"Thank you, Mrs Hume. That would be nice."

Luke had never seen such composure in a woman, her hands on no account leaving her lap, her eyes remaining calm and steady, her voice, and speech, clear and unfaltering. Yet Luke remembered his own recent grief, so it was easy for him to imagine how Elizabeth was feeling, realising her world had suddenly fallen apart. Her husband and the father of her children, was gone. No longer there to protect them from harm, or to love and adore them. Luke watched her get up, and walk to the window, gently moving aside the drift of lace hanging there.

"I'll tell my servant to ask your friend to come inside."

Returning to the sofa, Elizabeth pulled the bell rope beside the fireplace. There was silence while they waited, and presently the door opened, a small woman, wearing a grey flannel dress, a white apron, and mop cap, appearing.

"Thank you Edith. Can you ask the gentlemen waiting outside to come in? We'll take tea."

"Yes ma'am," she said, and curtseying, closed the door behind her.

"Please sit down, Luke," said Elizabeth, sitting on the sofa once more. "You look exhausted. Did you kill Whitton?"

"No. He got away. He took my watch, and my horse."

She smiled.

How stupid, Luke thought. What's a horse and watch, compared to losing a husband? Her love. Her life?

"I'm sorry, Mrs Hume."

"That's alright Luke."

At that moment, the door opened, and while Edith held it wide, John Baker walked into the room, Luke noticing the expression on Elizabeth's face suddenly change, as she glanced up at her new guest, the look of sorrow vanishing for a moment.

"Mrs Hume, may I introduce, Mr John Baker," Luke said. "John, I'd like you to meet Mrs Elizabeth Hume."

"Good day, Mr Baker," she said, holding out her hand. "Thank you for everything you've done for my husband."

John bowed his head solemnly.

"How do you do, Mrs Hume. I'm only sorry madam that we weren't able to do anything to prevent this terrible disaster. Your husband should be commended for his actions."

In the interim, Edith had returned with the tea things, laying them on a small table beside the window, Luke and John, helping themselves, while Elizabeth abstained.

"My husband sir was a brave man; born of good Scottish stock. I'm sure, if he'd been able to choose his end, it would be saving others before himself. Now please take a seat, and drink your tea."

A glance passed between Luke and John as they drank; the following five minutes spent in conversation regarding the children's progress at their lessons. Clearly, Mrs Hume was on the verge of giving way to her emotions, so the men drank quickly, returning their tea cups and saucers to the tray on the table.

"Thank you gentlemen, for your kindness today," said Elizabeth, ringing the bell once more. "It will not go unforgotten. But don't let me detain you both. I'll see Edith shows you to the door."

Riding on, and long after they left the house, Luke and John continued to hear in their minds the sound of children playing happily in the garden.

Chapter Ten

Hiding behind the rock, Elliot's palms ran with sweat, his heart in his mouth. They were following him. Why? What harm had he done? All he did was go into the cave, even keeping the torch low, so as not to scorch the walls, and damage the intricate paintings. Then why was it they continued to pursue him?

Earlier that afternoon, following dinner, Elliot told James and Mr Poney he was going for a walk. Therefore, heading for a distant steep escarpment, he made his way beneath its sheer face, spying a fissure in the rock, which, on closer inspection turned out to be a huge cave.

Even as a child, when his mother took him to Brighton for their annual holiday, exploring the caves at Black Rock had been Elliot's favourite pass time. He remembered them being made of soft white chalk, eroded by the sea into smooth shapes, resembling the icing on a cake. However, the rocks around the mouth of the cave looming before him, were rough and brittle, jagged edges, gouging at the tangled mass of vines encroaching its depths. All the same, the dark foreboding interior enticed Elliot with its mystery. So pulling together a bundle of dry gum branches littering the ground, he ducked inside, a cathedral of darkness enveloping him.

Feeling in his pocket for his sticks, Elliot crouched down. Mr Waldon had shown him how to light a fire, by making a hearth-and-spindle out of two sticks. He said this was how the natives made fire. By holding one stick between his hands, poking it into a notch on the other stick, on the ground, Elliot rolled it backward and forward with all his might, until the friction between one stick and the other caused the stick in the notch to glow white-hot. Next, placing the glowing ember into a pile of dry grass, it was simply a matter of blowing gently, while carefully adding more tinder, for a merry blaze.

The fire burned bright, illuminating the walls, Elliot astonished to see the marvels surrounding about him: mythical beasts, painted red, brown, yellow and white. Strange mysterious creatures, shimmering and transparent, as if hovering in space over his head, the flickering firelight causing the heavenly beings to pulsate to an unheard rhythm. Quickly, Elliot became intoxicated by the images, and the heat of the fire, relaxing on the ground to enjoy the panoply of fire and light above him.

It was then he saw the skulls. One on top of the other. Row upon row. Positioned against the wall. Leering. Unseeing.

Where am I, he wondered? Was this cave some kind of burial chamber, or temple to the dead? Whatever it was, he suddenly felt uneasy, smelling the scent of death under the reek of wood smoke, the acrid, sweet aroma of rotting flesh, filling his nostrils. And it was little wonder, because, amongst the pile of bleached skulls, climbing the wall, Elliot saw a head, the skin still lingering on the face, hanks of remaining hair, hanging in lank shards, the eye sockets crawling with white maggots. Elliot knew at last what the cave was. It was a trophy room, the sort of room his father had, where he hung the heads of stags that he killed.

Examining the skull closer, Elliot saw with horror that the skin, which hung in flails from the hollow cheeks, was not the colour that he would have expected. Instead of ebony black, it was pale green, the colour of pigskin in a barrel of salt. He shuddered; the head he was gazing at morbidly was of a white man.

Elliot stood up, leaving the fire to burn. It was time to go, he thought. However, before he could move, mumbled conversation, coming from the darkness beyond the fire, drew his attention. He should hide, and quickly. Better to be gone, before they see the fire.

Darting out of the light, Elliot tiptoed to the wall, and squeezing against it, he froze, as a group of eerie figures passed within a breath of him, Elliot able to see their silhouettes against the flickering flames. Elliot knew it was unwise to tarry longer. The more he remained, the more likely he would be discovered. Although, as the chanting began, something compelled Elliot to stay.

Between the figures, they carried a body, which they lay down beside the embers. He wondered why they had not been suspicious of the fire and questioned who had lit it. Perhaps there were more of their number already about, and maybe they thought that they had lit it. He was about to make his move, when the hatchets appeared.

They took them from the twine they wore around their waists and began to hack at the poor souls limbs, beating the bones, until they were nothing but pulp.

He watched in horror as the pulping flesh above the mush was cut up with sharp stone tools, which severed and seared at the white flesh.

"White Flesh! Oh! My God, another white man," Elliot said, under his breath. "If they find me here, that's me over and done with, I'm finished."

However, something compelled him to keep watching.

Once the legs and arms were removed, and the head hacked off, the task of disemboweling began. This was too much for the squeamish Elliot, and he turned away in disgust as the entrails spilled out over the dirt floor, the stench of excrement filling the air. Still unable to move, Elliot shut his eyes, wishing himself to be anywhere than where he was, but as he did so, the smell of effluent changed to the sweet odour of cooking meat.

He felt his stomach give a lurch, as the smell made him heave, his earlier dinner soon would be parting company with him, and he stifled a gasp.

There was little fear of being seen or heard, as the crackling fire, and the low wailing chant of the natives was loud enough to cover the smallest noise. Should he make his move?

Seeing the dark figures crouched around the fire, Elliot edged along the wall towards the dim light at the entrance of the cave, the further from the scene, the more confident he became. Until he was running and staggering over the stony ground, getting closer to fresh air, and freedom.

"Why you run?"

The voice startled Elliot, causing him to stop.

"What you do?"

Slowly turning, the sight Elliot saw filled him with terror, as inside the mouth of the cave, in the shadow of the ensnaring vines, stood an aborigine.

Six feet tall at least, and lean and muscled, his dark skin, glossy in the shimmering light, filtering through the foliage. Neither old nor young, the native held a spear in one hand, in the other, a shield made of hide, bleached white bones protruding through his ear lobes and nose, a swag of glistening shells around his neck. Other than this primitive weaponry and jewellery, the man was naked.

"Why you run?" he said again.

"I! I!" Elliot stammered. "I! I! I didn't do anything wrong. I promise."

The native stared at him, his golden eyes gleaming in the firelight reflected from the cave beyond.

"What you see?" the blackfella said.

"Nothing. I see nothing. I mean, I saw nothing. Honestly. I didn't see anything. I promise."

Sidling around him, Elliot pushed through the vines, and out into the sunshine. But the native followed, his eyes never faltering, burrowing into Elliot's mind, entrancing and entreating him mysteriously.

"Well yes! The natives. I saw the natives."

Elliot wanted to get away, but the man pursued him.

"What you see?" he said.

"Oh! Just some people singing."

"They bad people?"

"I don't know. I really don't know," Elliot said, trying to sound casual. "They might be?"

Endeavouring to run, the native's eyes held Elliot in their grasp.

"What they do in there?" the blackfella said, pointing inside the cave with his spear.

"I told you. They're singing. Well, chanting really."

Turning away from the hypnotic gaze, Elliot searched desperately for a means of escape.

"They not my mob," the native whispered. "They Maraket. Bad mob, Maraket. Hate whitefella. Take whitefella. Not my mob. My mob good. Wiradjuri good mob. We want friend with whitefella. Whitefella good. Give blackfella grog, bacca."

All the time he was whispering, he was coming closer, eventually, so near, Elliot could smell his sweat, musty and acrid, like that of a wild animal.

"Do you mind if I go please?" Elliot said, edging away. "My friends will miss me if I'm away too long."

Elliot began stumbling down the track, and away from the cave.

"Where you from?" the native said, following him.

"Oh! Just down there a bit."

Instinctively, Elliot felt it would be foolish, as well as dangerous, to tell the man where he lived.

"Me go with you. Maraket about. They kill you."

"Oh! Very well. If you wish," Elliot stammered. "But as soon as we reach clear ground, I'd rather be on my own, thank you."

The brush was thick, Elliot soon finding the effort of getting through exhausting. The native nonetheless, moved over the ground like an animal, sleek and silent, hardly disturbing the leaves and branches he passed.

"Hold up!" Elliot said, after half an hour. "I need to get my breath."

For several minutes neither spoke, Elliot clutching his side, waiting for a stitch to subside.

"Alright," he said finally. "When we get to the paddocks, I want you to go. I'm all right. I'll find my own way home."

On they went through the thicket towards the creek, and reaching the bank, Elliot turned to his companion.

"Thank you very much. I'll be all right now. You can leave me."

The native stopped and watched Elliot walk away along the creek.

"Whitefella look out!" he shouted, but Elliot was too far away to hear.

Back Creek formed the northern and eastern boundary of Luke's run. Therefore, Elliot knew that if he followed it south, he would eventually end up at Durra Durra.

Though where was the sun, he wondered, searching the sky? There! That's odd though. Instinctively he felt he should be travelling south, but the sun was behind him.

"That way must be south. Where the sun is, you silly man," he said aloud. "You're going in completely the wrong direction."

Turning, Elliot began stumbling back up the creek, although the water was running away to his left, the terrain becoming increasingly difficult to cover.

It was then he saw them, shadowy black shapes, darting in and out of the brush. Now here, now there, the shady outlines all around him. Was it the Maraket, Elliot asked himself? What should he do? He was heading straight towards them. Turning back, and staggering over the rocks, he began retracing his steps. But the figures were there, running low, springing from boulder to boulder, and tree to tree. Lithe. Black. Naked silhouettes, chasing him, hunting him. He must hide. Get away. Disappear.

Running now, Elliot tried to get ahead of them. But they were fast, their bare feet flying effortlessly over the rubble of rocks and shingle.

At last, he stumbled into a narrow, dark gully, the creek threading its way between giant cliffs, where, taking advantage of the humid air, tree ferns, and giant lilies grew in abundance, their huge leaves suddenly making a shady sanctuary. But there would be no saving Elliot. He stopped, trying to catch his breath, but the figures were advancing, splashing in the water, letting out woops and cries. They were closing in on their quarry, and they knew it.

Elliot's time was near. There was no escape. They would kill him. Kill him with a hatchet, or a spear.

Standing up from behind the rock, Elliot faced them, and whatever fate had in store, his father's words resounding in his brain. "Be a man Elliot! Be a man!"

Chapter Eleven

"Maraket leave whitefella." Elliot heard, dragging himself back to consciousness.

"Who say so?" a voice replied.

"King George say so."

Slowly opening his eyes, Elliot saw a pair of leathery black feet beside him in the mud. Then, with his eyes following the black skin of a leg, across a thigh, and upwards until they reached a head, Elliot saw it was his companion from the cave, the bones in his ears gleaming white against the dark green vegetation of the gorge.

"Whitefella belong King George," the native said, frowning down at Elliot.

"Hey! Wait a minute!" Elliot protested, while endeavouring to stand. "What's going on here?"

"Maraket have whitefella," the voice said. "Soon whitefella all gone Mungarbarreena. Plenny wadder before whitefella come. Plenny fish. Plenny kangaroo. Plenny opossum, plenny everything. Now all gone. Poor fella now, black fella. Bye and bye, that got nothin' at all to patter. Then that tumble down."

"Whitefella stay in talking place," King George said. "Many whitefella come. Many jumbuck. Maraket mob go."

By now, Elliot was on his feet, able to see his pursuers for the first time. All men. Strong, black, and naked, their bodies smeared with white clay, and carrying spears, hatchets and shields. He and his companion stood alone against ten. Surely, Elliot thought, this is the end.

The native doing all the talking stepped forward.

"King George and Billy Maraket fight for whitefella, yeh?"

"Hey now!" Elliot interrupted. "This is getting silly. Two grown men fighting over me. I'm my own man, I am."

His words went unheard, or ignored as both men moved across the clearing towards each other, and as if by a word of command, the remainder of Billy's tribe squatted on the ground.

Was this to be a long affair, Elliot thought? Dare he make a break for it? No that was foolish. The Maraket would be on him in a moment.

Watching intently, Elliot saw his protector King George, open his arms wide, a thin white spear in one hand, and a shield in the other. Then, bending his knees, he moved like a huge spider, encircling his opponent, King Billy taking the same stance, opposite him.

All of a sudden, Billy Maraket lunged at King George with his spear, George darting away, deftly avoiding the deadly barb at its tip. Crouching in the long grass, Billy Maraket's men mumbled, as their chief prepared to attack once more. But this time, King George made the first move, and hurtling himself against his adversary's shield, sent his spear into King Billy's foot, the chief leaping backwards, hollering and screaming, his shouts reverberating around the walls of the canyon.

Angry now, and with his blood staining the grass, King Billy lurched forward ferociously, but King George caught him with his shield, hurling King Billy Maraket to the ground, then rushing forward, brandishing his spear tip over his chest.

"Whitefella come King George, yeh?" George growled, menacingly.

King Billy said nothing, not attempting to continue the fight.

"You follow," George said to Elliot.

Meekly, and without protest, the Englishman complied, and soon they had left the Maraket behind, and were heading to Durra Durra, this time in the right direction.

***

Holding open the book reverently, Luke turned the page to the next day, seeing the graceful writing, in the soft brown ink. His mother was neat and precise in everything, he thought, from the way she kept house, to the way she wrote her journal.

After the terrible events at Gunning, Luke and John rode for the rest of the day, Luke silent and brooding.

The bastard was going to pay, he thought, stealing his horse, the pride of his life, and taking the only thing his father had given him. These were his most precious possessions, and he would get them back at all costs.

Reaching Yass, as the sun rode the ranges, Luke and John made straight for Charlie Blackman's station, where Luke's former overseer greeted John and Luke warmly, giving them a hearty supper.

The following morning, after an equally substantial breakfast, Luke and John bade Charlie farewell, and continued their journey, this time turning south, in the direction of Ten Mile Creek, a small township established on a river of the same name. However, there was still a day's ride ahead, and seeing there were no hotels as yet on the Great South Road, John and Luke made camp that night, in a clearing, the stars overhead as bright as diamonds, the darkness around, saturated by the sounds of the night.

"Here mother says," Luke said, squinting at the journal through the smoke from the fire, "the wisteria is in bloom again in Trinity's quadrangle. Such a beautiful shade of purple, the scent attracting the bees from hibernation at last."

Suddenly Luke stopped reading, and looked up.

"The date's April 8th, 1812. I was born in eighteen hundred and twelve, on April the sixth, but there's still no mention of me, just about Napoleon's invasion of Russia. Why I wonder?"

John shook his head, shrugging his shoulders,

"I remember the day well," he said quickly. "My father reading me the news in the Cock Inn, in Thurlow."

"Thurlow!" Luke said, looking puzzled. "There's that name again."

Gazing into the fire, smoking his pipe, while picking pieces of salt pork from between his teeth, John wondered how long he was going to keep Luke in the dark. After all, the man had a right to know. Nonetheless, John felt the time was still not right, worried how his new friend would take the news.

By now, John was well aware of the extent of Luke's love for his late parents, so he was beginning to feel uncomfortable, that he was about to tell this charming young man, information John was certain would devastate him. To discover he was adopted, and that they had kept it secret.

"Bath seems magnificent," Luke said, picking up another diary for two years earlier, leafing through at random. "It seems mother had a tremendous time. Lots of parties and balls. But wait! Here's the name!"

Taking up a stick, John began poking around in the fire, dragging fresh wood into its heart, well aware of what might be coming next, and preparing himself.

"Soame! Here we are!" Luke exclaimed. "Listen. June 6th 1811. Today at Lady Dobson's we met a delightful woman, Lady Edwina Soame. We chatted for hours. Such a charming person. I'm sure we are going to be great friends."

Luke suddenly looked up at John, frowning.

"Soame! Wasn't that the name of the man who founded the school?"

"My word Luke!" John said, feigning amusement. "I'm amazed. What a memory. You've not forgotten a thing.

"Of course not. I don't know why, but it seems important."

John smiled. How important the lad had no idea.

"Hey! But what a coincidence John. Did you know Lady Soame?"

"Luke! What me! A lowly blacksmith, know the Duchess of Thurlow."

"Then she was from Thurlow."

"Yes," John said, tired of the subterfuge. "And a more wonderful woman you would ever wish to meet. She was kind, and beautiful. The most beautiful woman in the world."

Staring at John, Luke was at a loss, not recalling him mention women previously.

"You say 'was', John. Then she died?"

"Yes Luke."

Luke began reading the journal again, John prodding the fire, sending showers of sparks into the night sky.

Would this be the moment to tell him, he wondered? Just burst out with the whole story, and give Luke his grandmother's letter to read as proof, causing him confusion, dissolution, and bitterness. Or should he bide his time? Allowing Luke to continue reading, in doing so, to discover how kind Edwina was. Then maybe, the realisation he was her grandson, would not be so difficult to comprehend.

As the evening wore on, by the light of the fire, Luke read his mother's words. At each turn of each page, a day went by. Day after day. Month by month. Until eventually, after an additional hour, he stopped.

"Mother and Lady Soame did become friends," he said. "Firm friends. It seems they saw each other every day. Then Lady Soame's husband died, and she left Bath. Who's the other Soame? He's mentioned after the old man dies. It looks like there were two?"

Turning away from the fire, John saw Luke looking at him, the firelight gleaming in his eyes.

"He's her son, Humphrey."

Luke's eyes were piercing, John needing to look away.

"What sort of man is he?" Luke went on. "Mother mentions him getting into a spot of bother, and being injured."

"He might have. He was a rascally fellow. Full of devil may care, and good spirits."

Hearing his own words, John felt bitterness deep inside.

"You mean he's a cad?"

"No no!" John answered, looking purposely into the fire. "Soame's a good fellow. Well respected in the village. Always doing good deeds for the poor and needy."

"Well I'm pleased. Lady Soame sounds a wonderful woman. I'm glad she has a son she can be proud of."

Filling the billy with tealeaves and fresh water, John placed it in to the embers.

What else could he say? Either tell Luke lies, keeping him innocent of the real facts, or tell the truth. Better to paint a rosy picture of Soame. Otherwise, should John do the opposite, when Luke discovers who he really is, he will never forget John told him his father was an evil scoundrel, a violator of women, and a pederastic swine. Such knowledge would reverberate in the lad's mind for the rest of his life. Luke possessed the goodness and purity of his grandmother. John must protect him from his father, even from the bones, mouldering in the villain's grave.

Watching Luke flicking through the pages, John wondered whether Mrs Reddall had mentioned John's sister, Emma. Had she told her journal about the night at the temple, when the arrangements for the adoption were made? John waited to hear with baited breath.

"Well John!" Luke said, snapping the book shut. "I'm to bed. It's good reading. But it'll have to wait for another day. I'm exhausted."

"Yes son. You get to your bed. I'll keep watch. I'll wake you in a few hours. Sleep well."

Luke unrolled his bed, and laid down, pulling a blanket around him, until all John could see was his black hair shining in the firelight.

Sipping his tea, John realised yet again that the lad sleeping just a few feet away, was his nephew. They shared the same blood. Lady Soame had been right. John's duty was to protect him, and with his life, if need be.

It was John's responsibility to see Luke knew the truth, and therefore his obligation to guide him towards his new life. Therefore, with a feeling of warmth filling his heart, John pulled the blanket around his shoulders, and gazed once more into the fire, searching for whatever mysteries might lie there.

Chapter Twelve

"You and that blackfella are very friendly, Elliot," James said, throwing the saddle over Dan's back. "You should look out. You can never really trust them, you know."

"He's alright, Jim," Elliot answered. "He saved my life remember, and I'm only teaching him a few words. He's really keen to learn."

"Just don't turn your back on him, that's all."

Elliot laughed nervously. Since the day in the gully, he had taken quite a shine to King George, Elliot considering him an honest sort of chap, always ready to please, fetching, and carrying for Elliot, almost becoming his servant. It was only right therefore, that Elliot did something for George in return. As a thank you for saving his life. A few lessons in English grammar, and pronunciation were the least he could do.

"When will you be back?" Elliot asked, watching James climb into the saddle.

"Half a day there. A night's sleep at The Woolpack. Then half a day back. Tomorrow night, I should think."

"What would you like me to do while you're away?"

"Ask Bill. He'll tell you."

"Can you do me a favour, while you're there?" Elliot asked. "Could you ask Mr Pabst, at the hotel, if he has any old books? Anything really. Even old newspapers would do. George is doing so well with his reading. But he needs something other than seed packets, and tin labels. He knows them off pat."

The lad was well intentioned, James thought, as he laid empty sacks across the back of the packhorse. He remembered his months on the convict ship, teaching the men and boys to read and write, oddly the face of Peter Fagan coming into his mind.

Whatever became of him? James wondered. He never tried to discover what happened to the sailors who caused the revolt that day, James almost certain they hung, since that was the penalty for mutiny. If Tom Fagan hung, then Peter would be facing life in the colony alone.

With the packhorse trotting behind, these thoughts occupied James, as Durra Durra disappeared from sight.

The afternoon wore on, James riding over the ranges, crags of whinstone and tall cedars, towering around him. Mr Waite's property, Waggarah, came into view, merely a cluster of slab huts, stockyards, and broad paddocks, quivering in the heat haze. Another few miles, and he would be at Ten Mile Creek.

All of a sudden, from out of the undergrowth, two fully-grown kangaroo dogs hurtled themselves at Dan's hooves.

"Get away, you buggers!" James shouted at the snarling dogs. But being feral, they paid no attention to his curses, continuing to snap at Dan's fetlocks, causing the horse to rear and buck, the packhorse, breaking its tether in fright, and disappearing into the brush.

"Woah! Calm down boy," James cried, trying to prevent Dan from rearing. "Steady!"

It was useless, nonetheless, and in a desperate bid to escape the dogs, Dan hurtled headlong into the bush, tearing through the thicket, without a thought for his rider. Clinging to his horse's neck, James saw with dismay that they were racing towards a large gum tree, a hefty limb crossing their path. James ducked, as Dan carried them beneath it. However, the butt of his gun, lying in the leather sheath on the saddle, jutted out just far enough, for a branch to catch in the trigger.

With a loud crack, the gun went off.

"Christ!" James shouted. "What was that?"

Hearing the shot, the dogs stopped, and curiously, so did Dan, everyone standing in the brush, breathing heavily.

"Now bugger off!" James shouted, the dogs slinking away into the undergrowth. "You've had your sport for today. Come on boy," he said to Dan. "Let's get to the road."

Hold on though. What was this? His right foot was wet. James wiggled his toes inside his boot. Yes. They were definitely wet. It could only be blood. If so, then where was it coming from? Feeling down his leg, the pain began, searing and agonising, slowly the realisation dawning. When the gun went off, the lead ball smacked into his calf muscle, and out the other side. But that was only the beginning, because, as Dan began to move, James realised with consternation, that the bullet had entered his horse's shoulder.

"Come on boy. Let's get to the track. We'll be alright then."

With James lying across his neck, Dan limped slowly back. Although, feeling weaker by the minute, his blood draining away into his boot, as they reached the track, James felt strange, a sensation of weariness and peace, overwhelming him. Was he dying? Is this what dying feels like? In and out of consciousness, he drifted, one minute on Dan's back, the next, lying in the dust, the only sound, the raucous cackling of cockatoos, and the buzzing of a million flies.

How long he lay unconscious, he had no idea. Except, waking for a moment, hearing a noise like ripping cloth; opening his eyes, he saw the face of a girl, her golden hair tumbling from under a bright straw bonnet, her ample breasts filling her white cotton blouse.

"Now, what have you done to yourself?" she said. "You look a sorry state, you do."

"Am I in heaven?" James said weakly.

"No my darling, you're not. But if we don't stop the bleeding you soon will be."

The vision of her breasts, and beautiful blue eyes was the last thing he remembered, as he slipped into oblivion.

Then, he was in an unfamiliar room. In a strange bed, sunlight filtering through cotton curtains at the window, the sound of children playing in the yard. James raised himself to see outside, but the pane was streaked with red dust. It was then he was surprised to discover, that he was no longer wearing breeches, and barring his shirt, was naked. Searching the room for them, all he saw were a few wax matches, a candle stub and candlestick, on the chair beside the bed, with only his jacket hanging over it.

It was clear to James that he was going nowhere. So he lay back on the pillow, folded his arms, and tried to recall what happened.

He remembered the gun going off, that was certain, and the pain. The bullet went into his leg, and out the other side. James felt for his leg under the sheet. Yes. It was heavily bandaged, from his ankle to his knee. The girl certainly did a good job.

That's right. There was a girl. A beautiful girl, with golden hair. James closed his eyes, and tried to remember her face, but oddly, a recollection of her breasts was all that filled his mind. They were enormous. Suddenly James became aware, that for the first time in a long while, he was becoming aroused. Perhaps it was the thought of her breasts, or the fact he was naked under the sheets. However, there was no denying the fact.

In the past, when a moment like this had arisen, he was loyal to his sweetheart Alice, fantasising they were together, and in each other's arms. Nevertheless, here was this stranger, a girl, young and pretty, causing his mind to wander from his darling sweetheart. James had only seen her for a moment, but here she was pervading his most intimate thoughts, and pushing back the past. The vision of her persisted, and resisting his feelings no longer, his hand moved beneath the sheet.

There was a knock on the door.

"Sir!" a woman's voice said. "Are you awake?"

James coughed, and took his hand away, quickly folding his arms, and drawing his knees to his chest.

"Yeah. Yes," he stammered.

"Can I come in?"

"If you like."

Turning on his side, he watched the door open, and a face appear. It was the girl from his mind.

"Good afternoon, sir. And how are you feeling?"

"Pretty well, thank you," James said, sensing himself blushing.

"Would you be up to having a cup of tea?"

The girl was standing half inside the room, wearing a grey cotton skirt, and a white blouse, a little mop cap on her head. Nonetheless, the clothes could hardly disguise her small waist, broad hips, and large breasts. The young woman was without a doubt, very handsome. However, after the initial shock of seeing her voluptuous body, her face now captivated James. She was beautiful, eyes the shape of almonds, and as blue as the ocean, all the while, her face enveloped by tumbling golden hair.

"Yes. Tea would be nice," he said, sitting up in bed.

"Then I won't be long."

She was about to leave, but James interrupted her.

"Excuse me. What's your name?"

She smiled.

"Catherine. Catherine Rhall. What's yours?"

"James. James Baker Waldon."

"What a lovely name. Very pleased to meet you, James Baker Waldon."

"Likewise, Catherine Rhall."

"I'll be back with your tea in a trice."

Relaxing into the pillow, a thought gradually entered James' mind. Who had taken off his breeches and underpants? Was it Miss Rhall? Had she seen his body, something that, other than his mother, only one girl had ever seen? Did he feel embarrassed? Strangely not. James had nothing to be embarrassed about in that department. Although, in the process of removing them, had she felt embarrassed. Miss Rhall hardly seemed the sort to take off men's trousers every day of the week, appearing to James to be most genteel.

Nonetheless, she must have needed to take them off, to treat his leg, but more than likely turned her head away. Well it's done! Miss Rhall might have seen him, or might not, and anyway, James probably would never know.

There was a knock on the door, and Catherine returned, this time carrying a cup of tea.

"Where am I?" he said, as she gave him the cup and saucer.

"Ten Mile Creek. At The Woolpack Inn. I found you on the road. You were lucky. I was out at Mr Waite's, buying milk. I managed to get you into the cart. You were very weak. Another hour, and you'd have been a gonner."

"But where's Dan?"

She looked puzzled.

"My horse. What's happened of him? He took the shot too."

"Now don't distress yourself. Mr Pabst got the bullet out. Your horse is doing fine."

"And my clothes?"

Catherine looked embarrassed.

"Oh dear! Mr Pabst took off your breeches, so I could dress your wound. But he was very thoughtful, and covered you with a sheet."

Oddly, James felt disappointed for a moment, the thought of her seeing him naked, having quite excited him.

"Would you care for something to eat?" Catherine continued. "I've just this minute, taken a loaf out of the oven, and there's some dripping. Would that do?"

"It would. Very nicely. Thank you." James said, suddenly feeling hungry. "How long have I been here?"

"Three days."

"Three days!" he said, choking on his tea. "But they'll be wondering what's happened to me."

He tried getting out of bed, but had second thoughts, considering his condition.

"Just calm yourself, and drink your tea. You have to mend your leg, before you go moving about. Otherwise you'll open the wound, and we'll be back to square one."

Her voice was firm. The sort of firmness a mother uses with a child, James feeling a rush of warmth surge through him. For the first time in a very long time, he was being cared for. Nursed. Looked after.

He watched her leave the room. Then finishing his tea, he pulled the sheets and blankets up to his chin, and shut his eyes, the sound of children playing outside, finally sending him to sleep.

***

"It'll have changed since I was last here." Luke said, as they rode down into the valley.

Nestled on the banks of the stretch of river baring its name, Ten Mile Creek, was simply a collection of huts and weatherboards, appearing peaceful in the afternoon sun, reminding John Baker of a sleepy English village. So, crossing a pebbly ford, he and Luke entered the hamlet, causing little interest from the inhabitants.

Along the main street, John and Luke approached a large hotel, an impressive sign above a veranda, announcing it to be The Woolpack Inn.

"This is new," Luke said, hauling the saddlebag off his horse. "A year ago there was no grog shop, only a couple of tents, where the fat German sold wine. Let's get inside. I've a thirst to quench. How about you?"

"Gutten abend meine herren," the landlord said, as Luke and John entered the taproom. "Vat can I get you boz?"

His accent was thick and guttural.

"What would you like John? Ale is it?"

"Thanks," John said, putting his bags over a chair.

"Two pots of ale, thank you Johan."

Screwing up his nose, the German squinted at Luke.

"Vhy! Herr Reddall!" he shouted, coming from behind the counter, shaking Luke's hand vigorously. "Wery goot to zee you again. You have, long time not been here."

"Long-time, Johan. Almost one year."

"Vhat you been doing, Herr Reddall? Growing many sheeps?"

"Yes Johan. Growing many, many sheeps."

"Hey girl!" Johan bellowed over his shoulder. "Commen zee here, frauline. Get zee men zee beer."

A door opened behind the bar, a young woman appearing, Luke noticing her flaxen tresses, blue eyes, as well as the biggest breasts he had ever seen.

"Yes sir," said the girl, her soft Irish brogue sounding like spring water beside the German's harsh accent.

"Unt no dilly dally," Johan shouted as she disappeared.

The girl returned almost immediately, carrying two large glasses of beer, and coming out from behind the counter, walked across the room to the table, where Luke and John were sitting. Placing the drinks down, she provided the men ample time to appreciate her breasts, bulging provocatively though her white cotton blouse.

All the while, Luke noticed that Johan never took his eyes off her for a moment, a broad smile across his wide, fat face.

"Thank you," John said, looking up at her.

"Not at all, sir," she replied,

"Goot for bizzinez, Mr Reddall," Mr Pabst chuckled, as the girl returned behind the counter.

"We'll bed and board here tonight, John," Luke said, after taking a gulp of beer. "Durra Durra's half a day's ride, and with Whitton about, I don't think we should travel by night. Have you rooms, Johan?"

"Ya Herr Reddall. Ve av vun uzzer guest, in zee uzzer room. Zo you av to share zee bed vis your friend. Goot bed ya. Gross!"

"How do you feel about sharing, John?" Luke asked.

"It's fine with me."

John was enjoying the strong ale, wiping the froth from his mouth.

"You men hungry, Herr Reddall? Ve av zee shinken, or zee swine rost."

"Indeed Johan! We are. I'll have roast pork. What about you John?"

"Sounds good."

With the dust washed from their throats, Luke and John relaxed, feeling the ale slowly helping them forget their aching bones, and sore muscles. Leaning back in his chair, John took an opportunity to scrutinise the room, while behind the bar, Johan lazily polished glasses, and the girl stacked shelves with china plates.

Although it was approaching winter, outside was warm, yet inside the hotel was cool, a wide veranda casting a deep shadow, preventing sunlight from entering. Except, with the open door to the veranda, plus several windows located in the outside wall, John could still feel air drifting in, watching it mix with the smoke from his pipe.

Although not a carpenter by trade, John could see the counter was well constructed from hardwood, the craftsman having fashioned mouldings and panelling along its front. Moreover, the furniture, consisting of several long tables, together with a dozen chairs, seemed stout and robust, appearing to be made specifically for the hotel. As were a pair of smaller tables, either side of an enormous carved fireplace, beside which he and Luke were sitting.

Cedar planks made up the floor, instead of the usual earth, polished by the girl on her hands and knees, no doubt, the image causing John amusement.

"What's funny?" Luke asked.

"Nothing," John said. "Just thinking. Do you reckon Johan made all this?"

"I shouldn't wonder. He's Bavarian. They know a lot about wood in Bavaria."

Once again, the door behind the bar opened, the girl sauntering through, carrying a tray.

"Your rost swine, meine herren," Johan shouted, as she placed two plates of steaming meat on their table. "Get zee men some brot girl. Brot mit mustard."

"Yes sir," she said. "Sorry sir."

"Hey Johan!" Luke said. "Don't yell at the poor girl. She's doing her best."

"Stupid dum koff, Irish bitch," the German growled. "All she goot for shagging, and digging potatoes."

"Come on! I've an Irish girl on my place. She's a damn good cook, and brews the best beer."

"Pa!" Johan said, spitting on the floor. "This one no goot. Since sick man come. Him, she think of all time."

"Sick man!" Luke said, looking at John. "What's wrong with him? No fever, I hope?"

"No Herr Reddall. Not zee fever. Zank got! He voonded."

"Wounded?" John said, through a mouthful of pork. "How?"

"I not know. He has zee voond in his leg. She goot nurse. Make goot bandage."

"There you are then," Luke said, laughing. "She can't be that bad. You German's! No one's good enough for you. Who knows what you say about us English, when our backs are turned."

Johan laughed loudly.

"Ha! Herr Reddall! You make goot joke ya. Us Germans like zee English. Zee English like zee Germans, ya?"

"Ya!" Luke joked. "Hey, Herr Pabst. How about another ale, ya? John and I are going to get goot, and drunk tonight."

"Frauline Rhall," Johan shouted. "Two more ales for zee gentlemen.

By the time Luke and John got up from the table, it was well after midnight, there having been a great deal of story telling, and laughter between them, Johan maintaining a steady flow of ale and wine, to keep the evening lively.

"Danke schone, gentlemen," he said, as Luke and John staggered across the room. "You're in za room, next to the voonded man. Gutten nacht, and sveet dreams."

Luke was too drunk and animated to think of sleeping, all the stories John and the German told of distant places, unsettling him, since, for the first time, he realised there was a world beyond his. A world he suddenly wished to see.

Lying back on the bed, folding his arms behind his head, Luke talked, while John undressed.

"This place Thurlow," he said, lighting a lamp on the bedside table. "Is it as big as Goulburn?"

John laughed.

"No. Much smaller."

John was sitting on a chair, unlacing his boots.

"It's just a collection of cottages," he said, "a handful of farms, a church, an inn, and Thurlow Hall."

"What's that like?"

"I've only been inside once. The time of the great flood. But I remember it being very grand."

"Big then?"

"Very big. You've heard me talk of my friend Henry. He was the butler. He told me it took him eight minutes to walk from one end to the other. Though it's shut up now."

John was relaxed, the strong wine having gone to his head, and loosened his tongue.

"Why? Was it closed after Lady Soame died?"

"No. She had an accident at the time of the flood, and become ill. In order to take the cure, she shut up the hall, and moved her household to Bath."

"Around the time she met my mother."

"No. Long after."

"Why haven't you told me this before?"

"I don't know," John said, pulling on his nightshirt. "You didn't ask, I suppose. Anyway, we'll talk about it in the morning. You should be getting some sleep."

"I can't sleep," shouted Luke irritably, undressing, kicking off his boots, and throwing his clothes on the floor. "All this talk of Thurlow seems significant. I want to know more, for a reason I can't explain. I know it might sound stupid, but when you talk about it, I get an odd feeling inside. Tell me more John! Come on!"

Luke was intoxicated, his speech loud and slurred.

"It's funny," he went on, as he turned down the lamp. "When I read mother's journal, around the time I was born, it's as if one day, I just suddenly appeared. Like a rabbit out of a hat. She never mentions how it was to carry me inside her, as she does when John's born. When he's born, the doctors tell her she's not to have another child, because it might kill her. Then I come along. There's never a mention of what she thought, when she found out she was going to have me. It's like 'pop' there I am. And then she goes and has Julia on the ship, but we hear all about that! Why not anything about birthing me? John! What do you reckon?"

While Luke rambled on, John rolled on his side, and began to snore, pretending to have fallen asleep.

"Oh bugger you then!" Luke said, under his breath. "But watch out! I'll be asking you tomorrow."

John's mind was also racing, hoping, that in the morning, Luke would have forgotten the conversation.

Hearing the voices in his sleep, James began to dream. He was inside the shed; it was hot and airless, the sheep coming thick and fast. His hand, gripping and releasing the shears, felt sore, fleece falling in hanks on the floor at his feet. When will it stop? On and on they come, an endless procession of heavy, bleating creatures. There was Master Luke, across the shed, also shearing. Sometimes shouting, sometimes laughing; talking to another man, shearing beside him. Master Luke was speaking as always like a gentleman. But the man beside him, hauling on the jumbuck between his legs, spoke softly, in a tone that seemed familiar to James. 'I must see his face,' James said, trying to catch a glimpse, but the man was bent over the sheep, "I must see his face!"

James woke with a start, the pulse inside the tight bandage, pounding.

The voice was real. He could hear it clearly through the wall. It was Mister Luke. He was shouting. He might be in trouble.

James looked for his breeches, at the same time, fumbling in the dark for the matches on the chair. Striking one, he held it to the blackened wick of the candle. Suddenly, with the room filling with yellow light, he was able to see them, laid across the bottom of the bed. Catherine had washed and mended them, and they looked as good as new. Also, his woollen long johns were there, washed, and ironed. So, throwing back the sheets and blankets, James pulled on his breeches, and stood up, picking up the candle.

Seeing it was the first time he had walked, his leg felt stiff. But slowly and painfully, he made it to the door.

With the candle flickering in a draught from an open window, James hobbled into the corridor, and the short distance to the next room.

He listened at the door. But everything was quiet, even hearing someone snoring. Though, there was Mister Luke again, babbling incoherently.

James knocked on the door.

"Who's that?" he heard Mr Luke whisper. "What do you want, at this hour?"

"It's me, Mister Luke. James. Are you alright?"

"Jim! What the hell are you doing here?"

"I'm in the next room. I heard you shouting. I thought you were in trouble. Are you all right?"

"Of course. Come in, and see for yourself."

James opened the door, and stood on the threshold, the candle illuminating the room.

"Are you the man who was voonded? I'm sorry. I mean wounded?" Luke asked, blinking in the candlelight.

"Yes. My bloody gun went off in the holster. The shot went clean through my leg. I've been here for three days."

"Are you alright?"

"I think so. It feels a lot better."

Even during this short exchange, James was aware his master was not alone, clearly making out the shape of a large person, lying beside him.

"Well I'm glad nothing's wrong, Mister Luke. I'll go back to my bed, and not disturb you any more."

"Hold on Jim. Don't go," Luke said. "While you're here. Hey John!"

James saw Luke nudge the fellow beside him.

"John! Come on! I know you're not asleep. Meet a fellow blacksmith. This is my man James. James Baker Waldon."

The man sat up in bed, his eyes gaping, and for a moment, there was silence, then a thud, as James fell to the floor in a dead faint.

"Come on Luke," John said, getting out of bed. "Let's get him back to his room."

"He shot himself. He must have lost a lot of blood," Luke said. "He's probably still very weak."

John crouched, and looked into James' face.

"He's only fainted."

Between them, they lifted James, carrying him into the corridor.

"He just dropped like a stone when he saw you." Luke said, picking up the candle of the floor. "Funny. But to me, it seemed he recognised you."

John opened the bedroom door, and he and Luke carried James inside, laying him on the bed.

Alcohol had not dulled Luke's senses, however, and watching John closely, he saw something unusual in the manner he was looking at the lad, and how he covered him with the blankets.

"John, I might still be a little drunk," Luke said. "But I'm going to say it anyway. I think you know this man. I don't know how I can tell, but I can."

Sitting on the chair, John stared at James, lying unconscious on the bed.

"Yes Luke. I do," he sighed. "I can't tell a lie. He's partly the reason I'm here."

"But he's my servant, James Baker Waldon. What's he to you?"

Luke stopped suddenly. "Baker!" he exclaimed. "His middle name's Baker. Of course! Is that the connection? He's your son. But then his last name is Waldon. What's it all about, John?"

For a moment, John remained silent, endeavouring to gather his thoughts. Discovering James was as much of a shock to him, as it was for anyone. Since finding Luke, he had almost forgotten there was another reason for his being there, his only concern to fulfil Lady Soame's dying wish, to reveal to Luke his true identity.

Now everything had changed. Here, unexpectedly, was Henry's son, and the boy taken from his family by the actions of Soame. How was John to explain this to Luke, without giving away Soame, his father, and the wicked man's motives and actions?

John reached for James' wrist.

"His pulse is strong. He's sleeping. Let's leave him."

Quietly, they shut the door, and went back to their room.

"So what's it all about?" Luke said, turning up the lamp, and getting into bed. "I think you should tell me. He's my servant after all. What's his connection with you?"

John climbed into bed, at the same time, gathering his thoughts.

"Very well," he sighed, pulling the blankets around him. "You remember me telling you about Soame?" Luke nodded.

"Well one winter's day, when James' father and I were boys, we got into a fight with young Soame. James' father and Soame ended up falling through the ice into the frozen river. They were about to be swept away, so I found a rope, and pulled them out."

"You saved their lives?"

"I suppose so. Well time went by, and we grew up. James' father met a girl, Lizzie, and they married, a baby coming along, not long after. It was a boy. The day he was baptised, Henry and Lizzie asked me if I would be his godfather. They named him James. But his father gave his boy my family name, as his middle name."

"As a mark of respect, and gratitude for saving his life," Luke added.

"Yes."

"Is that the custom where you come from?

"Not really. A boy's middle name is usually his maternal father's Christian name."

"Then this was quite different."

"Yes."

"Quite an honour."

"Certainly. A great honour to have a person bear your name for the rest of their life."

"So it must have been dreadful when the lad committed a crime, large enough to cause him to be sent here. You must have felt your name discredited."

"There was no such crime, Luke. It was all a misunderstanding. The man whose handkerchief they said young James stole, agreed so afterwards. Nevertheless, by then it was too late, and James was far away, and beyond help."

Shutting his eyes, John sank back on the pillow.

"What happened to him after that?" Luke said. "I asked James a long time ago, but realised he didn't want to tell me, so I didn't ask him again."

"That's James' story. Maybe he'll tell it himself one day."

"But he's a blacksmith, and so are you."

"Yes. He served his apprenticeship under my father. He and I worked side by side in the forge. Though, his father wanted him to better himself, and as the butler at the hall, got Jim a job as a footman."

"James worked for Lady Soame."

"Yes."

"Maybe he remembers my mother?" Luke went on.

"I shouldn't think so. He was just a baby when she visited the hall."

"Hey! Hang on! Mother visited Thurlow Hall! I never told you that. I've not read that in the journals. How did you know she visited the hall?"

John was cornered. He remembered the Reddalls. Her ladyship took Mrs Reddall riding one morning, and when Mrs Reddall's horse threw a shoe, Lady Soame brought her to the smithy.

"I don't know," John, said. "Maybe I saw them there. It was a very long time ago. Nearly thirty years. Anyway, didn't you say she knew Suffolk?"

Luke was silent, clearly endeavouring to understand the complex story in his tired mind.

"Alright. So what else are you here for?" he said, after a while. "You said Jim was part of the reason?"

"Come on lad! It's late, and I need some sleep, even if you don't. Blow out the lamp. We'll talk in the morning."

In the darkness, Luke pulled up the blankets, and turned over. He knew he should sleep, however his brain was in turmoil. Suddenly, the stranger he took from the ship; the man he had known for almost ten years; loyal, steadfast and faithful Jim, was linked by an amazing coincidence to his new found friend. Was it too much of a twist of fate, that James and John came from the same place as his mother's friend, Lady Soame? Now Luke knew his mother and father had visited Thurlow Hall; John had just told him. However, the strangest thing of all, was that the man in bed beside him; the man he now called a companion, was his servant's godfather. What was the connection? On the other hand, was it so far-fetched to be beyond comprehension?

Chapter Thirteen

"Good morning, Mr Waldon," Cathy Rhall said, pulling back the curtains. "Did you sleep well?"

"I did. Thank you," James said, stretching his legs in the bed.

"There's a cuppa there for you."

"Thanks Cathy."

She was about to leave, but James wanted company.

"Do you know," he said, taking a gulp of tea. "I feel marvellous. My leg feels quite better. I think I could be on my way today. They'll be wondering what's become of me at Durra Durra."

"Well just make sure you keep the bandage on for another week," she said, crossing to the window, and opening it.

"'Tis a lovely morning. I've a load of washing to do. This sunshine will dry it in a trice."

"Cathy?" James said. "Has Mr Pabst any old newspapers, lying about? A bloke on my place has taken to teaching a blackfella to read and write. He asked me to bring some back for him."

"I daresay he does. There's some in the cellar, I believe. But the boys will have messed them up I shouldn't wonder."

"Boys! What boys?"

"My boys of course. William and Richard. And a couple of little rascals they are to be sure."

"I heard children playing, but I thought they were in the street."

"They were," she said, laughing. "Little urchins. Take after their blasted father, they do, the devil take him!"

"Is he dead?"

"Not that I know of. But I wish he were. He up and left me a year ago."

"Sorry. I'm being nosey," James said.

"Oh! Don't you worry sir? I don't."

Cathy leaned on the windowsill, and gazed into the street, occasionally a breeze catching her golden hair.

"His name's John Clithero, if ever you come across him. He's a government man. Came out on the Mangles. We met in Sydney, seven years ago. What a charmer. He could charm all the ladies in George Street, including me."

James' eyes opened in astonishment.

"Oh! I beg your pardon sir!" Catherine said, seeing his reaction. "But I had to make a living. Times were hard. Although with my assets, what could I do?"

James' face began to colour, as it used to when he was a boy.

"But sir! I'm making you blush."

"No Cathy," he said. "Go on. I'll be alright."

"Well anyway, Mr Clithero was a servant in a big house in Pitt Street, and every day he'd pass by my pitch, on his way to the markets. He'd chuck me one on the cheek, and give me a farthing. I don't know how he thought he could do that, t'weren't his money to be giving away. He and I took to walking out of an afternoon, and it was on one of these days, he asked me to marry him."

It was a while since she had such a captive audience, so, beginning to enjoy telling her story, Cathy sat down on the end of the bed, twisting her behind, until she was comfortable.

"We were happy there for a while, and it wasn't long before I realised I was in the family way, if you know what I mean."

James nodded, at the same time feeling through the blankets her generous buttocks against his feet.

"When I started to show, he lost interest, and began carrying on with the other girls. This made me mad. So I followed him around, trying to catch him out. Well one night, I tailed him to The Rocks. He was in some house with a tart I knew, and she was no good. She had the pox you see. I kicked in the door, and caught them red handed, don't you know."

James nodded again. She was becoming annoyed, and the more she did, the more she wriggled her bottom against James' feet. It was more than the lad could bear.

"He jumps up see, all embarrassed, and I grab a saucepan from off the stove. I don't know what was in it. Could have been milk, or something. Anyway, I lay into the bitch, and hit her over the head. I knocked her stone cold. But he goes over to have a look. Then tells me she's dead. What a to do! I had to scarper quick, or they'd nick me. But something came over him, and he decided we'd both do a runner. So we did. We dressed ourselves as smart as we could, and took a Cobb and Co. Coach. Nobody thought we were absconders, and we ended up in a miserable scrap of a place called Goulburn."

"I remember Goulburn in those days," James said, edging his feet, to a safer part of the bed. "There wasn't much there."

"He went on about how he was going to open a butcher's shop," Cathy continued. "When all the while, we lived in a wretched tent, where I had the baby. We called him William. Then it was, he got a look at a newspaper in the grog shop, and came rushing home saying we had to move, because our names were on a list. So off we went again. This time ending up in Yass. A little while later, I found out there was another baby on the way, and then Richard came along. What a hole that Yass is. I think I was the only woman for miles around."

"You probably were." James said.

"I can't tell you how hard it was living there," she went on. "He did labouring jobs on places. But there wasn't much money. There were times when, after I'd fed his lordship and the boys, there was nothing left for me. I went to skin and bone, I did."

Gazing at her breasts, and generous thighs, James found the notion hard to believe.

"One morning, I wake up, and he's gone; scarpered, without a by your leave. High and dry I was, the three of us at deaths door. I tell you. I don't know what I'd have done if Mr Pabst hadn't chanced along. He saved my bacon, he really did."

"So he took you in, and gave you a job."

"Yes. He was on his way south, with a dray of stores, so we just hopped on. I obliged him for the favour, once or twice. But I've stopped all that. He's fat and heavy, and these Germans are rough buggers. They've no idea how to treat a lady."

James looked at her, sitting at the end of the bed. All right, he thought. She's not the sweet, demur girl he first thought, and not one to guard her honour greatly. But she was well intentioned. Cathy was honest and open, and he liked her. She made him feel warm inside. A sensation he had not experienced for a long while.

"Listen to me chattering on. I'll get you another candle," she said, getting up. "That one's broken."

"I won't need it, Cathy. I'll be leaving as soon as I've had a bite to eat."

James stopped suddenly, his train of thought interrupted.

"Hang on. You mentioning the candle has broken my dream. I dreamt last night, that I lit it. Now why should I have done that? I heard voices! That's right. My master Luke was shouting. I needed to get to him. To help him. He was in danger. I was searching. Searching for my breeches. I couldn't find them. Where had you put them?"

"They're on the chair," Cathy said. "I mended them, and put them there yesterday."

"They're not. I've got them on," James said, suddenly realising. "That's funny. Why am I wearing my trousers?"

"Are you alright?" Cathy said, putting her hand on his forehead. "You sure you're not starting a fever?"

"I'm fine. But it was such a strange dream. I dreamt I got out of bed, lit the candle, and put on my breeches. Then out in the corridor, I followed the sound of voices, to the room next door. I spoke to Mister Luke through the door, and then opened it, and there they were, my master Mister Luke in the bed, beside him, my godfather James Baker. I can't remember anymore. I think it was then I woke up. I've had some funny dreams, but that one takes the biscuit."

"Oh! You're such a silly," she said, ruffling his hair. "They're the two gentlemen who stayed last night. They're along in the parlour, having breakfast, right this minute."

James stared at her.

"What?"

"It can't have been a dream," she said, laughing.

James jumped out of bed.

"I don't believe it! John Baker here? It can't be true."

"I don't know his name. What's he look like?"

"He's a big fellow, with fair hair."

"That's him!"

"And Mister Luke has black hair."

"Sounds like both of them to me."

"Cathy! You're a wonder! I love you!"

Hugging her; then kissing her on the lips, and not bothering to put on his boots, James rushed to the door, and flung it open.

"Now just you be careful of that leg," James heard her say, as he staggered down the corridor.

Upon reaching the open door, the parlour was so flooded with sunlight streaming through the windows, James needed to squint. But sure enough, sitting at a table, mopping up the last of Mr Pabst's eggs and bacon, were his master and his godfather.

"Come in James," John said, smiling. "Have some breakfast."

"Yes. Come in Jim," Luke said. "We were going to see you when we finished. Your uncle and I looked in on you an hour ago, but you were asleep. We reckoned you needed the rest."

James opened his mouth to speak, but nothing happened, his eyes never leaving John Baker.

"You can thank Lady Soame for this James," John said, standing to greet his godson. "Her ladyship gave me the money to travel here to find you, and bring you home."

James moved as if in a trance.

"Come here lad, and let your uncle give you a hug."

Walking forward into his open arms, feeling them encircle him, the strong muscles gripping his shoulders, James was at home already.

"My mother?" he stammered.

"Your mother's well. And your father."

"But they must be angry with me."

"No James. They're not angry. They've never been angry for a moment. They love you. They want you back."

James looked up into his uncle's face, his eyes brimming with tears.

"Uncle, you don't know how I've prayed. Prayed for you to rescue me. Over and over. But you never came."

"I know lad. I know. But I'm here now, and everything's going to be all right. Now you've had a shock. Why don't you sit down, and drink some tea. It'll make you feel better?"

Luke got up, and drew a chair out for him.

"Do you want any breakfast?" he asked, once James was sitting down.

"No thank you, Mister Luke. I don't think I could manage anything right now."

"Hey Jim! Less of the Mister Luke. Any godson of Mr Baker is a cousin of mine. So let's cut out the Mister stuff."

"Yes sir. Sorry mister, I mean Luke," James stammered, John filling his cup with tea.

While James drank, John and Luke sat in silence, neither sure how to begin a conversation, at such a significant moment, the consequences of what had just occurred, still taking time to sink into their minds.

Finally, however, James spoke.

"How did you find me?"

"I didn't," John said. "You found me, I reckon."

John was thinking fast. His first task after he disembarked was to look for Luke, visiting the Colonial Secretary's office, and making enquiries. It was easy discovering Luke's location, John not giving it a thought to ask after James. Obviously, John was unable to tell James of this oversight. Not yet anyway.

"I had no idea where you were," he said, "but I followed my nose, and chanced to meet with Mr Reddall. And by the most amazing twist of fate, the meeting led me to you. I'm just as astonished as you are lad."

"What of home?" James asked. "How is everyone?"

"They're well. Still living in Bath. Except sadly Lady Soame died."

"So no one's ever returned to Thurlow."

"Yes. Your mother. She went back to Wratting, because your grandfather was very ill. I'm afraid he also died."

"I'm sorry. And Alice?

Seeing the look in his eyes, John realised James still cared for the girl, and leaning forward, he met the lad's gaze.

"You've got to be strong James!" he said, gripping his arm. "Promise me."

"I promise, Uncle John. What's happened? She's married, isn't she. I knew it."

"No James. She didn't marry. She died."

"Oh no! When?"

"Almost a year after you left us."

James felt the blood drain from his face, as a knot of anguish suddenly appeared in his chest. His sweetheart. The girl he would marry; dreaming of her night after night, and thinking of in every waking moment, was no more. His eyes filled with tears once more.

"But how?" he faltered. "What happened?"

"It's a private matter, James. I'll tell you later."

"No!" Luke said, getting up. "Please! Don't mind me. I've things to do before we leave. Stores to get. Bags to pack."

"Thanks Luke," John said. "We'll only be a moment."

When they were alone, John leaned across the table again, and took James' hands in his.

"She had a baby."

James gasped.

"A baby, James!" John continued. "Your baby. But it was all too much for her. Her heart was weak, and she died."

Quickly casting his mind back, James recalled the afternoon in the greenhouse. He tried to be careful. But Soame was watching through the window, startling them out of their wits.

"And what of the baby?" he asked. "Did the baby die as well?"

"No James," John said. "You've a daughter. A lovely little girl."

"But that's ten years ago. What's become of her?"

"She's adopted."

"Does that mean I'll never see her?"

"You'll see her alright."

"How?"

"You're going to find this hard to believe, but Lady Soame adopted her. She's a young lady, James. They called her Susan, after your grandmother."

"But why should Lady Soame do such a thing?"

"It was her way of making amends for the terrible sins of her son. Your father finally told Her Ladyship what Soame did that day. She was so grieved, that when Alice died, and with your mother away, and no one to look after the baby, she offered to care for her."

James sat silent, endeavouring to comprehend everything he had just heard.

"I've lived with the sight of him laughing at me, when they sent me down," James began, his voice trembling with emotion. "I've heard the screams of my mother, and seen the look of horror on my father's face. I want Soame punished for what he did, Uncle John."

"He's being punished Jim. Have no fear. He'll be punished for all eternity. He's dead, and rotting in hell I hope."

"How? What happened?"

"After they took you away, your father caught up with him on the bridge. There was a scuffle, and Soame fell into the River Avon."

"He drowned?"

"Yes. And it was my fault that he didn't drown all those years ago. If I'd let him, then these dreadful things would never have come to pass."

Even as he spoke, a picture of Luke appeared in John's mind. If indeed, he had let Soame drown that day, then the world would never have known Luke, and would have been a sadder place as a result.

"Do you feel better knowing he's dead?" John said.

"I think so. It's been awful carrying vengeance inside me. Over and over, I've planned what I'd do if Soame and I ever crossed paths. In my imagination, I've murdered him, time and time again. One day, I'd picture myself stabbing him in the heart, the next, shooting him through the head. It'll be good not to have to think such thoughts anymore."

John smiled. The lad was good; wholesome and modest, like his father and mother, and the rest of his kin. Except, how will he react when he hears his trusted master is the son of the terrible tyrant who caused all his misery?

"I think it's better you put all thoughts of Soame out of your mind, James," John said. "He's dead and buried."

"You're right, Uncle John. I'll never mention him again."

"Well," John sighed. "This has come as quite a shock to both of us."

"I should say so!" James said, able to smile at last. "I'll have some breakfast now, if I may."

"Certainly," John said, and rang the bell.

While Cathy served James bacon and eggs, and hot scalding sweet tea, John acquainted him with news of home, James eagerly devouring each word.

Not having visited Bath often, John was unable to tell him much of the goings on at the school. But he did amuse James, relating the story of the night he and James' father visited the inn, and of the antics of Mr Ives and Mr Denton.

After finishing his breakfast, James and John Baker took a walk in the sun, soon finding themselves beside the creek, after which the town took its name.

"What's your plan then lad?" John asked, staring into the water.

"What do you mean, sir?"

"Now I've found you, it's my duty to take you home. How do you feel about that?"

"I can't go home uncle. Of course, I'd like to, but I'm still working out my ticket. I can't go anywhere, until I've done another five years. After that, I get a certificate that says I'm a free man. Then I can do whatever I like."

"But couldn't I buy you out? Luke would let you go, I'm sure."

"It's nothing to do with Mister Luke, uncle. I'm a government man. I have to answer to them. That's why I must follow the rules. If I don't, they'll put me in gaol."

John was silent. He promised the lad's father, that as soon as he found James, he would send him home. This then was a turn of events, John unaware his godson was shackled by so many rules and regulations.

"You've to wait five years?" he said. "That's a long time."

"Not really sir. I can't tell you how quickly the last ten have passed. There's always things to do, and something new happening."

"I agree with you," John said. "The whole adventure's been a whirlwind for me also."

Back at the hotel, Luke was loading the packhorses with supplies, and seeing John and James returning, he waved, flashing a broad smile.

"Mister Luke's a good man. Don't you agree uncle?"

"I certainly do. I've grown to know Luke Reddall pretty well, since being here. It would be difficult to find a fairer chap."

"From the day he collected George and I from the ship, he's been nothing but a gentleman."

James was eager to talk, now that he had someone with whom to share his most intimate thoughts.

"But one thing has puzzled me from the beginning." he continued. "Have you noticed his eyes?"

"I can't say I have," John answered, endeavouring to sound nonchalant.

"They're extraordinary uncle. They're green. A vivid green. Can you remember another person having green eyes?"

John looked away from his godson's gaze, knowing to whom he referred, but hesitating to bring the name of Soame back into the conversation.

"Her Ladyship had green eyes, as I recollect," he said.

"Yes uncle. Who else though?"

James waited for a reply, but there was none.

"Sir! You must know. It was Soame."

"Did he? In truth, I never bothered to look that closely."

"In the early days," James continued, "every time I looked at Mister Luke, a thought of Soame entered my mind. But why? You couldn't find two men more different."

At that moment, they caught up with Luke.

"How are you fellows?" he shouted, from across the street.

"There must be lots to talk about. I still can't get over the coincidence. I'll have to look in mother's journals James, to see if she mentions you."

"Hardly sir. I was only a baby. She may mention my father, or Emma, Her Ladyship's maid. She's John's sister."

"Really John!" said Luke, frowning, "You never told me you had a sister. Your uncle's quite the dark horse, Jim. I'm forever discovering something new about him."

John laughed, however his laugh was hollow. This was far too close, he thought. Would Mrs Reddall have mentioned Emma? That morning, while Luke slept, John noticed one of the journals on the table beside the bed. It would have been easy to reach over him, and take look.

"I'm nearly ready men," Luke said, tightening the buckles of a saddlebag. "Are you packed Jim?"

"Not yet, sir. With all the excitement, I've clean forgotten."

"Get along quickly then. We'll be waiting for you."

James hurried across the street, and back inside the hotel. But before he could get to his room, an argument coming from the kitchen drew his attention. Mr Pabst was shouting. Catherine was shouting, and the boys, wailing.

"You and your two bastards can vamoose out of my place!" James heard Mr Pabst bellow. "I ask you one little favour, and you say nein."

"I thought you'd given all that up!" Catherine shouted, over the wailing children.

"I never ask for much," Pabst yelled. "I'm a patient man. But a man has his veakness' like anyone."

"I just don't want to do it!" Cathy screamed. "Not ever again."

"Then you get out! And take your bastard brats with you!"

"You bloody German fool!" she cried. "What you gonna do without me. Who's going to cook and sew, wash and iron?"

"I no worry Irish tart! I get other Irish tart, better than you."

James heard a sharp crack, sounding like a slap, and Catherine rushed out of the kitchen door, straight into his arms.

"Mr Waldon! Help me!" she screamed. "He's gone mad. He's

throwing the kids and me onto the street."

"Calm down," James said. "No one's going to harm you."

"You're a bloody madman if you get involved with her!" Pabst yelled from the kitchen. "She's a user. She'll bleed you dry, I tell you."

All the while, the boys were wailing, clinging to Cathy's skirt.

Suddenly Pabst went crazy, lunging at her from the kitchen door. But James was too quick for him, pulling Cathy and the boys out of the front door, onto the veranda.

"Leave her alone, Mr Pabst!" he shouted. "You can see she wants nothing to do with you."

Pabst stood in the doorway panting hard, because, being a big man, with a large belly, the effort of chasing her had exhausted him.

"You take her lad," he said. "Unt good riddance."

"But what am I to do with her?" James shouted, suddenly realising the situation.

"Go and talk to Mr Reddall," Cathy interrupted. "He'll take us, I'm sure."

"Yes," Pabst bawled. "Mr Reddall will have her. He'll have her, all right. I saw him eyeing her up last night."

"Shut up, Pabst!" James hollered. "You don't know what you're talking about."

Across the street, John and Luke were waiting. But the sound of James' voice alerted them.

"Come on," Luke said. "I think we'd better get over to the hotel. There's something's going on."

By the time they arrived, Pabst had James pinned against the wall, his hand grasping him by the throat.

"Get off him, Mr Pabst!" John shouted. "Or it'll be the worst for you."

"What! Zis bloody con talking back to me," he cried, leaning on James' throat. "I'll silence him for goot, I will."

Wasting no time, John launched across the veranda, and taking the fat man in his arms, lifted him in the air, and carrying him to the top of the steps, hurled him into the street.

"I warned you, Pabst," John said. "You've gone too far."

Quickly, James drew John and Luke aside, to explain the reason for the argument.

"She's nowhere to go," he said, "and there're the boys."

"We've got plenty of room on Durra Durra," Luke said. "We can take her. Anyway, I already miss Martha's cooking. It'll be good to have a woman around the place."

From the shade of the veranda, Cathy watched the men in conversation, and although she was unable to hear a word, she saw Luke smile.

"Thank you, Mr Reddall," she said, running to the men for safety. "You won't regret it, I promise."

Pabst stumbled back inside the hotel, cursing and grumbling in German. Meanwhile, Cathy and James went to their rooms, James to collect his saddlebag, and Elliot's old newspapers, Cathy, to gather together hers, and the boy's clothes, stowing them in a valise.

"How are we going to do this?" Luke asked, once they were together in the street. "I think the lady should ride with James, and we take a boy each. What do you say, John?"

"That seems the best option," John said, climbing into the saddle.

James was reluctant at first, since Miss Rhall was a big girl. Nevertheless, as she sauntered towards him, the sight of her caused him to change his mind.

"You know the way, Jim," Luke said, handing young Richard Rhall to John. "You'd better take the lead."

Thus, as James and his party embarked on the road south, leaving the town of Ten Mile Creek behind, and with Cathy's arms wrapped around his waist, her head on his shoulder, James pondered on the events of the morning. Who would ever imagine, he thought, such happenings should occur. He could hardly believe them, even if he read it in a novel. Nevertheless, they did happen, and everything was real.

Chapter Fourteen

Tom Whitton glowered into the fire, a smouldering pipe clenched between his teeth, his wide brimmed hat, and oiled canvas coat, running with rain shedding from a dreary grey sky. He was brooding over Luke's last words.

'I'll get you Whitton! If it's the last thing I do'.

"Not if I get him first," Whitton said aloud.

"Fuckin' leave it!" John O'Mealy sneered, spitting a spent chore of tobacco into the embers. "You already have his horse and watch."

"But he'll come after me for them," Whitton snarled. "You blokes heard what he said."

"If he does? We'll look after you boss. Don't worry."

They laughed, mockingly.

Hiding out, a few miles north of Albury, a small settlement south of Ten Mile Creek, Whitton's gang were resting, enjoying the spoils of their last two stick-ups.

The first, at Father Therry's property, at Billy Bong, a few miles north, was entirely successful, with plenty of easy pickings, the gang discovering a store of victuals, plus a good quantity of grog, as well as a couple of pieces of silver, on the side. The reverend was absent, with only a superintendent, and two aboriginal girls hanging around the place. Mick Bourke tied up the manager, while the boys satisfied themselves with the blacks.

Fowlers run, Mullingiandry, on the Great South Road, south of

Woomargama, was the next foray, Whitton and his men finding the house locked; consequently, smashing the door down, ransacking the place, returning to their hide out, on the heights of the Table Top Range.

Tom Whitton was surprised at the commotion the murder at Gunning had caused. How was he to know the stranger he gunned down that morning was the brother of the famous Hamilton Hume. The man was a good shot. After all, he and the gang were only protecting themselves. An act of self-defence, to say the least. However, the death caused the gang a great deal of trouble, since every place they went, be it town, or roadside hut, was plastered with posters, Tom's face emblazoned for all to see. The likeness was good, everyone in the neighbourhood now knowing Tom Whitton's appearance.

As a result, it was impossible to stay in one place too long.

Tom threw a log on the fire, kicking it into life.

"If Reddall hadn't stuck his nose in, we would have been clear away, and no one would have been the wiser. He's the bastard who told them who we were."

"But you told him your name," O'Mealy said, smiling slyly at the others. "I heard you tell him, when we were sticking up Cooper and his missus."

"Shut your mouth! It makes no odds whether I told him or not, I'm still going to get him, as sure as eggs are eggs."

The place the Whitton Gang had chosen to hide out was high and impregnable, a gorge leading to a lofty plateau, narrow and steep. A horseman navigating the chasm was a sitting target for a gunman hiding in the rocks above. The plateau was as flat as a table, as its name implied, with a sparse cover of scrub, and small trees. Also, a supply of fresh water, bubbling from a spring in the rocks near the top, making a course down the ravine, cascading into shallow pools, which, once heated by the sun, became welcome places to cool off at the end of the day.

As the walls of Table Top Mount were insurmountable, rising vertically almost five hundred feet above the plain, Whitton, O'Mealy, Burke and Dunn should have felt safe and secure in their hide out. To date, no one had discovered their lair, and they knew, as long as a man was posted on lookout, there was never a chance anyone could get to them. Therefore, unless man learned to fly, Tom Whitton and his men were untouchable.

Despite this, it still failed to reassure the edgy Whitton, who whimpered and moaned all the day long, biting his nails to the quick, his men looking on indolently, caring little for him. O'Mealy, who knew a little better, secretly believed Whitton was slowly going crazy, all the fighting and running, finally taking its toll.

Obviously, Whitton's neurosis was not good for moral, creating an uneasy and quarrelsome atmosphere, in which the men bickered, frustration finally driving them into the open, and on to yet more thieving and debauchery.

"Anyhow Tom," Mick Burke said, taking a hit of grog from a stone jar. "At least you know where to find him."

"Yeh! Thanks to the German. He's no friend of Reddall's. You can see that."

"You left the kraut alone, when you discovered he knew Reddall." John Dunn said, taking his turn with the grog.

"He's easy pickings. The fat bastard! All that grog and stores. With him around, we need never stick up again."

Whitton pulled a piece of paper from his pocket, staring at it closely.

"He drew me this," he said. "But I can't make it out. What's it say? It's sodding damp, and the pencil's faded."

Leaning over Whitton's shoulder, O'Mealy stared at the map.

"That's the river, I reckon," he said. "And there's the town."

"So by rights," Whitton said, pointing with a stubby finger. "All this, between the creek and the river, is Reddall's run."

"Look!" O'Mealy said, his finger following a pencil line. "He's marked a road. It goes from Ten Mile Creek, all the way down here, and ends up here."

"What's that say?" Whitton said.

O'Mealy squinted at the scribble.

"Durra Durra. Do you reckon that's him?"

"We'll have to go and find out, won't we. If it is, then Mr Reddall might just have to watch his back."

***

"When Mr Waldon gets back," Elliot said. "He'll have some better words for you."

"Me getting good yeh?" said King George, smiling a brilliant smile,

"Yes. You're beginning to know the words very well. But we need new ones.

It had rained persistently from early morning, Elliot and George doing little work all day. Although, as they sat on the veranda of Elliot's hut, enjoying the last rays of a magnificent sunset, the deep red sky predicted a fine day on the morrow.

"What we do if Waldon no come?" George said, poking a stick into the mud.

"I don't know," answered Elliot. "Poney will find us something, I'm sure."

"Me teach Herot!" yelled George, jumping to his feet. "Me show Herot."

Dancing with delight, George sprang around.

"Show me what?"

"We go bush. George show Herot dreamtime dragon."

"Yes. That would be nice," Elliot said, leaning back in the cane chair. "But what would Poney say if he finds us gone?

"He say notin' yeh. Like he say notin' when I left jumbuck."

George grinned.

"He told you to stay with them, so the wild dogs wouldn't kill them. He gave you the job of shepherd, to see how you'd get on. He wanted to know if he could trust you."

"Me fed up. Fire hot. George sleep."

"You were getting along fine. Then you disappeared. Where did you go?"

"George on own. Need jabber. Want mob. Jumbuck no jabber. Just 'Barr.'"

He made the sound with his mouth wide open, showing his gleaming white teeth.

"It took us a long time to round them up. Poney was very cross with you George. You're lucky he didn't whip you."

"Poney man no whip George. Poney man know George, King. Poney scared."

"He's not scared, George. He's just fair. We're lucky he's our boss."

For a moment, George was silent, putting the final touches to the drawing of a snake he had made in the mud.

"Poney look out. Maraket come." he said, quietly.

"Not that again, George! Always Maraket come. You've been telling me that for a month, and we've not seen hide nor hair of them."

"George say Maraket come, Maraket come." He tapped his nose with a bony finger.

"Alright, Maraket come," Elliot said irritably. "But if they do, we'll be ready for them, don't you worry."

The morning came, and as expected, the sun rose into a clear azure sky. It promised to be a glorious day. George stirred from his place on the veranda. He needed no blankets. No pillow for his head. The clothes Elliot gave him were enough to keep out the chill of the night.

"You really must start wearing something," Elliot said to him one day, once it appeared the blackfella was going to stay around. "Us whitefellas have our principles, you know. We just don't go around showing ourselves to all and sundry. We're modest about such things."

"George ain't ashamed. George proud."

"I know George proud. You've certainly no reason to be otherwise. But if you intend to stay on the place, you're going to have to abide by our rules, and show a little decency."

So the trousers and jacket that Elliot gave him, he never took off, and by now were shiny, dusty and stained. Even so, George walked around in them as if they were regalia, undoing and doing up the jacket buttons, and putting his hands in and out of his trouser pockets.

With the first rays of the sun warming his face, George yawned, and taking a great gulp of air, ran his tongue along his teeth. Then getting to his feet, he spat into the dust, and then shuffled to the edge of the veranda, his bony fingers unbuttoning his trouser fly. Sighing with contentment, he urinated onto the ground, turning the red dust to something resembling blood.

"Herot!" he called, "Herot!"

"Yes George?" Elliot replied, sleepily from inside the hut.

"We go bush, Herot."

"George! I hoped you'd forgotten about that."

"We go bush short time. Poney man won't see."

"Alright. Just short time. But we'll have a cup of tea, and something to eat first."

Therefore, once Elliot felt buoyed by his breakfast, they closed the hut door, and headed off.

"Where are you taking me?" Elliot shouted, seeing George striding ahead.

"You see soon," he called back.

Elliot looked for the sun, and found it. They were heading north, he thought, away from the river, towards the great escarpment, towering like the ramparts of an immense medieval castle. Away from any kind of track, Elliot began to find the terrain difficult to negotiate.

"Hey George!" he yelled. "Slow down, won't you. Your legs are longer than mine."

Making no sign of having heard him, George stepped effortlessly over the ground, his bare feet silently hopping over the gravel and rocks.

After walking for nearly two hours, Elliot was beginning to fade. However, they soon came to a creek, one of many cascading from the plateau above, George kneeling on the flat rocks of the bank.

"Herot drink," he said, cupping his hand in the water.

"Where are we going, for heaven's sake?" Elliot said, joining him, and taking a handful of water.

"I show Herot something. Herot will like. George sure."

"Alright. But just let's rest here a while."

Lying back on the rock, Elliot closed his eyes, cicadas ringing in the branches above his head, likewise from the shimmering white tree trunks and the brush close by. Elliot knew them to be bush Cicadas, small brown insects, flying from tree to tree, chirping gaily, the males, and females, enticing each other with high whirring calls. By now, however, Elliot was familiar with every kind of Cicada. He knew a few were quite large, some green or brown, others black, with particular names like green grocer, brown baker, and black prince.

One day, during the first weeks at Durra Durra, while felling trees, James showed Elliot a shell, clinging to a tree trunk, appearing to Elliot like nothing he had ever seen, only acquainting it to the pupae of an English dragonfly. Elliot found it difficult to pick the pale brown husk from the tree trunk, since the hooks on its feet gripped the bark tightly.

"That's how they look when they crawl out of the ground," James explained. "The skin splits down the middle, and out they come, fully formed. There's one up there. He's just this minute hatched."

Looking up the tree trunk, Elliot saw a huge fly, with a large head, and a pair of bulbous eyes, its long lacy wings quivering as they hardened in the sun. Elliot thought it exquisite. Like an enamelled jewel, and quite dazzling to the eyes.

"The female lays her eggs in the tree. Then she dies," continued James. "The larvae hatch, and drop to the ground, burrowing into the soil, where they stay for seven years, sucking sap from tree roots. Eventually the bugs dig themselves to the surface, climb a tree, shedding its old skin, and turning into a cicada."

"Seven years!" Elliot said, incredulously. "How do you know that? Did you wait for the thing to dig its way out?"

"I don't know. That's what Mister Luke says. And he should know."

"It doesn't matter. It's a wonderful story," Elliot said. "You wait till I tell mother."

Dozing to the murmuring water and whirring insects, Elliot reminisced.

How naïve he was in those early days; a wide-eyed innocent, recalling how the sight of a flock of cockatoos sent him into raptures, sending home a seven-page letter, describing the spectacle to his mother.

It was only natural that he had been surprised, since previously, the only cockatoo he ever encountered was on the shoulder of a sailor. Now, however, he hardly noticed the sound of cicadas, or the sight of a cockatoo, so much a part of everyday life, they had become.

"Herot! Wake," George said. "We go."

"Do we have to? It's heavenly lying here."

"George show Herot great thing."

"What is it then?" Elliot said, getting to his feet.

Pointing along the bank, George drew Elliot's attention to a large smooth boulder lying on its side. Except, on closer inspection, Elliot saw there was something rather peculiar about the way it moulded itself into the sand.

"Let's get nearer, George," he said. "I'd like a better look."

The closer they became, the more Elliot realised the rock was no ordinary rock, taking the form of a huge lizard, lying on its side. With a long neck, and a very small head, in proportion to its body, at the other end, Elliot noticing an equally long tail.

"It must be as big as a whale," he said, in amazement, "seeming to be half submerged in the rock it's lying upon, as if slipping into quicksand."

"Dragon, like in story." George whispered, proudly showing off his find. "Dragon like George kill."

"Yes," Elliot said. "Just like dragon George kill. But this was once alive, not something out of a storybook. This is a fossil."

Hearing a new word, George looked puzzled, mouthing it with his lips, endeavouring to combine the sounds and syllables.

"This creature lived and walked around," continued Elliot. "Long ago, here about, was a land of lush green forest, and swamps. This beast spent his days wallowing in water, eating leaves and grass. One day it died, and fell into the mud, the mud covering him slowly turning to rock, locking the creature inside. Millions of years passed, and the landscape changed, to what we see now. But the water in this creek wore away the rock, freeing the creature again. But this time, it had turned to stone."

George frowned, endeavouring to comprehend Elliot's logical explanation of the mythological beast that had been part of his culture, and revered by his people for thousands of generations.

"I've seen things like this in the museum, in London," Elliot continued, "but never such a perfect example. Will we be able to find this place again, George? People should see this. It must be the palaeontology find of the century."

George ignored his question, because he had moved away to the riverbank, and was sitting on a flat rock.

"Me hungry, Herot," he shouted. "George eat. Herot eat!"

"But we brought nothing with us."

"George have."

Shoving his hands into his pockets, George took them out again, Elliot noticing his fists, tightly clenched, George holding one out to Elliot.

"What have you got?" asked Elliot, suspiciously.

"Herot eat. Good."

Opening his fingers, George revealed a large white squirming grub.

"George!" Elliot said, looking away in disgust. "I couldn't. No! Not at all."

"Herot watch."

Elliot turned just in time to see his friend take the grub, and bite off its tiny head, spitting it into the water, then put the pallid creature into his mouth, and begin to chew.

"Mmmmm!" he said. "Now Herot."

George opened his other hand, in which another grub, as big as its predecessor, lay wiggling.

"What's it taste like?" asked Elliot, watching George chew the last morsel,

"Good! Good!"

"Good. Good. Is that all you can say? How do I know what good means?"

"Herot see," George said, putting the grub under Elliot's nose.

"Oh well. Why not. It's been an extraordinary day already, and it's not even seven o'clock."

Gingerly, Elliot picked up the larvae between his thumb and forefinger. Then brought it to his lips.

"Bite head!" George urged, "Head not good."

Elliot opened his mouth, and as he had seen George demonstrate, put the head of the grub between his teeth, and bringing them together, quickly bit off the head, spitting it into the water.

"In! In!" George cried, excitedly.

With the grub still moving between his fingers, Elliot shut his eyes, and put it in his mouth.

"Chew! Chew!" George shouted, jumping around happily.

Elliot did so. Biting into the grub. Feeling it pop in his mouth, the insides spreading over his tongue. If truth were told, the taste was not as bad as Elliot imagined. Rather like nuts. Almonds in fact! And chewing a little more, he realised he was enjoying the experience.

"Herot like?" George asked, as Elliot opened his eyes, once he had swallowed the last morsel.

"Yes George," he mumbled. "Very nice. But if I could get over the idea of having to eat the thing while it's alive, I would really enjoy it."

Letting the flavour of the grub dissolve in his mouth, Elliot returned to the giant animal, running his hand over its immense flank. Unlike a lizard, the skin was smooth, with no evidence of scales. It was so well preserved, Elliot could discern the folds and wrinkles around its eyes and mouth.

"I'm going to measure this beast," he shouted to George, while walking towards the tip of the tail.

Reaching it, he turned and faced the head, and pacing it out, by the time he had covered the entire length, it made eighteen paces.

"Over seventy feet," he shouted. "This could be the biggest creature ever found in the world!"

His excitement was curtailed, however, as George began to move again.

"George!" Elliot shouted. "No further. We should head back. You said short time, remember. And Poney will be wondering where we are."

Turning the way they had come, Elliot began to walk, hoping George would realise he was serious, and begin to follow. Nevertheless, the further Elliot stumbled, the more he realised George was not behind him.

"Where are you, George?" he shouted. But there was no reply.

"Hey! You're supposed to be my mate. You're supposed to look after me."

Echoing off the steep escarpment, his voice sounded hollow and frightened.

"Where the devil's he gone?" he said aloud.

Elliot stood for a moment, peering around, unsure of what to do. Which way should he go? Should he return to the creek, and look for George? Alternatively, he could find his own way back to the farm. But would he remember the way? Not having been concentrating on the way there. Simply following George, blindly.

"Where are you, George?" Elliot screamed, angrily. "Don't be a fool! If you're hiding, it's not funny, and I'm not laughing."

This time, the voice returning to him sounded sarcastic, as if mocking him. Elliot looked for the sun in the northern sky. It was higher now, well above the ridge of the escarpment. At least, he knew in which direction to go. He would never make that mistake again.

Suddenly, from nowhere, a huge Goanna Lizard ran across his path, and this time there was no confusion. This was no fossil. It was as alive as Elliot was. Stopping when the reptile saw him, it eyed him, for a moment, its tongue flicking the air, smelling Elliot's scent.

"What are you looking at?" Elliot said aloud. "If you've designs on me, you'd better think again! You're a big enough blighter. But I'm still too big for you, so scoot!"

Hearing Elliot clap his hands, the giant Goanna scuttled away into the brush.

Herriot shivered.

"For God's sake, George! Where are you?" he shouted as loudly as he could.

"What am I doing?" he whispered. "Blaring my head off. The Maraket could be about. If they hear me, I'm finished. I need to keep my wits about me. But how will I find my way back?"

Of course. Tracks! The soil was loose and sandy. He and George were bound to have left footprints. Elliot stared at the ground. Yes. There they were, heading off into the bush. All he need do was follow them.

Damn George! Elliot thought. He would go back on my own, and surprise him.

How far away he was, he had no idea. He and George left the farm after sunrise, which was about five o'clock. It was nearly seven when they found the beast. A two-hour trek, at Georges pace, could mean a number of miles. But now the sun was higher, and the air hot. It would be a long walk back, and Elliot had no water. Even if he returned to the creek, he had nothing to carry it in.

I'll fill myself up, Elliot decided, and hope it gets me home.

Back to the creek, he stumbled, and after drinking as much as he could, he followed his own tracks, returning to where he started.

Dare he shout again? Why not. Just one more try.

"George!" he cried, his voice ricocheting off the cliff face. "If you can hear me, I just want to say, I'm going back. If this is your kind of a joke, then it's not funny. Goodbye George. I'll not forget this in a hurry."

Peering at the tracks, Elliot began walking.

George's footprints in the sand were clear to see, the marks of his toes, deeper than those made by his heels. Doggedly, Elliot followed them, taking no interest in his surroundings, until his mind was mesmerized by the sight of sand and pebbles. On and on he stumbled, the sun beating down so strong, it caused the woven leaves of his cabbage tree hat to crackle.

Stopping, he took out his watch, flipping the lid.

"Ten o'clock," he said aloud, "and it must be eighty degrees already."

If only he could find some cover. Just for a few moments. A place to get out of the sun. Except there was nowhere, only low scrub stretching around him, as if forever. Struggling on, his legs began to weaken, as if he were about to faint? He needed to sit down. No! That would be suicide, Elliot told himself. He must keep on. The tracks were still clear, and the further he went, the closer to home he would be.

Though something began to puzzle him. George's footprints were clear as day. But what was this? Elliot knew his prints. He was wearing boots. But here were other footprints, beside, and on top of George's. Suddenly, the realisation dawned.

"We were followed!" Elliot said aloud. "Someone followed us."

Furthermore, it was not one person, since he could see other footprints on the ground around him. Who were they? Were they Maraket? If so, why had they not taken him? Perhaps, this time it was not Elliot they were after. George! They were after George! Of course. That was why he made no answer, when Elliot called.

They must have been watching when he and George sat by the creek, spying on him, as he measured the creature. Then, when George left for a moment, they sprang. What had they done with him? Elliot's mind was in a whirl. What should he do? Go back. He should go back. George was his friend, and Elliot must help him. If George was still alive, Elliot had to rescue him.

***

"It's good to see the place again," Luke said, dismounting his horse. "But where is everyone? It's deserted?"

Taking the best part of a day to reach the station, the heavily laden packhorses, and new travelling companions, significantly slowed the party's progress. Cathy's boys, riding along with Luke and John, were well behaved. Nevertheless, once or twice they did cause the men concern, by falling asleep so soundly, they were close to toppling off the horse's back. Finally, as a last resort, John suggested tying the boys to themselves, after which John and Luke were able to relax, knowing no harm would befall the youngsters.

Unlike her children, Cathy was safe, and thoroughly enjoying herself, as was James, if the truth were told. However, he could hardly breathe, since Cathy was clinging to him, her arms around his waist, hands clasped tight. Feeling the heat of her body against his back, and principally her breasts, by the time they reached Durra Durra, James' shirt was soaking with sweat.

Teasing him unremittingly, on one occasion, Cathy feigned falling from the saddle, hitching herself back on, and pulling him close, allowing her hands to fall perilously between his legs. She was a flirt, of that there was no doubt, James quickly concluding that Cathy was extremely experienced in matters of love.

With the rhythm of the plodding horse, plus the rubbing of her heavy breasts on his back, James' journey was fast becoming rather an erotic experience. And, leaning her head on his shoulder, feeling her breath close to his ear, Cathy told him her story.

"I was born in Ireland, but grew up in Sydney, in The Rocks. I never had any shoes until I was six."

Laughing, Cathy wiggled her feet in James' view.

"My mother's name was Cassidy before she married my father. Mary Cassidy. She was the worst mother a kid could have. She told the people at the orphan school I was a foundling. That way they let me in, though I was never there much. Mother was drunk most of the time, and I scavenged the streets and hotels for scraps of food. She didn't believe in cooking you see."

"What about your father?" James asked.

"Him? He was a lovely man. Christopher Rhall was his name. A private in the Royal Veteran Corps. Though Mother and I hardly ever saw him. He was either at the barracks, in the grog shop, or out with his fancy women, or so mother would say. All the same, he was handsome I can tell you. He would come over on a Sunday, and give mother money. I remember sitting on the doorstep watching him striding up the street, wearing his bright red uniform, with the white braid down the front, his shiny black helmet on his head. Those steps up to our cottage were steep, and I remember, when he got to our door, he'd take off his helmet, and wipe his forehead. He'd lovely hair! All golden it was, just like yours,"

She took off James' hat and ruffled his hair.

"Hundreds of curls. All over his head. He was tall too. And strong. With a lovely tanned face, and bright blue eyes. In fact, come to think of it, you remind me of him. He left the army. Governor Darling promised him, and other soldiers, land in Bong Bong, a place I always think sounds funny."

"I know Bong Bong," James said. "There was a terrible fire. Mr

Luke could have died."

"Mother and I left The Rocks," Cathy continued, "going with him to live there. It was a lonely, desolate place. No other women folk. Just ex-soldiers, living on their own, trying to make a living from the land, with just the public house to drink in, at the end of the day. My dad took to drinking too much, and came home to hit my mother, and throw things about the house. He even tried to set light to it once, with a lit candle. Tis a terrible thing the grog! Makes a man crazy. Anyway, there's an awful argument, a bloke called Kelly, one of my father's government men, goes and kills my dad. Hits him over the head with a branding iron. Mother wasn't much bothered. She went and married again soon after, but I was devastated. He was a lovely man, that he was."

In this way, Cathy helped pass the time, as hour after hour went by, until at last they came within sight of the great escarpment, distant and shimmering in the afternoon sun.

"We're nearly there," James said. "Just this side of the cliff."

"Blimey!" Cathy whispered in his ear. "Where's the nearest town?"

"We left it this morning."

She was silent for the rest of the ride.

***

Stealthily returning to the creek, Elliot tried not to make a sound. He was concerned the people he was tracking might hear him. On reaching the giant creature, he stood beside its tail, studying the ground closely. Yes. There they were. George's footprints clearly indented in the mud along the bank, heading north, towards the cliff.

So following them into the bush, finding one print after another, eventually Elliot arrived in the cool shadow of the towering escarpment.

Suddenly, he lost the trail, since it disappeared into a melee of footprints. In which direction were they heading Elliot wondered? Appearing to come from the south, they would belong to the people following George, he told himself. What about along the base of the escarpment? Those led west, Elliot convinced they were the ones he must trail. They would lead him to George.

Millions of years of wind and rain had eroded the rocks of the cliff face, causing them to fracture, and tumble hundreds of feet, to the valley floor, where they splintered and cracked into a billion tiny pieces. Across this incline of shale, and shingle, Elliot began his perilous quest.

In the shade of the great rock face, he laboured on, tripping and stumbling. Even so, it was cool in its shadow. Although, it would be different matter entirely, when the sun reaches its highest. Elliot was thirsty, because it was two hours since he had water, and he cursed himself not to have drunk more, when he returned to the creek.

"Why didn't I take a drink when I had the chance?" he said aloud.

He looked around amongst the boulders.

No possibility of any water here. It was too dry.

He did notice some plants, however, clustered amongst the cracks and crevices, appearing to Elliot to be well adapted to life in such a dry and barren place. So, struggling towards them, until he was able to peer into the centre of a specimen, to his surprise, he saw it filled with water. But was it water? He dipped his finger into the liquid, smelling it.

"Smells of nothing," he said to himself.

He licked his finger.

"Its water. But the leaves are so prickly. How on earth am I going to get a drink?"

Of course his hat! His Cabbage Tree Hat! Would it be waterproof? It should be. He wore it in the rain, and his head remained dry. Removing it, and laying it on a rock, Elliot put his hands underneath the plant, keeping well away from the spiny leaves, tugging it, until the roots gave way. Then, carefully carrying it to his upturned hat, he tipped the water inside, and after several journeys, and more plants, he had enough to adequately quench his thirst, and cool his face.

His spirits revived, Elliot continued on, doggedly following the footprints in the sand.

Above him, the cliff began to overhang the shale and boulders below, Elliot noticing a labyrinth of crevices, eroded into a honeycomb of holes, these now home to thousands of colourful finches. Darting in and out, to a chorus of chirps and twitters, the tiny birds fed chicks, venturing forth, or returning with fresh supplies from foraging excursions in the surrounding grassland. His eyes tracing the flocks of tiny birds, wheeling in the air above him, it was then that Elliot saw the smoke, curling ominously into the azure sky.

"No. They can't be."

Elliot refused to believe what his rational mind was telling him. It was too horrible to imagine.

George knew. He warned him, Elliot remembered. He warned them all.

'Maraket come', George said, knowing they would. After he stole Elliot from Billy Maraket, George knew Billy would want revenge. And now he had it. Elliot could feel his heart pounding. He must get to George as fast as he could. But would he be in time?

"Please God I am," he said, under his breath. "Please God I am!"

***

"It's strange there's no one about," Luke called from the bedroom, as he unpacked his saddlebags. "Poney would never go off and leave the place unattended. And where's Elliot? He's so timid of the bush. It's hard to get him to go anywhere."

In the other bedroom, John Baker dug his hands into his bags, pulling out his nightclothes, and shaving kit, his fingers brushing the cold metal of the little strong box, hidden deep inside.

"A good set up you have here, Luke," he said.

"Thanks! Poney and the boys did well. They built this hut for me, plus two for themselves. And now we've Cathy to cook for us, we'll want for nothing."

The evening was warm, with no need for a fire. All the same, the men were drawn to the hearthside.

"Now that I've some decent furniture," Luke said, sitting in a Windsor chair. "It's more comfortable. It was hell for a while, when all we had to sit or sleep on was made of bark."

He and John relaxed, John surveying the view from the window.

"It's spectacular! Don't you agree," Luke said, lighting his pipe. "It's the edge of Narra Narra. Well that's what the blackfellas call it.

Someone named it Mount Pleasant, when he came through years ago. Either Hovell, or Hume. One or other of them."

"It's like a gigantic wall," John said, puffing life into the pipe tobacco.

"Yes. And look at the colours. The rock is pale in reality. But it takes on every hue from the sunset. Reds, pinks, blues. It's never the same two evenings running."

The men sat in silence, appreciating the magnificence of the panorama spread before them.

"Forgive me, John," Luke said. "You must be hungry. I know I am. What's James done with Cathy? She should be here cooking something."

Luke was restless.

"How about a drink. There must be something in the larder?"

"You stay here, lad," John said. "I'll look."

Alone, and getting up from the chair, Luke went to the bedroom, returning with one of his mother's journals.

"What's your sister's name?" he called.

Coming back into the room, carrying a bottle of beer and a bottle of wine, John sighed to himself when he saw the journal.

"Emma," said John, reluctantly. "Where are the glasses?"

"In the cabinet beside the fireplace," Luke said, flicking through the pages of the diary.

Was it going to be another of those conversations, John thought, pouring Luke a glass of wine, and passing it to him?

"Thanks, John," Luke said. "This diary is one which begins when mother and father return to Cambridge. I've only read up to the month when they visited Lady Soame."

John sat down, holding the glass of beer against his chest.

"Here we are!" Luke exclaimed. "How marvellous. What a coincidence. Here's your sister. Mother mentions her."

John leaned back in the chair, and shut his eyes, feeling the strong, cool ale in his mouth, letting it drop down his throat in a gulp.

"Darling Edwina," Luke read aloud, "has been so kind to arrange this. Her personal maid, Emma, will travel with us back to Cambridge. I cannot say how appreciative Thomas and I are. We shall be the happiest of parents."

Luke stopped reading, and looked up.

"That's an unusual thing to say. What do you think she means?"

"I've no idea," John replied.

Luke read on in silence, John taking several more gulps of beer.

"Here mother describes the journey home to Cambridge," Luke continued. "After that, she seems to mention your sister every day. Yes. Here we are. The fourteenth of March, 'Emma is well, and flourishing'. And here on the seventeenth. 'Emma is a little exhausted, not able to join us on our walk beside the Cam'. Was she ill John?"

"I don't think so. As far as I recall, she was always a healthy girl."

John was drinking fast. However, he knew he must slow down, and keep his wits about him, or the alcohol would loosen his tongue.

"Emma was certainly in favour, and very popular with mother," Luke continued. "The way she refers to her, it seems your sister's more a friend than a ladies maid. Oh! Sorry John, that sounds terribly snobbish."

"That's all right. My sister was your mother's ladies maid. I remember her telling us at the time Her Ladyship was giving her to Mrs Reddall, because she had no maid of her own. The family were very surprised, and concerned. But we could do nothing. We must always oblige the gentry."

"Have another drink, John," Luke said, browsing through the diary once more. "There's plenty more in the pantry. Or would you like a glass of wine?"

"No thanks, son. My stomach's empty. And I'm afraid I'll get too drunk to stay awake."

"Of course. What's become of James and Cathy?"

Luke got up, and went to the window.

"James!" he called into the yard. "Where are you? And where's Cathy?"

The journal lay open on the chair, and it was easy for John to read the elegant handwriting, gliding across the page.

"Today," it said, "Emma begins her confinement. Only a few weeks to go. We are very excited."

He couldn't let Luke read that. It would ruin everything.

John left his chair, as if he were about to join Luke at the window. Except, in doing so, he pretended to stagger, causing some beer in his glass to splash on the page.

"Luke! I'm sorry," he said. "Look what I've done."

"That's alright," Luke, said, looking back into the room. "It's only one entry. It's smudged a little."

"You won't be able to read it."

"Don't worry, John. Just one entry. It probably wasn't important. I'll get you another beer."

Sitting down in the chair, John sighed. That was all very well, he thought. But he would hardly be able to do the same to all the pages.

***

The closer Elliot came to the column of smoke, the louder the noise. He had never ever heard the like. A droning, whirring, humming sound, rhythmic, and tuneful one moment, long, and drawn out the next. It was certainly not a human voice, nor the sound of insects, or animals. The humming was too variable and intentional, possibly issuing from a type of pipe.

With the lowering sun casting deep shadows across his path, crouching low, Elliot edged his way through the tangle of scrub, getting as close as he dared, then stopping, peering stealthily through the undergrowth.

In a clearing, a little way ahead, moving about in the evening light, naked people were dancing, their brown bodies smeared with white clay, all of them, pulsating to the rhythm of the droning resonance. Anxious to know what the natives intended to do with George, Elliot crawled across the ground, until he was close enough to the clearing, and almost directly under the overhanging rock of the cliff face.

Back and forth, Elliot's eyes darted amongst the weaving, throbbing figures. In and out, through old men, with long white hair and beards, their black wrinkled skin, hanging limp from their once manly chests; past young women, large pendulous breasts, bouncing and swaying, to the beat of the music; old women, whose breasts lay flat and useless, their thin legs, barely able to carry them in the dance.

Then finally, to young men, lean and muscled, pulsing and glistening with sweat.

Each individual appeared in a trance, the white smoke from the fire drifting in a rhythmic miasma around them.

Tugging his eyes away from the spectacle, something high on the cliff drew Elliot's attention, and what he saw, filled him with foreboding.

Underneath the hanging rock, some seventy feet above the ground, protruded a ledge, on its brink, bound hand and foot, George and William Poney, two black fellers holding them on leashes of twine, tied around their necks.

Poney! What was Poney doing there? Elliot had no idea. Where had he come from?

Before seeing Mr Poney, Elliot had reckoned, that with luck, he would be able to rescue George. But now, with two men to set free, it would be doubly difficult.

But why are they up there?

"They look frightened. Of course they're frightened. Stupid!" Elliot cursed under his breath. "It's a sacrifice. They're going to push them over the edge."

The dancing and music was becoming faster, and increasingly frantic, Elliot aware it was leading up to something. He would need to be quick. But what could he do? How was he, just one whitefella, to fight the whole tribe?

Urgently, he looked around for inspiration.

Noticing charred wood, littering the ground, Elliot presumed there had been fire through the area quite recently. Then suddenly he had a brainwave.

"I'll become a Willy Willy," he said to himself.

Once, in the desert, George pointed out a spiralling wind, zigzagging here and there, catching up everything in its path, spinning leaves and branches high into the air. George told Elliot it was a ghost. What his people call a Willy Willy. A spirit living in the wind. A mischievous little devil his people dreaded.

With the throbbing music pounding the sullen air, Elliot quickly took off his clothes, folding them neatly, and then piling them together under a bush. Next, picking up the largest piece of charred wood he could find, he ran his hands over it, until they were black. Then smearing his face and body. Without a mirror, this was difficult. Nevertheless, by twisting and turning, he became confident he was completely covered, with not a patch of white skin remaining. His hair though! What could he do about his hair? It was fair, and assisted by the sun, almost bleached white.

From nowhere, another idea popped into his head, and grabbing his cabbage tree hat, he began poking blackened sticks into the weave, until the whole object changed shape, looking like the back of a porcupine. Donning the strange hat, Elliot knew he was ready, or as ready as he would ever be.

As the doleful sound of the pipe grew faster, the drums began beating, Elliot realising the time for action was drawing near. Therefore, taking a deep breath, he began to creep through the scrub, keeping close to the ground, until he was within a stone's throw of the fire, and the dancing, chanting figures.

How funny he must look, Elliot thought. Whatever would his parents say if they saw him?

Crouching low behind a bush, Elliot peered between the branches. He was near enough now to see through the smoke, and the source of the droning music. A native was sitting on the ground, his legs stretched in front of him, an enormous tube of wood in his mouth, into which he was blowing.

I'll aim for him, Elliot thought.

"Willy! Willy! Willy! Willy!" he shouted, rushing from his cover. "Willy! Willy! Willy! Willy!"

"Jinbra! Jinbra!" the man shrieked, jumping up in fright, the pipe falling from his lips.

Stopping and reeling around, seeing Elliot spinning in wild circles, the terrified dancers ran for cover, Elliot chasing them, whirling like a madman, and shouting at the top of his voice.

"Willy! Willy! Willy! Willy!"

Looking up at the ledge, Elliot saw the two blackfellas guarding George and Bill Poney, drop their leashes, and flee down the rock face. Consequently, still shouting his war cry, Elliot waited at the bottom, until they reached the ground, chasing them away to join the rest of the scurrying tribe.

"Willy! Willy! Willy! Willy!" Elliot yelled, continuing to spin like a top around the fire. "Willy! Willy! Willy! Willy!" until he was certain not a single person remained.

"Now you two!" he called. "Just stay still. I'll be up to untie you, as soon as I can."

"Herot!" George cried. "Herot! My friend. You save King George!"

"I don't believe it!" Poney said. "I would never have guessed you had it in you lad."

"Now steady on," Elliot said, scrambling over the rocks. "I'll have you free in a moment."

As he quickly untied them, he took time to survey the landscape below.

"I can't see them," he said. "Let's hope I've driven them off for good."

"Maraket scared of terrible black devil," George laughed. "They hide in holes."

"You're a brave lad." Poney said, rubbing his wrists. "And clever too. That get up even convinced me."

"George too." George said. "I scared. I want run. But legs and arms stuck."

"Come on," Elliot said. "We haven't got time to hang about. I reckon the Maraket will begin to return. When they see you've gone, they'll think twice."

Descending quickly to the ground, George began leading them back along the way they came.

All of a sudden Elliot stopped.

"Do you know," he said, laughing. "Here I am strolling along with you chaps, and I've completely forgotten, I've not a stitch on."

They doubled back to the place where he had hidden his clothes, and waited while he dressed.

Then, with the sun low in the sky, they headed south, George striding ahead, Elliot and Bill Poney following.

"What on earth are you doing here, Mr Poney?" Elliot asked.

"You may wonder, lad. I caught the blacks spearing the pigs, and chased them into the bush. It was then they grabbed me."

"How did they pick up George?"

"He says he saw the Maraket had me, and followed them to the cliff."

"That's why he disappeared," Elliot said. "Their scouts must have captured him."

"Yes. But if it hadn't been for you lad, George, and me would be mincemeat by now. You're a brave man."

"Maraket not finished," George, shouted from up ahead. "Herot see."

He was pointing back, in the direction they had come.

Turning around, Elliot and Poney saw an enormous pall of black smoke running the entire length of the escarpment. The Maraket had set the scrub alight, the fire bearing down on the three men, coming nearer by the minute.

Chapter Fifteen

While Luke and John waited patiently for their supper, James showed Cathy around the farm, leaving the hut he shared with Elliot until last.

"You and the boys can sleep here tonight," he said, putting her bags on the floor. "I don't know what Elliot's doing, or where he is. But I'll put a note on the door, so he doesn't come blundering in and disturb you."

"You're so kind, James," she said, laying Richard on the bed. "Say thank you to Mr Waldon, William."

The older boy mumbled a reply.

"These two will sleep like tops tonight," she said, wiping their dirty faces with her apron. "The day seems to have gone on forever."

"Tomorrow, we'll fix up the lean-to for you," said James, turning to leave.

"Where will you sleep?"

"In Mr Poney's hut. He's not around either."

"Which one's that?" she said, going to the open door.

James pointed across the yard.

"The one close to Mister Luke's."

"Well, if I get frightened, I'll know where to go won't I." she said, winking at him.

Not wishing Cathy to see him blushing, James hurried onto the veranda, and down into the yard.

"I think Mr Luke will want his supper soon," he called. "Can you bring me something later?"

"Of course, dear. Just let me get the boys settled."

James headed towards Poney's hut, the sun sinking fast, although failed to notice the ominous pall of smoke hanging in the air ahead of the escarpment. Once inside he made straight for the bed, and lay down. His leg ached after the long ride. He needed rest, and wishing he could remove the bandage, he kicked off his boots.

James woke with the odd sensation that someone was kissing him on the lips a feeling he had obviously almost forgotten, and opening his eyes, saw Cathy staring down at him, over her shoulder, the blood red sky beyond the open window.

"What are you doing?" he said, struggling to get up.

"Be quiet, James," she whispered, laying her hand on his chest. "You want this to happen. I know you do."

"What to happen?" James said, as she forced him back onto the bed.

"You know you want me."

"No! No I don't," James stammered.

"Yes you do. Of course you do. You have since you first laid eyes on me. All the way from Ten Mile Creek, you've wanted me. A girl gets to know the signs."

While he had been asleep, Cathy had lain down beside James, and currently was moving against him, like a writhing snake, encircling its prey.

"What about Mr Reddall? James stuttered. "He'll be wanting his supper."

"All done! While you've been asleep, I went to the house, and found a chicken hanging in the larder, and roasted it for him and Mr Baker. So we've all the time in the world."

Her hand moved over his chest, and inside his shirt.

"Oh! You've lovely muscles, James. And just the right amount of hair!"

"You're tickling," he giggled.

Her hand moved on down his stomach, through the trail of soft hair, until it reached his navel.

"My! Yours pokes up, doesn't it."

"Yes," James quivered. "My mother did it, when I was born. There was no one to help her."

"I bet she's a lovely woman," Catherine said, her hand travelling further, until it came to rest on the fall front of his breeches.

"She is!" James gasped.

"Oh! But here's something else poking up!"

James could bear it no longer, and taking hold of her, he quickly turned her on her back, ardently kissing her open mouth.

"Phew!" Cathy exhaled, finally freeing herself from his embrace "It's been a while."

"Quite a while," James said, hardly daring to admit to how long.

"Now let's just take our time," Cathy purred. "Nice and slow."

Sitting back on her haunches, her fingers moved to the buttons on her blouse, casually undoing them, one after the other.

Up until that moment, what Cathy was proposing to show James, had possessed his imagination since the day she rescued him on the road. Now, however, the objects that had previously been a figment in his mind, were about to become reality, causing James' excitement to attain even greater lengths. Gasping as her breasts fell free from the constriction of her tight blouse, he took each one in his outstretched hands, drawing them close to his face. So close, he could smell the scent of her, strong, pungent, and alluring.

"Just enjoy it," she said, as his lips closed around one generous nipple. "We've plenty of time."

While he satisfied himself, Cathy eagerly pulled his shirt over his head.

"My! You're a beautiful man," she said, running her hands over his chest and arms. "It's no good. I can't bear it. I've got to see more."

Pushing him back on the bed, with nimble fingers, she unbuttoned his breeches, pulling them down to his knees.

"Come on James!" she whispered. "Don't be shy. You know you want me to see it. I had a quick peek when Mr Pabst took off your breeches, while you were unconscious. I bet it looks different now!"

James laughed, and no longer embarrassed, knelt, and pulled down his long johns, lying back on the bed, giving Cathy ample opportunity to appreciate what he was really made of.

"I knew it!" she screamed, taking hold of him. "Something good and meaty for a girl to get her teeth into!"

Doing just that, James moaned, as her mouth began to feast on him, while allowing him a chance to return the favour. Then releasing him at last, Cathy turned to face him, and grabbing him in both hands, straddled his thighs, easing herself down.

"Oh! James," she gasped, leaning forward, her breasts, now resting on his shoulders. "Be gentle with me, that's all I ask."

From that moment, a world of wonder and joy opened up to James. Cathy was his angel, and he was in heaven at last.

***

"What's the hell's going on?" Poney shouted. "Who's this?"

James leapt from the bed, quickly pulling up his breeches, Cathy covering herself with the blanket.

"Mr Poney sir! I'm sorry we were just..."

"So I can see," Poney said, his eyes fixed on Cathy.

"This is Catherine Rhall, Mr Poney. Mr Luke has taken her on."

"Has he now."

"We arrived this afternoon. We wondered where everyone was."

"Well get dressed, both of you, and be quick about it. The Maraket are coming, and they're burning everything in their way."

It should have been pitch dark. But pulling on his shirt, James realised, that while he and Cathy were making love, the sky outside the window had transformed from the red of a glorious sunset, to a sky lit by a million fires. The wind had caught the flames from one man's torch, sending fire ricocheting from bush to bush, and tree-to-tree, until it was a barrage of fire, towering into the sky.

"I'll tell Mister Luke!" James shouted to Poney. "Cathy! You get the boys and take them to Mister Luke's house. They'll be safe there."

Running across the yard, he hurtled, headlong into Elliot and King George.

"James!" Elliot yelled. "The Maraket are coming."

"I know. We're getting everyone into Mister Luke's house.

John Baker had woken minutes earlier, the smell of smoke dragging him out of a deep sleep. He quickly woke Luke, and by the time James arrived at the hut, John and Luke were on the veranda, staring at the sky.

"How close it is, Luke?" John asked.

"About a mile. And it won't take long to reach us, with the wind as it is."

"What can we do, Mister Luke?" asked James. "It'll burn the farm down. What about the livestock?"

"Get the horses into the stable. And make sure the pigs are locked in the stys. If they get a whiff of fire, they'll be off into the bush."

"We might be lucky, John," Luke said, as James hurried away. "There aren't too many trees on the place, and the yard's pretty free of debris. The fire could go around us."

"But in this wind, there'll be a lot of burning leaves flying about," said John.

"I know. We'll need to douse the roofs with water."

At that moment, Cathy, the boys, Poney, Elliot and George, ran out of the darkness, and on to the veranda, the towering cliff of flames behind them, advancing every second.

"Come on!" Luke shouted. "We've no time to lose. Let's get a chain happening."

Leaving the boys in the comparative safety of the house, everyone ran to the sheds and outhouses, and after collecting every type of container, soon a relay of people spanned the riverbank to the yard. Effective or not, they desperately poured water over the roofs, since, if the buildings did eventually burn, at least they could say they tried to save them.

Elliot and King George passed bucket after bucket between them.

"Where do you think the Maraket are George?" asked Elliot, nervously. "Will they attack when the fire gets here?"

"No Herot," answered George. "George know what Billy Maraket do. He wait. Sun just near. Then he fight. Bad witch people gone then."

"Does he know we tricked him?"

"When he no see me, and Poney man, he know."

Elliot felt his stomach lurch. Billy would be angry, he thought. Extremely angry.

"Do you think he knows it was me who tricked him?"

George shrugged.

As soon as one hut was doused with enough water, they moved to the next. However, convinced he must tell Luke what George had just told him, Elliot broke from the team, running to John and Luke at the head of the line.

"Thanks, Elliot," Luke said. "At least it gives us time to prepare. Let's deal with the fire first. Then we'll decide what to do next.

Watching the flames approach, Luke and John began to see the smouldering debris they feared, as leaves and twigs flew through the air, dropping to the ground around them. But as Luke predicted, the land was clear, rendering the incendiaries harmless, although it failed to stop everyone running and stamping them out.

Near enough to see the flames, licking across the ground, Luke saw eerie figures, flitting here and there. In and out of the light. One moment in smoke, the next in fire. Close by, Elliot also saw the figures.

"Get George please, Elliot," Luke called. "I'd like to speak with him."

In the blink of an eye, George was beside Luke.

"George," he said. "We've not met. I'm Mr Reddall, the boss."

"Yes Boss," George said. "Herot say. George many pleased see you."

"Elliot tells me you saved his life. I'd like to thank you."

George smiled, nodding his head.

"These Maraket people," Luke continued. "You think they'll attack at dawn."

George smiled, Luke suddenly understanding the reason Elliot found the blackfella appealing. Since he was handsome in his own way, his large brown eyes, full of compassion, showing wisdom that, up until then, Luke only ever remembered seeing in his childhood friend, the famous native scout, Bungaree.

"Yes Boss," said George. "Maraket scared of dark. When fire out, Maraket sleep."

"But fire not out. Fire keep on."

"Fire go out."

George grinned, and pointed to the sky, tapping his nose with his finger.

"Ah!" Luke said.

"George good nose,"

"What's he talking about, sir?" Elliot interrupted.

"He says it's going to rain," Luke said. "He can smell it."

"How can he smell it through all this smoke?"

"Well he says he can. He says he's got a good nose."

A short while later, as if to order, the heavens opened, large drops of rain falling, splashing into the dust of the yard. A smell of water on hot ashes saturated the air, the sky, a moment earlier appearing full of a million fireflies, now dark as pitch, the tower of fire just a glimmer on the ground.

Standing on the veranda of the hut, Cathy and James gazed into the darkness.

"It's a miracle," she said, putting her arm through his. "But I was praying like mad."

"Although, you'll need to pray some more," James said. "Because, somewhere out there, the Maraket are waiting."

Later that night, before anyone thought of sleeping, Luke gathered Cathy and the men in the parlour, to plan what would happen in the morning.

"How many firearms do we have, Bill?"

"You've two old muskets sir. But I wouldn't trust them. You've a fowling gun, and I've my pistol."

Luke turned to Elliot.

"What about you. Do you have a firearm?"

"Father gave me a pair of percussion pocket pistols, before I left England. But I've never opened the case."

"Well you're going to. How about you, James?"

"I've a fowler, and my old flintlock. Except, it takes a devil of a time to load."

"I fired one of the muskets at Nemmit, when he had his eyes on Martha, and it seemed to work then. As for the other, I've no idea. But we're going to have to use both, otherwise, they'll not be enough guns between us. James! You show Cathy and George how to handle a gun. How are we for shot, Bill?"

"Fine. There's plenty to go around."

Sitting on the arm of the chair, Luke looked at everyone keenly.

"We'll need to surprise them before they get the chance to rush us. Isn't that right George?"

"Yes Boss," answered George, clearly eager to be considered important in Luke's plan. "Maraket good warriors. Proud. Brave. Strong. When sun just show, they run with spears. They think they surprise us."

"Then we'll make sure we're ready. We'd better get some rest. We'll need to be awake before sun up."

Long before the Kookaburra on the fence, or the old cockerel in the yard, had a chance to wake them, everyone was up, and making preparation. Since there were seven of them, Cathy and the men were able to spread themselves around the farm, with every shed and hut covered. Each person carried a firearm of sorts, James giving Cathy and George quick instructions on loading and cocking a gun, and squeezing the trigger.

Luke's orders were to wait in position, until they heard him whistle, then count to ten, and open fire. In this way, Luke hoped the first rally of shots would sound like an explosion, and frighten away the Maraket.

He and John Baker, positioned themselves at the open windows of the house, each with an old musket, Luke determining that, rather than risk injury to the others, he and John alone would fire them.

Standing in the window, staring into the gloom, Luke tried to remember if he had ever heard both guns fire when he was a child.

He certainly recalled his father displaying them on the study wall at Glen Alpine, his father explaining that they were over two hundred years old, and fired during the civil war.

In the darkness, he and John primed the guns with gunpowder, wadding and ball, ramming it home with the ramrods. Then, all they could do was wait and see what would happen, when they finally pulled the triggers.

From their various positions, each person watched the eastern sky for a glimmer of light, Cathy and James huddling in the doorway of his hut, the boys sound asleep, oblivious to what was about to happen.

Although James had an arm around Cathy's waist, he could feel her trembling.

"It's getting light," he whispered. "We've to listen for Mister Luke's whistle. That's the sign to cock the gun."

From their places at the window, John and Luke stared into the dimness of the dawn.

"You're younger than I," John said. "Can you see anything?"

"I'm not sure," answered Luke. "Sometimes I think I see something move. But then it might be my imagination. We need to be sure, before we begin firing."

They were silent, listening to the birds calling in the darkness.

Unlike the dawn chorus John Baker was accustomed to hear in his homeland, where the sun rose to the twittering refrain of sparrows, and the melodious, yet repetitious song of the blackbird, from out of the gloom, a raucous, cackling laugh, echoed through the gum trees beside the river. Three Kookaburras were chattering noisily, preparing for a day of hunting lizards and snakes. Then, from the tops of the red gums, a tuneful carolling began.

"That's nice," John whispered. "What are they?"

"Currawongs. A type of crow. But with white markings. Kookaburras and Currawongs tell us more rain's on the way."

"That's handy."

"Wait!" Luke whispered. "Did you see that? Across the yard!"

Barely able to make him out, John saw the shape of a naked figure, crouching behind the fence, the stripes smeared on his body, confusing with the white palings.

"It's difficult to see," he whispered. "But it looks like a man."

With the light rapidly increasing, Luke's attention was drawn to the gate, where a group of warriors was creeping stealthily into the yard; their bodies bent double, white markings on their shields and skin clearly visible.

"John! Get ready," he whispered. "As soon as I see more I'll give the whistle."

Distracted suddenly by a footfall on the veranda, John and Luke watched a shadowy figure creep past the windows, and up to the door.

"Boss!" a voice whispered.

"George!" hissed Luke. "What's wrong?"

"Boss. Maraket come river. Many many Maraket."

"The clever buggers!" exclaimed Luke. "They're surrounding us,"

"They in canoe," George said. "Herot say, what we do?"

With all of his positions facing east, west and north, it had never occurred to Luke the Maraket would attack from the rear, and from the river. He cursed himself. Why hadn't he considered it? Perhaps he had underestimated them. Why shouldn't they think strategically? They were clever people, accustomed to the art of war.

"George," he said. "You cover the back window of the stable. And tell Elliot to stay in his position."

"Yes Boss."

"Thanks, George. Be careful."

Luke and John watched the black fellow tiptoe back into the shadows.

"John. Stay here and cover the yard," Luke said. "I'll take the kitchen window."

"Are you sure you'll be alright back there on your own?" asked John. "If it's true what George says, then they'll be more of them that side, than this."

Although, even as he spoke, John saw an additional group of warriors, sneaking into the yard, all of them striped in white mud, holding spears and shields.

Luke saw them too.

"You look out for yourself," he said. "If I need you, I'll shout. And you do the same for me."

There was very little time. The Maraket were massing their forces, quickly surrounding the farm, Luke realising he needed to do something immediately, or else they would be overwhelmed. So going to the kitchen window, Luke blew a long low whistle, sounding more like the call of a solitary owl than a rally to arms. Nevertheless, everyone heard it, and prepared for battle.

Raising the ancient musket, resting it on the window ledge, Luke began to count.

One. Two.

He watched the silent canoes, pull up to the riverbank, the setting moon reflecting in the water, sending a sparkle of silver spangles through the gums. Each boat contained three or four occupants, Luke watching them jump into the shallows, when they reached the bank.

Three. Four. Five.

Feeling his finger on the trigger, his thoughts went to the others. They were doing the same. Would his plan work? He could feel his heart beating in time to the numbers sounding in his head.

Six. Seven. Eight.

Luke squeezed the trigger.

Nine. Ten.

The explosion sent him reeling across the kitchen, slamming him into the side of the table, and onto the floor.

"Jesus!" he shouted, staggering to his feet. "What was that?"

Running back to the window, pouring gunpowder into the muzzle, he dropped in the ball, pushing in the ramrod. Then putting more powder into the pan, he pulled back the hammer, and checking the frizzen was closed, Luke was ready, and this time he would aim.

Pointing the gun out of the window, seeing eerie apparitions darting and leaping, Luke heard shots coming from the stable, two ghostly figures, falling to the ground.

This time, braced against the window frame, Luke aimed the gun at a group of running, crouching natives, squeezing the trigger once again. The explosion was deafening. Except, beneath the window, a body lay on the ground, other warriors scattering into the trees.

At the front of the house, John was also discovering the power of his weapon, the butt thundering into his shoulder, sending a spasm of pain into his arm. However, this failed to alter his resolve, as he fired round after round.

These blackfellas are brave, he decided, aiming the barrel at them. With only hatchets, spears and shields, with which to fight, they were attacking fiercely, unafraid of the searing shot that could rip through their naked flesh. Repeatedly, they regrouped behind the fence. Then charged across the yard, only to be cut down by a hail of shot from Poney, Elliot, Cathy, James, and himself. Would they realise, John thought, reloading, with such odds, the chance of taking the farm were slim.

In the meantime, at the back of the house, Luke and George were holding fast, keeping their attackers busy, by picking shots at them, as they broke from behind the trees.

With light increasing, the attacks from the riverbank were diminishing, Luke seeing the warriors running to the bank, and back into their canoes. Then, paddling into the main current, it swiftly carried them away, and out of sight. As a result, eventually, not a soul could be seen among the trees. Therefore, with no forays to repel, Luke joined John at the front of the house, where the battle still raged.

From the hut window, James and Cathy had a clear view across the stockyards to the gates of the farm, and down to the river, where, amongst the river gums, James caught sight of stealthy figures, dragging canoes out of the water onto the bank. Unaware of what Luke had seen, on the far side the house, James took this to mean there was about to be another invasion.

"I don't think Mister Luke can see them, Cathy," he shouted over the noise of gunfire. "They'll be along the front of the stables, and onto his veranda before he knows it. I must warn him."

"Don't go!" pleaded Cathy. "They'll kill you, for sure. And what about me, and the boys?"

"Just keep firing. You'll be fine as long as you've the gun and plenty of shot. I have to go. We're closest to the house."

He kissed her, and then grabbed his gun and a hand full of shot, lurching through the door, dodging a rain of white spears rattling, inoffensively, against the bark walls of the hut.

Escaping the hatchets and spears falling around him, at last James was in sight of the house, and able to see John and Luke at the windows. When they saw him, they ceased firing, Luke at the door, letting him inside.

"You can't see from here," James panted, "but the Maraket have landed near the gates. They came from the river. They're already in the chicken yard. They'll attack the house next."

"The sneaky bastards!" Luke laughed. "And I thought they were running away. I'll get into the lean-to doorway," he said, grabbing more shot. "I'll be able to see the front of the dairy, and stable from there. If any try coming up here, I'll pop them off easily."

Elliot, from his place at the dairy window, and George at the stable door, both had seen the natives, firing at them freely, attempting to force them back.

Therefore, with the farm buildings currently heavily defended, Bill Poney and Cathy were quickly becoming disadvantaged, and unaware a force of warriors, led by King Billy Maraket, were moving across the far paddocks, making straight for the huts.

As the boys huddled against the doorframe, Cathy had never seen them so frightened, clinging to her dress, screaming each time she lifted the gun to shoot.

"Get under the blankets, William!" she ordered sharply to her eldest. "And take Richard with you. Mother has to fire the nasty gun, otherwise the blackfellas will surly kill and eat us."

Her words sent them scurrying to the bed, and under the covers, where they cowered, not daring to move for fear their mother's words might come true.

Cathy loaded the gun.

"Now boys, get ready. Cover your ears."

Raising the muzzle to the open doorway, she was about to pull the trigger, when, without warning, the room suddenly filled with sweating, naked men, wearing nothing but white mud, and bones through their noses.

Cathy screamed.

"Don't move boys! They won't find you if you stay still."

Fortunately, Billy Maraket's command of the English language was not good, failing to interpret her words.

"Don't come near me!" shouted Cathy, backing towards the doorway. "I'll blow your brains out, I will!"

Running out the door, Cathy's exit was barred by further warriors, one of them grabbing the gun.

"Don't touch me!"

Billy paid no attention nonetheless, advancing on her, his golden eyes shining in the glare of the rising sun.

John, Luke, and James failed to see the men take the hut, their attention turned on the Maraket storming the house, and out buildings. All of a sudden, however, the warriors drew back, and ceased shrieking their war cries.

"What's happening, John?" Luke shouted. "Can you see?"

"They've got Cathy," he yelled, seeing the Maraket warriors manhandling her into the yard. "They've dragged her from the hut. It looks like the chief's with her. Is it the chief, James?"

There was no reply.

Standing naked in the centre of the yard, the sun casting their long shadows on the ground, King Billy, and his warriors waited, one man's arm firmly around Cathy's waist.

"Maraket got white lady," he shouted. "King Billy jiggy-jig white lady. White Boss give King George. White Boss take white lady."

"Well that seems quite clear," said Luke, standing in the doorway. "He's holding Cathy to ransom. He'll have his way with her, if we don't give him what he wants."

"And that's King George," John replied. "How will King George feel about that?"

"Or Elliot, for that matter. They're pretty friendly."

In the direction of the dairy, Luke could see Elliot peering from the open window. Then, turning his attention back to the yard, Luke caught King Billy take hold of Cathy, and try to kiss her. She screamed. Looking back at the window, Luke saw Elliot had gone.

In the meantime, James, having crept out of the back door, and around the side of the house, was waiting in the shadows. Aware of the design of the farm, he knew that, by crossing the yard, passing behind Poney's hut, it was possible to get to the rear of his and Elliot's hut, without being seen.

Therefore, moving stealthily out of the shade, and running noiselessly, James darted behind Bill Poney's shack, until he was in the protection of the back wall. Then, edging his way along it, listened to King Billy's words.

"King Billy jiggy-jig white lady."

"No bloody black bugger's going to jiggy-jig my Cathy," he said, under his breath. "And he's not having George either."

With the same idea, Elliot was hiding behind the wall of the dairy. He knew George was listening in the stable across the yard. Would he be silly, and give himself up to the Maraket? Elliot knew he must stop George at all costs.

The stable was in clear view of King Billy and the warriors, so Elliot would need to be swift running to it without being seen. He was about to launch himself into the open, when Luke began to speak.

"Billy!" he shouted. "Why you no leave white lady. She scared of King Billy. King Billy no big man. Frighten lady. White Boss thought King Billy brave man, not coward."

Luke's words caused consternation amongst the Maraket, and enough of a distraction to allow Elliot to scamper across the open space, and into the stable.

"George!" he called in the darkness. "George! Are you there?" But there was no reply.

The gunfire had upset the horses, and as Elliot moved along the stalls, they became agitated. But reaching the open window, his stomach churned at what he saw in the yard. As there, shambling towards King Billy, his black trouser cuffs dragging in the dirt, was George. Elliot was too late.

King Billy watched George shuffling toward him, the sight causing him sorrow.

This is what the white men are doing to his people, he thought. The lumbering creature, dragging his feet in the dust, was the man with whom Billy had fought many battles. Conflicts for land. Wars for possession of the talking place. Disagreements over burial grounds. King George had always been there, leading the imperious Wiradjuri people.

George was once a proud warrior. But look at the great man now, dressed in white man's clobber. How ridiculous he appears.

The men behind Billy began to laugh, and point. But King Billy held up his hand, warning them to stop, not wanting to see the great man degraded more than he was degrading himself.

He could kill him now, Billy thought. Throw his hatchet at his head, and send him straight to the spirit place. It would be a release for the fool, and far better to be dead, than be this walking spectacle.

"King Billy let white mistress go," said George, when he was close enough to be heard. "She tumbledown fearful."

"George come along Maraket." King Billy growled.

"Only after white mistress in boss house."

Billy made a sign to the warrior to let Cathy go.

"You go boss house," he said to her, and grabbing her skirt, Cathy fled across the yard, on to the veranda, and in at the door, slamming it shut.

"You come Maraket," Billy commanded.

George shook his head.

"Billy fool," he said laughing. "Billy remember. No trust word of Wiradjuri people. They good gammon."

Still laughing, George turned his back on the chief, and shuffled towards the stable.

From his position behind the pig sheds, Elliot was able to see everything, looking on as George turned, and walked in his direction. He was certainly a brave man, Elliot thought. Courageous to deny King Billy his triumph for a second time. Heroic. But stupid to put his life at risk. Transfixed, watching his friend, Elliot hardly noticed the thin white spear enter George's back.

Who threw it? Elliot noticing Billy was the only man without a spear. Then, looking back at George, he saw him fall forward into the dust.

"You've killed him you bastard!" Elliot screamed.

There was the sound of a shot, and King Billy dropped to the ground like a stone.

"Who fired?" Luke yelled. "Did you see John?"

"No! I don't know."

"Start firing," Luke shouted. "Or else they'll be on us."

Once more, the thunder of musket fire filled the yard. But this time, it was too much for the natives. With their chief lying dead, they lost all stomach for the fight, and fled like frightened children across the paddocks, into their canoes, and away down the river.

Elliot ran across the yard, knowing what he would find.

James and Bill Poney appeared from behind the hut. And at the house, John, Luke, and Cathy came out onto the veranda, everyone watching, as Elliot reached George's body.

"Should we go to him, John?" Luke said.

"No. I think it's best he's alone."

"You fool," whispered Elliot, staring at the spear in George's back. "Always so fearless. You should have known not to turn your back on him. If only I'd got to you first."

Elliot's eyes filled with tears.

"What am I going to do without you, George?" he sobbed. "You were my mate. I never had a friend like you before."

Elliot wanted to turn George over. But it was impossible, unless he pulled the spear from his back. And how could he do that, he asked himself? Weeping quietly, Elliot knelt beside the body, and putting his hand on George's head, his fingers touching the man's shining black hair, he bent forward and kissed his cheek. It was still warm.

"I think we'd better get over there, John," Luke said, after a while. "The day's warming up, and we should bury the bodies."

"Who shot King Billy?" John asked.

"I've no idea. It wasn't any of us in the house."

"That means it could have been James, Poney, or Elliot."

"That's right. Each had a clear view of James' hut, where Billy was standing."

James was the first to be at Elliot's side.

"I'm sorry, mate," he said. "He was a great man, and very brave."

"There was none better," Elliot said, wiping his eyes. "I'm going to miss him."

James found it hard to say more. Knowing how it is to lose someone you love, sometimes words are meaningless. Therefore, standing together in silence, as the others joined them, after a period of respect and reverence, Bill Poney removed the spear from George's back, then he and James carried George's body out of the sun, and into the stable, laying him in an empty stall.

"Good shooting, Jim," Poney said, as he and James carried King Billy Market into a vacant pig shed. "You got him right between the eyes."

"I didn't kill him," said James. "I thought you did."

"Not me. Well who did?"

"I don't know. It all happened so quickly."

Poney frowned.

"Elliot could have. He was in the stables, and had a clear view."

"Well," James said. "The person who did, knows who they are, and they've avenged George's death. Billy was looking for trouble by attacking the farm. I certainly feel no remorse for him."

Leaving the body, James and Poney crossed the yard to the house, finding Luke and John in the parlour.

"Where would you like us to bury them, Mister Luke?" Poney asked.

"In George's case, I think Elliot might be the person to ask. Although Billy should be with his people. John and I have decided to ride to the talking place, and speak with the elders."

"Are you sure that's wise, sir?

"There'll be no more trouble Poney. I promise you."

"But we've killed their King."

"Yes. But now they know how strong we are. They won't cause problems anymore."

"Not until the new King starts something."

"We'll have to wait and see. I want to do this properly. Billy should be honoured by his tribe. It's the least we can do, to let them have his body."

As it happened, it proved unnecessary for Luke and John to ride to the talking place, as later that day, a party of Maraket appeared on the riverbank, making it clear to Luke that they wanted the body of their chief. Therefore, after asking James and Poney to lay Billy's corpse in the cart, Luke escorted King Billy from the pig shed, and down to the river. When they saw their chief, the men, and women began wailing, a sorrowful, pitiful sound, like the whimpering of wounded animals.

Coming forward, taking the body from the cart, they carried it to a waiting canoe, laying Billy inside. And to a man, the Maraket disappeared beyond the bend in the river.

Luke opened the stable door, knowing he would find Elliot inside.

"Are you alright?" he said, his eyes searching the shadows, discovering Elliot leaning over a stall. "Can we talk?"

Bill Poney and James had put George in a manger, half submerging him in straw. Luke thought he appeared peaceful, as if asleep, with even the hint of a smile on his face. Though, Luke knew this to be misleading, as rigor mortis had surely set in, the muscles of George's face tightening.

"I can't leave him, Mr Reddall," Elliot whispered. "I go to the door, but when I look back he seems so alone. You don't mind me being here do you? He would want me to be with him. I know he would."

"Of course I don't mind," said Luke. "You and he were best friends. I completely understand. But have you thought where you would like to bury him?"

"Do they bury their dead? I thought they'd burn them."

"No. They dig a shallow hole, and cover the body with earth. Haven't you ever seen a native burial ground? Mounds of red earth, painted yellow and white. It's symbolic."

Luke stood beside Elliot, putting a comforting arm over his shoulder.

"You've heard me speak of Reverend Cartwright," he continued. "When he was chaplain at Collector, he'd visit Mutt Mutt Billy, to read a service, and stay for dinner. He was a great friend of my father. In fact, they came from the same town in England. Cartwright told him a good deal about the natives. He studied them, writing a paper, which he sent to the Royal Society in England."

Although he was listening, Elliot's eyes never left George's face for a moment.

"What was the paper about?" he asked.

"It described the religious rites and ceremonies of the aborigines, and did a lot to help people begin to understand them."

"But we can't just throw dirt over George. The Dingoes will dig him up and eat him."

"I'm sure that happens. But the natives believe, whatever happens to them after they die, their spirits become part of what Cartwright said was a dreamtime."

"Like heaven, you mean?"

"I suppose so. Cartwright said the aborigines believe they become part of everything they see around them. The rocks. The trees. Some going into the sky. Others to the earth."

Luke's words were having an effect on Elliot, because he was openly crying.

"Can I bury George wherever I like?" he said, his eyes brimming with tears.

"Of course."

"In the garden behind mine and James' hut? Mother's sent me some seeds. I think they're poppies. I could grow them on his grave."

"I'll ask Bill and James to begin digging."

Luke was about to leave, but hesitated, suddenly feeling concern for the young man.

"Are you alright in here, all alone?"

"I'm not alone, Mr Reddall, my friend George is here."

While they dug the grave, Elliot tidied his friend, in order he might be presentable for the afterlife, buttoning his jacket and breeches, and brushing his hair. Then the men carried George across the yard, into the garden, and laid him in the grave. Luke wondered what appropriate words to say over a native chief, finally resorting to those he heard his father say countless times. With the simple service over, James and Bill shovelled earth over George's body, filling the grave to the top, Elliot sprinkling the freshly turned earth, with poppy seeds.

"Whenever I look out of the window, I'll see them," Elliot said, as he and James walked back to the hut. "Then I'll always remember him, won't I?"

"Yes Elliot," James said. "Always. You see; people we truly love never die. They live with us in our hearts, right up to the day we join them in heaven."

"Thank you, James," Elliot said, comforted at last. "I'm going to look forward to that day."

Chapter Sixteen

Later that afternoon, James crossed the yard, heading for the river, since it was usual for him to enjoy a swim in the afternoon. But smoke coming from the chimney of the smithy, drew his attention, and going inside, found his uncle busy shoeing Luke's horse.

"I've got to say it, John!" James yelled, while sparks flew, the ringing of the hammer stinging his ears. "No one shoes a horse like you. You're the fastest blacksmith I've ever known."

John was rasping and clipping overgrown hoof off the horse's hooves.

"Years of practice, James. That's what it is. I've never done anything else in my life. So I should be good at it."

"You need the strength though!" James shouted. "And that's where you beat other men hands down."

"There you are, lad!" he exclaimed, wiping a broad arm across his forehead. "That's the last one. Do you still swim?"

"I do uncle. In fact I'm heading to the river right now."

"Then let's go! I need a dip. I'm hotter than hell."

Beneath the deep shade of the towering river gums, their trunks shining red in the hot sun, the men threw off their clothes; wading into the water, until it was up to their waists.

"Hey Jim! It's cold," gasped John. "I wouldn't have expected it."

"I know. Bracing though. It's always like this at the end of winter. Mister Luke says the river rises in the high country, where it snows."

John shivered.

"I believe it. I can't remember The Stour being this cold."

"It's because the sun's so hot."

James laughed, happy to be in his uncle's company.

"You like it here, don't you lad," John said, seeing James so cheerful.

"I do uncle. I've practically forgotten about my other life; it seems so long ago. Here I feel free, though I know I'm not. Well won't be for a while yet. I've been lucky to have a boss like Mister Luke. Some poor beggars have a terrible time. Of course, I miss father, mother, John James, and the girls. But I knew when I arrived, there was little point yearning for things I'd lost. It would have driven me crazy. I had to get on, and make a new life."

John smiled.

"There are lots of things we need to talk about lad," he said. "Come on! Let's swim."

The further into the river they waded, the stronger the current.

"This is dangerous!" John shouted. "It's towing me away."

"Enjoy it uncle!" James yelled, his head just above the water. "Let it carry you along. It'll drop us on that sandbar over there."

John looked to where his godson was pointing, seeing a thin stretch of golden sand, just out of the water, resting on it a flock of white egrets, preening in the sun.

"Alright!" he cried. "Here I go."

Lifting his feet off the bottom, feeling the current pick him up, and carry him out into the main stream, suddenly John felt a wave of panic, since the water was deep and he was out of control, a sensation he rarely experienced.

"Don't fight it, uncle!" shouted James. "Lay back and enjoy it."

Doing as James said, John let the current tow him along, feeling the power of tons of water around him.

"It's all very well you saying that, lad," he spluttered. "I can see you've done this before."

"You'll be alright," James, laughed. "Trust me. We'll be on the sand bank, before you know it."

As good as his word, the swell bore James and John across the river, dropping them on the edge of the sand spit, the water shallow enough to wade out, sending the sparkling egrets soaring into the sky.

"Wow!" John cried, flopping onto the sand. "That was something! I've never done anything like that before."

James shook the water from his ears.

"Good isn't it. Beats the Stour eh?"

"Oh no lad," John said, lying back. "Nothing beats The Stour. My old river's the best in the world. This is beautiful. But how could you ever forget the pastures, the cattle, and the willows. What could beat that?"

James lay down beside him.

"I remember you teaching me to swim," he said, allowing the hot sand to warm his back. "You were a good teacher."

"Everyone should swim lad. You never know when you might need it."

"Sometimes," added James, "when we're washing sheep, Bill Poney panics. He can't swim. And Luke's not much good either."

John chuckled.

"I know. He and I swam at Mutt Mutt Billy. Although, he never did more than splash about."

They lay silent for a moment, catching their breath, while their cold bodies grew accustomed to the hot sun.

Rolling onto his stomach, James was the first to speak.

"Okay uncle," he said. "What is it we need to talk about?"

Refraining from answering immediately, John turned over, resting his head on his arms.

"Something's about to happen Jim," he said, all of a sudden staring at his godson intently. "Something important. I can't put it off any longer."

James frowned.

"What do you mean?"

"Jim. The story I'm about to tell is going to shock you. But I don't want you to feel malice towards the person it concerns."

"What do you mean John?" James said, frowning, John seeing the rushing river reflected in his godson's blue eyes. "What's the mystery?"

John paused for breath. It was now or never. The lad had to know.

"Do you remember when Her Ladyship went to Bath?"

"You mean, when she closed the house, and took us all with her?"

"No. The time before. When His Lordship was ill."

"Hardly uncle. I was just a baby. Mother told me about it though. That's when father began working as a footman."

"That's right. Her Ladyship took His Lordship to Bath, for his bad health, taking with her William and Douglas, the footmen, Mr Ives, and my sister, Emma. They stayed for over a year. But His Lordship became worse, and then finally died, so Lady Soame returned to Thurlow."

Allowing the sand to cool his cheek, James listened, fascinated to hear a story from a time before he was old enough to understand.

"I remember how pleased we Bakers were to see our darling Emma, after such a long time. We thought that was the end of the story until, within a few weeks, Emma told us she was leaving Thurlow, to live in Cambridge. She said Her Ladyship was giving her to a friend. This friend had no ladies maid, so she was going to have our Emma. Obviously, we Bakers were stunned and annoyed, but powerless to say anything, for fear of causing Her Ladyship's displeasure."

Relieved to be speaking the words that had been on his mind for months, the story tumbled out of John's mouth, causing James' eyes to grow wider at each fresh revelation.

"After about six months," John continued, "suddenly Emma returned. The only explanation for her unexpected homecoming being that the family in Cambridge sent her back, taking pity on her, because she was so unhappy and home sick."

John stopped to draw breath.

"You see James," he continued, "this wasn't entirely true. During the time Emma was away, she had a child."

James gasped.

"But your sister was always so sensible."

"Obviously not as sensible as everyone thought."

James leaned on his elbows, by now engrossed in the story.

"How did you find out?"

"Two days before Lady Soame died; your father gave young George Jesshope a message. He rode like hell from Bath to Thurlow, to give it to me. It said Her Ladyship wished to see me immediately. George and I then rode, non-stop, back to Bath, arriving just in time."

"What did she want with you?"

"Lady Soame had a secret James. Something she'd never revealed to a soul. Emma told her she was going to have a baby, so Her Ladyship arranged for her friends to let Emma into their home, where she would have the child. Then they would take it as soon as it was born, to raise as their own."

"So that's what happened," James said.

"Yes. Emma still has no idea whether the child was a boy or a girl."

"Did Her Ladyship tell you what it was?"

"Yes. A boy."

"I'm sorry John. This might sound hard, but why should Her Ladyship care about your sister having a baby?"

"Because, that's the kind of person she was. Always thinking of others, never herself. Obviously she didn't want to see her maid in distress, or the Baker family disgraced."

John paused, gathering his thoughts.

"When I asked you not to feel malice toward the person in the story…"

"No John," James interrupted. "It wasn't Emma's fault. The father's to blame. Anyway, what became of him? I hope he was taken to task, and made to marry her."

"No James. It's not my sister who I'm asking you to forgive."

"It's the father!" James blurted out. "Who was the laggard?"

James stopped suddenly, his mind doing cartwheels.

"I know who it is! It's George! He always had an eye for Emma."

"Hardly Jim," John said, laughing. "Emma conceived the baby in Bath. George was a schoolboy then."

"Of course," James said, sounding disappointed. "It's so confusing! It's making my head spin. Then who do I have to forgive, and for what?"

"It might help if you know the baby's name," John said. "The friends called him Luke."

"Luke? What a coincidence. Luke!"

James sat up on his haunches.

"Hey! Hang on a minute. This is very strange."

Silently, John watched as the information sunk into James' mind.

"John. Do you know the name of Her Ladyship's friends? The people she went to live with?"

John nodded.

"What was it?"

"Reddall," John answered, not daring to look at his godson.

James stared at John in disbelief.

"Then Luke's your nephew," he said at last, staring into John's eyes. "Your real nephew. So he and I are sort of cousins."

James stopped, another idea emerging in his mind.

"You didn't really come here to look for me did you? You came to find him."

"That's true," John confessed, sighing. "I have to admit. Her Ladyship told me the secret she held all those years, and said she felt guilty that Luke didn't know his real mother. She wanted to put things right before she died, bequeathing money to me, so I could come here to find him. When I told your father I was going to Australia, I couldn't tell him the real reason, for Emma's sake, so I said Her Ladyship wanted me to look for you."

Flopping back onto the sand, James stared once more into John's eyes.

"But that explains a lot. Years ago, when I first arrived, Mister Luke came to the ship, taking off George Parry and me. That's how it worked in those days. He was looking for a blacksmith, and a ploughman for his farm. I remember we stopped at his mother and father's house, on our way to Mutt Mutt Billy. On the morning we were about to leave, Mrs Reddall began to talk to me. I was shocked. Why should such a grand lady want to talk to the likes of me? Anyway, she asked me questions about where I came from in England. When I told her I was from Thurlow, she seemed to come over queer, as if she were going to faint. No wonder. She must have been very worried to discover I was born in the same place, her adopted son's mother came from, and I was to be his servant. Nevertheless, I'm still none the wiser uncle. Who am I to forgive?"

John smiled.

"You like Luke, don't you Jim."

"Yes. And knowing what you've told me won't affect that. He's the kindest person I've ever met, or ever will. Does he know about this?"

John shook his head,

"If I told you something unfavourable about him, would it alter your opinion?"

"What could you tell me uncle?" James asked, looking puzzled. "He's a good man. What could he have done that's unfavourable?"

"Luke's done nothing. You were right Jim, when you said Luke's father's to blame, and God willing, he's taking his punishment as we speak."

"Is he in prison?"

"No. He's dead. And I hope he's in hell. However he's left a little piece of himself behind in this world."

James looked bewildered.

"For God's sake, uncle," he shouted angrily. "Out with it!"

John paused for breath.

"Luke's father is Humphrey Soame."

James was suddenly dumbfounded, the sound of the rushing river water, fading as memories and feelings he had endured for years, flooded into his mind. How confused he had been each time he looked at Luke. He had thought himself crazy, thinking he found a semblance to Soame in Luke's face, and in the colour of his eyes. Now, here it was, suddenly true.

Every peculiar emotion was genuine. Luke Reddall, the man James held in such high esteem since the moment they met, was the son of his archenemy, the devil James planned to murder; and whose villainy had sent him to a fate worse than hell itself.

His uncle had asked him to feel no malice toward Luke, and strangely, looking deep into his heart, James found none.

"And Luke doesn't know?" James said, breaking the silence.

"No," answered John. "And I can't summon the courage to tell him. You see, I'm worried he'll be distressed. I know he'll be terribly shocked to learn that he's adopted, the parents he still adores, having failed to tell him the truth about his beginnings."

"But he has to know."

"I know. Although, Luke must never know the kind of man his father was. It could destroy him, and even send him over the edge into madness. I'd like you to promise me, you'll never breathe a word."

James thought for a moment. Luke was virtuous. Incapable of being wicked, with no capability of being anything other than good. Luke would never become like his father.

"I promise," James said. "He'll not hear a word against his father from my lips."

John sighed.

"Thanks lad. That's a burden off my mind. I feel better now telling Luke the truth."

Dozing on the sand, listening to the roar of the water, while enjoying the heat of the winter sun on their backs, both men had a reason to feel relaxed and relieved. John Baker, had unloaded some of the burden he had been carrying in his heart, and James was completely at ease, his thirst for revenge, finally assuaged.

Despite being half-asleep, however, a thought entered James' mind, causing him to open his eyes.

"Hey John," he said. "You understand the consequences of this, don't you."

"I was wondering when you'd realise." John said, yawning.

"Her Ladyship's dead. Soame's dead. Doesn't that make Luke, The Duke of Thurlow? He'll inherit Thurlow Hall."

"And the village, " added John, "and the Soame fortune. But I haven't told you everything James. Your daughter. I told you Her Ladyship adopted her."

James nodded.

"She loved her dearly, and made her a beneficiary in her will. If the dukedom is not contested before she comes of age, she'll inherit the title."

"How many shocks can I take in one afternoon, Uncle John?" James said, laughing. "You're going to give me a heart attack. Then I'm to be the father of a duchess. Does that make me a duke?"

He and John laughed, both happier than they had been in a very long time.

"What's the little girl's name? You did tell me?"

"Susan."

"Susan! Of course. My grandmother was Susan. Lady Susan, Duchess of Thurlow. It has a ring to it, don't you think? Come on uncle! My back's beginning to burn. I'll race you to the bank."

Chasing each other into the water, and caring little, they swam strongly through the surging current, arriving safely on the other side.

Chapter Seventeen

The poppy seeds Elliot planted on George's grave during the last week of winter, germinated in the warm soil of spring, the young plants pushing through the red earth, reaching for the sun. Consequently, when he saw the flame red flowers dancing in the breeze every morning in early summer, Elliot wondered where in the world George's spirit might be, wishing it were in the flowers, because they were so colourful and cheerful.

Summer was now waning, the blooms faded and dead, leaving fat seedpods, which Elliot eagerly awaited to collect, and plant again, anticipating an even bigger crop next year.

A peaceful life resumed on the farm, after the native attack, with no reappearance of the Maraket. The last winter days were sunny and cold, thick frost staying on the ground until the sun was high enough to melt it away. Akin to Elliot planting his seeds, it was soon time to plough and drill the paddock for wheat. Thus, with the rainfall moderate and regular throughout the spring, by the end of November, as the season turned, the ground was awash with green plants struggling towards the warm spring sunshine.

As a result, with hot sun during the day, and early evening storms, the wheat grew tall, and the ears fat.

Everyone lent a hand at harvest time, since it was essential to reap the corn quickly, gather it in stooks, and afterwards into stacks. Storms, once beneficial, can easily ruin an entire crop, and not only torrential rain, but also damaging hail, which might flatten the wheat, making it impossible to glean. In addition, wet corn, in the humid air of February, might turn mouldy, and begin to germinate, rendering it useless.

Therefore, with Luke, John, and James using scythes and sickles. Bill Poney pitching stooks. Elliot driving the cart to the stack, and Cathy tying sheaves, they were making rapid progress across the five-acre paddock.

"I think we'll finish here by the end of the week, John," Luke said, bending to tie his bootlace. "We've done it in record time this year."

Doing so, a gunshot rang out, John Baker crashing to the ground beside him.

"John!" Luke yelled. "Are you hit?"

"I reckon," he said. "Though it's only a graze."

Peering over the corn, Luke could see a group of riders at the edge of the field, instantly recognizing the man in the white brimmed hat.

"Whitton!" he said, between his teeth. "It's Whitton, John! Everyone on the ground!"

In a moment, James was beside his uncle, seeing instantly the large wound in his chest.

"You'll be alright uncle," he said, kneeling beside him. "It's only a graze. But we must get you into the house."

"Son! I'm no fool," John said, gasping for air. "He's got me good and proper."

"No no! You'll see. I need to get you into the shade. You'll be alright then."

"No lad. Don't move me. Just let me lie still."

Taking out a handkerchief, James laid it over the bullet hole, and despite there being little blood, what damage Whitton had done inside his uncle's chest, James dared not imagine.

"They're coming closer!" Luke shouted. "And we've no weapons."

The gang approached through the corn, a cloud of dust rising high into the air, Whitton, firing rapidly, a shower of shot spraying over Luke's head, as he crouched on the ground.

"Reddall! Shame I didn't get you first shot!" Whitton bawled, reining Luke's horse Clarence to a stop. "Look at you! Running around in the corn, like a scared rabbit. Come on! Be a man. Stand up, and let me finish you off."

"You're a bloody coward, Whitton!" shouted Luke, "shooting down a defenceless man. If I catch you, I'll hang you from the nearest tree."

"Fine words Reddall. But somehow, I can't see that happening. I reckon I'll set the field alight, and burn every one of you, dead or alive."

Staring through the standing corn, Luke could see Whitton mounted on Clarence, Luke's horse appearing miserable, thin, and wasted, revealing the kind of life he had led since the day Whitton stole him.

"If I only had a gun," Luke said, under his breath. "I'd shoot him down in cold blood."

"Fire into the corn' men!" Whitton shouted. "We'll flush them out in no time."

John O'Mealy raised his fowling piece, just as a shot ricocheted across the field. And where O'Mealy's eye had been seconds before, there was now a gaping hole. Hovering in the saddle for a moment, the gun poised, an expression of surprise on his face, O'Mealy slowly toppled backwards off his horse. But his foot caught in the stirrup, and rearing, the horse galloped away through the corn, O'Mealy's body hurtling beside it.

"James! Where did the shot come from?" shouted Luke.

But James failed to answer. He was listening to John.

"I'm not going to make it, lad," he gasped, the blood gurgling in his throat and lungs. "Come close. You need to know something."

Leaning over him, James attempted to hide his tears.

"It's your job now Jim," John whispered. "You'll tell Luke."

"Don't say that uncle, please."

"Quiet lad. It's all right. It'll be over in a minute."

He coughed, James wiping the blood from John's face with the handkerchief.

"Uncle John, don't die. We've only just found each other. You can't die."

Tears filled James' eyes, burning his sunburnt cheeks.

"I'm just glad we had some time together. You're a good lad," John choked, gripping James' hand. "Your father and I are proud of you. But I'm afraid it's the end for me."

With John's lungs rapidly filling with blood, he was finding it difficult to breathe and speak at the same time,

"Jim! Be true lad, and always honest. You take care."

He shut his eyes, struggling to breathe, James seeing him fighting with death, refusing to let it take him before he was ready.

"When you get home," John whispered. "Shake your father's hand, and tell him I said he was the best friend a man could have ever had, and kiss your lovely mother. She's surely the best woman in the world."

"I will uncle. I will." James said, weeping uncontrollably.

"There's one thing more."

He was speaking in short gasps, his voice growing rapidly weaker.

"There's a strong box, hidden in my room. The key's in the back pocket of my breeches. Inside the box are two letters. They're for Luke's eyes only, you understand. Promise me you'll keep the box safe, until you're able to give it to him."

"Yes uncle. I promise."

John's eyes glazed, James knowing his uncle's life was coming to an end. However, for just a moment, he heard John murmur, and putting his ear close to John's open mouth, as the last flicker of life left him, James heard him whisper 'Edwina'.

Shooting indiscriminately into the corn, two bushrangers suddenly fell from their horses, landing on the ground, stone dead.

"Who's firing?" Luke shouted.

Whitton was looking around the paddock, frantically searching for the gunmen.

"The odds are better now, Whitton. Don't you think?" Luke laughed. "Now we seem to have found ourselves a gunman."

Frantically looking from left to right, wheeling the horse around in wild circles. Whitton rode Clarence further away, attempting to discover where the sharpshooter was hiding.

"You're a sitting duck," Luke shouted. "Whoever's shooting will get you next, as sure as eggs are eggs."

"If I can't get you Reddall, I'll get your farm. I'll torch the place. When you get back, there'll be nothing left."

Pulling the horse's reins, Clarence reared, and digging his spurs into the animal's flanks, Whitton galloped away towards the house.

"You're faster than me, James," Luke yelled. "Get the loose horse, and stop him. I'll look after John."

"There's no need," James shouted. "He's dead."

"What!" Luke screamed, "He said it was only a graze."

"He's gone, Luke!" screamed James. "I can't believe it. But the farm. We must save the farm."

James wasted no time. He needed to get to the house. If Whitton succeeded with his plan, the strong box would be gone, and everything lost. So running through the corn, and grabbing the reins of the loose horse, he jumped on its back and raced after Whitton. Reaching the yard, James jumped to the ground, and hurried into his hut, and grasping his pistol and shot, he ran outside, just in time to see Whitton leap from his horse, and dash up the veranda steps.

"Whitton!" James shouted, arriving at the door. "Where are you, Whitton?"

There was no reply, James hearing a noise from the back of the house.

"He's in the kitchen," he said to himself.

James ran down the hall, out of the back door, and across the yard, seeing the kitchen door partly open. And with his pistol cocked, he moved stealthily to the door, slowly pushing it open.

Whitton was at the range, lighting a large bundle of papers.

"Give it up, Whitton," James said. "It's useless. I'll blast you to hell if you move."

"Get out of my way!" Whitton shouted, lunging at James, running past him, and across the yard into the house, the flaming torch in his hand.

"'Oh no you don't!" James cried, sprinting after him.

Whitton was in the parlour, setting fire to the curtains and furniture, James raising his gun to shoot. But like a lunatic, the bushranger hurtled past him, running into the bedroom.

James turned and fired.

The explosion filled the hallway, James glimpsing a shard of cloth fly from the shoulder of Whitton's coat.

"You bastard," shouted Whitton. "You're the first fucker to put a bullet in me."

"And I won't be the last!" James yelled.

Before James had time to reload, Whitton had dropped the flaming torch, and fled out of the house, James chasing him, ready to fire again. But Whitton was on his horse, and away, before James had time to aim.

Turning back to the house, flames had quickly taken hold, smoke pouring from the open veranda doors.

Water! He needed water quickly.

Back inside the house, James ran down the corridor, and passing Luke's bedroom, saw the bundle of paper had set the bed alight. Then bursting into the kitchen, he looked around frantically, finding a bucket, and running to the sink, he began drawing water from the pump. But it was simply a trickle. Then noticing a bowl on the kitchen table, brimming with freshly peeled potatoes, ready for supper, he grabbed it, and ran back into the house. Making straight for the bedroom, James hurled the contents onto Luke's bed, instantly quenching the fire.

The curtains in the parlour were well alight. But James had an idea. So pulling his shirtsleeves down, while holding the cuffs in his fists, he ran across the room, clutched a set, and pulled them off the rings, dragging them out of the room, down the hall, across the veranda, and into the yard, throwing them on to the ground. Hurtling inside once more, he did the same with the remaining pair, until there was a pile of blazing curtains in the yard.

Since it was covered with tapestry, and stuffed with horsehair, the sofa was merely smouldering. So James had a moment to return to the kitchen for water, and then return to the parlour to douse the fire for good. By the time the fire was extinguished, Whitton was clear away, James realising it would be useless to follow. Anyhow, while the house was empty, it would be an opportunity to retrieve the strong box from amongst John's things.

James entered his uncle's bedroom with a feeling of deep sadness, since he could sense John everywhere. The smell of bay rum he splashed on his face after shaving, the soap he washed with, and even the tweed jackets he wore. Looking at the bed, James saw the impression his uncle had made in the patchwork quilt that very morning, while doing up his bootlaces, James imagined.

This was not the time for sentiment, however. Luke and the others might return at any moment. Therefore, going to the chest of drawers, James tried the bottom one first, pulling it out, seeing it packed with tightly folded blankets. Would this be too obvious, James wondered. But searching between each one, all of a sudden, his hand touched something cold and hard. The strong box!

"Here it is!" he exclaimed, and tugging it out, hid it inside his shirt, and then hurried from the room.

Reaching the front door, James was in time to see the cart carrying John Baker's body enter the yard, Mr Poney driving, the boys, sitting beside him, Luke, Cathy, and Elliot walking alongside.

"We'll need a hand, Jim," Luke said, as they stopped at the foot of the steps.

While Luke unfastened the tailboard, James walked to the cart, seeing his uncle, lying on a bed of straw, Mister Luke's jacket across his chest. Climbing into the cart, James and Luke took John's shoulders, while Poney and Elliot held his legs. As the men began to lift John out of the straw, and onto their shoulders, they suddenly became aware of the enormous weight of the man, since it took all of their combined strength to carry him inside the house, and into the bedroom.

"Luke. Please can I have some time alone?" James asked, once his uncle was laid on the bed.

"Of course," Luke answered. "We'll be in the parlour. Shall I shut the door?"

"No. That's all right. I'll only be a minute."

Once alone, James quietly drew up a chair, and sat down.

Putting his hands together, and closing his eyes, he said a silent prayer, all the while, feeling the ring his godfather made for his christening, when James was a baby, marvelling at the fine engraving.

James opened his eyes, and gazed at John's lifeless hands, lying across his chest. They were large and strong, his fingers thick, calloused from years of hammering at the anvil. How then could they have fashioned the ring on James' finger? Not only the tracery, but also the letters engraved inside the band. It was years since James last removed the ring, since by now his own hands had grown large by hard labour. However, it was unnecessary to remove it, in order to read the words, because they were etched in his heart.

"*JBW. Be good. Be great. Be steadfast.*'"

James gave way, his soul yielding to the sadness in his heart, tears running down his cheeks, stinging his face.

How long he wept, James was unable to tell, but opening his eyes, the cold sensation of the strong box inside his shirt, reminded him of what he must do. Therefore, with all his strength, he turned John on his side, putting his hand in the man's back pocket. There it was! Just as his uncle said it would be. The tiny key.

"What on earth are you doing, Jim? What's in your hand?"

Luke was standing in the doorway.

"Nothing. Nothing," James stammered, completely at a loss. "I was just wondering, that's all."

"What's in your hand?" Luke asked, angrily.

"I can't lie," James said. "It's a key."

"A key to what?"

"To this."

Putting his hand inside his shirt, James pulled out the metal box.

"My uncle wanted me to have it. I'm to look after it, and keep it safe."

"Safe from what?"

Luke was staring at him intensely; James feeling cornered. Why was he keeping the box safe, he asked himself? So that one day Luke would know the truth about himself. When would that day be? No day was a good day. No day bad. If it had to be sometime, why not now.

"I've to give it to you," James blurted. "It's yours. What you find inside is very important to you."

"Whatever do you mean, Jim," Luke retorted. "What could John

Baker have in his possession that would possibly be of importance to me?"

"Open it, and find out."

Noiselessly, Luke walked to the bed, and took the box from James' hand.

"Here's the key." James said. "Do you want me to stay?"

"Of course. Sit down."

James sat back in the chair, and watched Luke take the box, and place it on top of the chest of drawers. Then, putting the key in the lock, and turning it, he slowly opened the lid.

"There's money here," Luke said. "Plus two letters."

Taking them out, Luke went to the window, holding them up to the light.

The wax seals were strange to him, the handwriting flowing and neat, similar to that of his mother, but with more flamboyance and grace.

Perkins, Perkins, and Perkins. Solicitors. Belgrave Terrace, Bath, Somerset, was the address written on the first envelope, Luke tucking it under the second. The second was addressed, Mr Luke William Reddall Esquire.

Luke's hand began to shake.

"What does it mean, Jim?" he said. "Do you know?"

James wished he could tell the truth, but knew the letter would explain everything far better than he ever could.

"I've no idea Luke," he said. "It's as much a mystery to me, as it is to you."

Suddenly afraid, Luke stared at the envelope. What could be inside, he wondered? Whatever it was, he needed to know. Therefore, with trembling hands, he broke the red wax seal, and opened the envelope.

The folded paper inside was exquisite. Far finer than Luke had ever seen, feeling like silk between his fingers. Unfolding it, he held it to the light, and began to read.

Oakwood House, 1ˢᵗ November 1839

'My Dear Luke,' it began. 'By now, my friend John Baker has found you, and

given you the letters I entrusted to him. I am sure you will find him as good, and as trustworthy as I do, for if he were not, then I would never have given him this most important assignment. Undoubtedly, what you are about to read, John has already related to you. I am sorry then if I reiterate what you already know. Although, for my own sake, I feel I have to tell you the story myself, if only to relieve my own tormented soul in the telling.

A year before you were born, a few members of my household, and myself resided in Bath, a city in England you may well have heard of in the colonies. My dear late husband had died a few months earlier, therefore I no longer had reason to remain, making plans to return to my house in Suffolk.'

Suffolk, Luke thought. There was the name again.

'It was with mixed feelings I did so nonetheless,' the letter went on. *'After all, I yearned for my home, although would miss my new friends, Isabella and Thomas Reddall.'*

Luke gasped; feeling his heart leap in his chest, part of him yearning to turn the page, and read the end of the letter, except some strange force compelled him to read every word, slowly and deliberately.

'Within a few months of arriving home,' Luke read on, *'My personal maid, Emma, came to me in great distress, saying she had discovered she was going to have a baby, and fearful of the consequences it would cause her and her family. The revelation concerned me. Emma was an intelligent, educated, girl, with a future. If she had the child, her prospects would be ruined.'*

Was this John's sister Emma, he was reading about, Luke wondered? His mother's maid in Cambridge?

By now, the sun was low, shining into Luke's eyes, making it difficult to read the fine handwriting. Therefore, he pulled the lace curtain across the window, casting a shadow over his face, and the letter in his hand.

'I had invited Thomas and Isabella to stay at the house for the weekend.' Luke read.

"This is Thurlow Hall isn't it?" Luke said, turning to James. "This is in mother's diary."

James had no time to reply, as Luke began reading again.

'A year earlier, when I first met the Reddalls, poor Isabella had been so weak

and ill. The birth of her first child caused her so much pain, she was sick for months afterwards. The Reddalls had elected to visit Bath to take the cure, Isabella's doctors warning her that it would be unwise to have another child, and would risk her life in doing so. Therefore, Isabella and Thomas resigned themselves to having only one child. The weekend they stayed with us, I began to see a solution to their predicament and Emma's dilemma.'

Although it was late afternoon, in the middle of summer, and the room was cool, observing Luke closely, James began to see beads of sweat appear on his forehead. Clearly, Luke was beginning to recognise the way the story was unfolding.

'I spoke of my idea to young Emma, and she seemed most grateful, and very happy to do whatever she was asked. Then I consulted the Reddalls, who were overjoyed at receiving such an offer. We arranged that I should give Emma to Isabella, on the pretence she become her maid. Emma was to tell her family that it was my order. In this way, the Bakers were unable to dissuade me from my actions.'

John Baker's words echoed in Luke's mind. Words he had spoken only months previously.

'My sister was your mother's ladies maid. I remember her telling us at the time, Her Ladyship was giving her to Mrs Reddall, because she had no maid of her own. The family were very surprised, and concerned. But we were helpless. We must always oblige the gentry.'

'Here, my dear Luke,' the letter continued. *'I have to confess to my own dishonesty in this matter. In my entire life, I have only ever told one lie, and that was to Isabella and Thomas. Naturally, they were concerned about the father of their child, wishing to know something of his background. It was here I failed to tell the truth. I told them the father was a local farm lad, young, irresponsible, and already married. Up until now, only Emma and I know who he really is, and this will remain our secret, until the day I tell John Baker.*

Luke, I will now reveal to you the true father of Emma's child. He was Humphrey, my late son, who, I am afraid to say, was a reckless individual and would hardly have made a fit and proper father. Therefore, Emma and I agreed

the baby should be given to people who would love and care for it.
Luke. That baby was you.

You were quickly taken from your mother, as soon as you were born, Emma never knowing whether you were a boy or a girl. She still has no idea, or of what became of you. The Reddalls love you, as if you are their own. So please feel no malice toward them when you reveal you know who you really are. They adore you, and, like me, only had your best interests at heart.

It would have been unnecessary to disclose the truth of your real identity, had it not been for the sudden death of my son, since he was the rightful heir to the title, and its possessions and benefits, after my death. Barring my adopted daughter, I have no other family to inherit the dukedom. However, as my son's child, you have in your veins the direct bloodline of the Soame family, meaning you are the rightful and true heir to the title. You are then, Luke, and if I may be the first to proclaim you, Luke William Soame, Ninth Duke of Thurlow.'

The letter fell from Luke's hand, and fluttered to the floor.

"You're pale," James said. "Are you alright?"

Luke made no reply, gazing vacantly through the lace curtain, his mind suddenly in turmoil.

Unlike his brother, Luke was level headed. Always aware of himself. Content with his life. His love of the land, and the love he bore his mother and father. Unexpectedly, from the moment he read the letter, in an instant, all had changed. Luke was altered. No longer the person he knew, since the blood of two strangers ran in his veins. People he had only read about in his mother's journals.

There were also his mother and father. Those who once loved him, and Luke loved, grieving bitterly when they died. Who were they now? Were they to become strangers too?

Unaware James had spoken; Luke turned from the window, picked up the letter, and began reading once more.

'By the time you receive this letter I shall be dead, therefore powerless to influence your reactions, or the plans you may have for the future. Knowing a little of your character, knowledge I might add, gained from your mother's early letters, I feel you will not disregard what I have told you, and toss this correspondence into the fire.

Unlike your father, you are thoughtful, and not easily swayed by your emotions. Nevertheless, I have to leave the decision making to you. Inside the box John has given you, you will notice, a letter to Perkins Perkins and Perkins, of Belgrave Terrace, Bath.

Mr Perkins is my solicitor. I have entrusted him with a letter that he may only open should the title of Duke of Thurlow be challenged by yourself. He may then read my correspondence, and my conformation of the truth, both in the letter to himself, and the one you will carry. Should you however decide not to take the title; the estate will pass to my ward, when she comes of age.

Finally, Luke, I hope you will be able to find it in your heart to forgive your father and mother, as well as myself. At the time, we thought we were acting for the best. But now I see it was selfish to disregard the feelings of a child, for the benefit of our egotistic motives. I am only cheered by the knowledge that you have grown to become a steadfast, strong, and loyal young man, with also the ability to love, the most cherished of attributes we human's possess. It would please me to think, you will perhaps, find it in your heart to bring your presence and love into my beautiful old home, and make it live again.

I am, and remain, your ever-loving Grandmother, Lady Edwina Soame. The Duchess of Thurlow.

Folding the letter, Luke put it in the envelope, and returning to the chest of drawers, placed the letters in the strong box, closing and locking the lid. Finally, putting the key into his pocket, he walked to the bed.

"Why didn't you tell me, John?" he said, looking down at him.

"He was waiting for the right time." James said. "He wasn't sure how you'd take the news."

"You knew about this all along, didn't you?"

Luke's green eyes were piercing.

"You would've made me tell, if you'd known. I knew it was far better you read the letter first."

They were quiet for a moment, both looking at John.

"Would you mind not speaking of this just yet?" Luke said finally. "I don't know what to think at the moment. The most important thing is to bury our friend. Then I'm going after that bastard Whitton."

Chapter Eighteen

After washing and shaving his uncle, James dressed John in a clean shirt, fastening his cuffs with John's best gold cufflinks, and fixing into his cravat the gold horseshoe pin. James then dressed him in his worsted jacket and trousers, polished his boots, and finally, ran the tortoise shell comb through the man's golden hair. Quietly carrying out this last rite, James' mind flooded with memories of home, mostly recalling family gatherings in the cottage beside the river. At Easter and Christmas time, the little front parlour seemed to burst with people, John Baker always there, filling the room with his presence. How his father and mother loved him. They would be desolate to know their friend was dead.

That evening, James and Bill Poney searched for a site for John's grave.

"I'm sure he'd want to be near the river," James said. "He was brought up beside the Stour. A river has always been part of his life.

Behind the house, the paddock sloped gently down to the riverbank, a glade of red river gums overhanging the water. James had always found it peaceful, shaded and cool, at times full of the carolling of Currawongs. For this reason, he decided it would be a fitting place to bury the great man. Subsequently, it was here James and Poney proceeded to dig the grave.

After wrapping John in a blanket, and laying him on another, James helped Luke, Bill Poney and Elliot, carry him to the cart, Elliot then driving it down to the river.

Once beside the grave, each man took a corner of the outer blanket, and slowly lowered John's body into the grave, Cathy dropping in a posy of wild flowers. When everyone was ready, Luke came forward to read the funeral service.

"Does anyone know a hymn we can sing?" he said, when it was over.

"I do," said James. "We used to sing it at school. John will know it."

"Then would you sing it for our uncle?"

Looking up, James saw tears in Luke's eyes, and moving to the graveside, began to sing.

'Jesu, lover of my soul/ let me to your bosom fly/
While the nearer waters flow, and the tempest still is nigh/
Hide me O my saviour hide/ till the storm of life is past/
Safe into thy haven guide/
O receive my soul at last.'

The more James sang, the more he wept, until it was difficult to sing the words. But as he stumbled and stuttered, another voice joined him. It was Luke, and they sang the hymn together, right up to the end.

***

"Now boys, don't you go too far. I want to keep my eye on you."

Cathy was washing clothes, her arms up to their elbows in soapsuds, as she punched and rubbed the shirts in the tub.

"You can see I'm busy," she said, wringing out the water with her strong arms. "I don't want to be worrying where you are."

"Mother look!" William yelled, pointing towards the gate.

Cathy squinted into the sun, seeing what had drawn her son's attention.

"Not again." she said, under her breath.

Shimmering in the heat haze, across the open paddocks a group of riders was approaching fast. So, throwing the shirt into the tub, she ran to her two children, playing in the dirt.

"Come on boys," she said, scooping up Richard. "Let's get you inside."

Running into the kitchen, she slammed the door.

"You boys stay here," she said. "I've to see Mister Luke."

Cathy found him in the parlour, sitting at his desk, his eyes fixed in thought.

"Sorry to interrupt, sir."

"That's all right, Cathy," his eyes resuming their focus. "What is it?"

"Men are riding up to the farm. I thought you'd want to know, just in case."

"Don't worry, Cathy. It's more than likely Mr Stewart."

He got up, and walked to the window.

"Could you have some refreshment ready for them, please?"

Two days earlier, on the afternoon they buried John, James had ridden hard to the Great South Road, knowing Mr Hurley's coach would soon pass, on its way from Albury to Goulburn. So, taking his horse into the shade of a tree, he waited for the coach to appear.

In a short while, a cloud of red dust appeared down the road, and presuming it to be the coach, James dismounted, and walked into the glare of the sun, waving his hat wildly.

It was difficult to see through the heat and dust, but he could just discern two men sitting high at the front, the man on the left flailing the reins, urging on the six horses, beside him, the guard, holding on to the seat with one hand, while grasping an old blunderbuss with the other.

"Stop!" James shouted. "Stop! I've a letter for Mr Stewart the magistrate."

Had they heard him over the rumble of wheels and the rattle of the harness? They were certainly slowing, the coachman heaving on the reins.

"Stop!" James yelled again, waving the letter.

The coach and six pulled up, the horses blowing hard.

"I've a letter. It's from my boss, and meant for Mr Stewart, the magistrate at Goulburn." James gasped, as the dust from the road enveloped him. "Tom Whitton held up our place this morning. A man's dead."

James handed the letter to the guard.

"He gave us trouble around Tabletop," the guard said, tucking it into his jacket. "Except he bolted, after I got a shot at him."

"Did you hit him?"

"No. The bugger's as quick as a fox."

"I did," James said proudly. "I winged him."

The driver laughed.

"Good on ya mate. The bastards going to swing one of these days."

Watching the coach and horses gallop away, James smiled, recalling the years sitting behind Mr Ives. He knew how it was to be buffeted and rocked about, like those men on the top.

***

"Thank you for getting here so quickly, Mr Stewart." Luke said, as they shook hands.

"My pleasure, Luke. May I introduce my colleague, Mr McGuiness? Also, I don't think you've met my sergeant, Mr Freer."

"Very pleased to meet you, gentlemen. Won't you come in?" Luke ushered them into the house. "I've some refreshment prepared in the parlour. Please come through, and sit down."

"Very kind of you Luke," Stewart said, taking off his hat. "It's a long and dusty ride."

All day the hot dry wind had blown relentlessly from the north, sending the thermometer soaring, Cathy needing to shut the veranda doors, in the early morning. Subsequently, by the afternoon, the house was shady and cool.

In the parlour, the men took the opportunity to ease their tired muscles and aching bones. Nonetheless, all eyes were on Cathy as she entered the room, carrying a tray laden with glasses, plus a large jug of cordial, setting it down on the sideboard.

"Thank you, Cathy," said Luke. "There'll be four guests for dinner. Also, please include the troopers with the men's supper?"

"Certainly sir," she said,

Luke smiled, observing the men's expressions as Cathy left the room.

"Sorry gentlemen," he said, going to the sideboard. "She's spoken for, I'm afraid."

Having poured four glasses of cordial, Luke began to hand them around.

"We've been chasing Whitton for months," George Stewart said, taking his drink. "He's as devious as the devil. When we think we've nailed him, he slips the net again."

"We only wish we knew the location of his hide out." McGuiness said. "Then we could stake him out."

Taking the last glass for himself, Luke sat down.

"It must be around here somewhere," he said. "These days, Whitton seems to concentrate on the area along the road from Albury to Yass."

"I agree," Stewart said. "You know the region Luke. Where around here would you go if you wanted to disappear?"

Luke frowned.

"One of my men spoke to the coach driver and guard, when he posted my letter. They said they'd trouble with Whitton near Tabletop."

"That's the second time the name's come up in the last couple of days," said Sergeant Freer. "Whitton and his gang robbed two travellers down that way, only a few weeks ago."

"Tabletop is almost impregnable," said Luke. "He could easily hide up there for months."

"Then it's a lead," Stewart said. "And the only one we have. So are we're agreed we should explore Tabletop?"

Everyone nodded.

"Good. Then we'll set off first thing tomorrow. It's very kind of you Luke, to put us up. I hope we'll not be any trouble."

"We've limited accommodation, George. However, what we have is at your disposal. The bed in the other room is big enough for two, and Poney's hut has a spare cot. I take it the troopers have tents, and bed rolls?"

"They do."

"Then do feel free to come and go as you please. The washhouse is in the back yard. And of course, there's the river. Very pleasant on a day like today."

The heat had left Luke feeling exhausted. So he excused himself, retiring to his bedroom.

***

A breezy southerly caused the shutters to rattle violently, waking Luke suddenly. What time was it, he wondered? Instinctively he reached for his watch on the bedside table, then realised he no longer owned one. However, it was still light enough to see the small carriage clock, on top of the tall boy. Half past six. He had slept for three hours. What would his guests think of him, Luke thought? It would be dinner in half an hour.

"I'm sorry, gentlemen," he said, hurrying into parlour. "The hot weather's dreadful. I seem to doze all day. Then pace about at night, unable to sleep."

George Stewart drew Luke aside.

"A man who cannot sleep, usually has something on his mind," he said. "That's not the case with you, I hope Luke?"

"Of course not, George," Luke said, frowning. "What makes you say that?"

"Only I'm loathe to speak out of turn."

Stewart suddenly lowered his voice.

"I've been wondering how you are, regarding your brother John? You must be rather concerned."

"What about John?" asked Luke, sounding puzzled. "I've not heard a word from him for months."

"I'm sorry Luke. I didn't realise."

Stewart appeared uncomfortable.

"Well I hate to be the one who has to break the news," he said, after an embarrassed silence. "But John's behaving quite abnormally."

"Why? Whatever's the matter with him?"

"He and I have met on several occasions in Goulburn, of late. Committees, dinners, political meeting, that sort of thing. And I've noticed him behaving most oddly, to say the least."

"It's the first I've heard of it, George. Since father and mother died, John and I have barely spoken."

"It's a very delicate matter. I'm reluctant to say more."

"Please sir," Luke said. "I'd be grateful if you would make your concerns known to me."

By now, the conversation had taken Luke and George Stewart out of the parlour, and onto the veranda, where the breeze was cool and refreshing.

"Very well, Luke," said George Stewart, cautiously. "It's the general opinion of Goulburn society, that your brother's going insane."

Luke stared at him in astonishment.

"Yes Luke," Stewart said, clearing his throat. "He's behaving most irrationally, and drinking heavily. On several occasions, I've noticed him talking to himself, and he's let his appearance lapse considerably, looking for the most part like a tramp."

"I must say George," Luke said. "I've had my concerns about John, especially in relation to his drinking. But I never imagined it would come to this."

"Myself, being the town magistrate, also Doctor Cartwright, the new incumbent, are at odds as to what's best to do. With no immediate family, except you of course, Cartwright and I consider that you are the only person to decide on John's future."

"Have him committed. Is that what you're saying? It can't be as bad as that."

"I regret to say Luke, it is. I think it's strongly advisable, before he does himself, or anyone else, harm."

"But what about Martha, his wife; isn't she concerned?"

"Mrs Reddall hasn't been seen at Breadalbane for months. Not since the loss of their son."

"They lost a son!" said Luke, appalled. "I never knew. Nobody told me."

Stewart nodded gravely.

"Well George, my brother must be pretty far gone not to tell me about such a tragedy."

At this point, Cathy sounded the gong, announcing dinner, and Luke and the magistrate returned to the dining room in silence.

Luke found it difficult to remain sociable at dinner, his mind fixed on the fate of his brother. While he pondered on whether commitment was the right option, the others talked, and drank wine. Suddenly, however, the realisation dawned on him. In fact, John was not his brother. Would this effect his decision? Of course not. He loved John. When they were boys, John was always beside him, the big brother affectionately teasing him, because he was younger and smaller.

The wine was going to Luke's head, anger brewing dangerously in his mind.

The lives he and his brother John led, caused them to become estranged, Luke in one part of the country, John in another, their father's thirst for land, all those years ago, driving the brothers apart.

Had they not been granted land when they were children, their father opting instead to encourage his sons to become doctors or parsons, he and John would have been less apart. Luke supposed they would have married, their families celebrating joyous Easters and merry Christmas' together, rather than living solitary lives in out of the way places.

What was the answer, Luke wondered? Do the humanitarian thing. Have the papers drawn up, and sign away his brother's freedom. Or turn his back. Forgetting he had ever had the conversation with Mr Stewart. Except, Luke was certain the magistrate was correct. Soon John might become a danger to himself, as well as others.

Abruptly, an image of John Baker came into Luke's mind. John was sensible, and level headed. John would know what to do.

The room was beginning to spin, Luke struggling to see across the table, where Mr Stewart was telling Mr McGuiness a tale, causing them to laugh raucously. That was John's chair, Luke thought, suddenly seeing, through a haze of alcohol, his friend smiling.

Without warning, Luke's throat tightened, and staring at the food on his plate he realised he no longer had the appetite to eat.

"If you'll excuse me, gentlemen," he said, staggering to his feet. "I'm sorry, but I'm not feeling well. I think I might retire. I'll see everyone the morning."

Closing his bedroom door, Luke fell onto the bed, weeping uncontrollably, at the same time suddenly experiencing loneliness, beyond comprehension.

He no longer knew who he was. His mother and father, the two people he loved most in the world, were suddenly alien to him. Apparently, his dear brother was insane. And John Baker, the man Luke now realised, he loved more than reason itself, was dead. He had nothing, and no one. There was no point in living. Everything black, the desolation unrelenting.

In a final, desperate bid for his own sanity, Luke scrambled off the bed, and slumping to his knees, shut his eyes.

'God help me!' he prayed. 'Show me a way'.

***

"Where are you going?" Luke shouted, as James rode up to the house the next morning.

"You don't think I'm going to let you go on your own?" James yelled. "I'm coming too. Uncle John would never have let you out of his sight. So neither will I."

"I'm not going on my own," said Luke, laughing. "I've four troopers, Mr Stewart, Mr McGuiness, and the sergeant here."

"Even so, I wouldn't dream of seeing my cousin put himself in danger, without being with him. I know Uncle John would have wished it."

"You're right, of course. Certainly you can come. Are you armed?"

"Am I armed?" James said, opening his jacket, revealing three pistols. "Elliot's lent me his. And this one's Poney's."

"Good. Let's hope you get a chance to put another bullet in the blighter.

The party rode out at dawn, Mr Stewart taking the lead, Luke and the gentlemen behind, James and the troopers bringing up the rear, reaching the Great Southern Road, turning south toward the Tabletop Range. Eventually, after an hour of hard riding, Mr Stewart pulled the posse up below a rocky outcrop, beneath which appeared a ramshackle hut, declaring itself, by a sign over the door, as 'O'Brien's

Inn'.

"Maybe Mr O'Brien knows something," Stewart said.

"O'Brien!" he shouted. "Mr O'Brien!"

A shabby curtain at the window twitched, a ruddy, unshaven face appearing, squinting in the glare of the sun.

"Mr O'Brien! May we have a word?"

The face disappeared, and after a while the door opened, a short, stocky man, wearing a stained vest and long johns, standing in the doorway.

"Sorry to get you up, Mr O'Brien," Mr Stewart continued. "We were wondering whether you knew the whereabouts of Tom Whitton."

Luke thought he noticed O'Brien's tired eyes widened for a second, and then quickly narrow, his face assuming a hard and suspicious expression.

"Do you think I'm bloody crazy?" he muttered, through his teeth. "Around here, it's bad luck to even speak the name. There isn't a person in the district who hasn't had some dealing or other with that devil."

He looked about nervously, as if Whitton himself had heard his curses.

"Mr Hurley's guard told Waldon, Mr Reddall's man, they had cause to fire on Whitton, around here a week ago."

"Yeah," O'Brien replied, pulling at the front of his soiled underpants. "Ned told me he'd been held up."

"Where did it happen?" Luke asked.

"Down the road. Half a day's ride. At the bottom of Tabletop Gorge."

O'Brien lowered his voice, looking around furtively.

"I haven't told you right," he said. "They do say his hide out's at the top. Hang on though gentlemen. I don't reckon he's there. Because two government men came through yesterday, saying Whitton bailed up their boss, Whitton telling the men to scarper, or join up with him."

"Where was that?" Stewart asked.

"Mr Dickson's place. This side of Woomargama."

"What shall we do?" remarked Luke. "He could be on his way back to Tabletop. I don't think he'd hang around Dickson's run?"

Stewart thought for a moment.

"We can't take the risk," he said. "Mr McGuiness, Freer, and I will take two troopers, and go north."

"Then James and I will take the other troopers, and head for Tabletop."

Stewart nodded.

"That way," he added, "we've both options covered."

"But won't you come inside gentlemen, and whet your whistles," O'Brien interrupted. "I've a case of new wine come in last week."

"No thanks, O'Brien," said Stewart. "We'll need clear heads dealing with the likes of Whitton. Maybe when we've caught the bugger."

Luke and James watched Mr Stewart, McGuiness, Freer, and the troopers ride away, the dust from the horse's hooves soon obliterating the view.

"Can you describe the gorge, O'Brien?" Luke said. "Have you seen it?"

"I have sir. It's powerful steep, a mighty waterfall, surging under the road. They say there's a track following the falls, right to the top. They reckon that's how Whitton gets up there."

"Is there cover?"

"Trees at the bottom, as I remember. But if I were you, I'd leave the horses there, and go the rest of the way on foot. Just in case the blighter's on top, watching."

"Thanks O'Brien," said Luke. "Sounds like good advice. We'll be on our way."

"Good luck!" O'Brien shouted, as they rode away. "You'll need it."

Spitting in the dust, then turning, O'Brian went back inside the inn, and shut the door.

***

"I don't think it's wise to get any closer," Luke said, as the four men rode through the trees, the gigantic walls of Tabletop towering above them.

Galloping on, they soon began to hear the roar of the falls, the horses scenting the water, needing no encouragement to maintain the pace. Subsequently, as O'Brien suggested, Luke and his party dismounted some fifty yards from the chasm, and after tying the horses to the trees, crept stealthily through the stand of gums toward the sound of cascading water.

Years earlier, after the route to Port Phillip was discovered, the surveyor general, Thomas Mitchell, supervised the building of the Great South Road, and reaching Tabletop, the convict gangs constructed a heavy stone bridge, vaulting the cataract, as it plunged down the mountain, the resulting creek at the bottom, eventually meeting the mighty Murray River.

Luke, James, and the troopers could see the bridge above them, the massive stones still bearing the marks of a thousand chisel blows.

Emerging from under the tree cover, they moved silently through the rocks, climbing ever closer to the road, until they found themselves in a narrow gully, between the boulders.

"This looks a good spot," Luke shouted, over the thunderous, rushing water. "Jim! Can you see a track?"

"Yes," he answered. "On the left. Just as O'Brien said. It follows the falls all the way to the top."

Finding a shady place amongst the rocks, Luke and James settled down to watch and wait, the roar of the falls numbing their senses.

"James," Luke said, after a while. "Have you a brother?"

"Yes," James answered.

"How old is he?"

"Younger than me by three years. So he'll be twenty seven."

"What's his trade?"

"When we lived in Bath, he was a gardener. Perhaps he still is."

Where were the questions leading, James wondered? Luke had a way of talking around a subject, before he came out with what was really on his mind.

"What's his name?"

"John James. After Uncle John, I suppose."

"Is he married?"

James could see Luke staring at him intently, his eyes reflecting the glare of the sun, and the sparkling water.

"Yes." James continued. "Uncle John said he married three years ago, to a girl named Elizabeth."

"Did you and he get along when you were young?"

"Once I was at school, and living with the Bakers, we didn't see a lot of each other. Then I went to work at the hall, and he became a gardener's boy, helping Mr Denton."

James was becoming transfixed by the tumbling water, for a moment his mind transported back to those days, so long ago, now just shadowy memories, flitting here and there in the darkness of his mind.

"Did he go to school like you?"

"No. John James can't read or write. It was only the eldest boy of the family, allowed to attend the school."

For a moment, Luke was silent, his face fixed in a frown.

"My brother's insane," he said at last. "I've to sign the papers that'll commit him. Would you do that to your brother?"

James thought for a while.

"If it were best for all concerned, then I suppose I would. But can't someone else do it?"

"His wife Martha, I suppose. I just haven't the stomach for it. This bloody country!" Luke said angrily. "It's destroyed the love my brother and I once had for each other. We were so close. He was the best brother in the world."

Luke and James fell silent, wrapped in thought, and mesmerised by the deafening roar of the waterfall. Except, after a while, Luke spoke once more.

"You must have wondered why I haven't said anything about the letter."

James nodded. "I dared not bring up the subject, for fear of what you'd say."

"It's been on my mind the whole time."

"I'm sure it has. It must be a great shock. But you do realise what it means, don't you?"

"I think so," said Luke, turning his gaze to the tumbling, glittering tumult. "If I go to England, and see this Perkins fellow. Give him the letter addressed to him. He reads it, and then reads the one he has from Lady Soame. I become a duke. Is that right?"

"I don't think anyone could put it more simply. That's exactly the situation. But will you?"

"What do you mean?" Luke appeared confused.

"Will you leave all you have here?"

"But what have I here?" he said. "My father, mother, and sister are lying in the vault in St Peter's churchyard. My brother's mad, myself, or someone else, about to commit him to an asylum. I've lived the life of a monk for years, so far from society I feel embarrassed, and unsure when in the company of my own class. John Baker was closer by blood to me, than was anyone of my so-called family. John would want me to be there. Perhaps I should go. It's my duty. My Grandmother would have wished it. In fact, she's told me so in her letter."

"You're a Soame right enough," James said smiling. "You're just like her. My father always said there was no one who had a stronger sense of duty, than the Duchess of Thurlow."

"But Jim, the whole thing scares me," Luke said. "I wish I had your eyes to see what it's like. Mother's journals are all I have to inform me about England."

"You're lucky to have those. I didn't have books to tell me how life would be in Australia. All those months on the ship, I'd no idea what sort of place I was coming to."

"I'm sorry," Luke said, fixing his eyes on James once more. "That was selfish. Give me a clue. What's Thurlow Hall like?"

Turning away from Luke's hypnotic gaze, James stared into the water.

He was sitting at the back of the carriage, his scarf wound tightly around his neck, the wool tickling his nose, his gloves on tight, and his hat pulled over his ears. Looking over his shoulder, seeing the house diminishing, was the last time he saw Thurlow Hall. Nevertheless, the picture was etched in his heart.

"Beautiful, Luke," he said, gazing into the rainbow created by the falls. "You'll have never seen the like. Thurlow Hall, the thatched cottages in the village, All Saints Church, the Cock Inn, the countryside roundabout, the Stour. Everything picturesque. In Australia, the countryside's impressive and majestic. Grandiose almost. Though I'd never say beautiful. It's like the difference between rugged good looks, and classical splendour.

Surprising himself, James had never spoken so expressively. Luke, however, was entranced.

"Mother made drawings in her diary." He said. "There's a sketch of a great house, drawn at the time of mother and father's visit. Could it be Thurlow Hall?"

"Probably. But I can't say unless I saw it."

"I remember it had a grand front, like a Greek temple. The sort you see in books. With huge pillars, at the top of a great flight of stone steps. But the thing that sticks in my mind, is an iron lamp hanging above the door."

"That's Thurlow," James said dreamily. "My father lit that lamp, every evening. It shone into the night like a beacon, reassuring anyone who saw it. "

"And everything there belongs to me?"

"Yes. You'd be the Duke of Thurlow. Her Ladyship has willed it to you."

"Then I'm very fortunate."

"But all of that," James said, "is it really worth giving up everything you have here, and to travel to England, a place you barely knew as a child?"

"That's for me to decide, I suppose," Luke said. "But when I go; I'll go. There'll be no looking back."

Close to midday, the sun shone on them relentlessly, its heat searing through James' Panama hat, and the thin cotton duck of his jacket, feeling the spray on his face, the water gushing beside him looking dangerous, yet inviting. James wished he could strip and jump in. Although, as his eyes followed the rapids tumbling away below, it was then he saw Tom Whitton, weaving across the rocks, Luke's horse, Clarence, stumbling behind. Nudging Luke, James nodded in Whitton's direction.

"There's our man everyone," Luke said. "Keep him in your sites."

Whitton was now so close they could hear him breathing, the effort of the climb telling on him. Though, James' attention was drawn to Whitton's left arm, hanging limply beside him.

"He's still got the bullet in his shoulder," he said, turning to Luke.

"That then will be our advantage." Luke said grinning.

Luke, James and the troopers watched Whitton coming nearer. He was falling into their trap so easily, thought Luke. Whitton would soon be in the gully, and they would be able jump him. If justice were done, Luke would take Whitton alive. Shooting down the villain was too good for him. He wished to see him swing for killing John Baker, and all the rest of his hapless victims.

Luke gestured to one of the troopers to move further along the gully, thereby cutting off Whitton's escape, when he is finally cornered. However, navigating the wet rocks, the soldier stumbled, his gun hitting a boulder, a loud crack echoing in the gully as it fired into the air.

Looking back at Whitton, Luke and James saw him stop suddenly, attempting to discover where the shot had originated, a puff of smoke above the gully, betraying the ambusher's presence.

"Fire!" Luke shouted. "Before he gets away."

With a hail of shots ringing out, Whitton scurried over the rocks, darting for cover, leaving Clarence defenceless amongst the boulders.

"Don't kill my horse," Luke yelled. "Fire at Whitton."

Except it was useless shooting at something that was no longer there, since Whitton had disappeared.

"We know you're there, Whitton!" Luke shouted. "Give yourself up. You're outnumbered."

Luke scoured the rocks for any sign of movement, but saw none.

"Where is the bastard?" James yelled. "He's not going to get away! That's for sure!"

At that, there was a gunshot, and a scream, one of the troopers dropping dead in the gully.

"He's above us!" the other trooper shouted. "On the bridge!"

His words resounding around the canyon, another shot echoed in the canyon, and the trooper fell to the ground.

"The bastard!" Luke yelled. "He's killed him too. Get out of here Jim. He'll pick us off like lame ducks."

Dodging behind a barricade of stones, with Luke at one end, and James, the other, slowly James peered around the edge.

"Can you see him?" Luke shouted.

"No. I reckon he's behind the parapet. Is there a way we can get up there?"

"Not without being seen," Luke answered. "If you go up, you'd be in clear view. But my side is beyond his sight lines. You keep him busy."

Nodding to Luke, James began a tirade of shots at the bridge, while Luke, moving fast, pistol at the ready, scrambled up the cliff, hand over hand, rock over rock, until his head was level with the road.

Just as James predicted, Whitton was crouching behind the wall, evading the volley of shots, bursting over his head, the wall shielding him. Even so, he managed once or twice, to hold his pistol over the wall, with just enough time to pull the trigger. However, he had no idea which way to aim, his hand shaking violently. For the first time Luke could see the reason. Whitton was using his left hand to hold his gun. James had shot him in the left arm. Whitton must be left handed, the pain in his arm, causing his inability to aim correctly.

Luke's mind was spinning. He had Whitton to his advantage. He could shoot him now. Shoot him dead. He had the chance. But shooting him in the back would be cowardly. Luke wanted Whitton to see the man who would finally put an end to his wicked, crazed life.

Waiting for a break in the firing, Luke aimed his pistol.

"Whitton!" he shouted.

Half rising, Whitton turned, his face twisting into a gruesome grin.

"Reddall! At last," he growled, aiming his gun. "You're finished Reddall."

But by the look of pain on Whitton's face, and his shaking hand, Luke could see the effort of lifting the gun was agony.

"I don't think so, Tom," he said. And as Whitton's gun exploded, Luke flattened himself on the ground, and pulled the trigger.

The bullet slammed into Whitton's head, searing the bone of his skull, blood, spraying high into the air. He hung motionless for an instant, as if time itself had stopped, then plunged over the wall of the bridge.

Below, James heard the shot, seeing Whitton on the bridge take the impact of the lead, then tumble over the edge, and crash into the torrent below.

Watching Whitton's body surge past him, and down into the abyss of dark green water, in the briefest moment, the echo of a story flickered through James' mind, but then vanished.

"He's gone!" Luke shouted from the bridge. "The bastard's dead for sure."

Staring down at the falls, Luke caught sight of Clarence, standing listlessly amongst the rocks.

"Well I've got my horse back!" he yelled. "But the bugger's still got my bloody watch!"

Chapter Nineteen

While James covered the bodies with stones, Luke wrote an inscription in charcoal on a slab of wood.

"I hope it doesn't rain, and wash the words away before someone finds them."

James looked puzzled.

"We'll be telling Mr Stewart, won't we?"

"No."

"Why not?"

"I've thought about this long and hard, battling with my conscience. We're not going back."

James frowned, seeing the expression on Luke's face.

"Since John died," James said, "I've been thinking, you've not been yourself. What's happening? Where are we going?"

We're disappearing, Jim. It's for both our benefits. I want people to think Whitton's killed us. Don't you see! If I vanish, you can too. I'm your boss remember. If I'm not there to report you absconding, you can disappear. Change your name, and start a new life."

"Are you crazy? What about your things? All you've worked for."

"I'm not crazy Jim. If I don't do this now, I'll regret it for the rest of my life. I know if I return to Durra Durra, life will go on just as before, and I'll be stuck in the old rut again. My brother's already mad. Who's to say I won't be too. No. I'm getting out, while I'm sane enough to make a choice. I've had it with everything here. My family no longer exists. Whereas, across the other side of the world I've a mother, who doesn't even know I exist. You must see that I've a yearning to see her."

Completely bemused, James could only stare, hardly able to believe what was happening.

"Here, my life's finished?" Luke continued. "Since knowing your uncle John I've realised, there's more to life than living alone. He showed me companionship I'd never experienced before. Maybe I'll find the same friendship where I'm going. Not if I stay here though, where it's one lonely day after another. The same until I die. I'll certainly go crazy."

"What about the farm. The house," James pleaded. "All the lovely things."

"Poney and Elliot will have them. Or whoever buys the place. You see, I said if I made a decision, there'd be no going back. So now's the time to make a clean break. Our uncle would want it. My duty's in England, and to my grandmother. I must carry out her dying wish. I have far greater responsibilities there, than here."

"The letters though Luke. You'll need the letters."

"I'm not stupid, Jim," he said, patting the saddlebag. "They're my legacy? I'm not leaving them lying around."

Watching Luke burrowing into the bags, James shook his head.

"But Cathy and the boys?"

"Now's your chance," Luke said, pulling out the strong box. "Go back and grab them, and vanish like me. There's a thousand pounds of Lady Soame's in here. I want you to have it. You can start a new life."

"Luke!" James exclaimed. "But what about you?"

"I'm alright. I've my winnings."

James was astonished. Suddenly everything was happening so fast.

"But where will you go?"

"We're close to the border. I'll ride to Port Phillip, and pick up a ship. No one knows me there. It'll be easy to slip away without being noticed."

"Then what?"

"Go to Bath, and see this Perkins fellow."

Suddenly, James felt a stab of jealousy.

"You might meet my mother and father."

"If I do, I'll tell them that the last time I saw you, you were fit and well. Would you want me to say that?"

Completely bewildered, James nodded.

Looking on while Luke tightened Clarence's girth, James saw an expression, together with a particular glint in his eyes, he had never seen before. Was this the beginning of what James had feared? Was Luke becoming like his father, after all? However, the look vanished, replaced by a grin.

"I feel wonderful Jim," he said. "Invigorated. For the first time in a long while, something new is about to happen. Hey! Why don't you come too? We've enough money between us. We'd have a grand time."

"I can't leave Cathy."

"I know. You love her. And you also love this country."

"I do Luke. I lived in England for nearly twenty years. There, I was part of a system. I had my station in life. If I return, I'd be back in my place, and I'd stay there for the rest of my life. If indeed, I do as you say, and disappear, taking Cathy and the boys to a place where nobody knows us, I'll be free to become anything I wish."

"Then we'll both be happy. You with your freedom, and me with my duty."

Putting the roll of money into James' hand, Luke laughed.

"Jim," he said, suddenly looking at him keenly. "From the moment I saw you on the ship, I felt there was a bond between us. Who knows, maybe it's the good Suffolk soil running in our veins."

Luke held out his hand, and James went to shake it. But suddenly the enormity of the moment overtook them, and they embraced.

"Now Jim," Luke said, mounting his horse. "Be off! Find that lady of yours, and who knows, one day we might meet again at Thurlow."

Hardly able to believe what was happening, in the blink of an eye James' world had cart wheeled, and what was once order, was now madness. Dumbstruck, he watched Luke gallop away. Would he ever see him again, he wondered? Moreover, in which world would it be? In his? In Luke's? In this world, or the next?

Part Two
Separate Ways

Chapter One

Warily, James approached the farm. No one seemed to be about, with no horses tethered to the rail, Poney and Elliot off somewhere, about some job or other.

What was he doing, he asked himself? Was this complete madness? Yet, the roll of money in his jacket pocket, pressing against his chest, was reminding him of how life might be. Perhaps Luke was right. Why not disappear, and start a new life.

With money, he could do anything. Go anywhere. Far away from anyone who might know him. It was true. He could purchase land, and start a farm. Suddenly, he had a future, and could seek his fortune at last. All these dreams were possible. But first he must disappear. Vanish. It would be just as if he were dead.

Tethering the horses in the deep shade of the river gums, James walked towards the house. But the sight of John's grave beneath the trees stopped him. Walking to it, he stood for a moment, looking down at the sad little cross, and bunch of withered flowers.

"You know what I'm doing, uncle," he said. "I know you do. I only hope I've your blessing."

From somewhere close by, James heard children laughing, and walking around the side of the house, saw Cathy chasing the boys around the garden, imitating a native, pulling faces, causing the little ones to scream with terror and delight. James could have watched the scene forever, but there was no time. Bill and Elliot might be back at any moment, and he Cathy and the boys should be gone.

James whistled, and she turned, a smile spreading across her face. Although, seeing his expression, she knew something was wrong, and running across the yard, fell into his arms.

"We must go," he said. "Quickly. Get some things packed. I want to be out of here, before Poney and Elliot get back."

"Why?" asked Cathy, staring at him keenly. "What's happened? Where's Mister Luke? Did you get Whitton?"

"Luke's dead."

"Oh no!" she cried. "But how?"

"He and Whitton were fighting in the water, and they were washed away."

"How terrible. But why must we go?"

"I've done a wicked thing," James said, avoiding Cathy's eyes. "Please forgive me."

She stared at him in disbelief.

"James? You've not a bad bone in your body."

"Luke had money in his saddlebag. After he drowned, I took it."

James looked at her hard, wondering whether she would believe him.

"Well he won't need it where he's gone," said Cathy. "But it could mean a new life for us. Where's his horse?"

"I sent it into the bush. If Poney finds out, he'll get the constables."

"James! You did it for us, didn't you? Naturally, I forgive you. Come on!" she said, breaking free from their embrace. "We'll be out of here in a trice."

Cathy was as good as her word. Because within minutes, she had packed a bag with clothes, another with provisions, and quickly dressing the boys in their Sunday clothes, she was across the yard to the waiting horses.

"I thought you said you'd sent Luke's horse into the bush," she said, as James helped her into the saddle.

"I did. This one belonged to one of the troopers. Whitton shot them both."

"Deary me! You have had a time of it, haven't you."

With a boy between them, they rode north at a fast pace, making sure no one appeared to give away their escape, reaching Ten Mile Creek by nightfall, without meeting a soul. Resting for a few hours, concealed in the bush, they moved on, this time under the cover of darkness. Once the sun rose, hiding the horses in the shade of tress, James and Cathy made gunyas, for themselves and the boys to sleep under until the evening. When it was dark, they continued on.

In this way, James, Cathy, and the boys covered a considerable distance, and by the fourth day, were well clear of Durra Durra.

During the last year at the farm, James heard tell of a new settlement beginning seventy miles north, on the Great South Road. Knowing it to be called Gundagai, James, and Cathy decided it might be a suitable place to settle. By the sixth day, and now less anxious to be seen in daylight, seeing huts and homesteads along the road, the land cleared, sheep, and cattle grazing, they were convinced they must be close by.

Standing in the stirrups, Cathy and James looked down at Gundagai, nestled on a flat plain, beside the far bank of the Murrumbidgee River. The plain was expansive and open, with few trees, grassland stretching away beyond the spattering of tents, huts and houses, a large sparse hill in the distance, giving the settlement an imposing backdrop.

"Are you sure we should stop here?" James asked, turning to Cathy. "It looks quiet. You might be bored."

"We'll go where you want us to go, James," she said.

"But I'm a runaway. I had one more ticket of leave to be stamped, and I've ignored it. The ticket I have will soon run out. If I get caught, it'll be the last you'll see of me."

"Then we'll have to hope no one knows us," Cathy said. "We've money. We'll say we've just arrived. Free settlers from the old country. No one will be any the wiser. Look James! There's a nice place to camp."

She was pointing to a shady glade, amongst a stand of river gums. So, while the boys waded in the shallows, searching for crayfish, James and Cathy collected firewood, and once she was able to light a fire, and begin cooking supper, James rode off in the direction of the town, promising to be back for supper.

The river was wide. However, with no bridge to cross, James noticed a rope sweeping through the water to the opposite bank. In the shallows was a punt, alongside a sandy beach, a small hut on higher ground, then a track beyond, leading into town. This must be the way across, James thought, heading toward it.

"Cooee!" he called.

An old man came to the hut doorway, and waving, hobbled along the beach, and began untying the punt. Then, climbing aboard, he began poling it through the strong current towards James.

James' horse Dan, had never ridden on water; thus required coaxing onto the deck. So, bit-by-bit, James urged him forward, until they were finally ready to cast off.

On reaching the other side, James paid the halfpenny fare, mounted his horse, and rode away up the track.

Gundagai was the smallest settlement James had seen for a while, although he was impressed by the width of the main street, considering it wider than any he had encountered, six drays and bullock teams, able to pass each other, without brushing sides. Counting twenty or so, well-built houses, dotted here and there, James noticed some built of stone, and others wood, while trees and shrubs, beside a few, created a semblance of a garden.

Four impressive hotels dominated the main street, The Criterion and The Royal, appearing to be the largest. Joining the jumble of dwellings was a building announcing itself to be the town post office; then a schoolhouse, by the sound of children playing in the yard. A familiar ringing, betrayed a shed belonging to a blacksmith. And in one place along the street, several provision stores, adjoined each other, shaded by a wide veranda.

Everywhere seemed peaceful, and appeared to take on the indolent nature of the river rolling by, only furlongs away.

Suddenly James realised he was thirsty, so decided he needed a drink. Cathy would hardly mind if he had just one. Therefore, pointing his horse in the direction of one of the larger hotels, James dismounted, and tethered Dan to the rail outside. Then, stepping into the shade of the hotel veranda, he opened the door, and went inside.

Where previously, the room had been a place of muttered conversations, yarns and jokes, it was now silent, all heads turned, as James approached the counter.

"What can I get you?" a man said, standing there.

"Beer thanks," answered James.

While men around the room stared, James watched the man at the counter go to a barrel, and pour a glass of beer.

"There you go, mate," he said, putting it on the bar. "That'll be a penny ha'penny."

James paid, at the same time, hearing from somewhere in the room, a man speak, another joining him, as normal conversation resumed.

"Where are you from?" the barman asked.

"East mate," answered James, attempting to sound casual. "Sydney."

"Where in Sydney? I know it well."

Frantically, James tried to remember places he had visited after he arrived, because it was a long while since he had given those early days a thought.

"Parramatta," he said quickly, the name suddenly popping into his head.

"That's not Sydney, mate," the man said, laughing.

"Well we went there, after we landed."

"Where in England are you from?"

James began to sweat. The man was probing. If he told the truth, he might be traced. There were so many records taken. Except, thinking back, he remembered he never told anyone he lived in Bath, so crossed his fingers.

"Bath, in Somerset," he said, then swallowing a mouthful of cool beer.

"I thought I heard a West Country accent. I'm from the east. Suffolk."

James gulped.

"Which town," he said. "I know people in Suffolk."

"Sudbury."

This was too close for comfort.

"Here! Do you mind if I sit down?" James said. "It's been a long ride."

"Of course mate. Just make yourself comfortable. Think of The Royal Hotel as your second home."

The hotel was becoming crowded, men having finished work on nearby farms and stations, beginning to drift back to town, the hotel being first port of call.

Shoulder to shoulder, hunched along the bar, most wearing wide brimmed hats, and smoking clay or corncob pipes, the men were thirstily drinking beer, or spirits. But seeing their patched and dilapidated clothing, to James they appeared poor and browbeaten. Although, as he listened to their conversations, and took in their keen expressions, he began to see a pioneering spirit. Clearly, they were never going to allow the harshness of the land to beat them at any cost.

A young man, with a black beard, and wearing a large panama hat, sat down at James' table. He was drinking rum, and smoking a long clay pipe.

"Not seen you around here," he said, knocking out the pipe on the rungs of the chair.

"No," said James.

He hoped this was not the beginning of another interrogation session, because his capacity to lie was lessening by the second.

"Looking for work?" the young man said.

"Yeah,"

"Ticket of Leave man?"

"No."

"What do you do?"

"Most things. Although I'm an ironmonger by trade."

"My father's already got a blacksmith."

The young man drained his glass, and stood up, turning towards the bar.

"Sorry mate!" he said. "I should have introduced myself. Robinson's the name. Jim Robinson. Would you like one, mate?"

He raised his glass.

"No thanks," James said. "I'm going after this."

"Not yet though," said Robinson, "I reckon I can fix you up."

Going up again to refill is glass, he returned, slumping in the chair.

"Yeah," he went on. "My father's William Robinson. Daresay you've heard of him."

James shook his head, while the young man filled and lit another pipe.

"We came here five years ago, from Port Phillip," the man continued. "Back then this place was beyond the Government line of occupation, so father found land, and squatted."

"How much does he have?" asked James.

"I don't rightly know. About seventeen thousand acres maybe."

"Really!" James exclaimed. "That's a lot of land."

Secretly, he was astonished. James considered Luke's farm at Durra Durra as large. But the concept of a place more than twenty five times the size was staggering.

"Do you want work?" asked Robinson, swallowing his rum, and getting up to go to the bar once more. "Father needs shepherds and fencers. And by the look of you, you'd be handy at fencing. It's tough work."

"Yeah. I wouldn't mind." James said, finishing his beer. "How will I find the place?"

"There's a road heading west, before you reach the punt. Take it for twenty miles. Then you'll see a track on your right, and a sign. The name of the place is Kimo. Just say Jim sent you."

The following morning, Cathy, James, and the boys began their journey, and keeping to the river, took the road following Jim Robinson's instructions. They were happy, eagerly anticipating the thought of work, and settling down once more.

Setting out at first light, the journey still took all morning, so it was lunchtime by the time they arrived at the sign, where, leaving the road, they followed a track creeping around the side of a low hill, noticing in the distance a large stone house, enclosed by a deep veranda, the house appearing majestic and cool in the midday sunshine.

An old woman appeared at the veranda rail as they approached, shading her eyes from the sun.

"Good afternoon," she said, as James and Cathy pulled up beside the steps. "What can I do for you?"

"Good afternoon, madam," James said. "Jim Robinson asked us to come. He says there might be work here."

"Jim's my son," the woman said. "I'm Mrs Robinson. When did you see him?"

"Last evening."

"In the hotel, I dare say."

James nodded.

"Well he didn't come home, so we're not expecting you."

Mrs Robinson noticed William and young Richard fidgeting.

"Let the youngsters down," she said. "They look anxious to be running about. Why don't you take the horses into the shade, while I get my husband?"

"She looks a nice sort," Cathy said, as they waited in the shadows watching the boys playing chase through the rose bushes. "Very nicely spoken, don't you think James? Lovely dress. I've always liked crimson satin."

"You'd look very nice in it too, my dear," he said. "One day I'll buy you a dress like that."

"James! You're so sweet."

Mrs Robinson reappeared, this time not alone, but pushing a frail old man in a wheel chair. Waving to James and Cathy, she gestured for them to come nearer. So leaving the horses in the shade, they walked towards the house.

"My wife tells me you're looking for work," said the old man.

"Yes sir," James said. "Your son says you need shepherds and fencers."

"Have you worked on a farm before?"

"Yes sir. In England."

"Then you're new to the country."

James looked at Cathy, and by her expression, he knew she would rather he lied.

"Yes sir. We've been here a few months."

"What do you think of the place?"

"Very nice, sir."

"Well lad. My son's right. I do need shepherds and fencers. This place is large. I've a mind to fence part of it, so I have more control over my livestock. What did you do in England?"

"A bit of everything sir. Your son thought I'd take to fencing."

"You've certainly the build for it. I reckon he's right."

"Thank you, sir."

"I pay my fencers two shillings a week, plus rations. Would you be prepared to work for that?"

"Yes sir. Indeed I would."

"What about your wife. Would she like work?"

James glanced at Cathy.

"Yes sir."

"Very well. She can work in the house. My wife will show her what's expected."

Mr Robinson touched his wife's hand, as it rested on the handle of the wheelchair, his voice weakening, clearly exhausted by the effort of talking.

"Please excuse my husband," Mrs Robinson said, smiling, "he tires easily. He wishes to welcome you to Kimo, and wants to know your name."

"Waldon!"

James blurted out the name without thinking, his stomach churning as he realised his mistake.

"I'm sorry," Mrs Robinson said. "Your English accent. It's confused me. How do you spell it? W O R L D O N?"

"Yes Mrs Robinson. That's right," said James.

At least the name seen on paper would not be mistaken for his own, he thought.

Mr McIntyre, Mr Robinson's manager, directed James and his family to a vacant hut close by the calf pens, Cathy quickly setting about cleaning, making sure it was habitable.

"Mr Robinson won't expect you to work today, Mr Worldon," McIntyre said, as he and James stood in the doorway. "But if you find me in the morning, I'll start you on something. Enjoy the rest of your evening. And welcome to Kimo. I hope you and your family will be happy here."

Although his life on Durra Durra and Mutt Mutt Billy had been convivial, at the start, James sometimes considered he was still regarded by Bill Poney, Elliot, and even Mister Luke, as a convicted felon, serving out his sentence. However, here on Kimo it was different. In the few hours since their arrival, James had been treated with more regard than he had ever experienced, even during his life as a servant in England. Suddenly, he was a gentleman. A free man. Arrived in the colonies to seek his fortune. For the first time, he was on the other side of the fence. An honest working man. Not a person to be feared, watched, and made to feel a criminal.

That night, lying beside Cathy in the darkness, James took stock. Despite assuming a new identity, running away from his past, as well as failing to renew his ticket of leave, he was happy. The woman he loved was warm, and close beside him. Her children, whom he now protected, were sound asleep, and snoring on their cot across the room. He had a job. A good wage, and money hidden. Who could be more fortunate, he thought. And it was all due to Luke. Marvellous, Luke Reddall.

Staring into the darkness, James wondered what his friend might be doing. A week had passed since Whitton's death. Luke would surely be at Port Phillip. Maybe he was already at sea.

In James' mind, he conjured up a picture of a great sailing ship, ploughing through the ocean, on its way to England, her hold bursting with bales of wool, sails filled by a following wind. Standing in the bows, Luke looked resolutely toward his future.

With the picture firmly in his mind, James drifted off to sleep.

Chapter Two

"Merry Christmas, Mr Soame," Captain Taylor said, pouring Luke a glass of wine. "Merry Christmas Mr Carpendale. Mrs Carpendale."

"Merry Christmas, Captain," the couple answered in unison.

Sarah and Eliza Briggs raised their glasses, "Merry Christmas, everyone," Eliza said. "Merry Christmas, Doctor Jennings."

"Merry Christmas, everyone," Jennings echoed, "And here's a toast to a speedy, and uneventful voyage."

Everyone agreed, drinking a toast.

At sea for two weeks, the Diamond was continuing to keep the south coast of Australia in sight.

"How long before we reach the Indian Ocean, Captain?" Jennings asked, cutting into white breast meat on his plate.

"In a few more days doctor, we'll begin to feel the benefit of the north east trades."

"I must say, Captain," Mrs Carpendale said, spiking a roast potato with her fork. "It was so thoughtful of you to bring this lovely goose on board, before we sailed. I've never tasted such a succulent bird."

"My pleasure, madam. I was determined to see my passengers enjoy a traditional Christmas feast."

Sitting at the end of the table, quietly eating, Luke said little, smiling as the witticisms and jokes, bandied around, occasionally catching Sarah Briggs looking at him quizzically through her wire-framed spectacles. It unsettled Luke. As if, she were probing his mind, endeavouring to uncover his secret. However, at her every glance, he smiled, hoping to appear calm and confident.

***

Riding all day, and then camping under the stars, it took Luke a week to travel the distance from Tabletop to Port Phillip. He surprised himself, since he felt little regret, or sentiment at leaving the country of his childhood, perhaps forever, his exhilaration overwhelming any such emotion. Although the night sky still held in its spell, would the sky be as wonderful in England, he wondered?

As soon as he arrived in the port, Luke found a hotel, and leaving Clarence in the capable hands of an old ostler, went straight to his room to bathe. Once clean, and bolstered by a meal in the dining room, he walked to the quay, in search of a ship.

Along the jetty, leading toward an imposing sailing ship, a file of drays waited to deliver their consignments, each piled high with fat sacks of wool. Upon reaching the front of the line, Luke watched a string of men unloading bales onto a winch platform that would haul them into the hold.

On the gunwale, a gang of sailors observed the proceedings.

"When do you sail?" Luke called up to them.

"As soon as she's loaded, mate," one answered. "Tomorrow. On the tide."

"That suits me," shouted Luke. "Any room?"

"You'll have to go to the office, mate. See the sign over there? '*Were Brothers*'," he said, pointing to a row of warehouses, beside the quay.

Inside, the warehouse was cool and dark, Luke immediately smelling the familiar odour of wool. All was quiet, except for the scratching of a quill pen. Consequently, looking about, Luke spied an old man sitting at a desk, entering figures into a bulky ledger.

"Can I help you young man?" he said, continuing to scribble.

"I hope so," Luke said, taking off his hat. "I wish to book passage to England. I understand you've a ship sailing tomorrow."

"We do sir. The Diamond. She's almost loaded. As yet, we've five passengers, so you're in luck, as we only have four deluxe cabins."

"I thought you said you've five passengers?"

"We do sir. But Mr and Mrs Carpendale, and the Briggs sisters are sharing."

"I see. Then who's the other passenger?"

"Doctor Jennings. Do you know him?"

"I'm afraid not. I don't know any of them."

"Shall I put your name down?" the old man said, looking up.

"Yes please."

Opening another book beside him on the desk, poising the quill over a page, the old man smiled.

"Your name, sir?" he asked, his milky eyes gazing at Luke.

"Soame," Luke said, hesitantly. "Luke Soame."

"Thank you, Mr Soame. Twelve guineas, if you please."

He scratched the name into a column,

"We expect The Diamond to sail on tomorrow's afternoon tide. But of course, you may move your trunks into the cabin as soon as you wish."

Luke pulled out his purse to pay the man, but suddenly remembered, that in his enthusiasm, he had forgotten Clarence.

"I'm sorry sir," he said. "My horse. Is there space for him?"

"I'm sure we'll be able to accommodate your horse, sir. At a little extra cost for carriage and feed."

***

"Tell me, Captain," Mr Carpendale continued, dabbing goose fat from his chin with a napkin. "How many settlers were you carrying this time?"

"Five hundred and eighty. And all arrived safely, I'm pleased to say, thanks to my excellent surgeon, Dr Irons."

"You must have deployed very strict rules on board regarding the imbibing of liquor. I read in the arrivals report, the voyage hailed from Cork."

"Indeed sir, it did. And yes, we did. We found rationing the drink, as we did in the convict days, certainly saved us a good deal of annoyance."

"My sister and I read you had a celebrity on board, Captain," Eliza

Briggs said. "Quite a fuss it caused in The Patriot."

"We did indeed, Miss Briggs. We were instructed by certain persons, who must remain anonymous, that we were not to disclose the lad's real name, signing him up on the crew as John Smith. The first mate gave him duties in the galley. But he was boastful, telling his story to the cook, and in no time it was all over the ship."

Everyone laughed, including Luke, although he had no idea as to whom they were referring, and why they were laughing, the conversation moving on to another subject, even before he had a moment to ask.

By the end of the fourth week, the ship was almost half way across the Indian Ocean, the passengers and crew enjoying pleasant weather, a stiff breeze hastening The Diamond at a rate of knots.

Luke was enjoying the journey.

After breakfast at seven, brought to his cabin by his steward, Luke washed and shaved. Then, once dressed, he went on deck to walk, and take the morning air. Having been too young to remember his first voyage, Luke found life at sea a stimulating experience for the senses.

With the ship carving a swathe through the deep blue ocean, Luke strolled the deck, the sun on his face, his nose filled with the caustic aroma of tarred ropes, as well as the sweet scent of teak wood, accompanied by the sound of wind through the ropes, the creak of rigging, and the snap of canvas. He was fascinated to see flying fishes skimming across the ocean, as well as albatrosses and stormy petrels, following the ship. Once having walked, Luke would pay his horse a visit.

Below decks, in the forward section, Clarence was in good company. The reason being, that his stall stood alongside a row of pens; home to three fat porkers, a dozen or so chickens, and a rooster, two geese, a cow, and two very ancient ewes. In fact, it required only a donkey and a goat for it to be a complete farmyard. It also smelt like a farm, Luke keeping his visits brief, only five minutes or less.

For the rest of the morning, depending on the weather, he would idle the time away sunning himself, reading a book found in the ships library, or watching dolphins leaping in the bow spray.

Luncheon was served in the dining cabin, promptly at one o'clock. After which, Luke returned to his cabin to read, and take a nap, dressing for dinner, and joining the others at seven. It was an ordered, leisurely life, unusual and enjoyable at first, except after a month, Luke began to feel fidgety and bored.

The years spent away from polite society had hardly adapted Luke to idle chatter, and small talk. As a result, he was quiet at mealtimes, finding it difficult to converse with his fellow passengers. Living all the while at Mutt Mutt Billy, and Durra Durra, he had existed for the most part, alone. Consequently, Luke was accustomed to his own company, unconcerned whether he was sociable or not. Therefore, his silence and solitude on deck caused Luke to become rather a mystery to the other passengers, especially the ladies.

"Who do you think he is?" Mrs Carpendale whispered, as soon as Luke had left the dining cabin. "He's certainly very chivalrous the way he excuses himself after every meal, just at the time when we begin to gossip. I've not been able to discover a thing about him. How about you, doctor?"

Doctor Jennings shook his head.

"I'm afraid not, madam. He's a strange one. Keeps himself to himself."

"Do you think he has a secret?" Eliza Briggs said giggling.

"Well if he does," her sister Sarah said, haughtily, "he can die with it, for all I care. I think he's stuck up, and boring."

Captain Taylor cleared his throat.

"Mrs Carpendale," he said, "may the doctor and I smoke?"

"Of course, Captain," she said, getting up from the table. "Shall we take the air, ladies? Herbert! Are you coming?"

"Not yet my dear. I'll stay a while longer."

"Very well. But not too much port! Remember your gout."

Up on deck, the women sallied forth, their crinolines brushing against the ropes and cleats, as they strolled along the gunwale.

"There he is ladies," Mrs Carpendale whispered, once they reached the foredeck. "Up in the bow. Look at him. So handsome, don't you think? That dark hair, and those green eyes, as green as emeralds. Oh! If only I were twenty years younger."

"Mrs Carpendale!" Eliza whispered. "You're quite outrageous. Although I do admit, he has an air about him. Romantic. Like a vagabond gypsy king. You know. The sort you see on the stage these days."

"Soame!" Sarah Briggs said frowning. "I'm sure I've heard the name before. But of course Eliza! School days! Lady Soame! Don't you remember?"

"Oh yes!" exclaimed Eliza. "Lady Soame was the founder of our school, Oakwood, Mrs Carpendale. What a wonderful woman. Do you think he's a relation?"

Just at that moment, Luke turned, and noticing the women staring at him, stepped forward onto the deck.

"He's coming this way," Eliza whispered. "What shall we do?"

"Goodnight, ladies." Luke said, passing them. "I wish you pleasant dreams."

Watching him disappear into the darkness, Mrs Carpendale fluttered her fan.

"The nights are getting warmer, don't you think my dears," she said. "I feel quite flushed."

"Come along Eliza," Sarah said, taking the old ladies arm. "I think we should escort Mrs Carpendale to her cabin. I believe she'll need her bed very soon."

From the shadows, Luke watched the ladies go below. It was too hot to sleep. He would have one more pipe, and then call it a night. Suddenly, appearing like a scared rabbit, caught in the light from the lanterns on the poop deck, Luke glimpsed a small youth dart across the deck, then climb nimbly into the longboat, pulling the canvas cover back in place.

"That's odd," Luke said aloud.

Endeavouring not to make a sound, crossing the deck, he reached the longboat, and leaning on the place where he saw the lad disappear, Luke lit his pipe. Even with the creaking ropes, lapping water, and snapping sails, Luke could plainly make out the rustle of paper coming from inside.

"What are you up too, young man?" he said, loud enough for only the lad to hear.

The rustling stopped.

"It's no good," continued Luke. "I saw you jump in there. So I know it's you."

"Don't tell on me, mister," a voice answered. "It's me muvver see, she was desperate when I was sent out. I fear for her, I do. She ain't strong. I 'ave to get home quick, for fear she might die."

Tugging the cover back, Luke peered into the boat.

"Don't sir," the voice said. "If someone sees, they'll find me, and send me back."

In the light from the lamps, Luke came face to face with a lean, sallow youth, and for a moment, they stared at each other, then Luke pulled the cover back into place.

"Who are you?" he whispered. "Why are you hiding?"

"I'm Edward Jones, sir. They put me on this ship five months ago. Wanted to get me out of the way for good, they did. But they can't beat me, sir. I gets em' every time. Off to Australia I was bound. Never to see my homeland, or me darlin' mother again. Cruel sir, don't you think? Downright cruel."

"But what was your crime?"

"My sir!" the lad chuckled. "You're a good'n. Where have you been for the last five years? I'm Edward Jones. Or you might have heard of me as, The Boy Jones. Famous I am. Made all the papers, don't you know, from London to Timbuktu."

"I'm sorry. But I'm still none the wiser."

"Oh well," sighed the boy. "I've told the story so often, I could tell it in me sleep. How much time have you?"

"Enough," Luke said, knocking out his pipe. "It's a warm night, and I've plenty of tobacco."

"Alright sir. But if you don't mind. I'm starving. So I'll have the piece of bread and cheese I've just nicked, if I may?"

While the boy munched on his supper, Luke filled and lit his pipe, the aromatic smoke drifting through the night air.

"That's better," the boy said. "I can think now. There's nothing worse than being hungry. Don't you reckon sir! Here goes sir. I hope you're ready."

Smiling, Luke had a feeling the story he was about to hear, would be worth the telling.

"Me family lived in Islington," the lad began. "Me father was a tailor. He had a nice little business going. But then he up and died, all of a sudden like. With all the rest of his family, and me mother's family dead, Ma went to pieces. There was no money coming in and lots of mouths to feed. You've heard of The Fleet, I dare say sir?"

"I haven't, I'm afraid," said Luke.

"The Fleet! The debtor's prison! Well that's where we ended up, cos mother couldn't pay my father's debts. We were in there for six months. And when we got out, us kids split up, and I took to thievin', ending up in Tothill, the prison in Westminster."

"How old were you?"

"About ten."

"Anyway, Tothill weren't bad. Not strict or anything. So, because I was good, they let me out. All us kids were on our own by now. I didn't know what happened to mother. She could have been in prison, or transported, for all I knew. So when they let me out, I had nowhere to go. Outside the gates, there's a busy road, handsome carriages and the like, you know the sort of thing. I walked west for a bit. Then turned north, and found meself in St James' Place, this bloody high wall to the left of me. Must be another prison, I thinks. All of a sudden, I comes across a little door in the wall. I tries it, and it opens, so in I pop, thinking I might hide up for a bit. On the other side was a yard, across the yard, another door. So I runs over, and lets meself in. Inside I sees a great long corridor, stretching out in front of me, all around smelling of soap and polish, and boiling vegetables. It was nice. Homely like."

Realising Jones' story was appearing to be extensive; Luke leaned on the side of the longboat.

"Off I runs down the corridor," Jones continued, "as quiet as a mouse, until I comes to some stairs. I'm just about to run up, when I hears someone coming down, so I darts into a space underneath, and out of sight. Well, with what I saw when I peeked out, you could 'ave knocked me down with a feather. There's this flunky see, all dressed in white and gold, with a bloody white wig on his bonce, and he's carrying this tray. It looks like gold. He walks away down the corridor, opens a door, and vanishes. This don't look like no ordinary prison, I thinks. Better 'ave a nose around. So, making sure no one's comin', I runs up the stairs, quick as I can. When I gets to the top, there's two big doors, with brass doorknobs, so I open one slowly, and has a quick butcher's. On the other side, is another long corridor. The walls are covered with great big pictures, the floor in thick red carpet. 'Ere, I thinks! I know where I am! I'm in the bleedin' palace! That's where I am!"

Laughing aloud, forgetting for the moment where he was, Luke glanced around to see if anyone had heard. However, the deck was deserted.

"Sorry," he said. "But it's really very funny the way you tell it Mr Jones. You should be on the stage."

"It's queer you say that sir, because Mr Eltham, at The Prince of Demark, wanted me to play his music hall in Graces Alley. But that's another story. Anyway, I creeps me way along the corridor, looking in the rooms that I pass, but they're all dark and empty. Except, I take a good squiz into one, and there's this chair see, big and grand, sitting at the end, all on its own. That's her throne, I thinks. Can't pass a chance like this, I thinks, and with just the light from the door lighting me way, I makes towards it, and sits down. I'm the King of all England, I thinks. Me! Little Edward Jones. After this, I goes on with me exploring, and comes across a great marble hall, with huge columns, and pictures in gold frames, painted on the ceiling."

"Don't let me stop you," Luke said knocking out his pipe on the side of the longboat. Because, realising the story was going to be lengthy, he began to refill it, lighting it with a match he struck on his vesta.

"In the middle of the hall," Jones continued unabated, "there's this grand staircase, that goes on forever. No one's about, so up I goes, as quiet as can be, until I gets to the top, where there's another long corridor, with rows of doors all the way along. I'm just about to run to the end, when I hear one opening. So as quick as a flash, I opens a door beside me, and jumps into the room. It's all cosy inside. A big bedroom, with a lovely fire burning in the fireplace, candles twinkling everywhere, and lots of lovely pictures on the walls.

I'm looking at these, when I hears voices, and the door starts to open, so I scrambles under the bed. From where I am, I see a pair of small dainty feet, in fancy embroidered slippers, walk across the carpet, and stop. I reckoned, whoever's wearing them was sitting down at the dressing table. The door opens again, and in comes a pair of feet in shiny leather shoes.

'Only twenty times tonight, Lady Sandwich. I'm rather tired,' I hears a lady's voice say.

'Yes Your Majesty.' comes the reply."

Luke gasped. "You really were in the palace! Buckingham Palace! The Queen was having her hair brushed."

"Yes sir. And me being there, all a mistake. My fault for thinking it was just another prison. That's what I told the judge. But the bastard wouldn't believe me."

"What happened next?"

"Well sir, here's where me story starts to get sensational, as they say in the newspapers. But seeing it's you sir, and not the press, I'll tell all."

"What do you mean by, all?"

"All the sordid details, sir."

Luke was not sure he cared to hear. But saying nothing, he allowed the lad to continue.

"There I am crouched under the bed, the royal chamber pot next to me ear. Thank heaven's it's empty, I thinks. But for how long.

'Goodnight Your Majesty,' I hears neat leather shoes say, going out the door.

Pretty little slippers, sits on the bed. Off comes the pretty little slippers, and I hear the bedsprings squeak. I wait for the lamp to go out, but nothing happens. Except I start hearing the sound of pages turning. Pretty slippers is reading. Then, there's a knock on the door.

'Come in dear,' pretty slippers says, with such a lovely voice. Like tinkling bells, it is. I peeks out, and sees the door open, and a pair of brown leather slippers come in.

'Good evening, dear,' says leather slippers, in a foreign sort of way. 'Are you tired?'

'Not quite,' pretty slippers says, and I hears the rustle of blankets and the bedsprings squeak again. I'm holding me breath by this time, frozen, daring not to move.

'Oh my dear,' leather slippers says. 'How lovely you look tonight.'

'You always look so handsome to me, my darling,' pretty slippers says, and I hears the sound of a kiss. Not loud like. Just like the tick of a clock. But it was enough for me. What was gonna happen next, I wonder? I covers me ears see. But it all starts goin' on over me head. Rustling and creaking, breathing and panting. Then the bedsprings start going, slow at first, but faster and faster, mixing with the sound of moaning and groaning."

"Stop!" Luke said. "I don't think I need to hear anymore."

"Sorry sir. But that's how it was. Went on for half an hour, or more, until pretty slippers made a little cry, and leather slippers sighed, then everything went quiet. Even though I started to hear the sound of snoring, I daren't move. I'll have to stay here all night, I thinks. And as quietly as I could, I move away from the chamber pot, towards the foot of the bed, where I cuddle up. I never slept a wink for fear I'd snore, and give the game away."

"What happened in the morning?" Luke asked lighting yet another pipe.

"Pretty slippers had her breakfast in bed. Then got up, leather shoes coming in, and them both going out. I breathes a sigh of relief, and waits for a bit. And making sure the coast is clear in the corridor, I scarpers."

"How long were you in the palace?"

"Four days. It was nice. I found a room right up in the roof. A footman's room, I reckon it was, but it seemed no one was using it. I'd sleep all day, and mooch about at night, looking for scraps, and wasn't there some tasty morsels to be had. Food I'd never set eyes on before. Blancmange, fruit, black fishy eggs, grouse, cakes and pastries. Them kitchens and larders was bursting.

"What happened in the end?" Luke asked.

"I gets caught don't I. A footman catches me one night, and I gets locked up. Then the coppers take me off, and I'm up before the beak in the morning. I tells 'im me story, about the things I'd seen and heard, but he doesn't think it's very funny. Not like everyone else I've told since. He says I have to go to gaol, and I end up in Tothill again."

"What on earth are you doing here then?" Luke said laughing. "All that happened when you were ten, didn't it?"

"While I was in prison," Jones went on, "I couldn't get the palace out of me head. It was lovely there. The food was good, and I loved sneaking around listening in on things. I missed it. I sees it, because I had no family of me own anymore, it was like I'd found one at last. Pretty slippers was me mother. Leather slippers, me father, and the Princess Royal, me little sister. When they let me out, I found meself climbing back over the wall. I stayed for a couple of weeks, until I was caught. I reckon me luck run out. But this time, before they sent me down, they took me to see pretty slippers and leather slippers."

"You met the Queen?" Luke exclaimed.

"Yeah. I was taken to her parlour. The bloke who took me, said she sent for me special. She'd heard what I'd been up to, and wanted to meet me."

"What's she like?"

"Small," Jones said. "Real small. I thought I was short, but she's about as tall as me, and I've grown a bit since then. She's very pretty, in a sort of way. Except, I thought she had a big nose for such a little face. And no chin. That's right! She had no chin."

"What about the prince?" Luke asked, by now completely engrossed.

"Very 'andsome he is. Losing his hair a bit. But sports a fine moustache."

"What did they say?"

"Very kind they were really. Not angry, or anything. Just wanted to know why I kept doing what I was doing. So I told 'em, Her Majesty smiled, and said how sorry she was that I didn't have a family of me own."

"So then you were put in prison again."

"Yeah. This time for two years. Tothill again. So it wasn't that bad. When me two years was up, I thought I'd nip up to the palace, and tell em I was all right. But this time, I didn't get past the gate."

"Up before the judge again?" Luke said.

"Yeah. But he was serious and stern, even though everybody in the court was laughing as I told me story, the men from the newspapers writing it all down. The bloody judge brought in a verdict. His words were 'Removal from British soil.' I was to join a ship, and work my passage to Australia. I was given another name, and supposed to use it. The detective who put me on board said I wasn't to breathe a word to anyone about who I really was. Well, can you imagine that? I'm proud of what I did, and don't care who knows it."

"Which ship did you come out on?"

"This one of course! When we arrived in Port Phillip, they got me ashore as quietly as they could. But the word was out, and the reporters were waiting on the quay, though they wouldn't let me talk to them. Instead, I was driven off in a closed carriage, to a big house, and told I was going to work there as a servant or something. It turns out it's a judges house. I wasn't going to be a slave to no judge, so I ups, and runs away, following me nose back to port. A few nights before we sailed. I sneaked on board, and found a snug billet in here."

"And you're going back to England?"

"Yes sir. Too right! I wasn't staying in that bloody backwater. I want to be in London. London's the place I was born, and London's where I'll bloody well die."

"Well thank you, Mr Jones," Luke said. "That was the liveliest, funniest story I've heard in a long time."

"You're not going to grass on me, are you sir?"

"Of course not, Edward. That's not my way at all. It's up to you what happens. And best of luck I say."

"One thing you could do sir, if I may be so bold to ask."

"What's that?"

"It's going to be a long voyage, at least another two, or even three months. I think cook's starting to notice his rations getting short. Maybe you could oblige me with a few scrapings from the captain's table."

"And a bit of soap wouldn't go amiss either, I think," Luke commented.

"Yes sir. Sorry sir. Thank you, sir."

They said goodnight.

Still chuckling as he made his way back to his cabin, and laughing aloud, recalling moments in Jones' story, Luke turned down the lamp.

Chapter Three

A month went by, James, Cathy and the boys settling into life on Kimo Station. There were several additional families on the farm, so during the week, a cart collected the children, taking them to school in Gundagai, Cathy's boy William joining them a day or so after they arrived.

Richard, being too young for the classroom, accompanied his mother to the house, where Cathy sat him on the lawn, in the shade of the acacia trees, while she cleaned and polished, all the while keeping a close eye on him through the veranda windows. Her domestic duties completed, Cathy joined cook, the manager's wife, Hilda McIntyre, in the kitchen, putting Richard under the table, where he could play in safety.

Cathy's cheerful usefulness came in handy in the kitchen, busy there all day, preparing vegetables, washing dishes, and doing the laundry, that is, until she heard the children returning at four o'clock. Then, she would bundle Richard in her arms, say goodbye to Mrs McIntyre, and run down to collect William from the cart.

Occasionally, Cathy prepared James and the boy's supper in the morning, before they were awake. Other times, Mrs McIntyre gave her left overs from dinner, to take back for her family. Whichever way, there was always a meal on the table at the end of the day.

Every Sunday morning, before anyone was awake, Cathy quietly got out of bed, and tiptoed into the back kitchen. It was her habit on

Sunday, once she boiled the kettle for tea, to use the remaining hot water to have a proper wash. Therefore, pulling off her nightdress, and standing naked before the range, she poured hot water into a bowl, washing her face, neck, and then the rest of her.

Today, however, something seemed unusual, since her breasts felt sore, her nipples raised and coloured. She was a little late with her monthly bleed, but that hardly caused concern. Nevertheless, this development surely was confirmation. She was pregnant, and James would be a father. Cathy could barely contain her excitement, quickly dressing, and making his cup of tea.

"James," she whispered, crawling into bed beside him.

"Mmm?" he mumbled.

"Here's your tea."

"Mmm."

"Don't let it get cold."

James turned to face her, his eyes still full of sleep.

"Thanks. What time is it?"

"You don't need to worry. It's Sunday."

"Good,"

James leaned over and kissed her.

"I'll have an extra hour then."

"Drink some tea first. Don't waste it."

Sitting up, he took a mouthful of the hot sweet tea.

"Mmm! Lovely," he said, collapsing back into the blankets, pulling them around him. Nevertheless, Cathy was undaunted.

"James," she said. "I've a surprise for you. Well I hope it'll be a surprise."

"A nice one, or a nasty one?" he murmured.

"It depends."

"What do you mean?"

"Well. You know at the moment we have four mouths to feed."

James sat up in bed.

"You're not!"

"I am."

"How do you know?"

"I know. Don't you worry."

"When?"

"September, I think. A spring baby."

"Ha!" James said. "I was a spring baby. March, I was born."

"Spring here, silly!" Cathy laughed.

"How about that then! You've got me all excited now."

"So I have," she said, feeling under the covers. "We're going to have to do something about that, aren't we."

**

After hearing the news, James took to his work with added enthusiasm, the holes he dug for the fence posts, suddenly taking less time to sink. A week later, James was working across a dry creek bed, when he made a curious discovery.

Working ahead a day or so, it was James' job to dig holes twelve feet apart, the men following behind, dropping in the fence posts, and fixing the palings. Unlike the post men, James' job was solitary. Just himself, his horse, a spade, and a tucker box. Hole after hole went by, James losing count how many. Each the same. Nothing remarkable. Until today.

When James sunk his spade into the soil, levering it down with his foot, the blade normally cut through the dirt like a knife. However, today something stopped his progress with a jolt. So, lifting the spade once more, James sent it back into the earth with some force, hearing a crunching sound, as the blade hit something hard.

It would be difficult to choose another spot for a fresh hole, as the distance between them would be either too short, or too long for the palings. Therefore, he began shovelling out the loose soil, until he was able to see the obstruction.

Peering into the hole, his eyes growing accustomed to the dark, James saw something glittering, instinctively knowing it to be crystal. Partially transparent, faceted into geometric shapes, it sparkled like ice. So kneeling, he put his hand into the hole, and wiped away the soil.

Able now to appreciate its beauty, James marvelled at the way the mineral reflected sunlight back into his eyes. But something even lovelier was catching his eye. Since deep inside, he could see a thick streak of yellow metal.

He could hardly breathe. Could it be possible? No! He dared not even think it. Nonetheless, he might be right. Might it be gold?

James knew the appearance of gold. He had handled gold. Washed gold under running water, and scraped food from gold plates, so he understood the colour well. It certainly seemed the same.

How much of it was there?

Jumping up, he ran ahead across the creek, sinking his spade into the ground. There it was again, before it went halfway, jerking to a stop. Repeatedly, he did the same, covering almost the entire creek bed.

Exhausted after half an hour of frantic digging, James sat on the ground. He needed to think. To plan what to do.

Obviously, he must never breathe a word to anyone. Not even Cathy. He loved her dearly, but she would be so excited, the whole station would know in the blinking of an eye.

Nevertheless, James realised the men with the poles and palings would be along tomorrow, and would wonder why the holes were not as deep, discovering his find.

Was he brave enough to change course? James needed to go back far enough for the deviation to be imperceptible. Coming to a decision, he began refilling every hole. Next, he backtracked for half a mile, or until he was far enough away from the creek for the change of angle to be un-noticeable. Then he dug new holes, repositioning the line a good half a mile beyond his miraculous discovery.

At the end of the day, tired and hungry, James rode back to the creek bed, taking a long look at the place, imprinting it on his mind. It was vital he remember the location. This could be his and Cathy's passport to true happiness.

That afternoon, young William brought his chalk and slate home from school, with a request from his teacher. He was to copy his letters, and bring them back to school in the morning. Consequently, with Cathy preparing supper, James took William on his knee, and helped him with his alphabet. His younger brother Richard, however, also wished to draw on the slate, and began to grizzle. So to occupy the child, James gave him a portion of the crystal he found.

"Look at that, Richard," James said, putting it into his hand. "Isn't it nice? Hold it up to the light. You'll see lots of lovely colours."

Richard did so, gurgling with pleasure at the kaleidoscope inside the prism.

"What's that you've given him, James?" Cathy said, standing in the doorway.

"Just something I found this afternoon."

"He'll put it in his mouth, and swallow it. Give it to mother, Richard, there's a good boy."

Richard handed her the stone.

"My! Isn't it pretty!" said Cathy, peering at it closely. "It's like a diamond. Is it valuable?"

"I don't know. There's plenty where I found it."

"Will it make us rich?" she said, laughing. "Maybe you'll be able to buy me a satin dress after all."

It was Friday morning, a few weeks later, Cathy up at the house, busy washing vegetables in the kitchen. Mrs McIntyre cleaning two large fish.

"They looks like cod from the old country. Don't you think so, Mrs Worldon?" she said, cutting the fish open, pulling out the entrails.

"I don't know, Mrs McIntyre, I was…" Cathy stopped in mid-sentence. She was about to say, 'born here'. How close was she to giving away their secret?

"I was never one for fish," she continued quickly. "I've never seen a cod. Big though ain't he, I'll give you that."

Mrs McIntyre ran a blade along the length of the huge fish, the scales flicking onto the chopping board.

"Look at the monsters head, and the size of its mouth!" Cathy exclaimed. "It could feed the five thousand, it could."

"Back home, fish like this swim in the sea," Mrs McIntyre said, laughing. "Trust them to come out of the rivers here. Tis a remarkable country, to be sure."

There was a knock on the front door, and since it was her job to answer it, Cathy quickly dried her hands on her apron, and hurried down the corridor. Opening the door, she saw a man standing on the doorstep, dressed entirely in black, a stovepipe hat on his head, a white collar around his neck.

Cathy curtsied.

"Good afternoon," he said cheerfully. "We haven't met?"

Cathy smiled coyly.

"I'm Reverend William Branwhite Clarke. The clergyman hereabouts."

"Come in, reverend," Cathy said. "I'll show you into the parlour."

As she let him pass her, Cathy quickly appraised the new guest. For a start, he was extremely short for a man, and his face terribly sun burned and wrinkled. Also, he wore the thickest sideburns.

"Please sit down, reverend," she said. "I'll tell madam you're here."

Once Mrs Robinson and Reverend Clarke had greeted each other, and were exchanging conversation, Cathy went back to the kitchen.

"The reverend's an interesting sort, Mrs McIntyre," she said, returning to the vegetables.

"Isn't he!" answered Mrs McIntyre. "He usually pays a call every six months. He'll stay the weekend, I shouldn't wonder."

By now, Mrs McIntyre had cut the cod into thick slices, arranging them in a pan, ready for baking.

"His parish must be hundreds of miles wide," Mrs McIntyre continued, "with just his horse to get around. I think he's brave, going about on his own the way he does."

"He's a man of the cloth though," said Cathy. "God'll look after himself."

Cathy tipped the potatoes into a saucepan.

"Although, you wouldn't think to look at him," said Mrs McIntyre, "but Mrs Robinson told me, that two years ago he was at deaths door."

She opened the range, sliding the pan of fish inside.

"He was so bad with rheumatic fever in England, his doctors told him to take a sea voyage. So he comes out to the colonies. He must like it, because he's still here."

"Well you're right," Cathy said, putting the pot of potatoes on the hot plate. "I'd never have guessed he'd been ill."

"Right! That's all done." Mrs McIntyre said, shutting the oven door. "Apple pie next. I've apples in the pantry. Bring me two jars, Cathy dear, while I start the pastry?"

"Does the reverend do marrying then?" Cathy said, returning with the preserves.

Mrs McIntyre nodded. "He did three, last time."

"Mmm," Cathy murmured. "And christenings?"

"All the usual things a vicar does. Although, would you believe it! Mrs Robinson tells me the reverend's an expert on rocks, and knows all about minerals and the likes."

"Does he now," Cathy mused. "I can see he's going to be useful in more ways than one."

There was a party the following night, Mrs Robinson inviting many notable families from the district, to a dinner and a grand ball, Cathy and Mrs McIntyre having been busy all day, baking bread, roasting meat, and making dainty cakes and pastries, to provide for the guests.

It was a jolly affair, the house lit up like a Christmas tree, the French doors open, not only to let the fresh evening breeze circulate, but allowing people to spill out onto the verandas.

Folk mingled in the dining room, the table removed, in order they might dance, the table relocated to the parlour, where it groaned under the weight of numerous plates of party food. Everyone chattered happily, enjoying each other's company, after months of solitude on their distant properties.

Cathy was enjoying the party, eavesdropping on conversations, while handing around tasty delicacies.

"When will it finish, Mrs McIntyre?" she asked, as they replenished their trays. "I'm worried about James and the boys."

"You can go my dear once dessert is served. We'll bother about washing up in the morning."

"I've been trying to speak with the reverend," Cathy continued. "But every time I think he's available, someone manages to get in first."

"Why? What's the matter?"

Cathy had her reply already prepared.

"I'm going to ask him to marry James and me."

"But aren't you married already?"

"In a fashion. You see, we were married on the ship. But the captain was so drunk he couldn't remember our names. I thought this time we'd do it properly."

"You poor dears! The reverend usually makes an announcement at prayers tomorrow morning. He asks if anyone in the congregation requires a special service."

"Then I'll not bother him. I'll wait till then."

When Cathy finally arrived at the hut, it was well after eleven o'clock, and with the merry sound of the pianola issuing from the house, she quietly entered the bedroom, seeing the boys tucked up in their cot, James in the bed beside them.

Cathy gazed at him while he slept. He was a good man, she thought, and a fine man with whom to spend the rest of her life. The boys loved him, doing everything he asked. Also, he was a first-class father. Cathy had no doubts about marrying him. James was a wonderful, caring person. And to top it, she was wildly in love, just the sight and touch of him, giving her the shivers. Silently, Cathy undressed, and crawled into their bed.

Feeling the heat of his body next to hers, turning towards him, she put her arm across his chest, his hair against her skin. He moved in the darkness, his arms slowly embracing her, Cathy feeling him hard against her stomach. Their lips met. She had thought to tell him her plan. However, it would need to wait until morning.

***

"I didn't know there were Soame's in Australia," Eliza Briggs said, helping herself to bacon. "Lady Soame had only one son, and he died. So our mother used to say."

The question startled Luke, and for a moment, he was speechless.

"You knew Lady Soame?" Luke asked uneasily.

"Oh yes! Well. Not know her, you understand. We were just girls."

Eliza Briggs was removing the top of her boiled egg with her fingers, sprinkling the shell onto her plate beside the eggcup.

"Lady Soame was the founder of our school," she continued. "Such a wonderful woman. So kind! Everyone always received a lovely present at the midsummer ball."

Luke felt her sister Sarah's eyes, boring into the top of his head, daring him to look up from his breakfast plate.

"Mother met her on several occasions," she said. "She was so impressed. We enrolled in the school immediately. We were two of Miss Baker's first pupils."

"Miss Baker?" Luke asked, hesitantly.

"Our Governess," Eliza said, sighing. "The beautiful and mysterious, Miss Baker. Of course, all the girls had a crush on her."

Luke laughed nervously. This was his mother to whom they referred. The girl who carried him for nine months, enduring the pain of his birth.

"Eliza! Do you recall the other girls in the class?" Sarah said, scraping butter across a thin slice of toast. "They were the butler's daughters, remember. We thought them so lower class."

"Oh yes! Their faces used to make us giggle," Eliza said, laughing. "All red and shiny. Like tomatoes. We used to tease them. Weren't their names Rebecca and Mary Waldon, Sarah?"

Luke looked up, and straight into their eyes. How wicked and scheming they were, he thought. Just like a pair of snobbish schoolgirls. How James' sisters must have hated them, loathing their nasty snide remarks, and whisperings behind their hands.

"Was Miss Baker aware you teased them?" he said.

"Oh no. We only did it when we were out to play." Sarah said, laughing. "We girls called them Beets. Do you remember Eliza, because their faces were so red? I wonder what became of them, sister dear?"

"I wonder," Luke said under his breath.

"You still haven't answered my question, Mr Soame." Sarah continued.

"Was it a question, Miss Briggs? To me it sounded more like a statement."

She glared at him.

"You know what I meant. What's a Soame doing in Australia?"

"Visiting, Miss Briggs."

"Really! Visiting whom may I ask? We know positively everyone in Port Phillip society, don't we Eliza."

Eliza's mouth was full of egg and toast, but she nodded vigorously.

"A friend of the family has a place in the country," Luke said.

"Whereabouts?"

"A long way north. Over the border."

"Really!" Eliza said, able to join in the conversation once more. "Such a wild place, don't you think? We'll be glad to get back to England, and civilisation."

The unbounded snobbery of these women was beginning to infuriate Luke. As a result, when Mrs Carpendale entered the cabin, he saw it as a signal to leave, and dabbing his chin with his napkin, made his usual excuses.

Having enough of small talk, and meaningless chatter for one day, Luke decided to ask his steward if he could dine that evening in his cabin. Subsequently, at seven thirty the steward arrived with a tray.

"Green turtle soup sir!" announced the steward, laying the meal out on the table. "Mutton chops, peas and potatoes; with date pudding and custard for after's."

After two mouthfuls of meat chop, Luke was swiftly convinced there was now only one old ewe in the forecastle. However, he decided the entire dinner, washed down with a bottle of acceptable wine, in the peace and solitude of his cosy cabin, was far preferable to dining with his shipmates.

The chops were so tough, he could barely chew them, and with a copious amount of vegetables and date pudding remaining, Luke decided to make up a meal for young Boy Jones. So covering the plate with a linen napkin, he went up on deck.

"Feeding the fishes, Mr Soame?" a voice said from out of the darkness.

It was Doctor Jennings, smoking a last cigar before bedtime.

"Good evening, doctor," Luke answered. "No. I'm taking these leftovers to the pigs. I've pigs at home you know. It's always been my habit after mealtimes."

Glancing quickly at the longboat, he saw the canvas cover twitch.

"Well then, Mr Soame," said Jennings. "Don't let me keep the pigs waiting."

Luke hurried forward in the direction of the forecastle, and sensing he was out of sight, and in the shadows, stopped and looked back to see if Jennings had gone below. But all that was left of the doctor was a drift of tobacco smoke.

Returning to the longboat, Luke tapped softly on the side, almost immediately the canvas flipped back, and a hand appeared.

"Thank you, sir," Jones said. "I'm much obliged. When I get back to Blighty, I'm going to make it known to certain persons of your kindnesses. Don't you worry sir. Who knows, it might mean a knighthood for you."

Laughing quietly, Luke strolled to the gunwale, taking out his pipe. It was a beautiful night, not a cloud in the sky, a huge moon, glowing deep orange, skimming above the horizon. Below him in the water, surging along the side of the ship, millions of luminescent fireflies seemed to tumble and turn, while overhead the sky was filled with a trillion stars, each as bright as torchlight.

Being a romantic at heart, John Baker would have enjoyed such a night, Luke thought. How wonderful it would have been to travel back to England together. John, anxious to see his family, and Luke excited to unite with his real mother, and receive his inheritance.

Although now, there will only be sadness when he finally meets Emma Baker, Luke having to inform her of her brother's death.

Imagining the encounter, a wave of anxiety overcame him, because, since hearing the Briggs women mention Emma at breakfast, all of a sudden she was reality, instead of an idea, as she had been previously.

The Briggs sisters saw Emma as a goddess. A woman of mystery and beauty, Luke wondering what she would make of him. Firstly, he was to impart the worst news she would ever wish to hear, and then reveal that he is the son she gave up, nearly thirty years ago. Once again, picturing the moment sent a wave of fear through him. Nonetheless, looking out over the dark ocean, Luke resolved the meeting was inevitable. It was his duty. If not for himself, then for

John and Lady Soame.

A wind snapped the sails, and ruffled his hair. There was a change coming, Luke feeling the air freshen, a stiff breeze nipping his face, and whisking the tops of the waves into foam. A storm was approaching. He had better get below.

The Diamond had been fortunate with the weather since departing Port Phillip. Nonetheless, large banks of cloud toward the north west looked ominous, the sound of thunder, plus the sight of lightning, filling everyone with foreboding. Captain Taylor's instructions were to cut the canvas to a quarter, by taking in the topsails. And everything that could be, was battened down. Now all the passengers and crew could do was wait for the weather to do its worst.

Despite making a sea voyage as a small boy, with no concept of a storm at sea, Luke sat in his cabin, wondering what to do. When the storm hit, was it best to sit, or lay down on his bunk, or rather stand? What could he do to take his mind off things? However, as the motion of the ship became increasingly erratic, he had no choice.

Through the roar of the wind, and the crashing waves, the ship began climbing one precipice of water after another, each steeper than the former. Only to meet on the other side, more such waves, in an endless rolling torment.

Sitting by now was impossible. Standing precarious. The only safe position Luke found was lying on his back, gripping the sides of the bed to prevent from pitching on to the deck. Nonetheless, what he found hardest was the inability to prepare for what was coming next. If it were daylight, he would prefer to be on deck, where he could see the next wave approaching. In fact, the experience would more than likely be thrilling. Here, in the isolation of his cabin, the swinging lamp throwing devilish shadows on the walls and ceiling, he felt vulnerable and afraid.

Feeling the dangerous motion of the ship, and hearing the roar of the wind, Luke wondered about his fellow passengers. Were they also frightened? Mr and Mrs Carpendale huddled together on their bunk. The Briggs sisters praying loudly to the almighty, all the while asking forgiveness for their wickedness. Doctor Jennings playing Patience, and steadily getting drunk on his second bottle of port. The Captain standing stalwartly on the quarterdeck, shouting orders to the crew. The man at the wheel, slavishly keeping the ship on course.

What was on their minds, Luke wondered?

All of a sudden, there was a tremendous roar, the wind hurling against the ship, pitching her precariously to port, Luke imagining the spars dipping into the waves.

"We must be approaching the centre of the storm," he shouted to anyone who might hear. "God help us!"

Shutting his eyes, he prayed repeatedly.

"Dear Lord. Keep me safe. Keep me safe."

Climbing mountains, and plunging into ravines, the ship sailed on. Until suddenly, as if a giant hand had pacified the waves, everything became tranquil. The wind ceased. The sea grew calm, and the rain stopped, Luke aware that the eye of the storm was around them.

At Mutt Mutt Billy one afternoon, he had experienced the phenomenon once before, watching with dread a storm approaching, clouds the colour of indigo, the wind so violent it was ripping trees from the ground.

At the time, Luke was sure the house and the sheds would be swept away. However, as he watched the storm from the veranda, gradually everything became tranquil, the dark, vicious, clouds swirling about him and upwards, into a towering abyss. Despite this, around him was peaceful as paradise.

Unfortunately, such conditions are short lived, and soon the ship began experiencing similar weather as before, rain lashing the porthole, wind hammering on the pane. Still, the movement of the ship seemed less violent, dipping a little less deeply into the troughs, and rising less steeply over the summits. Although Luke found the motion more uncomfortable, because he began to feel quite sick.

How many hours of this tortuous movement passed by, Luke had no notion? He had vomited more times than he could remember. So sick, there was nothing more to vomit except yellow bile. Each time he heaved, the pain was agonising, as if every reach brought his stomach closer to his mouth.

Continuing to pray for the storm to end, Luke felt no change for the remainder of the night.

By eleven o'clock the next morning, the sea remained heavy, but thankfully, the wind had eased.

Grateful to be alive, and after cleaning himself as best he could, Luke emerged on deck feeling weak, hungry and listless. The ships conveniences were one deck below, in the bow, and Luke needed to use them badly. Though, approaching the fore hatch, a terrible stench hit his nostrils, the smell coming from the animal pens.

How was Clarence, Luke thought with horror. Could he bear to go further forward, and find out?

After using the heads, Luke staggered through the bulkhead into the forecastle compartments, where a ghastly sight greeted him. It was obvious no one had been near the poor animals the entire night, because the deck swam with water, and every kind of excrement. In the gloom, Luke made out the shape of Clarence his horse, leaning against the wooden divider of his stall. Half stooping. His head lowered, his eyes appearing fearful and exhausted, while his hooves slid under him, at every pitch and roll of the ship.

"It's alright boy," Luke shouted over the clamour of the waves. "Don't be afraid. It'll soon be over, you wait and see."

Back on deck, Luke saw Captain Taylor standing on the poop, in conversation with Mr Chadwick, the first mate. Pitching toward them, Luke climbed the companionway.

"Good morning, Mr Soame," Captain Taylor said. "I'm sorry for these dreadful conditions, but only another hour more I think."

He pointed west, and relieved, Luke saw the reason for his optimism, as amongst the grey clouds, a few patches of blue sky were showing, the sun shining on the ocean.

Suddenly there was a commotion coming from below, and a slender youth darted across the fore deck, and up into the bowsprit, the cook in hot pursuit.

"Give it to me you little bastard!" he yelled. "If I catch you, I'll tip you over the side I will."

"What's wrong cook?" Captain Taylor shouted.

"It's that little bugger Jones! He's back aboard. Stowed away. And he's nicked your lunch."

"Keep him there, Mr Walsh. Don't let him get away."

Following Taylor and the mate, Luke ran the length of the ship, reaching the bow, the waves washing over the side, and onto the deck. Through the spray, he could see the Boy Jones, clinging to the bowsprit, a large meat pie in his hand, cramming as much into his mouth as he could.

"Hang on lad!" the captain shouted. "We'll not be able to save you if you fall."

Ignoring him, Jones continued stuffing his mouth with meat and pie crust.

"Come down Jones!" the mate yelled. "We'll not harm you. You can have as much pie as you like."

Finishing what was left, Jones gingerly made his way through the jumble of ropes, until he was able to jump onto the deck, where Luke expected him to run. However, he stood firm, his face set in a stubborn frown.

"I was hungry, that's all," he said. "I got desperate in the end. I thought I was going to die, I was in need of victuals so bad."

"You're lucky to want food in weather like this," Captain Taylor said laughing. "What on earth are you doing back on The Diamond? We thought we'd got rid of you for good?"

Jones laughed,

"You'll never get rid of me Captain. I'm like a bad penny I'm told."

"Answer my question lad."

"I'm not going to stay in bloody Australia, like they wanted me too," he said, puffing out his chest. "I'm an Englishman, and England's where I belong."

The captain looked at Luke and the mate, and shrugged his shoulders.

"What can I do gentlemen?" he said. "The boy's impossible. You've heard the stories I dare say Mr Soame?"

Smiling, Luke nodded.

"He's incorrigible. I give up." Taylor said. "You can ride along with us Jones, until I've thought what to do with you. In the meantime, you'll resume your duties with Mr Walsh."

Scowling at the captain, the cook led the lad below.

Chapter Four

"May the grace of our lord Jesus Christ, and the love of God, and the fellowship of the Holy Spirit, be with us now, and forever more. Amen."

"Amen," everyone said in unison.

It was announced that Reverend William Branwhite Clark was to conduct the service in the garden, therefore, everyone gathered at eight o'clock, having first breakfasted, bathed, and donned their Sunday best.

The morning sun shone down on the little congregation, and not intending to miss a thing, Cathy insisted her family stand at the front. It hardly mattered to her that she was born a catholic. Cathy's mother never sent her child to a church of any denomination, so whatever the preacher's creed, little bothered her. She enjoyed the words and the ceremony, for some reason feeling comforted by them.

"Brethren," announced Reverend Clark, "at this point, it's my custom to enquire whether amongst you, anyone requires my special services. Therefore, please take this opportunity to inform me of the fact."

There was silence. Who would be the first to speak? Then a man at the back put up his hand.

"If you don't mind, reverend," he said. "We've a son, two weeks old. We'd like him baptised."

"Certainly my friend. Are there anymore christenings?"

Raising her hand, Cathy stepped forward.

"What are you doing?" James whispered, tugging at her sleeve. "Where are you going?"

"Reverend, sir," she said. "I've two sons. I'd like to have them done please. One's nearly six, the other four. Are they too old your reverence?"

"Indeed no my child. No one is too old to join God's flock."

"Thank you, your reverence. But there's just one thing more, if I may."

"Certainly. I'm here to do God's work, and completely at your disposal."

Cathy took a deep breath, and swallowed hard.

"I wonder. Could you marry me and my James?"

James turned to her in astonishment.

"Cathy!" he muttered. "What are you doing?"

"I want us to be married, James," she said under her breath. "Right and proper like."

Cathy looked to where the Robinson's were standing, seeing the old lady and Mrs McIntyre smiling, and nodding their encouragement.

"Trust me James," Cathy said, putting her arm through his. "It'll be alright."

"Yes of course. I'll be happy to," continued the reverend. "We'll have the service this afternoon. Right after the baptisms."

"Would you and Mrs McIntyre care to be our witnesses?" James asked the manager, as the families walked back to the huts.

"Of course, Mr Worldon. And we're very pleased you've decided to get married properly. My wife told me about the fiasco on the ship."

James looked at him vacantly, although said nothing.

"Just don't forget to give me the ring," Mr McIntyre said, going inside his house.

The ring, James panicked. Where would he get a ring? Then a thought struck him. He could use John Baker's, if only he could get it off.

James turned it on his finger. It was loose at least. But years of hard labour had thickened his thumbs and fingers, making it difficult to force it over his knuckles. Checking that nobody was watching, he put his finger in his mouth, and feeling the ring with his teeth, pulled out his finger, gradually squeezing off the ring. Seeing it in his palm, James hoped it would fit Cathy's wedding finger.

Reverend Branwhite Clark's visits were always an important occasion at Kimo, the Robinsons inviting their employees and their families to a special luncheon, presided over by Mr and Mrs Robinson. Accordingly, in the garden, as the clock struck noon, folk gathered around hastily erected trestle tables and benches, to celebrate the half-yearly visit of the reverend.

Women hurried back and forth from the house, carrying trays of food, gradually filling the tables with hams, roast chickens, barons of beef, and bowls of steaming vegetables. Everyone then enjoyed a great feast. Mr Robinson however specified that alcohol be excluded, cold cordial being the order of the day.

After the meal, it was time to perform the ceremonies, the families of the children being baptised assembling beside a table positioned in the shade of trees, on it a white china bowl filled with water. As one child after another came forward, Reverend Clark performed the baptism, dipping his fingers into the water, and then making the sign of the cross on each applicant's forehead.

Cathy and James were the only couple to be married that day. However, it was an indication as to the strength of the Kimo community that everyone chose to stay and take part.

Listening as the reverend began the service, James gazed into Cathy's eyes, marvelling at the treasure he had found. He was to marry an incredible woman. She had arranged everything. He would never have had the courage to speak up the way she did. Almost certainly, not even having the bravery to ask her to marry him, in case she said no. Cathy was a wonderful woman. Beautiful, as well as strong and clever.

"You may kiss the bride," James heard Reverend Clark say, and bending his head James and Cathy's lips met to the applause of the entire community.

"I couldn't help noticing your accent, my son," Reverend Clark said, as he and James appreciated their glasses of ice-cold cordial. "You've a Suffolk accent, I believe."

James was taken aback. Since arriving at Kimo, he made certain that everyone believed he issued from Somerset. How then was he going to lie to a clergyman? Swallowing hard, James confessed.

"Yes sir. I suppose I have. My family moved to Bath when I was a lad. But Suffolk's where I was born."

"Bless my soul!" the reverend chuckled. "Me too! I hail from East Bergholt. How about you?"

"Thurlow, sir."

"Ah! A little way from there, I fear. Although, not far from The Stour, is it not?"

"Yes sir."

"Then we do have that in common, at least."

"Have you been in Australia long, sir?" James asked.

"Almost three years," answered the reverend. "When I first arrived, Archdeacon Broughton wished me to take over the chaplaincy of Saint Peters in Campbelltown, the Reverend Reddall having lately passed away."

Hearing the name, James felt his stomach leap, yet managed not to allow the astonishing coincidence show on his face.

"I was there a week," the reverend continued, "when they sent me to Parramatta, Governor Gipps wishing me to head the staff at the Kings School."

Cathy, with her boys in tow, was chatting with Mrs McIntyre, but seeing the reverend and James in conversation, she ambled across the lawn to join them.

"I hear you've an interesting hobby, your reverence," she interrupted. "Why not tell us about it, if you please."

James looked askance at his new wife. What scheme was she hatching now, he wondered?

"I do my dear," Reverend Branwhite Clarke was saying. "It's not so much a hobby, more a passion. It bores people, I fear. However, my great love is, or rather are, rocks. And the study of rocks."

"Really reverend!" Cathy said. "How fascinating. You've found an interesting rock, haven't you James. Show his reverence. It's very pretty, your reverence, sir."

Digging into his pocket, James held up the lump of quartz.

"Well!" Clark said, eyeing it carefully. "It's the first time I've seen quartzite in this district. Where did you find it, James?"

"About eight miles away," he answered, "to the north."

"Is it valuable reverend?" Cathy asked.

"No dear," the reverend chuckled, "I'm sorry. Pretty though it is. There's far too much of it around to be of any worth."

"What did I say, James," she laughed. "That's me satin dress gone for a burton. Come on boys! I think it's time for bed. Please excuse us, reverend."

Smiling, while gathering up her boys, Cathy curtsied, walking away in the direction of the huts.

"Now my boy," the reverend said, as they watched her go. "If it's possible I'd like to see where you found the quartzite."

"Of course sir. But it's late. It'll be dark before we get there."

"Then perhaps tomorrow. Just you and me. At eight o'clock tomorrow morning."

"But I'll be at work, sir."

"Alright," the reverend said, winking at James, "I'll give the Robinson's the impression I'm taking an early ride, and meet you here at five."

"Very well, sir. I'm sure that'll be all right. Though why the secrecy?"

The reverend smiled.

"Just erring on the side of caution, my boy, that's all. I'll see you in the morning."

It was raining hard, torrents hammering on the roof. But the clamour was not the only reason James was wakeful. Reverend Clark's words were echoing in his mind. Could he be as excited at James' discovery, as James was himself?

With the thought dwelling on his mind, he watched the sky grow light, through the curtains at the hut window, and trying not to disturb Cathy, crept out of bed, collecting his clothes, and then going out on to the veranda to dress.

It was still raining, and James was worried. On hearing it, would Reverend Branwhite Clark prefer to remain indoors, snug in his bed? James' question nonetheless, was quickly answered, as a tall horse appeared from the direction of the house, on it, a short man, wearing a stovepipe hat, a large bag, and spade slung across his back.

"Good morning, James," Branwhite Clark said, reaching the hut. "Sorry about the rain. I heard it last night, and said a prayer. Although, the almighty obviously thinks we've not as yet had enough."

James laughed nervously as he climbed into the saddle.

"Let's be off, sir," he said, spurring his horse.

Galloping along, eating up the miles, the dawn rising beyond the ranges, James began to form the opinion that the man of the cloth, riding beside him, was no stranger to horseback.

Close to the creek, James suddenly pulled up.

"Of course," he shouted, over the sound of the lashing rain. "The creek's full."

"What do you mean?" Clark yelled.

"I found the quartzes in a dried up creek. It'll be full to bursting."

"That's no matter. We'll dig more holes. Keep going."

On they rode through the deluge, arriving at the fence, the posts and palings, now firmly in place. James knew where he deviated from the line, so turned his horse towards the creek, finding it as he feared, deep, and running fast, all his holes now filled with silt.

"Where was the quartz?" Clark shouted, rain pouring from the brim of his hat.

"Over there!"

James pointed to the steep bank, beside the surging torrent.

"Come on!" Reverend Clark said, dismounting. "Let's dig!"

Slithering his way up the bank, he jabbed his spade into the saturated ground, James hearing the familiar ring of metal hitting quartz.

"Here we are!" Clark shouted. "I've found some already."

James watched while Clark dug savagely, prizing the spade into the ground, levering the crystal to the surface. Holding it steady, wiping away the mud, he peered at it intently.

"Yes!" he yelled. "I knew it! I told everyone it was here. I was convinced. Why should it be in the Americas, and not here."

"What! What?" shouted James.

"Gold lad!" Clarke hollered, holding up the lump of quartz. "Look there! Running through. Pure gold. Pure beautiful gold. You're rich lad! Rich!"

"But sir," James said. "I don't own this land. It belongs to Mr Robinson."

"I'll say something now," yelled the reverend, when he was beside James once more, "I hope you'll hear, and then forget you ever recall me saying it. I like you lad. You're a Suffolk man like me. We Suffolk men stick together. Am I right?"

James nodded.

"My advice to you is firstly, keep this to yourself. Don't breathe a word. You've two options, as I see it. Have you any money?"

"A bit."

"Then ask Mr Robinson if you can buy this block of land."

"But won't that look suspicious?"

"Why? All you need to say is that you've a mind to strike out on your own. I know him. He won't refuse hard cash when he sees it."

All of a sudden, James hardly cared that rain was soaking through his coat and breeches, his boots rapidly filling with water. The reverend was revealing a way by which he could make his wildest dreams come true.

"Since my arrival," Clark continued. "I've been convinced there was gold in the colony, even telling the Governor I'd be searching for it. He said to me, however, that if ever I found it, 'I was to put it away, or we should have our throats cut.' Those were his very words. There's going to come a time, and it won't be far off, when the Government must admit to its presence. They'll need to realise the wealth it'll bring to the country."

Clark looked at James keenly.

"Now put it back, and fill in the hole," he said. "Only you and me know about this, you understand. I'll not say a word. But I said you've two options."

Clark watched James drop the quartzes into the hole, and begin shovelling back the mud.

"Yes," he continued. "You could buy the land, then sit and wait. Or you can quietly take as much gold as you can, then get as far away from here as possible. It's up to you."

Chapter Five

Talk at the captain's table centred on the Boy Jones, and the imminent occurrence of rounding the cape, the former Luke finding entertaining, the latter, and the idea of more rough weather, hardly appealing. Once again, the story of the boy's antics was retold, although, Luke deferred telling the assembled company that he heard it straight from the horse's mouth, so to speak.

As the February days passed, rounding The Cape of Good Hope did eventually become the soul topic of conversation, and after their previous experiences, the passengers, and crew hoped the passage might be calm.

Their prayers were answered, as the weather off the coast of South Africa was in their favour, The Diamond making good progress, arriving at Cape Town one bright morning in early March. After a few days spent victualing, the passengers, and crew enjoying some much-needed time ashore, The Diamond was under way once more, steering a north westerly course, this time, into the southern Atlantic Ocean, exploiting the South East Trades, Captain Taylor setting a route for South America.

Following the coast of Argentina, the weather continuing to be favourable, everyone enjoyed the fresh air, and warm sunshine.

"Are we to call at Rio, Captain?" asked Mrs Carpendale, at breakfast one morning.

"I'm afraid not, madam," Captain Taylor answered. "The bad spell in the Southern Ocean delayed us. We must make the best of the winds, if we're to reach England in a month."

"That certainly will be most desirable, Captain," she continued. "Our son Ruben is getting married. My husband and I would be very upset if we were the cause of any delay."

"What are your plans when we reach London, Mr Soame?" Sarah Briggs asked Luke, her abruptness taking him off guard yet again.

"I won't be going to London, Miss Briggs," he said, avoiding her icy stare. "I'm disembarking at Plymouth."

"Rather a backwater for the dashing Mr Soame." Mrs Carpendale said, darting a glance at the Briggs girls. "Surely the pleasures of London would be more to his liking."

"I've business in that part of the country."

Luke hoped his answer would curtail further interrogation, but being women, they were inquisitive, continuing to probe for more information.

"Really!" said Sarah. "We know the West Country well. Don't we Eliza. Which town, Mr Soame?"

He was cornered. He could go ahead and lie, but to what end. Who were these women anyway? Once he leaves the ship, he will never see them again. They were bored, and because he had refused to act in accordance with their silly games, were mystified and curious about him. He would tell the truth, and enjoy their reaction.

"Bath," he said, unhurriedly buttering a slice of toast.

"Really!" Eliza said, looking sharply at her sister.

"Yes," Luke continued. "I'm visiting friends at Oakwood House."

Glancing at the sisters, he saw with pleasure that Eliza was blushing, while Sarah sat stiff and upright, her lips stretched in a tight smile.

"Friends?" Sarah said, in a voice sounding like breaking ice.

"I'm visiting Miss Baker, the head mistress of the school. And more than likely will pay a call on the butler of the house. It happens he's the father of a very dear friend of mine."

In a fluster, the girls rose from the table.

"If you'll excuse us, Captain," Sarah said, glaring at Luke. "We must write up our journals. We're falling terribly behind, are we not Eliza dear."

With that, they flounced out of the cabin.

Luke smiled at the Captain and Mrs Carpendale, who were both perplexed by the girl's sudden departure. Still, as in the best society, the event was quickly forgotten, and conversation resumed. Shortly, however, there was a knock on the door, and the first mate entered.

"Sorry to interrupt, Captain," he said, tugging his forelock. "But I thought you'd like to know, the Emma Eugenia is off the port bow."

"Thank you, Mr Chadwick. Could you signal, and ask her to heave to? This could well be a solution to our problem."

***

Finding it impossible to get the Reverend Clark's words out of his mind, James battled with his conscience for days afterwards. Should he quietly plunder as much gold as he could, and sneak away? No one would be the wiser, because who would know he had taken any, when no one knew there was any to take. There again, should he ask Mr Robinson to buy the land, arousing suspicion from others on the station?

His principles told him he should do the latter, but his heart said take the gold, and run.

Night after night, James lay in bed, tossing, and turning, mulling the problem in his mind. Robinson was an old man. He would probably die within the next few years, James thought, and in due course, his son would profit from the gold discovered on Kimo. Whatever James did, everything would come to Jim Robinson in the end.

James was uneasy however. Never having stolen anything in his life, taking the gold would feel like stealing. 'But you found it,' a voice in his head kept repeating. 'It should be yours.'

Several days later, with his work done, James decided to ride to the creek. Arriving there, he wandered around, hands in his pockets, unsure of what to do. There was Cathy, as well as the boys and the new baby to consider, he thought, kicking the red soil. What a difference it would make to their lives. Instead of grasping and toiling for every penny, they could lead a life of leisure. Not only them, but also generations of the family to come.

There was too much to lose, if he tarried longer, resolving to begin digging the following evening.

"Where've you been, James?" Cathy asked, as he sat down to supper. "You're half an hour late."

"Sorry dear," said James, thinking fast. "I took a ride. I wanted to look over the fences we put up last week. I'll need to work on them in the evenings. If that's alright?"

"I suppose so. Work's work after all."

The next day, an hour or so before sunset, James rode away from the farm, a sack over Dan's withers, and a spade across the saddle. Lastly, making sure no one saw him leave, he reached the creek an hour later. The previous heavy rain, continued for several days, but eventually abated, the sun having since baked the creek mud, cracking it into a maze of fissures. Knowing exactly the spot where he would begin digging, and leaving Dan grazing on scrub, James headed to the place, and throwing the sack on the ground, sunk his spade into soil.

Hearing the familiar sound, feeling the spade hit the quartz, his excitement increased, James doing the same as Reverend Clark, by wedging the blade around the edge of the hard mineral, levering it with his foot. Then, dragging it gradually through the earth, he knelt, and shaking off the earth, peered at the crystal. Except there was nothing inside. No streak of yellow. No glittering thread. Only a grey lump of worthless mineral.

Digging repeatedly, each time it was the same.

The sun was setting. He must leave. Otherwise, it would be dark before he would reach home. There was always tomorrow, he told himself.

Every night, for the remainder of the week, James revisited the creek, inevitably returning empty handed.

"This job of yours, James," Cathy said. "How long's it going to last? The boys and I are getting lonely of an evening."

"I'm sorry, Cathy," he said. "It's turning out to be more difficult than I thought."

Secretly James was beginning to think he had dreamt the entire episode, the only thing keeping him sane, the knowledge that Reverend Clark had witnessed his find. Of course, the gold was there. It was just a matter of finding it again.

One morning, a few weeks later, James found himself near the creek. Robinson's men were building a shearing shed close by, James digging holes for the holding pens. Cathy always packed his tucker box with tasty somethings, so he decided to ride over to the creek, and have his dinner.

With Dan grazing on scrub close by, James sat in the sun, chewing on a cold mutton damper, studying the landscape, and the area covered by his diggings. He shook his head in bewilderment. Where was the seam? Surely, it must still be where he first discovered it. Nonetheless, there was no sign. It was as if it had moved.

All of a sudden, it hit James like a thunderbolt.

Of course! The rain shifted the soil. The torrent of water eroded one side of the bank, while building up the other. What looked to James like his original site of discovery was now transformed. He must imagine how it appeared before the storm.

Standing up, James' eyes searched the barren rocky landscape for a clue, looking opposite to where he had concentrated previously. Then suddenly, he saw a glint. A flash amongst the rocks on the opposite bank. Shimmering in the sun. There one minute. Gone the next.

Moving near to where it had been, James saw it appear again. A glitter. A sparkle. Like a mirror, or a piece of broken glass, reflecting sunlight back into his eyes.

Swallowing the half-chewed mutton, James staggered down the bank, and out onto the dry crazed mudflat, where, squinting in the glare of the sun, he searched the rocks and rubble. There it was again, shining, deep in a fissure. Stumbling towards it, keeping the reflection steady in his eye, the nearer he became, the more he saw. Until finally, there it was, half embedded in grey quartzite. An exquisite nugget of pure gold.

About the size of a small melon, it was as clean as if it had been under a shower of rain. Kneeling, James reached out, caressing it.

Running his fingers over the smooth surface, which, having absorbed the rays of the sun, was almost too hot to touch.

James was spellbound, only the sound of Dan scraping his hoof on the mud, waking him from the enchantment.

"All right boy," he said. "I know. You're thirsty. We'll be off in a minute."

His fingers clawed at the lump of quartz, twisting it this way and that. And once free of mud and rubble, James lifted the crystal and gold, wrapping it in his arms. It was incredibly heavy. Thirty pounds at least. Therefore, taking its weight, he staggered over to Dan standing panting in the heat, laying the treasure on the ground.

"Well boy! Will the saddle bag be big enough, I wonder?" he said, tugging at the straps. "I hope so. Otherwise I don't know what we're going to do."

Realising he would need to remove the saddle, in order to fit the rock into the bag, James did so. And after a deal of pushing and pulling, managed to get the nugget inside the saddlebag, although he was unable to fasten the straps. Furthermore, returning the saddle to Dan's back, called for all of his strength. Then breathing hard, James secured the horse's girth.

"Cooee!" a call came from a way off. "Cooee!"

Peering into the distance, through a shimmering mirage, James saw a man riding towards him, and from the glare of his white panama hat, knew him to be the manager, Mr McIntyre.

"How are the blokes getting on with the shed?" the manager asked, when he drew near.

"Not bad, Mr McIntyre."

James quickly picked up his tucker box, swinging it over the saddle, covering as best he could, the protruding lump of quartz.

"I reckon they've almost finished."

Once he was sure everything was secure, James pulled himself into the saddle.

"What are you doing out here?" McIntyre shouted, as they rode back to the shed.

"Having a bit of dinner." James answered.

"Funny place. Not a bit of bloody shade for miles around."

"Well sir," James said, thinking fast. "Since the reverend's visit, I feel closer to God. Sometimes I need to find a quiet place where I can gather my thoughts and pray."

Mr McIntyre cleared his throat nervously.

"Sorry, Mr Worldon. I had no idea."

James could hardly contain his excitement on his return to the hut, the question whether to tell Cathy, or remain silent his main preoccupation. Cathy had already fed the boys, because, while unsaddling Dan, James could see William and Richard, playing chase on the veranda, the older boy always the trooper, Richard forever the bushranger.

Leaving Dan in the paddock, James carried the saddle, and its treasure into the shed at the back of the hut, where, searching the gloom, he saw nowhere safe enough to hide it. Burying it would be the best option, James thought. Though, would he bury it before showing it to Cathy? Aware he would be unable to keep the secret from her for long, he left the saddle on the bench, covering it with a sack, shutting and padlocking the shed door.

"Here you are!" Cathy exclaimed, as James entered the hut. "I heard you ride up. What've you been doing in the shed? You're never usually in there that long."

What an inquisitive soul, James thought, always noticing anything out of the ordinary.

"I needed to do something."

"You look flushed," she said, putting her hand on his forehead. "Sure you're not coming down with the fever?"

"I've been in the sun, that's all. What's for supper?"

James sat at the table.

"Mutton stew."

Cathy looked at him seriously for a moment and sat down in the chair opposite his, taking hold of his hands.

"James," she said softly, "are you sure you're alright? You've been so quiet and distant lately. And don't think I haven't noticed you've not been sleeping."

James was silent, unsure how to begin.

"I know when you're asleep," she went on. "Every time I wake, and listen for the boys, there you are tossing and turning."

"I'm sorry. I've had a lot on my mind."

"You don't regret marrying me, do you? I rushed you into it. I should have told you."

"Of course not," he said, gently squeezing her hand. "It was a wonderful surprise."

"Then it's the baby. You're worried we won't be able to afford the baby."

"No. Nothing like that."

James stood up, and walking around the table, looked down at her.

"It's just that I've found…"

"What?" Cathy said, jumping up. "You've found somebody else. I knew there was a reason for these late nights."

"Of course I haven't," he said, taking her in his arms. "I've found something. I want you to see it, before I bury it."

"Whatever is it?" she said, with a mixture of horror and happiness in her voice.

"Get a candle and matches, and come outside."

Doing as he asked, firstly checking on the boys, Cathy followed James to the shed, watching him unlocked the door, and push it open.

"Go inside, and light the candle," he said.

The smell of grease and leather greeted her, as she stepped into the darkness.

"James," she said, shivering. "I'm frightened. What's going on? What have you found? It's not alive is it?"

"No," he laughed, joining her. "Just light the candle."

As it flickered into life, an orange glow filled the shed, lighting every corner.

Cathy shrieked.

"There're spiders in here, James! You know how I hate spiders."

Taking her hand, he led her to the bench.

"Is this it?" she said. "It's just your old saddle, covered with a sack. I thought you'd found something new."

"Shush!" he whispered.

Taking away the sack, James slowly pulled back the flap of the saddlebag.

Cathy gasped.

"James! Is it?"

"Yes."

"Are you sure?"

"Reverend Clark thinks it is. And he should know."

"James it's beautiful. Can I touch it?"

"Of course."

James watched her reach out, her quivering fingers gently gliding over the gold.

"Now you can understand why I've been quiet and distant," he said. "I found it a few days before the reverend turned up. When I showed him, he told me to cover it up. Then I lost it."

"That's why you've been working so late."

James nodded.

"It's like a dream come true." Cathy whispered. "We can have everything we've ever wanted."

"We will. One day."

"What do you mean?"

"Clarke told me the government won't accept anyone discovering gold. He said they're frightened there'll be a gold rush, that'll take people away from the land, and into the gold fields."

"Although, that's what'll happen?" Cathy said, frowning.

"Exactly. So we're going to wait. If we up and scarper, without a by your leave, people might get suspicious. Or if we try to sell the gold, they'll want to know where we found it, and then Robinson will claim it as his."

Cathy listened to him, the candle in her hand, illuminating their faces.

"We're going to keep quiet," James went on, putting his arms around her. "When the time comes, and gold is officially discovered, then we'll make our move."

"But when will that be?"

"Who knows? Maybe next week. Next year. Or in ten years?

Whatever happens, we know we have it."

He drew her close, and held her tight.

"We're happy, aren't we Cathy?"

She nodded.

"We're going to have a baby, and maybe have more."

"I hope so, James," she said, tears welling in her eyes.

"When we're ready we'll go far away, and sell the gold. We'll say we found it somewhere no one's ever heard of."

"Then our life will really begin."

"But will it? I care little for the gold. I already have my treasure. She's here in my arms. The gold is just something extra. One day our passport to a life of freedom and leisure."

"You promise me though, James," Cathy said, looking into his eyes, "when that day comes, you'll buy me a crimson satin dress?"

Smiling, he kissed her.

"I promise. And you'll look like a duchess my darling, I'll make certain of that."

For a moment, standing there in the candlelight, James fancied he was at Thurlow again, standing at the front door, his wife on his arm, and his children beside him.

What a day that will be he thought. What a day.

Chapter Six

It is a thrilling spectacle when two ships pass each other on the high seas, as it is easy to forget the magnificent sight of a ship in full sail, when one is on one's own vessel, and alone in a vast expanse of vacant ocean. Like The Diamond, Emma Eugenia was half way towards her port of destination, sailing from Woolwich on the 16th November, bound for Hobart Town, carrying one hundred and ninety one, female convicts.

To Luke, standing with the Captain and Mr and Mrs Carpendale on the poop, she made a splendid picture, cutting a path through the sea, her bow spray shining white against the blue of the ocean, her sails stark against the cobalt sky.

With a seaman aboard, running up flags, a multitude of colours fluttering gaily in the breeze, Luke watched as both ships changed course, and steered toward each other.

"Breakout the longboat, Mr Chadwick!" ordered the Captain. "And ask a man to bring Mr Jones on deck."

Luke smiled, realising the Captain's intentions.

"We'll scupper any plans the lad has for getting back to Blighty," Captain Taylor said, laughing. "Her Majesty will be most grateful, I'm sure."

The longboat and oarsmen were winched over the side, the sight of a seaman escorting Edward Jones from below, catching Luke's attention.

"Some of the crew got together, collecting clothes for the lad," Captain Taylor said. "He's not a bad'n, just too crafty for his own good."

"Let's hope he stays put this time," Mr Carpendale said.

Suddenly Luke had an idea.

"Could you hold on one minute, Captain?" he said. "There's something I must do."

Hurrying to his cabin, he quickly returned carrying his panama hat.

Jones was standing beside the gangway, about to climb down the ladder into the boat.

"Here lad!" Luke said, giving him the hat. "It'll be of little use where I'm going. But you'll certainly need it. Anyway, I hope it brings you luck. After all, it's to the lucky country you're bound. Don't give it up too hastily. It's a wonderful place. You'll see."

"Thank you, sir," Jones said. "I'm much obliged. And thank you for your kindness. I'll do as you say. Who knows! Maybe there is a life for me there. The best of luck to you sir, you're a gent, good and proper."

Jones scrambled down the side of the ship, and into the longboat. And as the oarsman pulled on the oars, Luke saw him don the Panama, holding it resolutely as the longboat steered a course toward Emma Eugenia. Then, looking closely, the white hat was all Luke could see, as the lad climbed aboard, disappearing amongst the maze of masts and rigging.

It pleased Luke to think a little piece of him was going back. He could not deny Australia was still his home, after all. Nevertheless, he must travel on to other worlds, with his destiny to fulfil.

***

"Where are all the other Perkins's?" Luke asked, looking around the dingy office, all the while listening to Mr Perkins sifting through mountains of documents on the dusty shelves.

"My father and grandfather died many years ago, Mr Soame," Mr Perkins said. "They made me a partner when I was a man in my thirties. In those days, Lord and Lady Dobson lived at Oakwood."

Sitting in the musty leather armchair beside the window, Luke watched the old man's crooked fingers darting over sheets of paper, and hundreds of envelopes.

"I know I had it here somewhere," he said. "I saw it only last year."

Unable to decide whether the knot in his stomach was due to the irritation of waiting for the old solicitor to find Lady Soame's letter, or the anxiety of being so close to finally realising his dream, Luke turned his gaze to the grimy window, and into the street below.

It was still early, the gas lamps shining on the wet cobblestones, a steady drizzle falling from a steel grey sky. A milk cart was drawn up at the curb side, a milkman collecting metal churns from the entry of each house along Belgrave Terrace, returning from the cart with churns brimming with fresh milk.

Since his arrival in England, Luke was continuing to find odd the closeness and smallness of things around him. Coming as he did from a land of infinite horizons, and endless skies, the little amount of England he had already seen, he found pretty, yet circumscribed and claustrophobic.

It was a Sunday, and the last day of March when the Plymouth pilot came aboard, steering The Diamond safely past Eddystone Rocks, through The Breakwater, leaving her anchored off the northern shore of St Nicholas's Island.

Feeling excited, and with little sadness at leaving his fellow passengers, Luke quickly packed his belongings, arranging with Captain Taylor to go ashore.

So within the hour, a harbour tug arrived to carry Luke and his horse to the jetty.

After four months at sea, the stillness of his bedroom at The Dolphin Inn was disconcerting. The motion of the ship was so imprinted on Luke's mind it seemed the room was bucking and rolling on the high seas. As a result, with Clarence, tethered to the back, Luke was glad to climb into the Bath mail coach the following morning, pleased to be experiencing the sensation of movement once more.

With the scenery passing by the window, a landscape of rolling hills, copses, and small fields, to Luke, the labyrinths of hedgerows and walls of stone seemed unfamiliar. Furthermore, instead of the shining, elegant white gum tree trunks, to which he was accustomed, thick brown trunks of oak trees replaced them, their wide canopy of branches, already sprouting an early sprinkling of green spring leaves. Quaint villages came and went, with rapid haste and frequency, each claiming an ancient church, plus an inn or two.

Crossing rivers and streams, up hills and down dales, the coach journeyed on, until the dark ominous mass of Dartmoor, loomed ahead on the horizon.

Higher and higher, they climbed, the air turning damp and cold. And with no adequate clothing for such weather, Luke huddled in the corner, feeling colder than he had ever been before, until that is, a thoughtful travelling companion lent him a scarf. Thanking him, and in a desperate bid to keep warm, Luke wrapped it around his face and neck, while pushing his hands deep into his jacket pockets.

Rain and mud spattering the pane of the coach window obliterated any view Luke might have of the moor. But he hardly worried. It sounded a dreadful place, according to the conversation his travelling companions were having.

As evening drew on, the coach approached the city of Exeter, and since it was the first time Luke had seen such an English city, he was fascinated to observe the ancient black and white, timber framed houses, and majestic cathedral, as the coach rolled and rattled through the ancient gate in the crumbling city walls.

After a supper at The White Hart Inn, nestled within the peal of the cathedral bells, then a sound sleep in a comfortable bed, afterwards a hearty breakfast, Luke was back inside the coach, and prepared for the next leg of the journey.

Luke noticed a distinct change in the landscape once Exeter was left behind, the hills, and pastures of Devon now exchanged for flat meadowland, slow meandering rivers, and the wide drainage ditches of the Somerset Levels. Rolling along at a good rate, the coach made steady progress. And as dusk began to fall, Luke and his fellow travellers were at last able to glimpse the southern outskirts of Bath.

By this time, Luke and the man who lent him the scarf were on good terms.

"Where are you lodging?" asked the man.

"I've no idea," Luke said, as the coach clattered over the cobbles of an old stone bridge.

"Do you recommend anywhere in particular?"

"I always lodge at Mr Hayward's, in South Parade. It's near the centre of the city. The beds are comfortable, the rooms spacious, and the board excellent."

"It sounds just the place. How about a tailor?"

"Marshall and Lord, of Milsom Street. I wouldn't go anywhere else."

From that moment, everything Luke saw beyond the coach window amazed him, from the gas lamp's shimmering green light, to the elegant facades of houses passing by, some windows aglow, allowing him a glimpse of the graceful interiors.

So entranced was he, Luke endeavoured to recall if he had ever seen the like.

Sydney was the only large town he knew, but was small and simple compared to this grand city, with its wide streets, bounded by opulent terraces and stately mansions.

Mr Kinchela's house on Hyde Park was grand and comfortably furnished, although simple, compared to the ornate interiors Luke glimpsed as the coach sped along.

The nearer they came to the centre, the more shops lined the street, brightly lit windows showing off their wares. Fashionable hats, gowns, and bonnets. Fine lace shawls, and dainty shoes. Everything displayed on glass stands, or stiff mannequins. Grocery shop windows, brimming with ripe cheeses, darkly smoked sides of bacon, and juicy legs of ham. Then butcher shops, skeins of sausages hanging on hooks, beside carcasses of pigs and mutton. Luke stared at everything in astonishment, since to him it was paradise, a wonderland of colour, light, and extravagance.

The following morning, after breakfasting at Haywood's, and a short visit to Clarence in the stables, Luke made his way to Milsom Street, and to Marshall and Lord's establishment. There, an assistant measured him for two new suits of clothes. Next, it was time for a haircut and shave, after which, he felt well prepared to meet Mr Perkins. Subsequently, with a feeling of happy expectancy, he sought his way through the maze of crescents and squares, finally arriving at Belgrave Terrace.

"Here it is!" old Perkins exclaimed. "I knew I'd find it somewhere."

Luke turned away from the window.

The old man was holding a vellum envelope, his fingers shakily breaking the thick red seal. Then, sitting at the desk, he slowly took out the content, unfolding it.

In the ensuing silence, while the old man read the letter, the ticking clock on the wall kept abreast with the beats of Luke's heart.

Seeming like a lifetime to Luke, Mr Perkins finally laid the letter down, and peered at him coldly over his spectacles.

"Now may I see your letter, Mr Soame?"

Luke passed him the letter addressed to Mr Perkins and his late departed father, and grandfather. The old man broke the seal, and took out the letter, pushing his spectacles up the bridge of his nose with a stubby finger. Watching him reading, his heart pumping like steam engine, Luke wondered whether Perkins was finding the moment equally exciting.

"You say the man, John Baker delivered the letters," Perkins said at last. "He sought you out in Australia?"

"That's correct, Mr Perkins," answered Luke. "Mr Baker said Lady Soame instructed him to find me, and give me the letters. Mr Baker told me it was her dying wish."

"And now you say Mr Baker is dead."

"Yes sir."

Perkins stared hard at Luke, his mouth twisting into a smile.

"Then he would be the only person to verify your identity."

Suddenly, Luke felt a cold chill appear in his heart.

"Yes."

"You can see what I'm getting at I hope, Mr Soame, or should we still call you Mr Reddall."

Perkins removed his spectacles, and rubbed his eyes.

"You see," he continued, "without proper identification, obviously I cannot hand over the title. I'm sure you understand my position."

"I suppose so," Luke replied. "But are you saying I'm lying?"

"I cannot say either way Mr Reddall. The plain fact is, until I can positively state you are the person to whom Mr Baker delivered the letters, I can take this matter no further."

"But how am I expected to prove it? The other person who knows anything about this is twelve thousand miles away?"

"I take that to mean they're in Australia."

Luke nodded, beginning to feel desperate.

"Perhaps we could send for this person. They can then explain the situation."

Perkins began to tidy his desk, returning the letters into their respective envelopes. While watching him, Luke felt a sense of hopelessness overwhelm him.

"I've no idea where the person is." Luke answered.

"Oh dear! Then we're in a fix. There's no one in England able to prove who you are?"

"No. I was six when we left for the colonies. I had an uncle living here, but he died recently. And my grandparents, my father, mother, and sister are dead, and my brother's in an insane asylum."

The old man slowly shook his head, a long silence ensuing.

"Your letter from Her Ladyship mentions Miss Baker," Perkins said at last. "Would she be able to help us?"

"I'm afraid not. She knows nothing of this. She never saw me when I was born, and has no idea whether she gave birth to a boy or a girl."

Leaning back in his chair, his elbows on the armrests, Perkins put his hands together, and gazed icily at Luke.

"I'm sure you're telling the truth, Mr Reddall," he said, endeavouring to smile once more. "But there's a great deal at stake, as you can imagine. Along with the title, comes not only the estates of Thurlow and Oakwood, but also the right to sit in the House of Lords. We must be certain you are who you say you are."

"I can see that, of course," he said. "So what do you suggest I do Mr Perkins?"

"You could perhaps think of someone else in the colonies, who could verify you to us."

"But that would mean them coming here?"

"I'm afraid it would."

By now, flustered and confused, Luke looked out of the window, thinking desperately for a way out. Had he been too reckless he thought, running away as he did without telling anyone other than James where he was going, or what he intended? No. He was still convinced it had been the right decision, cutting all ties, and making a new start. There must be something he could do, some conclusive proof, although as hard as he thought, he found it impossible to come up with an answer.

Therefore, with a heavy heart, Luke closed the solicitor's front door and stepped into the street, the wet pavements and leaden sky only adding to his depression. Walking back towards the city, he pondered on his situation. What had the future in store for him? He dreamt of wealth and position. A life of duty and philanthropy. This now seemed a flight of fancy. His money would hardly last forever, and then what would he do. He must work for his living. But all he knew was farming. Perhaps he should return to Australia. He still had money enough for a passage. After all, he owned property there. But then again, did he? It was four months since he disappeared. By now, everyone would think him dead, and Mutt Mutt Billy and Durra Durra sold.

With these preoccupations filling his mind, gloomily Luke trudged the rain washed streets, oblivious of people, and the goings on around him, until finally, he arrived in Abbey Square, finding it deserted, save for a black carriage, drawn by two black stallions, standing at the doors of an imposing building.

Through the rain, Luke gazed up at the west front of the great church, seeing on each tower, flanking the enormous west window, angels carved in stone, climbing stone ladders. One, Luke noticed was sculpted to appear falling from the ladder, toppling, backwards towards the ground. The image caused him to smile. Perhaps things were not as bad as they appeared, he decided. There must be a way out of his predicament. He would go inside the house of God; say a prayer, and ask him for a solution.

The interior of the Abbey was dark and cold, the only light issuing from a cluster of flickering alter candles at the eastern end of the nave. Walking down the north aisle, Luke listened to the sound of his own footsteps echoing in the vastness surrounding him. After a while, with his eyes becoming accustomed to the gloom, he saw to his left, the wall of the north transept, covered with monuments and plaques, all sad memorials to the long departed.

Suddenly a name caught his eye. 'Soame'. Yes. There it was. On a large marble plaque, surrounded by weeping marble putti, an inscription carved upon it, inlaid with gold.

Luke read aloud the epitaph.

"In memory of Sir Stephen Soame, Seventh Duke of Thurlow. Died in this city. Fourth day of July, in the year of our lord, eighteen hundred and eleven. Sadly missed by his devoted wife and son."

Luke's eyes filled with tears.

"This is my grandfather," he whispered. "My real grandfather."

Staring at the words for several minutes, the truth of his ancestry finally a reality, his attention was drawn to another smaller plaque, lower down the wall.

"My father!" Luke gasped.

Silently, he read the inscription.

'Near this place, lies the body of Sir Humphrey Soame, Eighth Duke of Thurlow. Died in this city, aged forty-two, on the eleventh day of March, in the year of our lord, eighteen hundred and thirty one. A tragic accident taking his life.'

At that moment, Luke realised he failed to ask James the circumstance of his real father's demise. The epitaph said it was an accident. How and where did it happen? Certainly, Miss Baker would know, Luke making up his mind up to see her that very morning.

From somewhere in the depths of the gloom, an enormous cacophony startled Luke almost out of his skin, as an organ began playing deep resonating notes, thundering and vibrating the air, like a thousand rapid drumbeats, with no apparent melody, and simply a discordance of sound. Unable to tolerate the unexpected noise, Luke fled outside into the daylight.

Back in the Abbey Churchyard, the carriage remained in place as before, the horses appearing miserable and stationary in the pouring rain. Sheltering against the wall of the west front, Luke watched the coachman suddenly jump down from his seat, and open the carriage door. A woman appeared on the steps of the building, and running to her with an open umbrella, the coachman protected her from the rain, as she hurried to the carriage, Luke briefly catching sight of her face, beneath her black bonnet.

In her middle years, he thought her beautiful, her golden curls shining, although the day was dull. Suddenly, he had a peculiar sensation, since her face appeared familiar. Except, in an instant, she was gone, hidden inside the dark interior of the carriage.

Then, with rain pouring off the rim of his bowler, the coachman climbed into his seat, cracked his whip, and the carriage rattled across the square, around the corner, and out of sight.

Luke pulled his coat tight around him and his hat down hard, and then ran around the side of the Abbey, across a little square and into Pierpont Street, down which he hastened to South Parade.

An hour later, Luke was riding Clarence, following the road beside the river, until he reached a bridge, deciding it unusual, having never seen one with houses along its length. Yet, once on its span, he realised, the houses were individual shops, passing confectioners, a bookshop, a coffee house, several milliners, and a drapery establishment.

How significant was Pulteney Bridge to Luke's destiny, he was scarcely aware, because on a day, twenty seven years previously, on that very bridge, Luke's journey into the world was about to begin.

Today, however, Pulteney Bridge was almost deserted, the wet weather keeping people indoors. Nevertheless, a few brave souls were venturing forth, hurrying along under umbrellas.

"Excuse me, sir," Luke asked a man, sheltering in a shop doorway. "Which way to Bathwick Hill, if you please. I'm looking for a school by the name of Oakwood?"

The man pointed past a little fountain, to a grand avenue, bordered with graceful houses.

"Down to the end of Great Pulteney Street," he said, "turn right at the Sydney Hotel, then straight on. You can't miss it. I believe the school's at the top."

Thanking the stranger, Luke rode on through the rain, keeping Clarence at a steady trot.

Bathwick Hill certainly lived up to its name, being indeed a hill, and very steep at that. Up and up they climbed, Clarence finding it difficult to maintain his footing on the wet cobblestones. To help his horse, Luke eventually dismounted, continuing the ascent on foot.

Bounded by stately dwellings, as most streets are in Bath, the hill ascended in a procession of terraces, each owning a basement yard, leading to a kitchen door, accessible by a flight of descending stone steps.

Trudging along in the rain, looking down through the railings into the 'entries', to Luke, each appeared a repetition of the other. However, despite this similarity, in passing, differing concoctions of aromas emanated from each kitchen door, and up every flight of stone steps. Here was a house where a cook was roasting beef, and boiling cabbage. Next door, a steaming suet pudding sat on a stove, beside it, simmering, a saucepan of creamy custard. Rapidly Luke realised he was hungry.

It must be almost lunchtime. It would be rude to arrive at the door of Oakwood unannounced, just as the occupants were about to sit down to their midday meal. So Luke decided he would find an inn. Have a bite to eat, and wait for a more convenient hour to call.

At last, Bathwick Hill became almost level, at which point the rows of houses ended abruptly, to be replaced by large mansions, hidden behind lofty limestone walls. One such house backed on to the road, masked by one such wall. Interestingly, Luke noticed it to be unlike the adjacent architecture, observing a belvedere turret, inset with windows, and a red tiled roof.

The house seemed approachable by two entrances in the wall, one wide enough to take a carriage and horses, the other a front door, black, and shining with new paint, and a gleaming brass knocker and letterbox. A solemn stone portico was above the door, a name painted there in large black letters.

Luke read it aloud.

'Oakwood'.

Luke thought himself fortunate as he sat in the snug of the Claverton Hotel, enjoying a pipe of fine Turkish tobacco. The menu said steak and kidney pudding. Therefore, encouraged by earlier encounters with the aroma of steaming suet pastry, he ordered lunch.

Happier than he had felt previously, Luke was unable to decide whether the ale was causing his state of excitement, or the fact he had found Oakwood, and was close to meeting Miss Baker. Nonetheless, by the second glass, he was positively euphoric, having enjoyed the best meal in a long while. Consequently, with a bright fire burning in the hearth, Luke settled into a deep leather armchair to read The Times.

It was not long before he was fast asleep.

The clock on the mantle chimed, waking Luke with a start. Four o'clock! From being too early to visit Oakwood, he was now very close to being too late. Hastily, putting on his hat and coat, and paying Mr Packer, the hotel proprietor, Luke hurried to the stables to collect Clarence.

In no time, they were cantering through Claverton village toward Bathwick Hill.

Luke hastily dismounted, and tugged the bell pull set in the wall, hearing from somewhere deep inside the house a bell ring. A minute later, the door was opened by a serious young man dressed in a black suit, a white wing collar and black tie.

"Good afternoon sir," he said, regarding Luke haughtily.

"Good afternoon," Luke replied. "I'm very sorry for not leaving a card, but is it possible to see Miss Baker?"

"I'll enquire if she is receiving callers," the butler said. "Would sir come in?"

Taking off his hat, Luke stepped inside the hall.

"Who shall I say is calling, sir?"

"Mr Reddall."

"Please be seated Mr Reddall."

The butler indicated a small occasional chair positioned against the wall, and Luke sat down, watching him cross the hall, and climb the stairs.

The house was quiet; the loudest sound the ticking of the grandfather clock in the corner of the hall. Although, listening hard, Luke faintly heard children singing from somewhere far away.

His heart was beating fast. How would he begin? The name Reddall was sufficient to ignite her curiosity. No doubt she would be wondering why the name had returned to haunt her. Not only must Luke tell her that John, her only brother, was dead, but also the man providing this terrible news, was her relinquished son.

Footsteps on the stairs announced the butler's return; Luke standing as the man solemnly crossed the hall.

"Miss Baker will see you sir. May I take your things?"

Luke removed his coat, and handed it to him, along with his hat and riding crop, the butler stowing them in a cloakroom.

"Follow me sir," he said on his return.

The butler led Luke up the stairs, and then along a short corridor lined with framed watercolours. When they arrived at a pair of double doors, the butler knocked once.

"Come in George," Luke heard a woman say from inside.

Opening the door, the butler stood aside allowing Luke to pass.

"Mr Reddall, madam."

"Thank you George."

She was standing at the window, and turning, smiled. Luke was astounded, since it was the woman in the carriage. The lady he had seen that morning entering the carriage in the Abbey Churchyard.

For a second, there was silence between them. Then she spoke.

"Good afternoon Mr Reddall. Please take a seat. I've asked George to bring tea."

"Thank you Miss Baker. That's most kind."

Two sofas bordered the fireplace, Luke sitting down on the one facing the window, while Miss Baker sat in an armchair beside the window.

"What can I do for you, sir?" she said, folding her hands in her lap.

Luke cleared his throat.

"This is going to be very difficult Miss Baker," he began. "My duty is not a happy one I'm afraid."

"Oh dear. Not sad news of your mother or father I hope."

Luke frowned.

"You are their son John, are you not? Your mother and father were very kind to me once. Very kind indeed."

"Well yes Miss Baker," Luke said, already confused. "They died several years ago. There was a terrible epidemic, but…"

"Really! I read nothing of this. I remember thinking at the time that Cambridge had been lucky."

"Miss Baker. I'm sorry. But Mr and Mrs Reddall died in Australia."

Miss Baker was clearly surprised.

"Australia! Really! What were they doing in Australia?"

"The family moved there over twenty years ago. The Reverend was asked by the Governor to begin a new schooling system."

"My word!" Miss Baker exclaimed. "Edwina said nothing of this. Then she always said she'd lost touch with them. This must have been the reason. Dear me though, my manners. I'm sorry John. What must you think of me? You would have been terribly distressed by their loss."

Luke began to panic. What could he do? By not telling her who he was, he was getting into deeper difficulties and greater confusion.

"Australia!" Miss Baker continued. "My brother's visiting Australia. He's been there for almost two years. We haven't heard from him in all that while. Up to some wild adventures, I shouldn't wonder. Maybe you've run into him Mr Reddall?"

This was too much for Luke. Although, at the very moment he was about to speak, the door opened, and the butler, and a footman brought in a tea trolley.

Emma and Luke watched in silence as the men laid the table with teacups, saucers, plates, trays of little sandwiches, and a stand of dainty cakes. Bowing, they left the room, closing the door behind them.

"Miss Baker," Luke began again. "Your brother is part of the reason why I'm here."

"What do you mean?" she said, looking at him inquisitively.

"As I said, this is terribly hard for me. There's no easy way of saying what I have to say."

"Something's happened to him. Some awful accident. I knew it would. I told him when we kissed goodbye."

She stared at Luke.

"Are you going to tell me what I've been dreading since he left?"

Luke lowered his eyes, not wanting to see her grief.

"Sir," she sobbed. "Please don't tell me he's dead! Not my wonderful brother!"

Luke nodded his head, the tears already flooding his eyes.

"My poor mother and father. What will they do?" she said, weeping helplessly. "It'll kill them."

"I'm so sorry Miss Baker," Luke murmured. "He was a magnificent man. He and I were more than simply friends. I miss him terribly."

Getting up from the chair, taking a handkerchief from her sleeve, holding it against her eyes, Miss Baker walked to the window, and stood with her back to him, Luke barely able to listen to her weeping uncontrollably. After several minutes, nevertheless, her sobs subsided.

"What I can't understand," she said, wiping her eyes, "is how you and he met. It's somewhat of a coincidence. I understand Australia's a vast country."

"It is Miss Baker. But your brother was sent there to find me."

"Whatever do you mean young man?" Miss Baker said, turning sharply. "Lady Soame left everyone an annuity. She gave my brother a sum of money. He told me he was going to seek his fortune."

Miss Baker rounded on him, Luke seeing her suddenly grasp his meaning.

"But why should he be looking for you?"

"Lady Soame requested it. It was her dying wish."

"Why would Lady Soame wish to send my brother halfway across the world searching for John Reddall?"

By the manner in which Miss Baker frowned, and then turn her attention to the window once again, Luke could see she was becoming angry and bewildered. He must tell her the truth. Otherwise, she might dismiss him out of hand.

"I'm not John Reddall, Miss Baker."

"What's going on here, young man? I'm not sure where this conversation is leading."

Unperturbed, Luke continued.

"My name is Luke. Luke William Reddall. I'm John Reddall's brother."

"But Mr and Mrs Reddall only had one son, and he was John."

Watching Miss Baker keenly, Luke saw her shoulders suddenly tense, as the true revelation struck her like a bolt of lightning.

"My God!" she whispered, her back still toward him. "What are you saying?"

"You're my mother."

Miss Baker gasped, faltering as if she might faint, using her hand to steady herself against the windowpane.

"And what causes you to assume this young man?" she stammered.

"Your brother gave me a letter written by Lady Soame. In her very own words she told me who I am."

Miss Baker turned to face him, Luke seeing in her eyes a look of anguish and despair.

"I'm sorry Miss Baker. I'm truly sorry."

"You'll have to forgive me young man," she said, looking at him steely, "if I do not appear overjoyed. You must realise that fifteen minutes ago my life was ordered and regulated. Although, in a matter of minutes you have turned it upside down."

Luke hung his head, feeling shame at causing her such grief, unable to look at her, her words lashing at him like a whip.

"For years, I've hidden from the word you've just said. 'Mother'. I'm a mother. How I tried to run away from the thought, but failed. What was it? Boy or girl? Alive or dead? Near or far? Many times, I longed to ask Lady Soame if she knew. But at the last minute, stopped myself, fearing the knowledge would drive me mad. Now, here you are telling me the dearest person to me in the world is dead, and that you are my son, the child I gave away one night. The baby that's haunted me ever since."

Sinking into a chair, Miss Baker sobbed helplessly, while Luke sat in silence, unable to think of a way to console her. But after a while, she blew her nose, and wiped her eyes.

"I'm truly sorry Miss Baker," he said. "But everything I've told you is the truth."

"You've no reason to lie. Lady Soame obviously had a plan for you. Otherwise, she would never have put my brother in such danger. Nonetheless, this is going to take a while to come to terms with young man."

Tucking her handkerchief in her sleeve, Miss Baker tidied her hair inside her lace cap.

"In the meantime Mr Reddall, would you pour us a cup of tea. Suddenly I feel I'm in need of one?"

Luke went to the table, and poured the tea, Miss Baker taking hers without a word. Then, pouring his own, he returned to the sofa and sat down, but aware Miss Baker was staring at him intensely, Luke averted his eyes to the carpet.

"Now that I look at you," she said, "I can see you've something of your father about you. You definitely have his hair, and the same shape face. But your eyes. You've your grandmother's eyes. Your father's were also green, but the shape's your grandmothers."

Luke was embarrassed, her sudden interest taking him off guard, causing him to blush.

"Although," Miss Baker continued, "I'm pleased to see that you don't appear to have inherited your father's impetuous nature."

"Yes," Luke said, trying to restore his self-control. "Lady Soame said something of the sort in her letter. Could you tell me a little about him please?"

"Do you honestly wish to know?" she said, gazing at him sternly. "I'm sorry! But I cannot find a good word for him. He was a rogue."

"That's alright Miss Baker. I'd rather know a little, than nothing at all."

She smiled coldly.

"Where would you like me to begin?"

"At the start I suppose. When you and he became properly acquainted."

"That my dear boy is a tale too ghastly to tell."

"I'm sorry Miss Baker. I'm causing you anxiety. Perhaps then you'd feel better telling me the circumstances of his demise."

"My brother John and your father were not on good terms," she began. "I understand at school, Soame, as he was called, was a dreadful bully. For reasons I shall not go into, he and my brother fought a duel, which it appears your father lost. Ever after, he swore to reap revenge on my brother, part of which was fulfilled by getting what he desired from me."

Miss Baker paused, the memory causing her visible distress. So, finishing her tea, and getting up, she placed the cup and saucer on the table, and walked again to the window.

"Your grandmother adored this house, Mr Reddall," she said. "She'd sit here for hours. You see, she loved Bath, having many fond memories of happy days spent here with Lady Dobson, and Mr and Mrs Reddall, your mother and father. Oakwood was Lady Dobson's house when Edwina first came to Bath; she bequeathed it to Edwina in her will. But sorry, I digress."

The city, beyond the window, was bathed now in the rosy glow of a glorious sunset.

"You'll forgive me," Miss Baker continued, "since what I'm about to say may shock you. When I said a moment ago that your father was a rogue, it was an understatement. He was far from that. A rogue gives one the impression of a man, artful, yet loveable. Your father was neither. He was downright evil."

By the expression on her face, Luke knew she was in deadly earnest.

"I know you're shocked," Miss Baker said, while noticing Luke's reaction. "However, it's best you hear it from me, rather than others. He was a wicked man. Driven by lust, anger and a thirst for vengeance. Not only did he act out his retribution on my brother, but also on John's childhood friend, since your father was jealous of the love they shared. John's friend had a son, and Soame had wicked designs on him. When the lad refused to comply with your father's wishes, he got rid of him, for good and all."

"What on earth did he do to the lad?" gasped Luke. "You're not saying my father killed him?"

"Not quite. But he was responsible in having him transported for life, retribution seen by many to be equally as terrible. Your father made it appear the boy had committed a crime, even standing in court to testify he had seen him perform the deed."

"Where was the lad sent? The colonies?"

"Yes."

Miss Baker turned away from the window, and going to the fireplace, pulled the bell rope.

"I'll ask George to light the lamps. It's growing rather dark."

"What a wicked thing to do," Luke said, as Miss Baker sat down in the armchair. "How then did my father die? I saw his memorial in the Abbey. It said there was an accident?"

"It's true. After the trial, the boy's father followed Soame. I understand the reason was to challenge him, to persuade Soame to retract his evidence. There was a scuffle on the bridge, and your father fell into the river and drowned."

Luke was silent as the picture penetrated his mind, Miss Baker respecting the moment.

"Although he was my father," Luke said after a while. "By what you've said, I think the end was right and fitting."

Miss Baker smiled.

"Indeed, young man. I too believe this, and so at the time, did everyone else. It was a great relief to have Soame out of our lives forever."

There was a knock on the door, and a footman entered the withdrawing room, Luke and Emma, sitting in silence as he moved, noiselessly, from one lamp to the next, lighting each in turn, and thus gradually filling the room with warm orange light.

Once they were alone, Luke was the first to speak.

"What happened to the man's son?"

"Nothing's been heard of him since. It's as if, on that dreadful day, he vanished out of our lives, never to be seen again. He did leave something of himself behind, however. Alice, his sweetheart, had a little girl, but sadly died giving birth to the child. Your grandmother was mortified when she heard the account of your father's merciless act. Consequently, in a bid to make amends, she adopted the little girl. She's been the light in our lives ever since."

Luke was pleased to see Miss Baker smile at last.

"Well, at least part of the story ends happily."

As the smile spread over her face, Luke realised why she seemed so familiar. In a feminine way, Emma Baker was the image of her brother. The warmth in her eyes. The golden sparkle of her hair. The laughter around her mouth, so reminding him of his dear, dead friend. Sensing a lump appear in his throat, Luke knew he was about to cry.

Except Miss Baker began to speak.

"I hope you can understand, young man, why it's a great relief to see you've inherited nothing of your father's temperament. Meeting you today, you seem to be completely sane, loving, and kind. Most admirable qualities for a man to process."

"Thank you, Miss Baker," Luke said.

"What then are your intentions?" she continued. "Obviously Her Ladyship informed you in her letter, that you're the heir to the dukedom?"

Luke nodded.

"Are you prepared for all the responsibilities that incurs?"

"I hope so. But I'm in a fix. My solicitor, Mr Perkins, needs evidence to confirm I am who I say I am, before he's able to grant me the title, and release the estate. I've nothing to prove it. Either here, or in Australia."

Miss Baker smiled again, getting up from the chair.

"Follow me," she said.

After collecting a lamp from an occasional table, Miss Baker took Luke's arm, and led him from the room into the corridor. Silently they descended the stairs and crossed the hall, Miss Baker opening a door, allowing him into a dining room. Here, in the lamplight, Luke saw a large table dominating the room, shining black as jet, at its centre, a lone silver candelabrum, complete with six candles.

Warm light caressed the table and twelve chairs drawn underneath, as well as danced on the white silk walls and dark portraits hanging there. Miss Baker directed Luke's attention to the mantle however, holding the lamp high, its glow shining onto a portrait in a gilt frame.

The painting was almost life size, depicting a young man, posing in a misty landscape.

Dressed in black doublet and hose, he wore an enormous white, starched ruffle around his neck, his black silk stockings, gartered below his knee breeches, his black leather shoes sporting shining silver buckles. A musket leaned languidly against the young man's right forearm, while at his feet slept a deerhound. However, the most remarkable feature of the portrait was the man's face and hair, which was black and shining, comparable to the wing of a raven, and worn to his shoulders. Moreover, a small moustache, and neatly pointed beard adorned his top lip and chin. But, had it not been for these hirsute additions, astonishingly, Luke realised, the man in the painting could well have been himself. It was as if he were looking into a mirror.

"Here's your proof," Miss Baker said softly. "The portrait once hung on the stairs in the Marble Hall at Thurlow. Edwina had it brought here when we established the school."

"Who is he?"

"Sir Stephen Soame. Your great, great, great, great, grandfather. He built the alms-houses, and founded the school at Thurlow, and was Lord Mayor of London during the reign of Queen Elizabeth."

Staring at the portrait, it amazed Luke to see it so life like. The man would be about the same age as himself. Except, he owned an air of confidence and grace that only the aristocracy possess. Completely trusting in the divine right of his position, as head of his house and lineage. Suddenly, Luke felt a surge of pride, recognising he shared the same blood as the proud young man in the portrait.

"I can't thank you enough, Miss Baker," he said turning to her. "May I show Perkins?"

"Of course," she said, smiling. "Mr Perkins could never doubt it. It's positive proof you are a Soame."

Leading Luke from the dining room into the hallway, and turning, Miss Baker took his hand in hers.

"I'd be pleased if you would visit me again," she said, looking into his eyes, "as I'm sure you have a great deal to tell me. I feel you've led a fascinating life so far. Both of us have a great deal to catch up with, before we can call each other mother and son."

She kissed his cheek, and they said goodbye.

His heart bursting with joy, Luke rode back to South Parade.

Miss Baker had accepted him. There was no doubt. It mattered little to Luke whether Perkins believed the portrait. To him, at that moment, the fact his real mother had taken his hand, and kissed his cheek; and that she wanted to see him again, was the most wonderful thing in the world.

Chapter Seven

Hayward's Boarding house was comfortable and commodious, taking up two large houses, numbers five and six, South Parade, the elegant terrace of houses, facing south, as suggested by the street name. The front windows commanded extensive views, offering the guests panoramic vistas across the River Avon, the Kennet and Avon canal, and Mr Brunel's new railway line; this outlook then continuing up Widcombe Hill, to Prior Park, Mr Ralph Allen's magnificent mansion, then across to the romantic hanging woods of Beechen Cliff.

At the eastern end of the parade, behind shrubbery and trees, a grassy bank led to the River Avon, where a small wooden jetty played host to watercraft, which, after collecting their passengers, idly cruised the waterway, passengers enjoying splendid aspects of the crescents and terraces, forming the glorious backdrop of Bath.

The dining room was situated on the ground floor, with three lofty windows, opening to a wide pavement outside, thus, enabling light to penetrate the otherwise, dark room, since the panelled walls were black, stained by years of tobacco smoke, and fumes from the fire. No drapes hung in the windows, rather, long shutters; closed at night, and then, unclipped and unfolded by a male servant in the morning.

Served in the dining room, between the hours of seven and nine, breakfast was a busy time.

"And what will sir be having this morning?" the waiter asked Luke haughtily, his pencil poised over an order pad. "The side of bacon I saw in the kitchen looks delicious."

"No thank you," Luke said, sitting down at the table. "I'll have a boiled egg, please."

"How would sir like it? Light, medium or well?"

"Medium, please."

"And bread, sir?"

"Er? Yes please."

Luke watched the waiter weave his way back through the labyrinth of tables, toward the corner of the dining room, and place the order inside a dumb waiter. Then pulling a rope, the paper disappeared, Luke presuming it would reappear in the kitchen below.

Aromatic pipe and cigar smoke wafted in the air, accompanied by a fragrance of fried bacon and fresh bread. With the morning sun streaming through the windows, casting wide shafts of milky light onto the customers, Luke noticed every patron was male, either tucking heartily into his breakfast, or reading the morning newspaper.

Considering the early hour, each gentleman seemed to respect the other's privacy, conversation remaining at a minimum. All were of varying ages, ranging from youthful to elderly. The old, Luke supposed, were visiting Bath in order to take the waters, desperately attempting to push back the advancing years, and ease their aching joints. The middle aged, he theorised, were men of business, or commercial travellers, skilfully plying insurance, or investments upon the more susceptible amongst the population. The youthful, Luke imagined, were in Bath to make a catch. Numerous widows, spinsters and unattached young women filled the hotels and boarding houses, all of them living by independent means and fat annuities, Luke considering them to be well worth the chase.

Watching the waiter approach, carrying Luke's boiled egg on a tray, he noticed the door open, and a young man enter the room. He stood looking around for a place to sit, and seeing Luke sitting at a table, an empty chair facing him, he headed towards him.

"Do you mind?" he said, as the waiter put down Luke's breakfast plate. "There doesn't seem to be anywhere else."

"Please. Be my guest." Luke said, gesturing to the opposite chair. "But do you mind if I carry on. I don't wish my egg to become cold."

The young man laughed, flicking away his coat tails, and sitting down.

"Of course, my dear chap," he said, at the same time, attracting the waiter's attention. "There's nothing worse than a hard egg. I'll have my usual Lyall."

"Certainly sir," the waiter said, walking away scribbling in his pad.

Unfolding his napkin, the young man spread it across his lap.

"William Cater Denby, at your service sir," he said, looking up at Luke and smiling.

"Luke William Reddall," Luke replied. "Pleased to meet you, I'm sure."

"I've not seen you at Hayward's before."

Luke swallowed a mouthful of egg.

"No sir. It's my first visit."

"Really. And what do you think of Bath?"

Splendid! I've never seen anywhere as beautiful."

Cater Denby laughed.

"Then you can't have seen Paris, Florence, or Rome. Although, I do admit Bath has its charm. But the cities of Europe are beyond compare."

"It's true," said Luke, a little embarrassed. "I haven't seen many places. But when you've lived as far away at I have for most of your life, any city seems wonderful."

The waiter returned, carrying a tray, putting a plate of fried eggs, bacon, breakfast sausages, and fried slices of bread, on the table in front of Mr Cater Denby, placing beside it, a cup and saucer, a milk jug, and a steaming pot of tea.

"Didn't he ask if you wanted tea?" Cater Denby asked Luke.

Luke shook his head.

"Bring another cup, Lyall. I'm sure Mr Reddall would also like tea."

The waiter flared his nostrils.

"Yes sir," Lyall said, raising his eyebrows, and walking away.

"Don't take any nonsense from him, Mr Reddall," said Cater Denby. "He's been here years, and thinks he owns the place."

They continued to eat in silence until Lyall returned, the second cup and saucer in his hand.

"Here you are," Cater Denby said, proceeding to pour Luke a cup.

Sipping the hot tea, Luke took a moment to assess his companion.

Mr Cater Denby was handsome, maybe a year or two younger than himself, showing a fair complexion, yet suntanned. Also possessing a smattering of freckles across the bridge of his nose and cheeks, his fair hair long, reaching to his collar; Luke noticing he preferred the current fashion of waving. Similar to Luke, Cater Denby sported sideburns. His were almost flaxen, however, and well frizzed. Moreover, he wore a moustache, a most continental fashion, perhaps to compliment a somewhat small mouth. Overall, his face was pleasing, open and honest, his blue eyes taking in his surroundings as he glanced here and there.

Luke having finished his boiled egg, took a moment, between mouthfuls of tea, to secretly watch his table companion devouring his breakfast. As Cater Denby cut the fat bacon and sausages with his knife and fork, dipping bread into the egg yolk, Luke noticing his hands and fingers were fine; not at all those of a man who worked for a living. Then again, neither were they feminine. Cater Denby's fingers tapered, his nails were well kept, and polished, Luke observing a gold signet ring on his right hand, although no wedding ring on the left.

Physical appearance aside, it was Cater Denby's outfit that thoroughly enthralled Luke. Since, prior to meeting his fellow diner, Luke considered the suit he ordered from the tailor in Milsom Street, to be the height of men's fashion. Yet, his attire appeared positively conservative beside the assemblage the young man sitting opposite wore.

Over a white silk shirt, and high, starched collar, a crimson silk cravat, tied in a lavish bow, Cater Denby was wearing a yellow and white, striped silk waistcoat, over this, and undone, a deep green, velvet morning jacket, finely cut to the waist. Glancing nonchalantly beneath the table, Luke noticed a pair of tapering, pale grey woollen trousers, finishing in a pair of neat, shining, pointed, black leather shoes.

After a quick appraisal, Luke decided that Cater Denby was in fact, the best-dressed young man in the room, a positive dandy in comparison to the uniformly black clothes of the old men, and the grey frock coats, and morning jackets of the youthful and middle aged.

Suddenly conscious of being scrutinised, Cater Denby glanced up from his breakfast, and flashed Luke another dazzling smile. Then, pouring a cup of tea, resumed his meal.

"From whence do you hail, Mr Reddall?" he asked.

"New South Wales," Luke replied, having swiftly deduced the young man's question.

"Ah! Yes," said Cater Denby, through mouthfuls. "I'm sure. That's an extremely long way away. Things must be very different there. Hot I hear."

"It can be."

"Savages?"

"Sometimes."

"And sheep."

"True. But also cattle."

"Are you planning to stay a while in our fair city?"

"Just until I sort out a business arrangement."

"Ah!" Cater Denby exclaimed. "There perhaps, I might be of assistance. My brother in law's a solicitor. Mr Albert Williams. Perhaps you've heard of him. Oh! But of course you haven't! How silly of me."

"Thank you, Mr Cater Denby," Luke said. "But I've a solicitor of my own."

"Then do let me be your tour guide. I've the rest of the day free. There's not an inch of this city I don't know."

Cater Denby poured Luke another cup of tea, offering him cream or lemon, Luke preferring cream.

"I'd planned to see my solicitor this afternoon," Luke said. "Although I'm not doing anything this morning."

"Have you bathed?" Cater Denby said, looking at him keenly.

Luke felt slightly affronted.

"Yes! Bathed and shaved."

Cater Denby laughed.

"No! No! By bathed. I mean bathed at the spa."

"Oh!" Luke exclaimed. "Not yet."

"You can't come to Bath, and not visit the baths. It's the thing. Everyone does it."

Cater Denby was sipping his tea, at the same time, mopping his plate with a hunk of bread.

"Really!" Luke said, hesitantly.

"Will you let me take you? I know you'll adore it. You will've never experienced anything like it."

"But I'm not a good swimmer."

Cater Denby laughed aloud.

"You don't need to swim! Please! Let me show you?"

"Very well, Mr Cater Denby," Luke said, reluctantly. "But first, I must drop a note to my solicitor in Belgrave Terrace."

"Why not get Mr Haywood's boy to deliver it," suggested Cater Denby. "Then we'll have the whole morning to ourselves. And for heaven's sake! Call me Denby! All my friends do. And what do you go by, Mr Reddall?"

"Luke," Luke said shyly.

"Come along then Luke! Let's collect our hats and canes. The baths await!"

Leaving the waiter to clear the table, Luke and Denby stepped out into the sunshine.

The wide pavement in front of South Parade offered a splendid setting along which to promenade, and even at that early hour, ladies and gentlemen, old people in Bath chairs, plus nannies, pushing infants in perambulators, were taking advantage of the fresh air.

Denby and Luke stood on the doorstep, putting on their gloves and hats.

"How do you find Hayward's?" Denby asked.

"Most agreeable," answered Luke, "and very reasonable. Two pound ten shillings a week, including meals. And for five shillings extra, I get a private sitting room."

"A necessity for a gentleman," Denby said smiling, revealing a row of perfectly white teeth. "One never knows who may be dropping in."

As the two men walked along Pierpont Street, it fascinated Luke to see Denby use his black ebony cane, flourishing it; employing it not as a walking stick, but as an accessory, and another means of expression. Striding confidently beside Luke, he spoke of this and that, indicating with his cane the places of interest, as well as the houses of famous residents that they passed. Crossing the Abbey Church Yard, the immense bell tower, soaring above them, Denby pointed out the architectural features of the ancient church.

"Have you been inside?" he asked.

"Yes. It's most impressive."

"Gloomy though, don't you think? Depressing. All those memorials. Not my cup of tea at all."

Denby pointed at an imposing building with large windows across the square.

"That's the Pump Room,"

"Is that it!" exclaimed Luke. "I've seen it before. What do people do there? I know my mother and father went there when they visited Bath."

"Drink the waters, of course," Denby said, brandishing the cane. "Everyone does it. It's supposed to do you good."

"Where do the waters come from?"

"The ground."

"Have you drunk it?"

"Oh yes."

"How does it taste?"

Denby shrugged his shoulders.

"Like hot water, I suppose. With a sort of metal flavour."

Luke shook his head.

"There's nothing like it where I come from," he said. "Not that I know of, anyway."

Walking beneath a colonnade of Doric columns, Luke and Denby entered Stall Street, arriving at the entrance to the treatment rooms, and the baths themselves.

An old man sat behind an elegant table in the vestibule, obviously employed to take money and hand out towels, as well as bathing clothes and robes. He peered at Luke and Denby through his thick spectacles.

"Good morning, gentlemen," he said. "That'll be one and sixpence each, please."

"Thank you, Mr Green," Denby said, taking out a small change purse, handing him three shillings. "May I introduce my friend, Mr Reddall? It's his first time at the baths, and to Bath itself, if truth be told."

"You're very welcome, Mr Reddall," the old man said. "I hope you enjoy yourself. And I must say; you've found an admirable guide in young Mr Denby. He's most knowledgeable."

Mr Green picked up a small brass bell, and rang it.

"Mr Ridley will see you down, gentlemen."

A door at the end of the hall opened, and a middle-aged man gestured them forward.

"Good morning Ridley," Denby said. "Lead the way."

Mr Ridley led them down a short passage beyond the door, and after descending two flights of stairs they arrived at a stout half-glazed oak door, its frosted glass etched with the words 'Kings Bath'.

Grasping a shining brass handle, Ridley pulled open the door, allowing the men to pass into another corridor, along which ranged doors, leading to the changing cubicles.

On entering, the smell Luke encountered was like nothing he had ever before experienced, deciding it resembled a mixture of steam, and the smell of a foundry.

"Is it busy Ridley?" Denby asked, as the man opened the door to the first cubicle.

"No sir. They say it might rain. That always keeps the crowds away."

While Luke and Denby waited, Ridley went inside, in order to lay fresh towels on a couch, and a clean mat on the floor.

"Why should a drop of rain put people off?" whispered Luke. "You're wet anyway."

"Because there's no roof."

"But what's the difference," Luke continued. "When you're wet, you're wet, whatever the weather."

"The reason being, my dear chap is that some dandies of my acquaintance spend a fortune on their coiffure. They certainly wouldn't want to spoil their waves and ringlets, with a sprinkle of rain."

"So it's not the done thing to put your head under?"

"No Luke!" exclaimed Denby. "Never! For a start, it's too hot. You'd scald. And you wouldn't want to swallow the water either."

"All ready for you, sir," Ridley said, inviting Luke to enter the cubicle.

Nervously, Luke turned to Denby.

"I don't know whether I'm going to enjoy this."

Denby laughed.

"Now get along with you, my good fellow. I'll see you in the water."

Lit by a single skylight, the cubicle was small, just big enough for a couch, a cupboard, and a chair. Luke sat down and began unlacing his shoes; then to undress, hanging his clothes on a hook on the door.

Squeezing into the bathing costume Mr Ridley had given him; Luke hardly thought it the height of fashion, being made of knitted wool, consisting of a shirt and breeches, woven into one. Luke supposed, that once its previous occupant had discarded it, the suit was boiled, since it was stiff, rough on the skin, and tight. He also found difficulty fastening the row of buttons down the front; hoping contact with the warm water would soften the costume once more.

A long canvas curtain, hanging from a rail, on tarnished brass rings, was all that separated the cubicle from the bath, Luke able to hear people splashing in the water on the other side. Standing at last in the woollen costume, feeling somewhat ridiculous, together with experiencing the hot stone under his bare feet, and the heat through the canvas curtain, he finally pulled it back and peered out.

Through a great cloud of vapour, he realised he was standing on the border of a pool, open to the sky, enclosed by lofty walls, and filled with steaming green water. Several large windows, more likely belonging to the Pump Room, were set high to one side, giving the inside observer a clear view of the baths below. Since even now, Luke could see several people standing at the glass, gossiping and laughing.

Facing him along the sheer walls on three sides, fixed rings were positioned at intervals, just above the water line, their once shining copper, now tarnished a bright green by mineral water, and the humid atmosphere.

A stone plinth was positioned in the middle of the bath, from which hot water flowed freely from vents at its base. A life size statue of a man stood atop the plinth, dressed in robes, and sitting on a throne, a crown on his head.

A dozen or so old men occupied the bath, wandering about, water up to their shoulders, some holding their arms above their heads, wisps of white hair mingling with the steam drifting around them.

Each cubicle had a row of stone steps leading into the water, so tentatively Luke began taking one step after another, until he reached the water's edge.

"In you come," a voice said from somewhere in the steam, and recognising it to be Denby, Luke searched for him through the mist.

"How deep is it?" he called.

"Deep enough! You won't drown. Just keep finding the next step."

Slowly, Luke walked into the water, each step taking him a foot lower, until his toes touched the sandy floor. The water felt luxurious. Hot; but not scalding; soft, nonetheless abrasive, causing his skin to tingle.

"How hot is it Denby?" he called.

"One hundred and four degrees at the outside," Denby shouted out of the fog.

Luke had experienced hotter days in Australia. But somehow, this heat was different, seeming to seep into his body, penetrating his bones and joints. It was little wonder ageing people enthused about the water's medicinal powers, because he could feel it working even on his relatively young body.

Suddenly, Denby was beside him, his blonde hair plastered over his brow, his skin as red as an apple.

"Who's the King?" Luke asked, pointing through the steam to the statue on the plinth.

"That's Bladud," answered Denby. "He's supposed to have discovered the spring. It all happened hundreds of years ago, before anything was here, just the woods and a river. Bladud was the son of King Rud. The old king wished to improve his son's education, so sent the boy to Athens. But when he came home, he was suffering from leprosy, and his father banished him from the court. The poor lad ended up looking after pigs, in a place by the river, near this spot. Clever young Bladud noticed his pigs liked to wallow in a patch of hot bubbling mud. He also saw that they never suffered from skin complaints. So what does Bladud do? He plasters himself with the stuff. Then low and behold! No more leprosy! It's a miracle. He goes back to court, and all's well. When he becomes king, he never forgets about the mud, and builds a town on this spot, and these baths."

Luke laughed.

"What a wonderful story," he said. "Are the baths really that old?"

"Certainly. You only need read the inscriptions next to the rings you see along the wall. Some of them were put there by people who bathed here three hundred years ago."

Luke was amazed. Cater Denby was truly astonishing. He had such a head for facts, and history. The way he explained it all, brought everything to life. In fact, rather as his father once did, when Luke and his brother John were boys, back in school, at Mr Meehan's Castle.

"Come on!" Denby said. "Walk with me to the middle. It's hotter there."

Cautiously, Luke waded toward the statue, seeing several old men gripping a brass rail encircling its base, at the same time, bobbing up and down. Presumably, they were undertaking some kind of exercise, their heads, and shoulders protruding from the scorching water, their skin redder than cooked lobsters.

"Hot isn't it," Denby said, when he and Luke reached the rail.

Luke nodded, squinting as the scalding water seared his skin.

"What's the temperature now?" he gasped.

"About one hundred and sixteen, where the water hit's the air. But it's hotter through the vents near our feet. Can you feel?"

Luke edged one foot forward, until his toes touched an iron grill in the sandy floor. It was indeed, scorching hot, and he quickly took his foot away, Denby finding Luke's trepidation amusing.

"You're a funny fellow," he laughed. "I'm growing quite fond of you."

"But Denby," Luke said in his defence, "all this is new to me! I would never have done this in a million years. But tell me. How is it the water is so hot?"

"Beneath us is a great reservoir, in which the hot water that's coming out of the ground, from way down, deep is collected."

"Is it the only source?"

Denby shook his head.

"There are several places nearby, where it bubbles up, baths built on each of them. How do you feel?"

"Marvellous! I don't think I've ever been as clean."

Denby smiled, clearly pleased to see his new friend enjoying himself.

"If you've been hunting," he said, "playing racquet ball, or exercising in the gymnasium. It's tremendous to come here afterwards. Very relaxing, don't you know. Have you had enough?"

"I think so. How long do you stay in for?"

"Not too long. Old chaps who've dallied a while, have been known to fall asleep in their cubicles afterward; then never wake up. A nice way to go I suppose; but a caution."

"Come on then," said Luke, laughing. "Don't you think we better get out? Race you back."

"Put your robe on before you dress," advised Denby, when they reached the steps. "You'll find you'll sweat like the blazes. Just lie back on the bed, and relax. Give yourself a good half hour. But for goodness sake! Don't fall asleep."

Pulling back the cubicle curtain, with Denby's words ringing in his ears; Luke ducked inside, the sudden change of temperature causing him to shiver. He quickly climbed out of the bathing suit, flung it on the floor, and towelled vigorously. Then, after wrapping himself in the thick robe, slumped onto the bed.

Denby was right, for as Luke lay there, the perspiration began flowing from every pore. Even in February, the most humid month of the year in the colonies, Luke had never perspired as much. He could feel his heart pumping, blood in his temples, pounding, and his ears ringing. Was bathing as good for you as they say, he thought? He could be having a heart attack.

Soon, however, these violent sensations began to subside, his breathing becoming slower, feeling himself relax, a wave of tranquillity overwhelming him. It was a strange, but pleasant sensation, as if he were floating, his arms, legs, and torso melting into the mattress. Listening to the sound of people splashing in the bath beyond the curtain, as well as water lapping at the bottom of the steps, Luke's mind began to wander.

How far from his old life could this be. Definitely a long way from the dry dusty plains, hot summer sun, and cold frosty winter mornings. Closing his eyes, a vision of sheep and cattle, grazing over an endless plain, filled his mind, the sound of squawking cockatoos resounding in his ears.

Feeling himself suddenly sink, Luke pulled himself up with a start.

He was falling asleep, and Denby told him not to. If he fell asleep, he would end up like those poor old chaps, never to wake up again. They would carry his lifeless corpse from the baths, and bury him in some strange place. Perhaps someone might give him a memorial plaque in the Abbey.

'Fell asleep in the Baths. Never to wake again'. People reading it, shaking their heads, and sighing.

Down he went again. No. He must stay awake.

Pattering on the window glass roused him, and opening his eyes, Luke stared up at the skylight. It was raining. Mr Ridley, the bath man, was correct in his forecast. Luke wondered how the baths might look in the rain. So climbing off the bed, he peeked around the curtain, just in time to see the old men wading through the water, making for the cubicles, the once smooth surface, now obliterated by pelting rain.

There was a knock on the door.

"Are you ready?"

It was Denby.

"I'll be with you in a moment, Denby," Luke said. "I need to dress."

"How do you feel?"

"Tremendous."

"Fit for lunch?"

"Lunch would be most appreciated."

Chapter Eight

By the time Luke and Denby left the baths, the rain had stopped, the streets wet and shining. It was only a spring shower, and now the sun shone from a cloudless sky. Being nearly midday, Stall Street was filled with horses, carts and carriages, folk shopping, Luke seeing for the first time, people in Bath Chairs, a peculiar three wheeled invention, allowing invalids access to the thoroughfares of the city.

Soon, the narrow lanes gave way to a wide and elegant byway, lined with superior shops, Luke recognising it as the street in which he bought his new clothes.

"Where are we taking lunch?" Luke asked, as they sauntered along.

"Mother's," Denby answered. "She'll enjoy meeting you. And you'll like her, I'm certain."

"Then she has a house here."

"Has for years. Since father died. She met her next husband in Bath. But Kimber met the same fate as pater. She's well over men for good and proper. Just enjoying herself, and living off her shares and investments."

"But why are you at Haywood's," asked Luke, "and not residing with her? If you don't mind me asking, of course."

"Not at all my dear Luke. For the simple reason, there's no room for me at present. You see, I've been abroad, don't you know, touring Italy and Greece. While I was away, mother took a lodger.

Well everyone does in Bath. A governess. They've grown quite attached. Now I've returned, mother hasn't the heart to ask her to leave. So that's how you find me at Hayward's."

"And I'm glad!" Luke said. "Otherwise we would never have met."

Cheerfully, they strolled along, Denby naming the streets as they passed.

"This is Milsom Street," he said. "If you wish to buy anything of quality, then this is the place."

Turning left into George Street, Denby directed them up Gay Street, until they arrived at the magnificent Circus, a complete circle of gracious houses, three tiers of decorative columns and shining windows, climbing toward the sky.

"How about this Luke!" Denby exclaimed, waving his stick in the air. "Come on! You must admit, you've never seen anything so fantastic. Can you see the columns between the windows? Each is a different order, with different capitals. Doric on the bottom. Ionic. Then Corinthian."

"Yes. I see," said Luke. "It's amazing."

"There's nothing like it in the entire world. It's quite unique."

"I know there's certainly nothing like it in Sydney."

Denby was proud of his city, Luke listening as he chattered about architects, masters of ceremonies, balls, parties, and the theatre. Also, fashionable ladies, and handsome dandies, Luke's mind swimming, deciding everything was very different from Goulburn or Yass.

Arriving at the end of Brock Street, Denby pointed to a street on the right.

"Mother lives up there," he said. "Upper Church Street. Not as grand an address as The Circus, but a desirable residence all the same. Although, what I'm about to show you, I'm sure will astound you. I give you the famous Royal Crescent. "

With a sweep of his cane, Denby introduced the most splendid vista Luke had ever seen, since an immense semicircle of noble houses curved away from where he and Denby stood, appearing to Luke as if a giant hand had taken a splendid Bath terrace, and bent it into a perfect arc.

Each house was in complete symmetry with its neighbour, having the same façade of elegant columns, classical architraves, all finely chiselled from golden Bath stone. Strolling along the wide pavement, Luke marvelled at the hundreds of windows, glittering in the midday sun. Passing shining black railings, glossy front doors, and brightly polished brass door-knockers, and letterboxes, all the while Denby talking eloquently about the Royal Crescent, and its history.

"Obviously," he said, waving his cane. "The people living here care little for the window tax. Do you know how much Bath paid last year?"

Luke shook his head.

"Eighteen thousand, eight hundred and fifty six pounds. The tax is daylight robbery."

Luke laughed.

"You're simply a mine of information Denby," he said. "How do you remember such things?"

Walking on, chatting about this and that, Luke noticed a large park below the crescent, folk taking the air, or riding horses, all around, an atmosphere of leisure, beauty and grace. It would be pleasant living in such a place, he concluded, and most beneficial for health and well-being.

"Well I'm getting hungry," said Denby. "It seems a long time since breakfast. Let's make tracks for mother's."

Turning tail, and in less than five minutes, they were again in Upper Church Street, standing on the doorstep of number six, the door opened by a footman; a lean young man, dressed in grey livery, white stockings, and black buckled shoes.

"I trust mother's at home, Shell?"

"Yes sir," he said, standing aside, allowing the gentlemen to pass. "She is in the drawing room, sir."

"Don't worry, Shell," Denby said. "We'll see ourselves up."

As Luke and Denby climbed the stairs, Luke took in the dark and narrow hallway, noticing a large chandelier, hanging in the centre, pictures ranging along the walls and up the staircase. Dark oil paintings of ancestors, some even dressed in similar clothes to that of his own forebear in the portrait at Oakwood.

With a thick carpet on the stair muffling their progress, reaching the first landing, Luke could finally appreciate the elegant plaster moulding on the ceiling, forming garlands of flowers, trophies and sweeping arabesques, reminding Luke of piped icing on a wedding cake.

A panelled door appeared at the end of the landing, and after knocking softly, Denby opened it, Denby and Luke entering the drawing room.

Mrs Cater Denby was sitting beside a window, working at an embroidery screen. She looked up when they entered.

"Good morning, dear," she said, turning her cheek towards Denby. "How lovely to see you."

Denby crossed the room, and kissed her.

"Good morning, mother."

Then turning, he gestured to Luke.

"May I introduce my friend, Mr Luke Reddall? It's his first visit to Bath. I've been showing him around."

"How do you do, Mr Reddall," Mrs Cater Denby said smiling, at the same time holding out her hand to him. "I'm very pleased to meet you."

"How do you do, Mrs Cater Denby," Luke said, shaking her hand.

"Please sit down, both of you."

Luke and Denby sat together on a sofa facing the fireplace, while Mrs Cater Denby returned to her embroidery, peering through her pince-nez, painstakingly threading the needle with a newly chosen coloured thread.

"Your first visit to Bath," she said. "How wonderful. It must be exciting seeing everything for the first time. Breathtaking is it not, Mr Reddall?"

"It is madam," Luke said. "Truly breathtaking."

"Luke's from Australia, mother," remarked Denby. "He's in Bath on business."

"Well I hope you won't be rushing back too soon, Mr Reddall," said Mrs Cater Denby. "The season is about to begin, and we have such fun, don't we William."

She stopped her stitching for a moment.

"I must say," she said peering at Luke, "You're a handsome young man. You've the air of a romantic about you. Something akin to Mr Scott or Lord Byron. My son always chooses the handsome ones. Don't you dear."

"Mother!" exclaimed Denby, his cheeks flushing. "You're incorrigible!"

Sat beside him on the sofa, Luke could only smile. And while Denby and his mother conversed, he took time to consider the room.

It was of medium size. Bright, and cheerfully decorated. Dominated by three sash windows, extending from the carpeted floor to the decorative, plaster ceiling. Through the windows Luke noticed an iron balcony appearing to run the width of the house. Also, with the windows raised, he supposed a person might easily be able to stand upon it, and take in the air. Comfortable chairs and sofas were positioned here and there, each upholstered in tapestry, representing exotic birds, and brightly coloured flowers, the design repeated in the curtains. Opposite him, a white marble mantelpiece surrounded a shining steel grate, where undoubtedly in winter a bright fire would burn. On the mantel, a large black onyx clock, adorned with gilded cupids, ticked the seconds away. A pair of silver candlesticks flanked the clock, keeping company with pretty porcelain figurines and beautiful miniatures, in black ebony frames. Plus, at either end, as if for protection, two large china dogs gazed devotedly into the room.

Luke was also astonished to see how many gilt framed watercolours covered the walls of the room, each depicting an English rural scene.

"Pretty aren't they, Mr Reddall," Mrs Cater Denby said, seeing Luke admiring them. "They're painted by quite a well-known artist, who once lived in Bath. Perhaps you've heard of him. Benjamin Barker?"

Luke shook his head.

"Sorry Mrs Cater Denby. I haven't. We know little of such things in the colonies."

"I'm sure there must be far more important things to do than paint pictures," Mrs Cater Denby said. "I've read life in Australia is very hard."

"It can be, Mrs Cater Denby," agreed Luke. "The country is young, and the land unrelenting. However, we're discovering ways of taming it to our uses. The more the land is opened, the greater it will become."

Mrs Cater Denby smiled, once again changing the thread in her needle.

"I'm pleased to hear it. My late second husband, Alexander Kimber, wished to send my William to Australia. Mr Kimber used to say it would make a man of him. My William doesn't need making a man of. Do you dear. Thankfully, Alexander died before he could put his plan into action."

Denby laughed.

"Mother!" he said. "You're outrageous. Come! Let's go downstairs. I'm sure I heard the gong."

Luncheon was a jolly affair, Mrs Cater Denby in full flight, telling comical stories of the bygone days, when Bath was filled with the notable and the notorious, Luke and Denby laughing uncontrollably, while Shell and a housemaid, waited sedately at table.

As the meal wore on, Luke began to feel drowsy, most certainly the effects of the hour spent at the baths. But politeness prevented him from nodding off. Then, once the last morsel was eaten, and the final glass emptied, Mrs Cater Denby dropped her napkin on her plate, and rose from the table.

"Well gentlemen," she said, "and what will you be doing this afternoon?"

"Luke has a meeting with his solicitor," said Denby, glumly. "I don't think he wants me tagging along."

"On the contrary, Denby," Luke said. "It would give me the greatest pleasure. I haven't enjoyed a person's company as much for many a year."

A while later, Denby and Luke stepped into the street once again.

"I've to meet Mr Perkins at Oakwood House, at three o'clock," Luke said. "It's on Bathwick Hill,"

"That's quite a walk," said Denby, laughing. "Let's hire a handsome."

Managing to hail a cab in Brock Street, Denby shouted the destination to the driver.

"He looks fine in his blue coat, and shiny black hat." Luke said, climbing inside.

"It's the driver's regulation uniform," commented Denby, "which sets them apart from cab drivers in any other city in the country."

Luke settled back into the interior and the comfortable cushioned seat.

"I must say," he said, "Bath certainly has a way about it. Everything seems to run so efficiently."

Denby smiled proudly.

"That's all due to the Bath Corporation, Luke. They take immense pride in the city, and show it off at every opportunity."

The carriage clattered across The Circus, down Gay Street, then reaching George Street, the driver steered the horses over the cobbles, heading down Broad Street, and on to Pulteney Bridge. As they rattled across its span, looking out of the window, Luke saw it differently, aware now of its significance, causing him to recall Miss Baker's account of the events on that memorable day.

It must be there, that he fell, Luke surmised, seeing a low stone parapet appear. Then, as if fate had taken a hand, the driver pulled up the horses, to allow an old woman to cross the street, thus giving Luke a clear view over the edge of the wall, and down into the water. The sight of the surging, churning weir, sweeping away in a great foaming arc, made him shudder. Recoiling at the thought, he turned his attention to the other window, yet the image of his father, being swept away in the heaving water remained in his mind.

"Your mother's very nice," he said, in an attempt to shake off the feeling of dread. "She seems to have an interesting time."

Denby produced a silver cigar case, offering Luke a cheroot.

"She does," he said, taking one for himself, and tapping it on the case. "Ever since her aunt died, leaving her the money, she leads a wonderful life. Mother's met all of society, both the good and the bad. She knows everyone, and everyone knows her."

Luke wondered if she had ever met his father.

"She seems so ordinary though," he said. "Not commonplace, of course. I mean unaffected."

"I agree," Denby, said, lighting their cigars. "Mother's pretty steady. She keeps everything in proportion. Her lineage is partly the reason."

"How do you mean?"

"Mother comes from good country stock. Her family owned an old manor in Bedfordshire called 'Kempston'. Mother's father was Beckford Cater. The Caters tied in with the Beckfords hundreds of years ago. They owned plantations in Jamaica. That's where mother's money comes from. Mother can trace her ancestry back to the days of Queen Elizabeth. "

"Really!" Luke exclaimed. "How impressive."

Except, he could not help thinking, that if Perkins believes the portrait, he would be able to do the same.

The gradient of Bathwick Hill increased, the cab driver cracking his whip, urging the horses towards the halfway point, where he would allow them to drink. Having arrived at the stone water trough, the cab pulled up, giving Luke a clear view of the city. When he rode Clarence up the hill, the day before, it was raining, the view obscured by a veil of cloud. However, today the sky was clear, afternoon light playing indiscriminately over the parks, terraces, and crescents of the city. Luxuriating in golden sunshine, it was truly a glorious sight, settled within a bowl of green hills.

While waiting for the horses to finish drinking, Denby also gazed out of the window.

"I don't think I know anyone up here."

"Really!" Luke said. "Oakwood House is a school for girls. The headmistress, Miss Baker, is the sister of a late friend of mine."

"Miss Baker eh?" Denby said, eyeing Luke quizzically. "A sweetheart maybe?"

"Not at all, Denby. An acquaintance. Her brother John became a friend, when I lived in the colonies. The closest friendship I've ever had."

For the first time in a long while, Luke mentioned John without feeling sad. Also, he suddenly realised he had revealed to someone his true feelings for John Baker. Plainly, Denby was having a profound influence upon Luke, and he felt better for the friendship.

"Such a bond is unparalleled!" Denby said, looking Luke squarely in the eye. "Greater by far than any experienced with the so called, fairer sex. You say late. What happened to him?"

"He was murdered! Shot by a coward!"

"I'm extremely sorry Luke! Although, you have led a fascinating life. So why then are we meeting your solicitor here?"

"Because I have to show him something. Something very important, which will change my life."

"Really Luke! Might I ask what this could be?"

"You'll soon find out."

Denby frowned.

"Luke Reddall! You're a mysterious fellow, to be sure! I've an impression that you're keeping something from me. I like to know everything concerning the man with whom I am about to become firm friends."

"You'll have to wait, Denby. I'm not going to tell you anything until I know I'm to be believed."

Suddenly, the coachman cracked his whip, and they were off once more, Denby sitting back in the corner, looking petulantly out of the window.

It took George Jesshope several minutes to answer the bell.

"He must be a long way off," Denby said, as he and Luke waited on the doorstep.

Nonetheless, the sound of a key turning in the lock, preceded the butler opening the door.

"Please come in, gentlemen," he said. "Madam is expecting you, Mr Reddall, and is waiting with Mr Perkins in the library."

After giving the butler their hats, gloves and canes, Luke and Denby followed him along the corridor, Denby finding it hard to constrain his curiosity.

"What's going on?" he whispered. "It's all very mysterious."

Although Luke's stomach was full of murmuring starlings, he smiled, enjoying keeping Denby in suspense.

"Hush!" he hissed.

Reaching the library door, George opened it, standing aside to allow Luke and Denby into the room.

Mr Perkins was at the window, looking into the garden, the fresh spring leaves, dappling the glass with dancing washes of green, while Miss Baker stood at a table, turning the pages of a book. It appeared to Luke that he and Denby had hardly interrupted a lively conversation.

"Good afternoon, Luke," Miss Baker said. "How good of you to be so punctual. Also, I see you've brought a friend."

"Yes Miss Baker. May I introduce, Mr Cater Denby?"

"How do you do, Mr Cater Denby," Miss Baker said, crossing the room to greet him. "But surely! And please forgive me. Hasn't your mother recently taken one of our teachers as a companion? Miss Newcomb recently retired."

Denby was taken aback.

"Why yes, Miss Baker!" he said. "She has. What a coincidence. Miss Newcomb and my mother are quite inseparable. In fact, they are about to travel abroad. The tour; don't you know."

Hearing the conversation, Perkins turned away from the window, hovering in the background, waiting for an introduction.

"I beg your pardon, Mr Perkins," said Miss Baker. "You've met Mr Reddall, of course. May I also introduce, Mr Cater Denby?"

Miss Baker turned to Denby.

"Mr Perkins is Mr Reddall's solicitor," she explained.

"Good afternoon, sir," the old man said, holding out a wrinkled hand. "I'm very pleased to make your acquaintance."

Stealing a horrified glance at Luke, Denby shook Perkin's hand.

"Good afternoon," he said courteously. "Pleased to meet you, I'm sure."

Miss Baker moved to the fireplace.

"I'll ring for tea," she said, turning a small brass lever in the wall. "Please sit down everyone."

"Seeing you're of the same profession, Mr Perkins," said Denby, as he and the solicitor sat down in opposite armchairs, beside the fireplace, "maybe you're acquainted with my brother in law, Mr Albert Williams."

Luke was uneasy, nonetheless, and catching Miss Baker's eye, gave her an anxious glance, at the same time gesturing to the window.

"Can we get on with this?" he whispered, when Denby and Perkins were out of earshot. "I can't bear the suspense much longer."

Miss Baker smiled, touching his arm.

"Then again," she said, looking back into the room, "perhaps we should get to the business at hand, and then take tea. What do you say, Mr Perkins?"

"Anything you wish, madam," he said, getting up from his chair. "I understand from Mr Reddall's communication this morning, I'm here to investigate something that will help verify his identity. Am I not correct, Mr Reddall?"

Denby looked at Luke, and shook his head, the expression on his face communicating to Luke as 'What the hell's going on here?'

The face caused Luke to smile for a moment, somewhat calming his nerves.

"Yes, Mr Perkins. That's quite correct," he said. "Would everyone please follow me?"

Luke led them out of the room and down the hall to the dining room.

Unlike the previous evening, the room was now full of afternoon sunshine, filtering through the lace curtains, casting snowflake like patterns on the walls, as well as shedding light above the fireplace, and on to the portrait of Sir Stephen Soame.

With everyone assembled, clearing his throat, Luke moved to the mantel.

"I hope, Mr Perkins," he began, "that when you take a close look at the painting you see behind me, you will no longer have doubts as to my true identity."

Perkins shuffled around the table, and stood beside him, followed closely by Miss Baker and Denby.

For a brief moment, the solicitor fumbled inside his breast pocket, taking out a pair of spectacles, exchanging them for the ones he was already wearing.

"Now let me see," he said, peering hard at the painting.

Luke saw Denby's mouth open in astonishment.

"Reddall!" he whispered. "Is that you? But the painting must be three hundred years old?"

"Shush!"

Luke put his finger to his lips, and pointed to Perkins.

"Yes!" the old man said slowly. "I can certainly see a resemblance."

Mr Perkins looked at Luke intently, and then back at the picture.

"A very strong likeness," he said. "It could be you Mr Reddall, I must admit."

"Of course it's him!" Denby exclaimed. "Can't you see it? He's a dead spit. The hair. The eyes. The mouth. The chin. Everything! Exactly."

"Well?" said Perkins, frowning up at the picture.

"Oh come off it, old man!" scoffed Denby. "You must be able to see it. I don't know what this is all about! Something concerning Luke's identity, you said. Well whatever it is. That chap up there is definitely related to this chap down here. No doubt about it."

Unable to contain themselves, Miss Baker and Luke laughed aloud, followed very shortly by Denby. They stared at Perkins, who once more stared at the portrait.

"Very well," he said, turning to Luke, a quiver of amusement appearing in his voice. "I see it. It's remarkable. You have the family resemblance, undoubtedly. I will state that I've identified you, Mr Reddall, and begin drawing up the documents relating to the title. Everything should be complete within a couple of days."

"Yes!" Luke shouted, unable to restrain himself further.

"Thank you, Mr Perkins!" he yelled, clapping the old man on the back, and shaking his hand vigorously. "Can I call myself Soame now?"

A smile spread across the old man's face.

"I don't see why not. You are one, after all."

"Can someone tell me what's going on?" asked Denby. "What's all this about a title? Moreover, just when I've gotten used to calling you Reddall, I've now to call you Soame."

Luke and Miss Baker laughed.

"Let's have tea," she said. "Luke will explain everything."

As they climbed the stairs, however, she caught Luke's sleeve, and pulled him close.

"But not absolutely everything, Luke dear," she whispered.

It was Sunday evening, and Luke and Denby were dining late, there being much cause for celebration and considering it would be a private affair, Luke asked Mr Hayward if they might take supper in Luke's sitting room.

"It doesn't matter how much wine you ply me with Denby," Luke said, quaffing back his fourth glass. "I'll not tell you anymore. You know most of the story anyway. Although, how I came to be a duke is a deadly secret. When I take my seat in the House of Lords, only the highest in the land need know the truth."

"Which means you don't trust me, you bounder!" Denby said, draining his glass, and pouring another.

"I have no idea what a bounder is, Denby," Luke said, feigning indignation. "Neither do I wish to. And yes! Exactly! I do not trust you."

"But we're chums, Luke. Chums don't have secrets from each other."

"The secret involves a dear friend. And it's their wish the secret remains a secret until such time as they allow the true story to be told. I'm sorry. But that's all there is to say on the matter."

Both men having tucked their napkins under their chins, in order to protect their fancy silk waistcoats, Denby leant back in his chair, and folding his arms, watched Luke carve the first cutlet from the roast rib of beef.

"Very well," Denby said. "What will you do once the papers are signed?"

"I'll take the mail to London," answered Luke. "Then another to Cambridge."

"And pay your country seat a visit, no doubt," Denby said, sarcastically.

"You sound jealous."

Luke put a chop on Denby's plate.

"I am. I've always wanted to be a duke, an earl, or even a baron. If mother's cousins hadn't sold Kempston Hastingsbury, I'd more than likely be the Duke of Bedford by now."

Luke laughed, helping himself to the second rib.

"What's the significance of Cater?" he said. "I've never heard it used as a middle name."

"No. And you won't again for a long time, since I've no plans to marry."

Denby gnawed savagely on the bone.

"Anyway!" he said, having wiped his mouth with his napkin. "How much have you drunk? I told you this afternoon. The Caters go back to the days of Queen Bess and beyond."

"So do the Soames," Luke said.

"Of course! I forgot. You're nobility now. I must try to remember."

"Hey! That's a little near the mark," Luke said, pretending to be angry.

Denby smiled.

"Sorry Luke! But if you really want to see more of me, you'll need to get used to my sarcasm. It's just my way. I never mean it."

For a moment, no one spoke, as the friends enjoyed the flavour of beef, the taste of the wine, and a sensation of becoming drunk.

The young man was handsome and amusing, Luke decided, as he topped up Denby's glass, at the same time watching him vigorously nibbling on the meat bone. It was a while since he had as much fun with anyone. In fact, not since he last enjoyed a day with John Baker. But unlike John, who was considerably older, Luke and Denby, except for a couple of years, were comparable in age, which made a difference in their friendship. John Baker entered Luke's life at an opportune moment; Luke having recently lost both adopted parents. Therefore, it was hardly surprising that Luke regarded John, almost as a son would a father, sheltering in the big man's protection. He and Denby, however, might well be brothers, and like most brothers, their personalities were poles apart. Denby was wildly extravagant, and highly-strung, prone to sulks and petulance. And also spoilt, Luke clearly seeing why, having met his mother.

As different as chalk and cheese, Luke was happy in his own skin, understanding his personality perfectly, the years of solitude, having taught him introspection. Generally, unless he was drinking, he was quiet and thoughtful, and a little suspicious of strangers, but definitely honest, with a strong sense of fair play.

Watching Denby enjoy his supper, Luke wondered how their personalities would manage to exist together. Only time would tell, he told himself, as he filled his glass again.

"Here's a toast to me," he said, standing unsteadily. "It's my birthday tomorrow!"

"Hear! Hear!" Denby shouted, pushing back his chair, and joining him. "Happy birthday for tomorrow."

They brought their glasses together in a toast.

"I'll be thirty," Luke said, pretending to be miserable. "An old man!"

Denby laughed.

"What's tomorrow?"

"Monday, the sixth of April."

"Hey! I'll be twenty seven, on October the fifteenth," Denby yelled. "There's three years six months difference between us. You realise my good fellow, I was born in a good year. The year Napoleon lost at Waterloo. No one can ever forget that. Here's a toast to good old Wellington!"

"Here's to the grand old Duke!" Luke exclaimed.

"And I was born the year Napoleon retreated from Moscow! Here's to the Ruskies!"

The wine was well and truly taking its toll, both men feeling the need to resume their seats.

Looking at Luke, Denby frowned.

"Hey! Does that make you an Aries? I can't remember."

"A what?" Luke slurred.

"It's a sign of the zodiac! A ram, old chap. Aries the ram."

Denby laughed loudly, taking a mouthful of wine.

"It's the new thing," he said, putting down his glass clumsily. "Astrology. Haven't you heard? Our lives and behaviour are supposed to be governed by where the stars were on the precise date and time of our birth. I'm a Libran, don't you know. Can't you tell by my well balanced nature, and keenness for fair play?"

"For heaven's sake!" Luke shouted.

"Exactly!" Denby exclaimed.

Leaning back in their chairs, they laughed helplessly.

"Now!" Denby said, once some semblance of normality had resumed. "If I'm not mistaken, I heard you say you'll take the mail to London?"

Luke nodded.

"The mail!" scoffed Denby. "Why on earth do you want to take that outmoded contraption, when at the end of the road, you've Mr Brunel's magnificent Great Western Railway, to whisk you off to London, in just a few hours? The station's only yards away."

"Because," replied Luke, leaning across the table, his napkin dangerously close to draping in the gravy left on his plate, "I've read in the Times, that railway travel's dangerous."

"The Times!" exclaimed Denby. "What does The Times know about it? It's the most marvellous modern day invention. It'll change our world. You mark my words."

"That's all very well. But it worries me. I've read that sometimes the trains go at speeds of fifty miles an hour. How can a person breathe travelling at that rate?"

Denby shook his head.

"Luke!" he sighed. "Forgive me. But last year mother and I took the train on its very first run. Mr Brunel and mother are acquainted, and we travelled with him in his private carriage as far as Chippenham. After a night at the Angel, we caught the morning train back. It was fantastic. So exciting."

"What speed did you go?"

"I don't know. Something like a fast gallop. Anyway, you should be used to speed. You told me you were a jockey."

"I suppose so," Luke said doubtfully. "But I've also read, the thing to be feared the most is Box Tunnel. The papers say it's the longest in the world, and might deafen, or even suffocate a person."

By this time, Denby was reeling with laughter.

"Luke. You shouldn't believe all you read in the papers. Am I deaf? Do I look suffocated? Mother and I loved it. It's loud, I grant you. But we covered our ears. If you're that afraid, I'll come to London with you."

Luke stared hard at his new friend.

"No thanks, Denby," he said, sounding serious all of a sudden. "I'm sorry. And please don't be offended. I find you delightful company. In fact, I haven't had such a marvellous time with anyone for a long while. We're going to be good friends. Firm friends, of that I've no doubt. But I really must do this on my own. I've a lot to think about before I get there, and I know what'll happen if you join me. You'll show me London, which rest assured my friend, I would certainly enjoy immeasurably. It's just that, at the moment, I have my responsibilities, and they come first. Although, as soon as things are settled, I'll write. I'd be keen for you to join me at Thurlow."

Denby silently refilled his glass.

"Thank you, Luke," he said. "Thank you for being honest. I know how important all this is to you, and I'm beginning to see that you're a person of strong convictions, and fierce loyalties, and I admire that in a man. I'll do as you wish. But please take the train. You'll love it."

Luke laughed.

"Alright. But if we crash, I'll blame you."

The evening continued in much the same way, until it was time for Luke and Denby to say goodnight. By now, both men were extremely drunk, and putting Denby's arm over his shoulder, Luke helped him across the landing to his bedroom.

"You can join me, if you wish," said Denby, when they reached the door. "I wouldn't mind the company."

Luke propped Denby in the doorway, and searched for Denby's door key, in his friend's jacket pocket.

"At the moment," he said, turning it in the lock and opening the door. "I don't think that's a very good idea. Do you? Don't worry, I'll see you at breakfast."

"Well, if you get lonely," Denby said, entering his bedroom. "You know where I am."

Standing in the open doorway Denby leaned forward.

"Good night, sweet prince," he said, kissing Luke on the cheek. "And flights of angels sing thee to thy rest."

Luke kissed Denby, and watched him close the door.

Later, lying in bed, Luke mused over the events of the day, deciding it had been the most enjoyable of his life. He was cleaner than he had ever been; also a new participator in Bath society. His title had been recognised, and he had eaten and drunk well.

Nevertheless, the most miraculous occurrence of all, and something that Luke still found difficult to believe, was that he had discovered a marvellous, intelligent and attractive friend. Therefore, with this realisation warming his heart, and the sound of steam locomotives shunting in the station sidings, Luke finally fell into a deep   sleep.

Chapter Nine

At breakfast the following morning, Denby and Luke were subdued, both nursing headaches derived from drinking copious amounts of wine. Despite sore heads, however, they ordered a full breakfast, including black pudding, which was Denby's particular favourite.

Having laid the tea things on the table, Lyall moved away to serve other guests, leaving the men to tuck into their food, Denby starting by slicing the pudding of cooked pig's blood.

"Was I totally outrageous last night?" he asked. "I don't remember anything after you told me today was your birthday."

Denby suddenly dropped his knife and fork.

"Hey!" he exclaimed. "Today's your birthday! Happy Birthday, Luke," he said, clapping him on the back.

"Thank you, Denby. And no you weren't."

"Weren't what?"

"Outrageous. You were fun."

"Thank heaven's for that!"

There was silence as they hungrily devoured the bacon, fried eggs, and juicy breakfast sausages. But once their initial hunger was assuaged, Denby was the first to speak.

"We should do something special today."

"I've to see Miss Baker this morning. I'll be leaving tomorrow, so it'll be the last I see of her for a while."

Denby frowned, and ceased eating for a moment.

"What's the thing you have for this teacher Luke?" he said. "I'm sorry. I know! It's not my business."

"Miss Baker's the sister of the man who came to Australia to find me."

"That's right. Of course she is. I've a brain like a sieve."

"I was the one to tell her he was dead," Luke added. "I feel I've grown close to her since, that's all."

"Very understandable, my dear chap. More tea?"

Luke nodded.

"But we can get together this afternoon," he said, passing Denby his empty cup. "And I'm not doing anything this evening."

"Splendid! Then I'll see you at mother's at one. We'll take luncheon. Now I wonder whether Lyall has anything for a hangover. My head's splitting."

"Madam is in the garden, Mr Soame," George Jesshope said, taking Luke's hat, gloves and riding crop. "I'll take you to her."

"No thanks, George," said Luke. "Don't worry. I'll find her."

George led Luke into the dining room, opening the French windows onto the terrace.

"Madam is beside the lower lake, sir. Just follow the path. You can't miss it."

Positioned below the house, the steep and extensive garden tumbled in a series of ascending terraces, each abounding in shrubbery and trees, plus a limpid lake, partially covered by water lily leaves, on which moorhens strutted piously.

The garden was landscaped pastorally, as was the fashion, taking on a natural ambiance, not unlike scenes of Arcadia, apparent in the paintings of Poussin. Therefore, wandering along rustic stone paths, and descending steps, Luke followed the bubbling streams, and trickling cascades, linking one lake with the next. Until, reaching the last stretch of water, he stopped, and looked about for Miss Baker, discovering her stood beside a stone grotto, an easel in front of her.

Miss Baker was painting, and by the angle of the easel, Luke realised she was painting in watercolour. Rather than disturb her concentration, he remained at a distance.

"Luke!" she said, finally aware of his presence. "There you are. How pleasant to see you again. You must have slept well after such an exciting day."

"I did, Miss Baker," he replied. "It's a great relief to know that Mr Perkins believes the portrait."

Emma smiled, returning her brush to a water jar beside her paint box.

"As you see," she said. "I do a little painting myself. Just simple sketches really."

"May I take a look?"

"Of course."

Emma stood away from the easel.

What Luke saw was a small, exquisite, delicate painting, executed with the minimum of fuss, keeping the subject matter as the prominent feature. In this case, the dark, mysterious, romantic grotto.

"It's beautiful!" he exclaimed.

"Thank you, Luke. You're very kind. I very rarely let anyone see them. Showing them causing me to feel vulnerable. Don't ask me why."

"That's because you value them highly, as you put everything you have into them."

"Exactly," Emma said, laughing, Luke suddenly seeing a resemblance of John Baker in the manner in which her eyes danced gaily. "I feel quite exhilarated when I've finished. Naturally, they're nothing like Mr Barker's watercolours. He painted in this garden, when Lady Edwina was alive, using it as a setting for many of his best pictures. Sometimes, I'd slip away from my desk to watch him. From a distance of course."

"Would that be Benjamin Barker?" added Luke.

"Yes. He's quite a famous artist, and lived in Bath. Sadly, he died four years ago. Except these days his work has become very popular."

Suddenly, a memory of the parlour at Upper Church Street filled Luke's mind, and the wall opposite the window, crowded with a collection of watercolour pictures.

"I know," he said. "I've seen his paintings. Mr Cater Denby's mother has dozens."

"Really! How interesting. I'd love to see them."

"I'm sure that's possible, Miss Baker. I'll talk to Denby."

Miss Baker looked at Luke seriously, and touched his arm.

"Luke. I think it's about time you called me Emma," she said.

"Very well Miss B… Sorry! Emma," he said, blushing.

"I really cannot agree to you calling me mother. Not just yet, anyway. There's a problem nevertheless. Your visits are beginning to cause some gossip below stairs, so my butler Mr Jesshope informs me. Who is this handsome young stranger from over the sea, the servants are wondering? Why is he visiting our mistress? I've told Jesshope you're a distant relative of Her Ladyship from Australia, and laying claim to the title. This is entirely true, of course. So I feel happy I'm not lying to him. Yet I cannot see you divulge our true relationship to anyone. Am I being unreasonable, Luke?"

"Certainly not, Emma," replied Luke. "You can trust me."

"Thank you."

Emma began her painting again.

"When will you be leaving us?" she asked. "I'm sure you're anxious to see Thurlow."

"Tomorrow morning," answered Luke, rather sadly. "By the eleven o'clock train. I shall miss Bath. I feel I'm quite at home already."

"Yes," said Emma. "Bath does that to a person; the city gets into your blood. It's always hard to say goodbye. But I'd love to see Thurlow again."

Emma gazed over the shimmering lake.

"It's been years since last I was there. I've not even seen mother and father in all that time. There's never been the right moment."

Luke watched her expression change.

"I've dreamt of it though. Horrid dreams about the night in the temple. The night the arrangement was made. Going back would be good for me. Maybe I'd lay some ghosts forever. The day will come when I'll feel strong enough to face my demons, and as your mother, I'll take your arm, and show you all the treasures that wonderful house possesses. Treasures that now belong to you."

She touched his face tenderly.

"Now off with you," she said, "before I cry. There's enough water on this painting as it is. Have a marvellous journey, and write to me often."

Emma turned her head, and Luke kissed her cheek.

"I will," he said, "and thank you."

When Luke arrived at the second lake, he looked back. Emma was painting once more, but she glanced up and waved, a broad, brilliant smile on her face, causing Luke's heart to surge with a sense of love, hitherto unknown. A feeling that had lain dormant, since he remembered embracing his adopted mother, Isabella, a recollection so far removed from his present life, it seemed to exist in another time and place.

At the house, George Jesshope, the butler, was waiting in the hall, holding Luke's hat, gloves, and riding crop.

"I've asked the groom to bring your horse around, sir," he said. "He'll only be a minute."

"Thank you George," Luke replied.

For a moment, they stood in silence, the ticking of the grandfather clock the only sound.

"May I be so bold as to ask you something sir?" George said suddenly.

"Certainly," Luke replied. "Go ahead."

"Well sir. Is it true you're from Australia?"

"Yes. That's right."

"I've read sir that Australia is a very big country."

"It is indeed George."

"You'll probably think my question's a bit odd sir. But in your time there, did you ever come across a man named James Waldon?"

Luke stared at George in disbelief.

"James Baker Waldon?" he gasped.

"Yes!" George exclaimed. "You have. You've met him! How amazing!"

Luke felt faint suddenly.

"Do you mind if I sit down George? I had quite a night of it last night, and your question has come as rather a shock to say the least."

George helped Luke sit on the chair positioned against the wall.

"Are you alright sir? Would you like me to fetch a glass of water?"

Luke shook his head.

"No thanks. I'll be fine."

"We were good friends James and I sir," continued George. "He and I were footmen at Thurlow; and here in Bath. That was until that terrible day sir."

"James would never tell me what happened," Luke said.

"In those days, James' father, Henry Waldon, was butler to Her Ladyship, and we heard her ladyship's son, Sir Humphrey had some sort of quarrel with him when they were boys at school. Soame took vengeance on Mr Waldon by taking it out on his son."

Luke's mouth dropped open in astonishment. He knew this story.

"Do you mean Sir Humphrey Soame implicated James Baker Waldon in a crime he never committed, and in consequence had him transported to Australia?"

"Yes sir. That's exactly right. But how do you know that?"

"Miss Baker told me the circumstances of Sir Humphrey's death, but failed to tell me the names of the persons involved."

"It was an awful day sir," George continued. "James was tried and sent down, and there was nothing anyone could do, so damning was Sir Humphrey's evidence. On that day, I lost a best friend. His mother and father, a loving son, and my dear, late departed sister Alice, a sweetheart. And all because of the wickedness of one man."

Luke stared at the opposite wall in dismay, the full realisation finally flooding his mind.

His father was the cause of James' pain and torment; suffering so terribly, he had never spoken of it to a living soul. Soame was responsible for wrenching the young man from everything he loved, sending him to a fate worse than death.

Suddenly, in his frenzied mind, Luke realised, James knew Soame to be his father. Since the day John Baker died, and Luke read the letter, James had known that he, Luke, was the son of this evil man, and yet had remained silent. Why? For the simple reason that James had a heart the size of an ox. Brave. Strong. Steadfast James. Always there to lend a hand. Never showing anger, or malice. Luke felt ashamed, tears welling in his eyes.

"Are you sure you're alright Mr Soame?" said George. "Shall I call a doctor?"

"No, no!" Luke stammered. "I'll be fine. I've had a dreadful shock that's all."

"How did you and James meet, sir, if I maybe so bold to ask?"

"He was a servant on my farm," answered Luke, quickly wiping his eyes with a handkerchief he had taken from his top pocket.

Now it was George's turn to be amazed.

"You don't say sir! That's incredible!"

"It is George. Quite incredible. Over the last ten years, James and I have shared many adventures, becoming firm friends."

"You mean he's alive?"

"Oh yes George. That is, up until the last time I saw him. Don't you worry my friend; it'll take a great deal to kill off James Baker Waldon."

There was a knock on the door, George opening it to reveal the groom holding Luke's horse by the reins.

Luke rose from the chair unsteadily, and went to the door.

"Well thank you George," he said. "With what you've told me this morning, I can safely put the last piece of jigsaw into the puzzle."

"It's my pleasure sir. And thank you for telling me the good news. Do you think we shall ever see James in England, sir?"

"Stranger things have happened George," Luke said, climbing into the saddle. "Stranger things have happened."

***

At Upper Church Street, having left Clarence in the stable at the rear of the house, Luke crossed the yard, and descending the entry steps, knocked on the back door. It slowly opened, around it appearing the startled face of a young girl.

"Yes sir. What can I do for you sir?" she said shyly, wiping her hands on her apron.

"I'm to meet Mr Cater Denby here at one o'clock."

The girl stifled a giggle.

"But sir should have come to the front door."

"I had to stable my horse."

"Mr Shell would have arranged that sir. Come along in sir. But I'll have to call Mr Shell. He'll need to announce you. Madam is entertaining Miss Newcomb."

"Thank you."

The hall was quite unlike the entrance hall at the front of the house, being plain, with cream painted walls, above a dado rail, beneath which Luke noticed brown painted and grained wood panelling.

The maid led him down the passage, passing an open door, where a woman stood at a kitchen table, kneading dough. She stared at Luke as he went by.

"Somehow I think I've done the wrong thing," he whispered, as the girl opened another door.

"Yes sir," she said. "Beg your pardon sir. Gentlemen never come to the back. It's not done sir."

"I'm sorry. But where I come from, we can come and go from any part of the house."

"I see sir. Well Mr Shell will see you up."

Leading him along another short passage, the maid knocked on a door. It opened, revealing the tall figure of Mr Shell. Frowning, he peered down at Luke.

"What can I do for you sir?"

Luke was about to reply, but the maid interrupted him.

"Mr Shell! The gentleman was unable to call at the front. He left his horse in the stable, and thought it quicker to come through the back."

"That's right," said Luke, glancing up at the butler nervously. "Thank you miss…"

"Rebecca, sir."

"Yes. Thank you Lovelock," Shell said, haughtily. "That will be all. I'll see Mr Reddall up."

"Mr Reddall," Shell said stiffly, upon opening the drawing room door.

"Come in Mr Reddall. How lovely to see you again," Mrs Cater Denby said, getting up from the sofa. "May I introduce my companion Miss Newcomb?"

"How do you do Mrs Cater Denby," Luke said. "Miss Newcomb. I'm very pleased to meet you."

Mrs Cater Denby gestured to the armchair beside the fire.

"Please be seated Mr Reddall. William dropped by this morning on his way to the gymnasium. He said you would be joining us for luncheon. He also told me that today is a rather special day for you."

She turned to the elderly lady sitting on her right.

"It's the young man's birthday Rachel dear. Isn't that wonderful. How lovely it must be to look forward to one's birthdays, instead of dreading each one, as we do."

Laughing, the ladies nodded their heads in agreement, while Luke sat in the chair, smiling. It was good to be in the pretty room once more.

"William tells me you'll be travelling soon Mrs Cater Denby," Luke said.

"Yes Mr Reddall. We will indeed. And we're so looking forward to it, aren't we Rachel dear?"

"We certainly are," Miss Newcomb said. "Mary's promised to show me all the places I've only read about in books."

The ladies were of similar age, Luke noted, as well as very intimate, Luke clearly noticing the closeness, by their expressions as they gazed at each other. Was this perhaps more than just a friendship? Denby did say his mother had given up men for good.

Alike in years they may be, however, they were total opposites in stature and general appearance.

Mrs Cater Denby was short and stout; Miss Newcomb, tall and thin, the spinster's hair, steely grey, and pulled back into a tight bun, appearing beneath a white lace cap, tiny ringlets at the side of her smooth, scrubbed face.

On the other hand, Mrs Cater Denby's flame red hair appeared lavishly from under her lace cap. However, not an ordinary red Luke observed. More as if, while the owner aged, the natural colour had lost some of its glory, and was now being assisted by the addition of vegetable dyes.

Mrs Cater Denby's coiffure was flamboyant, her hair parted down the centre, two spaniel ears, tied with blue bows, hanging voluptuously on each side of her plump jolly face. A face Luke observed to be thickly powered, cheeks rouged, lips a dark red, with a hint of charcoal around her light blue eyes.

Miss Newcomb's face, conversely, was long and thin, with no trace of makeup, although her cheeks were as pink as little cider apples, however naturally so, from sunshine, and copious fresh air.

Their disparities continued into their apparel, Luke never having seen the like of his hostess' ensemble. Not in the colonies that is.

Mrs Cater Denby was wearing a corn coloured calico gown, covered in a pattern of tiny blue cornflowers, and gathered into numerous pleats at her tightly corseted waist. While her sleeves were puffed and capped with white lace, bows and ribbons appearing to cover everything.

Overall, Luke thought it a pleasing assemblage, and although perhaps rather young for Mrs Cater Denby's years, nonetheless, fashionable and gay.

Miss Newcomb's attire was considerably less flamboyant, her skirt and bodice made from shining black satin, the tight bodice above her corseted waist, fastened by a row of tiny jet buttons, ending with white lace at Miss Newcomb's throat and wrists.

Around her neck, as if to heighten the severity of her appearance, Miss Newcomb wore a fine silver chain, from which hung her pince-nez.

In general, her appearance was one of sternness and severity. Miss Newcomb, Luke surmised, must have commanded great respect in the classroom.

"Are you visiting anywhere nice Mrs Cater Denby?" Luke asked.

"Oh yes dear," she answered. "All the old haunts. Places William's father took me on our honeymoon. Then of course, the war was still on, so it was difficult to move about Europe. Except we did manage to see a great deal of the Mediterranean. Especially the Italian coast. So romantic! My dear little girl. The first of my three children was conceived at Amalfi, I'm positive of it."

"Mary!" Miss Newcomb exclaimed. "You'll embarrass Mr Reddall."

"Mr Reddall's a man of the world; aren't you Mr Reddall."

"I think so Mrs Cater Denby," he said, trying not to blush. "You've other children Mrs Cater Denby?"

"Two now Mr Reddall," Mrs Cater Denby said, sighing. "My first, a little girl, died poor thing. Then William came along. We spoiled him terribly, the little dear. We were so worried we'd lose him too, even though there was nothing ever the matter with him. Next came darling Anne Elizabeth. She married my son in law, Albert Williams, last year. They live in a lovely house in Notting Hill Square. Do you know it? Of course you don't! Silly thing that I am. Mr Reddall's from Australia, Rachel dear. He's a relative of Lady Soame."

"I taught at her school for many years," Miss Newcomb said, "Such a wonderful person. So kind and caring."

"Yes. So I've heard," Luke said.

"Mr Reddall's come all the way from the colonies. Sorry Mr Reddall. Should I tell Miss Newcomb of your good fortune?"

Luke smiled, and nodded.

"Rachel. Mr Reddall has laid claim to a title. And it seems we must soon need to call him Your Lordship. Isn't that so Mr Reddall?"

"I think so Mrs Cater Denby."

"Well I hope you set a better example than the last Duke of Thurlow," Miss Newcomb said, unaware Mrs Cater Denby was glaring at her. "He was a complete scoundrel. Lady Soame had no control over her son, so we at the school were led to believe. He carried on the life of a wastrel, and a licentious pervert. No one was safe when he was around, if you understand my meaning."

It was too late, since there was nothing Mrs Cater Denby could do to stop her friend when she was in full flight. She looked helplessly at Luke.

"I'm sorry, Mr Reddall," she said. "Miss Newcomb is a person who speaks her mind. William tells me Sir Humphrey was a distant relative of yours. I do hope her harsh words haven't offended you."

"Have no fear Mrs Cater Denby," Luke answered. "I'm quite aware, Miss Newcomb, of the man's failings, and I'll endeavour to restore the good name of Soame in everyone's hearts."

"That's a worthy sentiment, young man," Miss Newcomb said, sternly.

At that moment, and to Luke's relief, there was a knock on the door, and Denby walked in.

"Hello everyone," he said, "You look cosy. What have you been gossiping about?"

"We don't gossip, William," his mother said, indignantly. "We converse. We were conversing, were we not, Mr Reddall. Anyway, that was the gong. Let's go down."

As Shell and Rebecca moved quietly around the table, holding salvers of cold collations, and tureens of vegetables, the chief topic of conversation was the ball scheduled for that evening.

"I adore living so close to the upper rooms," Mrs Denby said, serving herself a smoked trout. "It saves me such a lot in carriage fares, to say the least."

"But mother!" Denby protested. "You never walk. You always take a cab, and the rooms are only five minutes away."

"It wouldn't do to arrive at a ball on foot, dear. How plebeian. What would they say? I wouldn't want people to think that a Cater, or a Denby for that matter, couldn't afford a Hackney."

Helping herself to cold buttered potatoes, Mrs Cater Denby spooned mayonnaise on to the side of her plate.

"I wish I could run to a carriage of my own," she continued. "But they're so expensive, Mr Reddall, and such a waste really. Though I miss our rides in the country, don't you, William dear? Then again, most of our friends have either a chariot, or chaise, so we still have many opportunities to ride in the fresh air."

"Then are we going to the ball tonight mother?" Denby said, smiling at Luke. "It'll be Luke's first. And it's his birthday after all."

Mrs Cater Denby stared at her son in disbelief.

"William! Have I ever not attended the first ball of the season? Even when I'm old and decrepit, you'll have to wheel me there in one of those dreadful contraptions. Sorry, Mr Reddall, I mean Bath Chairs. I'll never miss a ball!"

Everyone laughed.

"How much does it cost?" Luke asked Denby confidentially, since he was worried that, after all his other expenses, he might be unable to afford the admission.

"Quite cheap really," Denby replied. "If you only wish to attend one ball, it costs five shillings. Mother buys a family ticket, don't you mother. That's three guineas for the entire season, and all of us can attend every ball, between April and June."

"Isn't that rather exhausting?"

"Not at all, Mr Reddall," Mrs Cater Denby said. "It's well worth appearing at every ball, because if one misses something scandalous, one simply cannot ever forgive oneself, and then it's impossible to catch up. Am I right, William dear?"

"Yes, mother," said Denby sighing. "But I must admit Luke, I do get rather tired, or actually," he whispered behind his hand, "Rather bored. The same old faces, and I mean old."

"I heard that William," protested Mrs Cater Denby. "Isn't he naughty, Mr Reddall! It's not true at all. We've some extremely handsome young men, and pretty young ladies come down for the season. Do we not Rachel dear?"

Quietly eating her lunch, Miss Newcomb was nevertheless listening to the conversation.

"Well Mary," she said. "I do agree with William. Sometimes, it can become rather tedious."

"Rachel! Admit it. I can't keep you away by mid-season. You're rapacious."

They laughed, falling silent as Shell and Lovelock cleared the course ready for dessert.

"Denby, if we're going out tonight," Luke said, as they smoked cigars. "I'll need to get back to Hayward's to bathe and change. Also, I must pack for tomorrow. There'll be no time in the morning. And there's Clarence to think of. His tack will need cleaning. I'll not have him on the train looking like a nag."

"Then come on!" urged Denby. "Let's say goodbye to mother, and Miss Newcomb and be on our way."

Chapter Ten

The afternoon was spent pleasantly, by smoking, playing cards, in between, Luke packing. Subsequently, once the men had bathed, shaved and dressed, it was time to hail a chariot, and head off to the Upper Assembly Rooms.

It seemed to Luke the whole of Bath society was about that evening, folk strolling along the elegant streets, riding on horseback, or in open carriages. Everyone enjoying the spring evening.

What had he done on his last birthday, Luke pondered? He spent it with John Baker, at Durra Durra, he remembered, enjoying dinner, and drinking wine, afterward playing a game of cribbage.

Who would ever have imagined, a year later, that he would be in another country, in a beautiful city, and on his way to a grand ball.

As Luke and Denby stepped from the carriage, heads at the door turned to see who was arriving. Quite a queue had formed under the entrance portico, a resplendent gathering of elegantly dressed ladies and gentlemen. Everyone excited to be at the first ball of the season. Denby and Luke joined the end of the line, Luke hardly feeling out of place, dressed in his new clothes, fresh from the tailor in Milsom Street.

Appearing spruce, and at the height of fashion, who would have believed, that here, standing in line, and about to enter Bath's Upper Assembly rooms, was the man who once sheared and washed sheep, fought and killed a bushranger, as well as quelling a native uprising.

Luke's velvet frock coat was a deep shade of indigo, with a large collar that brushed his ear lobes. Over the collar, his neatly cut, black hair, hung in glossy locks, a morning visit to the barber certifying his chin was smooth, and his side burns deftly combed.

Beneath his coat, Luke wore a white silk shirt, under a yellow chequered silk waistcoat, fastened, at the front by bright brass buttons. Inside his coat collar, his standing shirt collar was high, and well starched, a white silk cravat tied around his neck, ending in a large bow under his chin. He had on a pair of high waisted, grey, fall front, woollen trousers, tapering to the ankle; on his feet, a pair of neat black shining leather shoes. Along with everything, a pair of white cotton gloves were tucked into his inside coat pocket.

Luke certainly looked a dandy from head to toe, and quite the part, if he were to begin revealing to Bath society his true identity.

On the other hand, Denby's taste in clothes was slightly more outrageous. His collars just a little higher, the colour of his coat, somewhat brighter, his blonde hair set and waved to perfection, his side-whiskers frizzed, and his moustache waxed.

Inevitably, Luke and Denby found themselves scrutinized, not only by the young ladies in the queue, but also a few young gentlemen. It promised to be an interesting evening for them both.

Once they paid their admission, Luke and Denby proceeded to the gentlemen's cloakroom.

"What do we do, Denby?" Luke whispered, passing his hat and cane to an attendant.

Having done the same, Denby ushered Luke down a long corridor, taking in the faces of the people around him as they went.

"Wander about, and look interesting," Denby said. "A footman will give us a cordial. Then we'll walk around catching people's eyes. They'll talk to you, if they find you interesting, and I don't think you'll have a lot of trouble on that score. You look terribly interesting to me."

"Shut up!" Luke said, laughing. "Quiet. Here comes that footman."

Following Cater Denby as a sheep dog follows a shepherd, Luke marvelled at the warren of corridors and rooms, passing as they went, a refreshment room, maids, and footmen dressed in grey uniforms, busily arranging plates of food on a long buffet table. In addition, Luke was surprised to see a large octagonal room, where ladies and gentlemen were already sitting at card tables.

"What are they playing?" Luke asked, as they stood in the doorway.

"Bezique most likely," answered Denby, "and Whist. And most certainly, Beggar my Neighbour. Come on. I'll show you the library."

"A library!" Luke exclaimed. "Here?"

"Of course. Just in case things become boring."

"I can't imagine how things could get boring at a ball."

"They can, my dear chap, rest assured. Besides, the library can be an extremely convenient place to hide, should one be receiving avid, unwanted attention from a person one wishes, wholeheartedly, to go away."

It was already nine o'clock, but the rooms were only half-full.

"When does it begin?" Luke asked, as Denby led him down yet another passage.

"Soon. The orchestra gets going around now. Then they serve refreshments. Afterwards, the serious dancing begins."

"What time does it finish?"

"Officially, at twelve. But one has to pay extra if one wishes to stay. Pays for the musicians, don't you know."

"Can we smoke?"

"Of course! Whatever next! Where've you been, where a gentleman couldn't smoke?"

Luke shrugged.

"Nowhere, I suppose."

Walking down the corridor, toward a pair of glazed and frosted doors, the sound of an orchestra began drifting toward them. Two footmen stood in front of the doors, and as if on cue, took hold of the polished brass door handles, and pulling them open, allowed Luke and Denby into the ballroom. The music of a Mozart waltz filling his ears, Luke gazed around in wonder.

Never in his life had he seen anything as beautiful as the grand ballroom of the Upper Assembly Rooms, finding it impossible to take in the brilliance of everything at once. As a result, Luke allowed his eyes to stray over each magnificent detail in turn, describing them to himself, so as to make sense of every detail in his mind.

The ballroom was enormous, soaring to a spectacular ornate plaster ceiling, from which five glittering chandeliers hung from decorative ceiling roses. The overall impression was white, akin to the whiteness of a wedding cake. White, crystal, as well as gilt. Encircling Luke, a classical stucco frieze encompassed the room, a third of the way below the ceiling. Upon the towering wall facing the windows, appeared pilasters, and then equally spaced niches, occupied by marble statues, the wall resembling the side of a Greek or Roman temple, and lastly capped by a grand architrave, a frieze, and then a cornice.

A wide alcove and balcony featured mid-way along the wall, and it was here the orchestra were playing, the conductor wildly waving his baton.

Along the wall below the sparkling windows, and conveniently located, were two white marble hearths, plus an additional pair at either end of the ballroom. Around these, people gathered, laughing and gossiping, everyone embracing a merry fire, burning in the grate. Between the fireplaces, large cedar doors led to various corridors and vestibules beyond.

"I've never seen a room as enormous," Luke said.

"It's one hundred and sixty five feet long, and forty three feet wide," Denby said proudly, having noticed his new friend's expression of amazement.

"How do you know?"

"There's an inscription in the entrance lobby, informing the patrons. I've read it numerous times, while waiting in line as one does."

"Look at the fancy ceiling," gasped Luke, gazing upwards.

"Forty two feet high," Denby said.

Denby was also watching couples already dancing a minuet.

"Ah ha! I see the Napier's are here."

Turning his back on the dancers, Denby shouted in Luke's ear.

"They were very conspicuous last year. Took a house at

Freshford. Only here for the election. The old man, Sir William, is quite a writer these days. He's written a marvellous series of volumes on the Peninsular Wars. You must read them. He's also quite a radical, don't you know. I heard they wanted him to stand for the seat of Bath, but he persuaded young Roebuck instead. Until last year, we had Viscount Powerscourt as our parliamentary member. Then at the election, Roebuck got him out by a landslide."

"You surprise me, Denby," Luke said. "I didn't know you were interested in politics."

"One needs to have something to talk about with the fellows, when the ladies retire," answered Denby. "Personally, I'd far rather be with the women. Most men are so stuffy, don't you think."

Luke noticed a man standing in the centre of a group of adoring females. He was tall, middle-aged and sporting an elegant moustache, and goatee beard, plus a flamboyant dark brown coiffure. Although, his most impressive feature was his deep blue tunic, resplendent with medals and ribbons.

"Who's that?" Luke said, directing Denby's attention to the man.

"My word!" gasped Denby. "He's back. Don't let him see we're looking. He's dreadfully vain. Then of course, he would be. He's French, don't you know."

"But who is he? He looks very important."

"That because he is I suppose. If he has his way, he'll rule France. That's Charles Louis Napoleon Bonaparte. Boney's nephew."

"Really!" gasped Luke. "Does he live in Bath?"

"On and off. He buzzes back to Paris, after one coup or another. Then scarpers back here, when things start to look dangerous."

Luke was beginning to enjoy seeing the notable and the notorious.

"Any other famous people here?" he asked.

Denby scanned the growing numbers, milling around the ballroom.

"Hang on!" he said. "Now that's interesting. I'm amazed he has the effrontery to show his face."

"Who's that?" Luke said, following Denby's gaze.

"You see that handsome gentleman, standing with two women, and an old man, underneath the orchestra gallery."

Immediately, Luke could see the man to whom Denby was referring.

"That's Sir John Conroy. You must have heard of him. It was a dreadful scandal."

"No Denby," replied Luke. "I'm sorry. We never hear of such things in Australia. Mary Kinchela was the only person to write to me, and she would have been too modest to mention a scandal. If indeed, she ever heard of them. What happened?"

"Up until the coronation, five years ago," Denby began. "Conroy was comptroller of the household of the Duke and Duchess of Kent."

Luke frowned.

"The Queen's mother and father!" continued Denby. "Well! When the old Duke died, Conroy stayed on with the family. For years it was rumoured, he and the duchess were lovers, and even bandied about..." at this point, Denby spoke close to Luke's ear, "He's the queen's father."

Luke looked at him in amazement.

"But mother and I don't believe it," scoffed Denby. "Look at him. So handsome! How could her majesty possibly be a child of his? If ever you saw her father the duke, you'd say, he and her Royal Highness were like peas in a pod. Round faces. Big noses, and small chins. A typical Hanover head, as mother and I would say."

"I've heard she's not vastly pretty," remarked Luke, "and I have that from one who's seen her first hand. Has the Queen ever visited Bath?"

"Certainly," Denby said, leaning towards Luke, clearly about to impart more scandal. "She arrived to open Victoria Park, when she was the Princess Victoria. The park I showed you yesterday, below the Royal Crescent. But she's never been back, and do you know why?"

Luke laughed, realising he was about to hear another choice snippet of gossip.

"Because, my dear Luke, at the opening ceremony, one of mothers friends, and I've been sworn to secrecy as to her identity, was heard to say quite loudly, that the princess had thick ankles. Well it got back to Her Royal Highness, didn't it, so she's shunned Bath ever since."

"Then what happened to Conroy?" asked Luke. "Why has he the gall to be here?"

"One of the Queen's ladies in waiting was Lady Flora Rawdon Hastings," Denby began, taking a gulp of cordial. "She was the daughter of Sir Francis Rawdon Hastings, Governor General of India. Now, Lady Flora had been to Scotland on a visit. But when she returned, she looked considerably larger, than before she left."

Denby gave Luke a knowing wink, while once more leaning close to Luke's ear, since the gay music was growing louder, and the noisy chatter increasing.

"Understandably," Denby said, "as Lady Flora was unmarried, and in her early thirties, tongues began to wag. But not only was her waist growing, but she was experiencing considerable pain. Consequently, Flora paid a visit to the Queen's physician, who told her she was pregnant. The doctor saw her for a whole month, keeping his findings a close secret."

"How on earth do you keep up with all the gossip, Denby?" asked Luke, laughing.

"Talk of the clubs, and the Pump Room, Luke old chap. It was quite common knowledge in polite circles, and even made The Times."

Unperturbed, Denby continued with his scandalous story.

"However, that chatter box, the Marchioness of Tavistock got wind of it, and told Lord Melbourne, the Prime Minister. Then of course, it got to the ears of the Queen."

By the expression on his face, Luke knew Denby was nearing the climax of his story.

"Lady Flora was not a woman to keep her feelings to herself. She outwardly disliked Baroness Lehzen, the queen's friend and confidant, and neither was Flora keen on Lord Melbourne. She was also a close friend of Sir John Conroy, whom by now, the Queen detested, having sacked him from his job as equerry. As a result, Victoria hardly held Lady Flora in her favour, allowing it to be presumed around the court that Conroy was the father of Lady

Flora's unborn child. Poor Flora's honour was stained, and despite the testimony of two physicians, discounting the pregnancy, the Queen failed to be convinced, and Flora was shunned at court. Sad and wretched, Flora stayed on at the palace, but the Queen would have nothing to do with her. Finally, after several months Flora took to her bed, and died."

Luke looked at Denby in astonishment.

"But how was that?" he asked. "Surely, she must have received the best possible care during the delivery. And what happened to the baby?"

"There was no baby," Denby said, mysteriously. "Flora's family always believed Flora was chaste, insisting on an autopsy, revealing a huge cancer of the liver. They were outraged of course, the story making all the newspapers. The behaviour of the Queen throughout the entire tragic affair was the talk of the country, and has done her a great deal of harm since. Last year, I went to the opera at Covent Garden, and the Queen was in her box, sitting behind a curtain. Although people were unable to see her, she was booed all the same. People calling out, 'Where's Flora?' I was quite taken aback, I must say."

Suddenly, from behind them they heard a familiar voice.

"Now what are you boys up to?"

It was Mrs Cater Denby.

"I was telling Luke about the scandal."

"Now which scandal is that dear?"

"Lady Flora."

"That's old news, William. I'm sure it'll all be forgotten in another few years. It was her mother, the Marchioness of Hastings who finished up the worst, poor thing. The woman was so devastated by the loss of her daughter; she passed away six months later. They say she died of a broken heart."

"Where's Miss Newcomb?" Denby asked, searching the crowd.

"She's one of her heads, dear. She's taken a powder, and gone to bed. So I'm foot loose and fancy free, as they say."

Mrs Cater Denby was wearing yet another remarkable costume, Luke admiring the bright red satin ball gown, trimmed with white lace, and yellow ribbons.

"If I may say, you look wonderful, Mrs Cater Denby," he said.

"You may, Mr Reddall. And thank you, kind sir. I hope you'll mark my card for a polka. It's quite the new thing, don't you know, and I think far more fun than the waltz."

Taking a glass of cordial from a footman, Mrs Cater Denby gazed at the dancers, presently dancing a quadrille. A row of ladies and gentlemen, entwining, changing sides, bowing, curtsying, and promenading the full length of the ballroom.

"I don't dance," Luke whispered into Denby's ear.

"You what!" he said loudly.

"Shush! I don't dance Denby. Father hired a dancing master at the school, but my brother John and I were only about ten. I won't be able to remember a thing. Anyway, they were dances, danced in those days, not any of this up to date stuff."

"What do you mean?" Denby said, clearly amused to see Luke's embarrassment. "You saw the minuet just now. That's been around since old King George. And we always finish with a Sir Roger De Coverly. You must know that!"

"I think so," said Luke nervously. "I don't know."

"We have Scotch Reels," added Denby, "and La Boulangere. They're great fun."

"I suppose so. Although your mother wants me to partner her in the Polka. I haven't danced for years."

Denby laughed.

"Don't worry old chap," he said. "Just follow the others. But don't wave your arms about, or lift your knees high. Look at them."

He pointed to a row of gentlemen, advancing and retreating to the music of the violins, reflecting their female partners, on the opposite side of the dance floor.

"See how they dance from the hips downward. They hardly move their chests or shoulders, and mostly keep their arms behind their backs. If you're in a corkscrew, or a thread the needle…"

"What on earth are they?"

"Look!" Denby said, pointing again to a row of ladies and gentlemen, meeting in the middle, turning back-to-back, and gaily revolving to the music.

"That's a corkscrew."

The couples then parted, the ladies joining hands, and holding their arms above their heads. While the gentlemen wove their way between them, thus changing sides.

"And that's a thread the needle."

Luke shrugged, looking miserable.

"Oh well," he sighed. "I'll have a go. That's if anyone asks me."

"Who's going to ask you?" Denby exclaimed. "You have to be the one to ask. What am I going to do with you?"

He clapped Luke on the back.

"Cheer up old chap! You'll be fine. Come on. Let's get something to eat."

By now, the tea room was bursting, people eagerly consuming the cold banquet. At a point nearest the door, a queue had formed, ahead of a long, linen covered table, ranging from one end of the room to the other. Each person, having collected a plate, was helping him or herself, to either cold ox or lamb tongue, roast pork, roast beef, quail, partridge, pigeon, pheasant, rabbit or hare. Presented in silver dishes, and china tureens, along the length of the table, the cooked meats were accompanied by various steamed vegetables, sweet or spicy pickles and preserves.

Positioned beside Denby in the queue, Luke marvelled at the plaster decorations on the ceiling above his head, and the magnificent chandeliers, recently fitted for gas, causing the room to shine as bright as day.

Ahead of Denby and Luke, the Napier sisters were serving themselves with poached salmon, now and then, turning to Luke and Denby, and smiling. Then, when they returned the gesture, the sisters fell into fits of giggling.

"What's that all about?" asked Luke.

"Take no notice!" Denby said, helping himself to a plate from the stack provided. "They're a bunch of silly women. All spinsters. They've got their eye on you because you're a new face."

As it was now their turn to begin to fill their plates, Luke became overwhelmed by the assortment of food on offer.

"What are you having Denby?" he asked.

"Certainly not fish," Denby answered. "We had trout for lunch. I'll probably have mutton and pickles. I'm not really very hungry. But you have what you please."

Luke helped himself to cold pheasant, and potatoes in mayonnaise.

"There've been pheasants in the colonies since it was founded. But not many," he said, as they slowly made their way along the table, putting food on their plates.

"How extraordinary!" Denby exclaimed. "Then there can't be much to shoot?"

"There're native pigeons and quail," Luke said, pointing to the roast game displayed on various dishes. "But nothing like this. We've rabbits and hares, brought by the first fleet."

"Then you only eat sheep, cows, and pigs?" added Denby.

"But there are Kangaroos, opossums, ducks, geese, and brush turkeys."

"My!" Denby said in astonishment, "What's Kangaroo like?"

"Pretty tasty. Apparently, much the same as English deer. But since we've no deer either, I wouldn't know."

"Ah! Then if it tastes like venison, I wouldn't mind it."

Once their plates were filled, Luke and Denby broke out of the queue, and looked around the refreshment room for a table, observing most were occupied. Denby, however, noticed one vacant on the far side, near the doors, so he and Luke headed towards it. Nonetheless, the Napier girls had also seen it, arriving first.

"Damn!" cursed Denby, under his breath. "Those girls are a trial. Come on. There are two seats unoccupied. We'll have to sit with them."

Getting closer, Luke realised the Napier girls had seen he and Denby approaching through the crowd of hungry patrons, and had begun to whisper, and excitedly flutter their fans. Reaching the table, the gentlemen bowed.

"May we join you, ladies?" Denby asked. "There seems to be no other seats available."

"Certainly," the elder sister said, gesturing to the chair beside her.

"Please," the second sister said to Luke, waving her hand languidly at the other chair.

Placing their plates on the table, the men sat down.

"What will I call you?" Denby whispered in Luke's ear. "Reddall or Soame?"

"It's my birthday," Luke said, from behind his hand. "And the first day of my new life. From now on, I think I'll be Soame."

"Good evening, Emily," Denby said. "How very nice to see you."

"Good evening, William," answered the elder sister. "It's pleasant to see you also."

"We've met on many occasions," Denby went on. "But please allow me to introduce my friend, Mr Luke Soame. He's new to Bath."

"Good evening, Mr Soame," Emily said, the other girls smiling, while blushing coyly. "We're the Napier sisters. May I introduce my younger sister, Louisa Agnes?"

"How do you do?" Louisa said, looking at Luke from under her long eyelashes.

"How do you do," Luke said, smiling.

Blushing behind her fan, Louisa took over the introductions.

"This is my younger sister, Caroline, and her twin sister, Pamela Adelaide."

Nodding at Luke, the twins smiled demurely.

"It's Caroline and Pamela's first ball," Emily said. "They're terribly excited. I'm sorry if they've been unruly, by paying you too much attention."

"Not at all," Luke said. "It's also my first ball, so I know how they feel."

"Will you mark our cards, Mr Soame?" Caroline and Pamela said in unison. "We so wish you would."

Luke shot a glance at Denby, seeing him look away, and smile.

"Well I'm a little rusty," said Luke. "We don't do much dancing where I come from."

"We're sure you're a terribly good dancer," said Caroline. "Anyway, we'll help you if you make a mistake. Won't we sister."

Giggling into their fans, they hurriedly produced their dance cards, which Luke reluctantly marked.

"Would you care to dance this evening, Miss Louisa," Denby asked.

"I'm terribly sorry, William," she replied. "You know how I usually adore dancing with you. You're such a wag. However, my card is already quite full. Dear Emily has a quadrille, and a polka free. Have you not, Emily?"

The elder sister appeared embarrassed, fluttering her fan.

"Yes Louisa," she answered, secretly glaring at her sister. "I do have several dances available."

This hardly surprised Luke, thinking Emily a rather plain young woman, short and verging toward the plump. Homely, would be the way to describe her, he thought, having not the tall, elegance of her younger sister, since Louisa was quite the opposite in her expression and figure. In fact, Luke decided she resembled a young deer, graceful, elegant, with a fine neck, and gently sloping shoulders; her attractive face, framed by a collection of dark brown curls, falling from beneath a pretty lace cap. Except her eyes were Louisa's most alluring feature, being soft, brown and doe like, shining through long dark eyelashes, Louisa using these to their best advantage.

Therefore, Luke could easily see why she was unable to fit Denby onto her dance card.

Luke was having fun talking to the twins, finding their animated conversation fresh and amusing.

"Is it really your first ball, Mr Soame?" Pamela asked, fanning herself breathlessly. "It's the first Caroline and I have ever attended. We're sixteen. Well, just sixteen. Our mother took such a lot of persuading, didn't she Caroline."

"In Australia, which up until recently, I called home," Luke explained. "The nearest town was a long way away. So it was difficult to attend parties. I know in Sydney, there's nowhere one can attend a ball, night after night."

"Oh dear!" the girls said, frowning. "That must have been dreadful for you. How did you manage?"

Luke smiled.

"Now which dances are you putting me down for?"

In the ballroom, the music and dancing were becoming louder and faster.

"Look at mother!" Denby shouted. "She's managed to get Viscount Powerscourt on her arm. She didn't waste much time."

Luke and Denby were pushing their way through the crowd of onlookers, finally arriving at a position where they could see the revels clearly.

"Is your mother looking for another husband?" Luke asked.

"If she is, my dear chap," answered Denby. "Then she's barking up the wrong tree with His Lordship. Richard Wingfield's marriage to Lady Elizabeth is as strong as a rock. And he's a little young for mother, don't you agree."

"I thought you said she was over men for good."

"I know," Denby said, shaking his head. "But she says she seems quite happy being on her own, and with the friendship of Miss Newcomb. Even so, she enjoys the money side of marriage. Both Denby, my father, and Kimber, her last husband, left her with heaps. But mother's the kind who can always do with more."

Their position beside the dance floor was ideal, since it was directly under the musician's gallery, where they could see, and be seen, both equally as important, when attending a ball.

"How about you, Denby?" yelled Luke, over the clamour of violins, cellos, flutes and piccolos . "How do you manage to live without working?"

"Luke!" Denby exclaimed. "That's not the done thing to ask a gentleman. A gentleman might very well take offence, and refuse to answer."

"Sorry. I beg your pardon. I wasn't thinking."

"Don't worry," said Denby, putting an arm over Luke's shoulder. "Remember! No secrets! Friends tell each other everything. Father died when I was a youngster. Consumption, mother said. We lived in Mecklenburgh Square, in London. But he took a house here, so he could visit the baths for the cure. I was born in Gloucestershire, a few miles north of Bath, at Yate House, my mother's family home. Then, two years later, in London, my sister Anne was born."

Considering their position under the musician's gallery, Luke was finding it almost impossible to hear Denby. But, concentrating hard on his face and lips, he was able to follow his story.

"Father went on for a few more years. But steadily became worse. This meant Anne and I spent most of our time in Bath; when we weren't at school, that is. After father died, mother sold the London house, calling Bath her home. We were well off. Father's pension from the war office, don't you know. But then my paternal grandfather died, and left me an annuity. So that's how I came to be a gentleman of independent means."

The music from the balcony above them was both boisterous and rollicking.

"Wouldn't you ever wish to work?" Luke shouted.

"What would I do?" Denby answered, laughing.

"Teach history! You'd be marvellous."

"What! To a lot of snotty little boys, farting and picking their noses. No fear, Luke old chap! One day, maybe I'll take a professorship at my old college. But then again, I don't think they'd have me. I was a rascally fellow at Cambridge."

Luke laughed, as he could well imagine the larks his new friend must have played.

"Here's your quadrille with Pamela," Denby said, as the orchestra struck up a new tune. "Look! She's fluttering at you."

Pamela Napier had promised to look after Luke, and was as good as her word, steering him through what he later admitted to Denby to being a 'damn difficult dance'. Miss Napier moved Luke here, and tripped him there, as they cavorted, promenaded, bowed, and curtsied their way through the complicated figures. Everyone in his circle, which included Denby, partnering Miss Caroline, together with Miss Louisa, plus a dashing young army blade, who turned out to be her brother, John Moore Augustus Napier, were more than generous, laughing gaily at Luke's mistakes. Therefore, by the end of the quadrille, Luke was feeling rather more relaxed with the entire business of dancing.

"Ladies and gentlemen!"

A voice drew everyone's attention to the musician's gallery, where a stout young man had appeared, his arms in the air, Luke amazed to see his huge side-whiskers, as well as great mop of brown hair.

"Welcome everyone," he said to loud cheers. "Welcome to the Assembly Rooms, and the first ball of the season. For those of you unfamiliar with our gaieties, may I introduce myself? I have the pleasure to be your host, James Chute."

Enormous cheers, ringing around the room.

"Some call me Jimmy," he continued. "Wee Jimmy."

The cheers turning to laughter.

"Those amongst you who I call my friends, that is. Therefore, I hope everyone whose first time it is tonight, will come to call me by the same."

Another great cheer.

"We're enormously fortunate to have with us this evening, the orchestra of our very own, Theatre Royal."

Yet another raucous cheer, and round of applause.

"They come to us fresh from a highly successful engagement in Paris. Where they were rightfully acclaimed."

A further roar ringing around the room.

"Then without further ado, let the frivolities continue. I leave you with the Patta-Cake Polka. Thank you Maestro, please."

The fiddlers began playing the merry tune, the conductor waving the baton with great aplomb over the players, and the dancers below.

From out of nowhere, Mrs Cater Denby was suddenly at Luke's side.

"Mr Reddall!" she cried, tugging his sleeve. "You marked my card. Remember?"

"Did I?" he said, frantically turning to Denby.

"Mother!" Denby said. "He's not to be called Reddall anymore. He's decided tonight, and forever after, he's to be Soame. Isn't that right Luke?"

Luke nodded.

"And please call me Luke, Mrs Cater Denby, Mr Soame sounds so serious."

"Very well, Luke," she said, anxiously looking toward the dancers. "But come on! We're missing the polka."

With that, she dragged him into the melee. And flinging one hand on his shoulder, gripping his hand with the other, whisked him away into the wild, stamping, galloping polka.

It was traditional to end every ball at Bath Assembly Rooms with the 'Sir Roger De Coverly', and tonight was no exception, the entire gathering forming two enormous lines, stretching from one end of the ballroom to the other. Once everyone was in position, the orchestra struck up the familiar tune, and the fun began.

Old gentlemen and ladies. Dowagers. Duchesses. Viscounts. Lords and Earls joined together in whooping, calling, yipping, and whinnying, as they tripped and capered up and down. Side to side. Back-to-back. Dainty feet pointing. Hands clapping. Heads bobbing, and backs bending. All in time to the merry music. Thus, with the last braying blast from a hunting horn, a night of frivolity was over. Although, in Luke's case, not quite over.

***

"You'll pop down and see us once in a while, I hope Luke," Mrs Cater Denby said, the hackney cab driving them to Church Street, the duration of the journey taking all of five minutes.

"Of course," he said, looking at Denby. "Wild horses couldn't keep me away."

"And now with Mr Brunel's lovely railway, it's so easy," she continued.

Sitting opposite them in the carriage, Luke smiled.

"I've only been in Bath a few days, but I've grown much attached to the city, and very fond of you both."

"And likewise, old thing," Denby said. "You're a breath of fresh air to us staid city folk, coming as you do from that wild and exciting country."

The coachman stopped outside the house, where Shell waited to help Mrs Cater Denby out of the carriage. Once she was safely down the steps, she looked inside.

"You boys say your goodbyes," she said. "And have a pleasant journey, Luke. I hope to see you again very soon. Goodnight."

"Goodnight," Luke said. "And thank you."

Sitting inside the carriage in the dark, neither man knew what to say.

"Hayward's is it, gentlemen?" the coachman called down.

"No wait cabby! Just a moment," Denby called.

He turned to Luke.

"You know!" he whispered. "We don't have to go back there."

Luke looked puzzled.

"Why?"

"We could stay here."

"But I thought you said your room was being used by Miss Newcombe."

"It is. But my sister's is empty. It's always made up in case she comes down from London unexpectedly."

"I suppose so," Luke said. "All the packing's done. And Clarence's tack is ready. Will anyone mind?"

"Mother will be fine. And Shell won't care either way. It's no work for him. The room's ready anyway. What do you say?"

"Alright."

Denby smiled in the darkness.

"No thank you, driver!" he called. "We've changed our minds. We'll get out here."

Then, after paying the man, and with the clatter of the hackney cab disappearing into the night, Denby let them both in through the front door.

The house was quiet, Mrs Cater Denby having gone straight to bed, the servants nowhere to be found.

"Do you fancy a drink?" Denby whispered, as they climbed the stairs, the gas turned so low they could barely see each other.

Luke shook his head.

"No thanks. I'll need a clear head in the morning."

Arriving on the landing, tiptoeing past the first door, Denby put his fingers to his lips, and mouthed, 'mother'. Then, as they passed a door on the second landing, he did the same; this time mouthing, 'Miss Newcombe'.

Finally, arriving at Anne's bedroom door, Luke and Denby quietly slipped inside.

"There's usually a matchbox on the washstand," Denby said in the darkness, "You stay at the door. I can just see by the light from the hall."

A flicker from the oil lamp on the table beside the bed, announced to Luke that the matchbox had been found, and with a warm glow filling the small room, he was able to appreciate its cosy interior.

Papered throughout with a blue Chinese print, on a white surround, the same was echoed in the curtains and upholstery fabric. Placed around the room were various small pieces of furniture; a writing desk; dressing table and chair; a cabinet, filled with tiny porcelain figurines, and lastly, a bureau full of books. Against one wall stood a large, four-poster bed, high, and draped with lace, the bed covered expensively in a deep blue satin quilt. Two small tables were either side of the bed, Denby placing the lamp on the one facing the window.

With silk cushions arranged at the bedhead, and completing the ensemble, Luke thought it was definitely a sister's room.

"Hey!" he said, suddenly. "I've no nightshirt. What do I do?"

"I've not worn a nightshirt for years," Denby said, closing the curtains across the window. "Not since I left Eaton."

Luke laughed.

"That's very risqué of you, Denby," he said. "I'm fast forming the opinion you're something of a bohemian."

Denby took off his jacket, hanging it over the back of the chair.

"It's just that I can't bear the feeling of clothes when I'm in bed," he said. "I like to feel free. Like when we swim in the river."

"You swim in the river?"

Luke was hurriedly undressing; then embarrassed to be naked, bundled his clothes on the floor, pulled back the quilt and blankets, and quickly ducked beneath them.

"Oh yes!" continued Denby, languidly unbuttoning his waistcoat, and untying his cravat. "It's great fun."

Luke had pulled the blue satin quilt up to his chin, in order to watch Denby slowly undress, at the same time sensing an odd fluttering of anticipation in his stomach. Another portion of himself was beginning to stir beneath the quilt, Luke aware that this might perhaps be the moment to end all the years of loneliness, when at last he would finally be able to reveal his true self to another person.

"I wish I could swim," he sighed. "It must be wonderful to feel your body floating free. My friend John Baker tried to teach me. But I wasn't brave enough to take the final step. Are you good?"

Luke looked on as Denby took off his shirt and folded it neatly, laying it over his jacket.

"Not bad," he said, sitting on the chair, in order to remove his shoes. "We race across the Avon and back. And more than once, I've beaten all the other chaps. It's good exercise. I'll teach you, old man."

Denby stood to remove his shirt, and in the glow of lamplight, Luke could see by his friend's well-developed arms, chest, and stomach, that he was indeed an extremely fit young man.

"There's a gymnasium in Broad Street," continued Denby, beginning to unbutton the fall front of his trousers. "I go there once or twice a week, to swing clubs, wrestle, and lift the medicine ball. What with that, and a spot of shooting, and hunting, I reckon I'm a pretty athletic type of fellow."

With Denby now naked, all his clothes neatly laid upon the chair, Luke was able to fully appreciate, and agree with Denby, that he was indeed, a fit, and well-proportioned young man in every respect.

Denby climbed into bed, and reached across Luke in order to turn down the lamp.

"Denby!" said Luke, out of the darkness. "I want to thank you for the last few days. I can honestly say I've never enjoyed myself more. And you're the one responsible. You've filled every hour and minute with laughter and happiness."

"My pleasure, old chap. I too had a tremendous time. You're very good company, my friend."

"Your mother enjoyed herself tonight," Luke said, rolling onto his back, the sensation of cool linen on his bare skin, curious, yet appealing.

"She did!" Denby whispered. "But then she always does. She'd give anyone the run around, as my poor late departed father found to his cost."

"What do you mean?"

Luke turned to face him, seeing his profile in the lamplight.

"Mother got her claws into father, when he was just a lad."

Denby laughed quietly.

"Snatching him from the cradle, so to speak."

"Really?"

"He was a mere lad of nineteen, and she was twenty seven."

"No!"

Denby turned toward Luke, and laughed again, so close, Luke could smell lemon cordial on his breath, as well as a hint of bay rum from his cheeks.

"She's no doubt told you that my poor, dead, little sister was conceived somewhere up or down the Amalfi coast. Well! If my calculations are correct, her conception, more than likely occurred in the next county, in the woods behind Yate House."

Now it was Luke's turn to laugh.

"You're marvellous, Denby!" he said. "You're so good for me! I can be a reflective, gloomy sort of a chap sometimes. But your every word lifts my spirit."

All of a sudden, conversation ceased, the men suddenly aware of their own heartbeats, the thrill of being so close; the heat of their nakedness, exciting a passion that had existed between them, since the moment they met.

Out of the darkness, Denby was first to speak.

"Would you mind?" he whispered, "and would you be terribly embarrassed, if I kissed you?"

"Not at all," Luke answered. "and I won't be. And I wasn't, last night."

"Did I kiss you last night?"

"Yes."

"And you didn't mind?"

"Not at all."

"Well then, here goes."

Chapter Eleven

Clarence shied, as the screaming whistle pierced the air, a surge of steam belching from beneath the locomotive.

"You'd better get him on board, sir," shouted the guard, as he lowered the side of the wagon. "We'll be leaving in a minute. And no need to worry, sir. Your horse will be fine once we get underway."

"He'd better be," said Luke. "We've come a long way, he and I."

"Then I dare say he'll enjoy seeing a green field, sir."

"He will indeed."

Two hours earlier, Luke woke with a start. What was the time, he wondered, his heart raising? In the glimmer of light leaking around the curtains, he reached across Denby as he slept, checking the man's pocket watch that lay on the bedside table. Ten minutes to nine. Two hours before the train was due to leave.

"Denby!" Luke whispered, touching him on the shoulder. "Wake up. I have to go."

Denby stretched luxuriously.

"Good morning, Luke old chap," he yawned. "How did you sleep?"

"I had the best night I've ever had. But I must get up. It's nearly nine o'clock."

"Oh yes! The train. The damn train!"

"I know," said Luke. "But I have to go. I really must."

Denby grabbed him, pinning him to the pillow by his shoulders.

"I won't let you," he laughed.

"Get off me!" protested Luke, laughing.

"Never, never, never."

Denby tugged at the blankets, Luke initially resisting his efforts, until the younger man's strength prevailed, Luke vainly attempting to hide his embarrassment.

"We haven't the time," Luke said, seeing Denby's expression, once Luke had nothing with which to cover himself.

"But it'll be an age before we see each other again," Denby pleaded. "I'll not be able to resist you."

"All the more reason to be patient," said Luke.

Denby was not to be placated nevertheless, and the two men wrestled like schoolboys.

"Look," Luke said, when he was finally able to speak. "I'll write to you as soon as everything's settled. And you can come on a visit."

"Of course," Denby said, panting. "You can count your eggs on that."

There was a knock on the door.

"It's Shell," gasped Denby, pulling the quilt up to his chin. "Come in, Shell."

Luke attempted to dive for the covers, but was too late, since Shell was already in the room, walking to the washstand, holding a steaming jug.

"Your hot water, sir," he said.

"Thank you, Shell."

"Will you and the gentleman be taking breakfast, sir?"

"We shall, Shell. Thank you."

"Will that be all, sir?"

"Yes thank you, Shell."

"How did he know we were here?" whispered Luke, as the door closed.

"Shell knows everything," Denby said, mysteriously. "The all-seeing. All-hearing, Shell."

Laughing, they leapt out of bed, and ran to the washstand.

"I'm only washing," said Denby, wiping his face and body with a cloth. "Can't shave. My kits at Hayward's."

"So's mine!" Luke said. "Will anyone mind me being here?"

"This time of the morning, we'll be eating breakfast alone. Mother won't be up for hours. And Miss Newcomb's at her morning walk."

Later, at Hayward's, the men went to their rooms, shaved, and changed into clean clothes. By which time there was only half an hour before the train would leave.

***

Luke and Denby watched the guard lead Clarence up the ramp into the horsebox.

"I've put your trunks in the luggage wagon, sir," the guard said, replacing the side, pulling the heavy bolts into place. "They'll be quite safe until you reach Paddington."

"Thank you," said Luke. "Which is my carriage, please?"

"The yellow one, sir. The one with first class on the door. You're in the middle compartment sir."

"Are you alright?" Denby asked, as they walked toward the end of the train. "You're very quiet. Are you nervous?"

"I know what you're saying," said Luke, looking askance at him. "I hear the tone in your voice. It's alright for you. You've been on a train. You know what it's like. This speed thing is all new to me."

"But you were a jockey! Surely, you're used to travelling fast."

"I suppose so. But it's the locomotive, and the wheels. At least when you ride a horse, you're in control. Maybe it's because I'm not driving."

"Alright," Denby said. "So now, not only do you want to be a duke, but you also wish to be an engine driver. There's no keeping up with you, old chap."

Denby laughed, at the same time as clapping Luke on the back.

"Don't worry," he said. "You'll like it. You've enjoyed every other new experience you've had in the last few days."

Luke turned on him in astonishment.

"You've the cheek of the devil, Mr Cater Denby!" he exclaimed, feigning indignation. "You're outrageous. But yes. It's true. I have. And I'm sure you're right."

Denby opened the compartment door.

"Come on," he said. "It's time you were getting along."

Luke climbed inside the carriage, the locomotive bursting into life once again, steam, and smoke erupting from the wheels and funnel.

"I nearly forgot!" Denby shouted over the roar. "This is for you."

He handed Luke a small, red velvet box.

"What on earth is it?" Luke said, leaning out of the window.

"Open it, and see."

Lifting the lid, Luke saw, lying on a cushion of white silk, a solid gold pocket watch, attached to a gold chain.

"Denby!" he gasped. "It's wonderful. I haven't had a watch since that villain Whitton stole mine, over a year ago. You really shouldn't have."

"Yes I should," replied Denby, casually. "I saw you didn't have one, and a gentleman must always have a watch, especially on a train journey. How else is he going to check the speed?"

"How do I do that?"

The guard blew his whistle, and waved his flag.

"Never mind," added Denby. "Look! You're moving."

The locomotive was belching steam and smoke, far greater than before, this time the large driving wheels beginning to turn, the wooden carriages, rolling and clanking together.

"You know how I feel, Denby," Luke shouted, as the train pulled away.

"Me too," Denby replied.

Denby was walking beside the carriage, keeping up with the train.

"I want you to know. I've never felt like this before!" Luke called.

"Me neither!"

Denby was running to keep up.

"I'll miss you terribly!" Luke shouted.

The figure of Denby standing at the end of the platform, receded into the distance.

"I'll write!"

Luke watched Denby waving, until the train made a great curve to the left. Then suddenly he was gone, and sitting back in his seat, Luke saw through his tears, the great panorama of Bath pass before his eyes. There was the bell tower of the abbey, standing majestically in the centre of the city, the spires of smaller churches throughout, also pointing to the sky. Then the mighty River Avon, deep, green, and dark, slowly winding its way through the valley, toward Bristol and the sea. The remarkable Pulteney Bridge, spanning the river, the churning weir no longer turning Luke's heart to ice. Then finally, the tiers of terraces and crescents, ascending gloriously, to meet at last the green pastures of the surrounding countryside. Luke had seen many wonderful visions in his life, timeless landscapes, remarkable sunsets, and endless skies, but here, before him was a vision that would endure in his heart forever. The true beauty of Bath.

"Going far?" a voice said.

Turning away from the view, Luke was surprised to see a middle-aged gentleman, sitting at the opposite window.

"I'm sorry," Luke said, taking out his handkerchief, and blowing his nose. "I didn't realise there was anyone else here. Yes. London. I'm going to London."

In saying so, he felt a flutter of excitement. He was bound for London. How incredible! London! The biggest city in the world. He was both thrilled, and nervous; an odd, unfamiliar feeling.

"How about you?" Luke asked.

"London."

The gentleman took a silver case from his inside jacket pocket.

"Cigar?" he asked, holding it open.

"Thank you," replied Luke. "Don't mind if I do."

Leaning across the compartment Luke took a cigar, the gentleman striking a match on the cigar case, lighting Luke's, and then his own.

"Allow me to introduce myself," he said. "William Day Wills."

"Very pleased to meet you, Mr Wills. Luke William Soame."

They shook hands.

"Do you travel often?" Luke asked, puffing on the large cigar.

"A couple of times a year," Mr Wills replied. "In fact, I've been up twice since the line opened. I used to make the journey on the mail. This is considerably more comfortable, don't you think."

"Indeed!" Luke said, endeavouring to give the impression of a seasoned traveller. "Do you have business in London?"

"Two factories, and several warehouses. I'm a cigar manufacturer."

"I see."

Which explained the fine quality of Luke's cigar.

"The railway opened last June," Mr Wills continued. "It's proving extremely successful. By the time we reach London, this compartment will be full."

Sitting back in his seat, enjoying the sensation of speed, together with the sound of the wheels on the track, and a good cigar, Luke surveyed his surroundings. The seats were comfortable, furnished in deep blue velvet, cushioned, and buttoned, separated by comfortable armrests. Teak trimmed the windows, and panelled the walls, leather straps in the doors, allowing passenger to open and close the windows. Every modern convenience had been considered, even down to a ventilator in the ceiling, lest the compartment become stuffy.

As the train rattled and clattered along, Luke sensed it gradually gaining speed. Therefore, endeavouring to relax, he gazed at the meadows of the Avon valley, passing ever rapidly beyond the window. Presently, the railway joined a canal, Luke noticing several barges gliding ponderously through the languid water, towed from the towpath by straining horses.

Yet, the faster they went, the image vanished in an instant, the rhythm of the wheels on the track, the passing trees and shrubbery, indicating the rate at which they were travelling.

With the clouds now flying by, Luke felt exhilarated by the rush of speed.

"We're moving along now," he said to his companion. "How fast do you think we're travelling?"

"Thirty five miles an hour, I'd say," said Mr Wills, consulting his pocket watch.

"But my friend says the train reaches fifty," Luke continued. "Do you mean we go faster than this?"

Mr Wills smiled.

"First time eh?"

Luke nodded, sheepishly.

"Until recently," he confessed. "I lived in Australia. There's no railway there. Not yet, anyway."

"And it'll be a long time before there is," Mr Wills commented, "by what I hear of the inaccessible terrain."

"Indeed. The land is harsh. The geography and vegetation unyielding. It'll be difficult to cut a swathe through."

Mr Wills stubbed out his cigar in the brass ashtray beside the window.

"Talking of cutting a swathe," he said. "We've Box Tunnel coming up soon. Although we'll stop before we go through."

"Why?"

"To allow people to get off. Some find the idea of the tunnel frightening."

Luke sat up, interested to hear what Mr Wills might say about Box Tunnel.

"A few believe it'll burst their eardrums, or suffocate them."

"I've read much the same in The Times," Luke said. "But what happens to those who get out?"

"They catch a coach. Taking the turnpike over the top to the other end of the tunnel. Then wait for the following train."

Luke laughed, since it did seem rather ridiculous. Nonetheless, he was nervous, wondering whether there was any foundation to their fears. Denby, and now Mr Wills, had been through Box Tunnel, and they seemed unharmed.

Once the train left the valley of the River Avon, the following section of track between Bathford and Box was as straight as an arrow, allowing the engine driver to open the valves, and let the locomotive show off its full potential, since they were positively flying.

"Heavens!" Luke shouted, the thrill causing him to forget himself for a moment. "How about this! This railway is incredible."

Mr Wills laughed.

"Pull down the window," he said. "Then you'll get a real sense of how fast we're going."

"You don't mind?"

"Not at all. Go ahead."

Unbuckling the leather strap from the brass stud, Luke lowered the window, a blast of air bursting inside, filling the compartment with the scent of fresh meadows and ploughed fields. Luke stood up and faced the window, feeling the air rushing past outside.

"Put your head out, and look at the engine," Mr Wills shouted. "Be careful though. If you get a smut in your eye, they're a devil, and hurt like hell."

At first, Luke was fearful, the sight of the trees, roads, and bridges rushing by in hap hazardous confusion, confounding him. The train must be travelling at over fifty miles an hour, perhaps nearer sixty. However, summoning the courage, he did as Mr Wills suggested, and looked toward the front of the train.

For a moment, the speed snatched the breath from his mouth. Even riding at full gallop, was nothing in comparison, the rush of air stinging his face and eyes. Squinting, lest he encountered a deadly smut, and seeing the track taking a bend to the left, suddenly he saw the locomotive, in all its glory.

A magnificent monster of smoke and steam, shining in its green and Indian red livery, the brass fire hood, chimney top, rails and pipes, sparkling in the sunshine. Thick black smoke belched from the funnel, while white steam spewed from the wheels and pistons. And through it all, Luke could just make out the engine driver, busily adjusting valves. While the fireman swiftly shovelled coal into the firebox, the great driving wheel turning at a rate faster than Luke had ever seen before, the connecting rod, hammering back and forth; pushing the train to even greater speeds.

A loud whistle pierced the air, Luke seeing a lane crossing the track, and approaching fast. A man stood beside a closed gate, waving a red flag, at the same time shouting to another sitting high on the seat of an empty hay wagon, three children beside him.

The children caught sight of Luke at the window, and waved, Luke waving back. Then the whole picture vanished, lost in a kaleidoscope of green leaves and grey branches.

Almost immediately, a cluster of houses, and the tower of a church emerged from amongst the trees, the train beginning to decrease its speed.

"Box!" said Mr Wills, as the carriage drew alongside a short wooden platform. "Now watch the antics."

Leaning out of the window as far as he was able, Luke noticed several porters, standing beside empty trolleys, waiting for the train to stop. While ahead, in the hillside, an enormous tunnel loomed ominously, Luke comparing it to the entrance of a terrible immeasurable abyss.

When the train finally came to a halt, people began climbing down from the carriages onto the platform, the guard who had Clarence in his charge, opening the luggage van, distributing bags and trunks to waiting porters. Meanwhile, the ladies and gentlemen who were shunning the tunnel, made their way to a waiting coach. They seemed resolute, convinced the tunnel would do them harm. Except, Mr Wills' confidence continued to reassure Luke, and he smiled, and shook his head, as the anxious people hurried away.

With everyone attended to, the guard blew his whistle, and the locomotive thundered into life once more, slowly edging away from the platform, the wheels picking up the rhythm of the joins in the track, the now familiar, 'clickety clack, clickety clack' sounding merry to Luke's ear. Happy though he was, he could hardly ignore the mouth of Box Tunnel, coming closer every second.

"Mr Soame," Mr Wills said, "you'd better shut the window. It'll get rather noisy."

Having closed the window, Luke sat back, and put his hands together in front of him. Although, he quickly realised their position might be construed as one of prayer, so he let them fall into his lap instead.

Suddenly, the compartment was plunged into darkness. They were inside the tunnel, and there was no going back.

As they tore along, at first, Luke thought the noise extremely loud, and actually rather frightening. Fearsome, yet thrilling. And staring wildly into the dark, he could feel his heart thumping like the wheels of the train, or the pounding of pistons.

"How long is it?" he shouted.

"Nearly two miles!" Mr Wills yelled from out of the darkness. "At the beginning it's about seventy feet deep. Then about three hundred, in the middle."

Hurtling along, Luke found he was growing accustomed to the roar. It certainly was never going to deafen him.

"How is it we can breathe?"

"There are five ventilation shafts, sunk from the surface," Mr Wills explained, "each thirty feet wide. The motion of the speeding train pulls the air down into the tunnel."

"Can two trains pass each other?"

"Absolutely. There's a double track. But I haven't experienced it yet. At this speed, it'll take us about three minutes to get from one end to the other. Just about long enough to boil an egg."

All of a sudden, Luke began to panic, since he was encountering a strange heaviness, and a thickness in his ears. Could this be the first symptoms of deafness?

"What's happening Mr Wills? I feel my ears are blocked. Can you feel it?"

"Don't worry. Its pressure due to our depth, plus the speed we're travelling. I'd say we're almost in the middle. Don't worry, Mr Soame. The feeling will pass. Swallowing hard helps the ears unblock."

Luke decided not to let his mind dwell too much on the thought of three hundred foot of solid Oolite Limestone above him, looking forward instead to the light that would eventually return; which indeed it did, flooding the compartment, to Luke's great relief. It had been a thrilling ride, but he was glad it was over.

The train began to slow, no doubt approaching another halt.

This time a handful of people waited on the platform. And in a short while, once everyone was occupying seats, with bags and baggage safely stowed, the train was on the move once more.

As Mr Wills predicted, at each station along the way more people boarded. Consequently, by one o'clock, he and Luke had the company of four other passengers, leaving just two seats to fill.

An elderly lady got on at Pangbourne, taking the seat opposite Luke. Dressed from head to toe in black satin, and wearing a black bonnet, the front draped with black net, she was obviously in mourning. A black cocker spaniel sat on her lap, Luke smiling courteously, as the old lady made herself comfortable. Several minutes later, nonetheless, once the train was on its way, the old lady became uneasy, all of a sudden lifting her veil, Luke observing her concerned expression.

"I'm so sorry," she said. "Would you kindly do me a service, young man?"

"Certainly," replied Luke.

"Would you change seats with me? I'm afraid I'm not keen travelling with my back to the engine. It causes me to feel quite queer."

"Of course."

Luke stood up, and assisting her into his seat, settled into hers. However, he had to agree, because it was indeed a somewhat disconcerting feeling, travelling backwards. So it pleased him to know there was merely an hour before the train would arrive in London.

At Reading, an extremely large old gentleman, wearing a heavy coat and a broad brimmed hat, filled the remaining seat. He was a jolly chap, insisting on introducing himself to everyone.

"Ambrose True!" he said loudly. "Very pleased to make your acquaintances."

Everyone nodded. Nonetheless, no one responded.

"Butchery's my trade," he continued. "Butcher of Reading. Been established a hundred years, don't you know. Anyone finding themselves in Reading, and looking for a choice bit of meat, then I'm your man."

Luke and the rest of the passengers smiled, although no one uttered a word. Perhaps this was an example of the English reserve, Luke heard so much about.

After Reading, the towns and villages passing by became increasingly frequent and extensive, Luke marvelling at the number of houses, side-by-side, marching up roadways, and down streets. Each appeared the same as its neighbour, with single upstairs and downstairs windows, owning an identical front door, plus a slate roof, and four clay chimney pots.

To Luke, having lived all his life in a country where one's neighbour could well be twenty, or even fifty miles away, this proximity appeared incomprehensible. The concept of thousands upon thousands of people, crowded together, carrying on their daily lives, working, eating, living, and dying, all within a few feet of each other, was completely alien to him.

Steaming through the fringes of the metropolis, the engine picked up speed, Mr Wills informing everyone in the compartment that they were travelling, almost certainly, at sixty miles an hour. Cuttings, embankments, and road and river bridges, sped by in a giddy swirl of colour and light, making it impossible for Luke to focus on one thing at a time.

Eventually, however, the train began to slow, and he was able to see terraces of elegant houses, painted white, stretching away to the countryside beyond. Could they be the new desirable, outer suburbs of Maida Vale and Paddington, Luke read about in The Times?

Then the run into the terminus itself, shunting yards and coachwork sheds to the left and right, locomotives standing, some in steam, and prepared for another run, others idle, their work complete for the day. Next, the stop. The last turn of the wheel. The final blow of steam, and the journey over.

After bidding farewell to Mr Wills, and thanking him for his gift of a box of cigars, Luke hastened along the crowded platform, past jostling passengers and porters with barrows, eventually arriving at the horsebox at the end of the train, where the guard was unbolting the door.

"Did you enjoy the journey, sir?" he asked.

"I did," answered Luke. "Thank you. I think I could get addicted to train travel. It's quite exhilarating."

"If you would care to saddle your horse inside the wagon, sir," the porter suggested, "you'll find it easier. I've so many people claiming luggage."

"Of course."

Luke climbed up the ramp.

It was dark and cool inside the horsebox, smelling of fresh hay, Clarence pleased to see his master, nuzzling his hand.

"What did you think of that then, old lad?" Luke said. "Pretty good, wasn't it!"

Chapter Twelve

Denby recommended Luke stay at the White Lion, in Edgeware Road, so it was to the inn Luke arranged for the guard to send his luggage. Then, riding Clarence cautiously into the street alongside the terminus building, Luke asked himself why a modern marvel such as The Great Western Railway possessed just a small wooden station. Yet his query was answered, when he noticed a huge edifice under construction across the road, a vast span of iron tracery, vaulting almost seventy feet from one high wall to the other. A breathtaking piece of engineering, which would eventually become the roof of Paddington Station.

The guard said it was merely a matter of yards to Edgeware Road, and he was correct. Since before Luke knew it, he had ridden down bustling Praed Street, and was turning into even busier, Edgeware Road, completely ensnared by horses, carts, carriages and wagons, the noise and dust overwhelming.

To a man of the open plains, and soaring ranges, it was unnerving to Luke, nonetheless, as vendors shouted their wares, young and old hurrying about their business, appearing entirely at ease in the hurly burly in which they inhabited. Finding everything altogether alarming, Luke searched desperately for a place of refuge, and found it, a quarter of a mile up the road, at the junction with Harrow Road, at the fine old inn, The White Lion.

White Lion Passage ran behind the inn, where Luke discovered, amongst a maze of outhouses, stables, an ostler with whom to leave his horse. Then, letting himself inside the inn through the back door, he followed twisting, dark passageways, passing heavy doors and thick oak pillars, arriving finally in the taproom.

It was crowded with men, the beams above them blackened by hundreds of years of grime, small leadlight windows hardly allowing enough light from outside, to be of any use. Luke pushed through the throng, and reaching the counter, caught the eye of a young man working there.

"Good afternoon, sir. What can I get you?" the young man asked, wiping the counter with a cloth.

"I'd like a room, please," said Luke.

"Certainly sir. Mr Smith will see to you, sir. Although he's inconvenienced at present. Would you care for a drink, until he returns?"

"Actually," Luke said, "I'm just this minute off the train, and quite hungry. Could I perhaps have something to eat?"

"I can't say, sir," answered the young man. "Mrs Hensy will have finished dinner. But she may have something left. I'll ask. Drink sir?"

"Yes please. A glass of wine, if I may."

Enjoying the warm effect of the wine, Luke remained at the bar, until the young man returned.

"Yes sir," he said, cheerfully. "Good news. Mrs Hensy says she's a pig's trotter left over, and will warm up some vegetables. If you'd care to take the door beside the window, sir, you'll find yourself in the hall. The door opposite leads to the dining room. Agnes will bring it to you."

Thanking the young man, Luke edged his way through the crowd, and out into the hallway.

The dining room was large and airy, appearing to be an extension of the old inn, Luke presuming it to have been added in recent years. Dark oak tables and chairs, extended along the centre, a drinks bar close to the door. Also, Luke was curious to see at the end of the room, a platform under an arch, appearing to be a stage, judging by a plush red curtain, gold ropes, and tassels, ranged above a row of footlights. Obviously, the dining room had a secondary function.

Feeling somewhat odd and uneasy, sitting alone, and sipping his wine, it pleased Luke to see the door open, and a young woman bustle in, carrying a meal on a tray.

"Your pig's trotter, sir!" she said. "And Mrs Hensy's heated some parsnips and a few turnips. I'm Agnes, sir. Pleased to meet you."

Agnes put a plate and a steaming tureen on the table.

"Thank you, Agnes," said Luke. "And I'm very pleased to meet you also.

"Mr Smith will be with you presently, sir," Agnes said, tucking a lock of her hair back under her mob cap. "It's a room you'll be wanting, is it not sir?"

"Yes Agnes. A room for the night, and a stable for my horse. Thank Mrs Hensy for me."

"Certainly sir."

Agnes hurried away, leaving Luke alone once more.

Eating in silence, his thoughts dwelt on Denby. Luke wondered what his friend might be doing at that hour. So, taking his new watch from his waistcoat pocket, and flipping the lid, he saw it was approaching four o'clock.

Would Denby be taking tea with his mother? Otherwise, could he be swinging clubs at the gymnasium. Since it was Tuesday, and considering the first ball of the season had been held the previous night, there would be no ball that evening.

It was only five hours since Luke last saw Denby, but he already missed him, and felt lonely. A small part of him wished he had asked Denby along, but logically he knew the next stage of the journey must be carried out alone.

The door opened again, and a young man hurried to the table.

"Good afternoon, sir," he said. "My name's Smith. George Smith. I'm the proprietor of The White Lion. No sir! Please don't get up. I'd not wish to interrupt your meal. I understand you'd like a room.

Luke nodded, his mouth full of succulent pork meat.

"Mr Watts and his son left after dinner," continued Mr Smith. "So I've asked Agnes to make up a fresh bed for you in the upstairs front. Everything will be ready by the time you finish. To whom am I addressing, sir? So I can put you in the register?"

"Soame," mumbled Luke. "Luke Soame."

"Thank you, Mr Soame."

"Excuse me, Mr Smith," Luke said, between mouthfuls, seeing Mr Smith was about to leave. "But I'm intrigued. This room. Do you use it for theatrical entertainments? I notice it has a stage."

"We do, Mr Soame," said Mr Smith, proudly. "We're licensed for singing and dancing. Not so much your dramatic performance, sir. More a variety, you might say. My father built the room six years ago, when parts of the inn were modernised. At the time, father said he would like to pull the whole lot down, and build a music hall. He said there was money in musical entertainment."

"Well!" Luke said. "Maybe it'll happen one day. Who knows?"

A while later, Agnes returned to clear the table, also informing Luke his room was prepared.

"Just go back into the hall, sir," she explained, "and up the stairs. Second door along at the front. Charlie's put your trunk in there."

On opening the door, Luke was immediately impressed by the room's dimensions, also finding it unusual, because, considering the age of The White Lion, he calculated that his bedroom would be at least three hundred and fifty years old, Luke finding the concept of age hard to fathom, coming as he did from a country barely claiming fifty. Therefore, in order to take in his surroundings, he stood for a moment in the doorway.

He also noted the height of the room, because the thick oak beams above him were low enough to touch. Calico curtains hung at two lead light windows, facing the road, these locked fast, since if opened, Luke imagined the clamour from outside would be unbearable. Rush mats covered dark floorboards, and against one plain plastered wall, stood a carved oak tallboy, obviously intended as a wardrobe. An ancient crazed, framed mirror hung between the windows, while beneath it stood an oak chest, on it a water jug, inside a plain china bowl, clearly meant for his ablutions.

However, situated against the wall opposite the windows, was the one item Luke could hardly miss, this being an enormous four poster bed. Quite possibly the biggest Luke would ever see. Thick crimson brocade bed curtains were tied back against four deeply carved oak posts, and seeing the height of the mattress and pillows, Luke considered a ladder might be necessary to clamber into bed. Appearing entirely insignificant beside its oversized neighbour, a bedside table played host to a pewter candlestick, and a fresh candle.

Although austere in appearance, the solid oak furniture, plus a slight aroma of wood smoke issuing from a large inglenook fireplace, facing the foot of the bed, gave the room a warm, inviting atmosphere.

Luke climbed on to the bed, and sat on the edge, wondering what to do. It was already five o'clock. Should he explore the sights of London? A little late perhaps. Maybe a nap. Just a quick one. The sights could wait. Therefore, taking off his jacket, he laid back, the softness of the mattress enveloping him. So, shutting his eyes, and with a warm feeling of a pig's trotter in his stomach, memories of Box Tunnel, and Denby's smiling face filling his mind, Luke drifted into a deep sleep.

Music, and a woman's sweet warbling tones dragged Luke from his slumbers. And opening his eyes, he lay for a moment staring at the ceiling. Downstairs the entertainment had begun. It would be fun to take a look.

He checked his watch. Nine o'clock!

"I've slept for four hours!" he said aloud. "This won't do. Better get up."

Luke went to the chest, and picked up the jug, pouring water into the china bowl. Then, splashing his face, drying it on a towel, he combed his hair in the mirror. Putting on his jacket; then after checking his pockets for cash, and ensuring his trunk was firmly locked, he ventured out into the corridor, where, with a mixture of fear, as well as excitement, he closed the door behind him.

The quiet, empty dining room, where Luke had sat only hours earlier, had now been transformed by a seething mass of humanity, into a music hall, the air so thick with tobacco smoke, Luke could barely see the stage. Men and women around about him were sitting at tables, leaning against the walls, or standing at the bar, everybody swaying to music coming from an orchestra positioned below the footlights. In front of the musicians, a conductor waved his baton, while a young woman, dressed in white, stood on the stage in a spotlight, singing for all she was worth, her voice as clear and as lyrical as a nightingale's.

Luke's entrance into the music hall was not entirely unnoticed, because a pair of brightly painted ladies were sidling through the crowd towards him.

"Hello ducks," one said, tugging his sleeve. "Want some company?"

Luke turned to face them.

"No thanks," he said, smiling. "I'm not staying."

"Where're you going, lover boy? We'll tag along if you don't mind. Won't us Mavis. We'll show you a good time."

"Although, I'm not going yet," Luke stammered. "I thought I'd watch for a while, that's all."

Wishing whole-heartedly that they would go away, nonetheless, Luke could see the women were quite determined.

"You're not from round here, are you ducks." the other one said, nudging him in the ribs.

"Quite a looker, ain't cha. And that tan! Who gets a tan like that in April, eh? Do you think it's all over Marge? Do you reckon he'll let us see? Then he might give us a squiz at what he's got down there."

"By what I sees in his breeches, Mavis, he looks like he's enough to share. I don't think he'll disappoint us."

"I'm all of a quiver." Marge said, putting her arm through Luke's. "Come on! Give us a look ducky! Come out in the alley, and show us. It's nice and quiet out there."

"No! I'm sorry," Luke exclaimed, feeling his face flush with anger and embarrassment. "I won't. And it's not all over. And I'll not show you anything. What do you think I am?"

"A queer!" Marge said, under her breath. "That's what you are. A fucking queer! Who'd turn down two such lovely ladies like me and Mavis here, unless they were bent?"

Luke was dumbstruck.

What could he say? Admit to these women something he had known in his heart since he could remember. The something, which was his only way of expressing his love for anyone. Why must he hear this simple natural emotion derided by the dreadful word 'Queer'?

He bit his lip, refusing to answer. Then turned his back, and walked away.

"Oi! You think you can get away that easy?" Mavis shouted, hurrying after him. "We could get the runners on to you. Oh yes we could. Then you'd be for it. You'd swing."

They were like blowflies, buzzing around him unmercifully.

Luke saw the landlord, Mr Smith, standing beside the bar, keeping an eye on the patrons. So purposefully, he headed toward him.

"Good evening, Mr Soame," Smith said, seeing Luke approach. "I hope you're enjoying the entertainment."

Quickly glancing over his shoulder, searching for Marge and Mavis, Luke was pleased to see they had disappeared into the crowd.

"I certainly am, Mr Smith," Luke answered. "Thank you. The young lady is a tremendous singer."

"We're very lucky to have Miss Lind with us tonight. It might be her one and only performance in London. She's on a lightning visit from Paris. Would you care for a drink?"

Luke smiled.

"Thank you."

Mr Smith beckoned to the young man who had served Luke earlier that afternoon.

"Wine is it not, sir," the young barman said.

"Thank you. That's right," Luke answered.

"So, what do you think of my music hall, Mr Soame?"

Obviously Mr Smith was taking pleasure impressing a newcomer.

"Most agreeable, is it not."

"It is sir. As yet I've not seen the like anywhere."

"Music Hall is fast becoming popular," continued Mr Smith. "I'm sure it won't be long before establishments such as this will be cropping up all over London."

Miss Lind burst into another song, the crowd joining in the chorus, everyone raising their glasses, and swaying to the music.

"Where are you heading tomorrow, Mr Soame?" shouted Mr

Smith, over the singing.

"Sudbury; in Suffolk," answered Luke. "Haverhill to be precise. I've been told I've to take the coach from the city. Is that correct?"

"Yes, sir. From the Belle Savage Tavern, on Ludgate Hill. All the eastern county coaches leave from there. I'm sorry I'm not able to tell you the times. Though my advice is to rise early. You can settle your room with my sister on your way up."

Luke thanked him, and looking at his watch, realised the lateness of the hour.

"If I don't see you in the morning, Mr Smith," Luke said, finishing his wine. "Thank you for your kindness and hospitality."

He shook Mr Smith's hand, and hurried through the crowd. Then, after paying for his bed and board, Luke climbed the stairs to bed.

Chapter Thirteen

Although exhausted, Luke found it difficult to sleep, the sound of the revellers below, together with the caustic ridicule of the prostitutes, ringing in his head.

'Queer! Queer!' they accused, repeatedly. And he was about to answer, 'What if I am!' Nevertheless, to say as much would have been dangerous, and entirely foolhardy.

Denounce him to the law! What constable would believe the word of two women of the street, against that of a gentleman?

Although they were right! Six years previously the hanging of James Pratt and John Smith, at Newgate, even made the Sydney Gazette. The crime, a word Luke dared not even bring himself to think of, let alone say.

This would be a lesson to Luke and Denby, that they must be on their guard, for men such as they, it was hazardous to show their true feelings, especially in that respect. Why had the women launched at him in such a fashion? Simply because he refused to take them to some dark secluded place, and violate them, as a brutish man would do.

They called him queer. Although there was nothing odd about him, Luke was convinced. He was gentle, kind, and in touch with his emotions. Yet, not in a feminine way. On no account was he feminine. He observed femininity in some men, finding it amusing, except unattractive, as well as, rather disconcerting. Therefore, if being honest and caring made him a queer, then he would say 'to hell with it!' He was a queer, and there it would end.

Now that he had finally recognised his demon, and faced it, there was no going back. And anyway, the demon was no longer anything to fear. Rather, it was a way of life, an alternative path to follow; especially now he had a companion to share the journey.

While he listened to Miss Lind singing so lyrically from the music hall below, Luke recalled his childhood. Had he known all along this hour would come? Was discovering his true self, an enormous shock? Certainly not. If he were honest. He always knew.

Even as a boy, Luke was aware of his feelings toward his own sex. His father would often take his brother John and himself to Sydney, on some jaunt or other, ultimately ending at Government House, considering father was a good friend of Governor Macquarie.

Luke remembered being fascinated to watch the soldiers, marching up and down, impressed, even at that tender age, by their manliness and handsome faces.

Then the native men on the farm, running naked. How splendid they appeared, wild and free, their black skin glistening in the hot sun.

All these emotions, however, lay locked away in Luke's heart. Dark and secret, Luke never imagining a time these covert passions would be revealed. Not until now, that is. To Denby at least. Dear Denby.

Aware of his true nature, in order Luke exist in the world of men, he had striven to cultivate a persona for himself. A devil may care attitude. Cavaliering sense of bravado. The pioneering spirit. An affable man. A man's man. The man everyone liked. Someone who could take or leave the ladies. Living the life of a gay bachelor. All the while lonely, existing as he did, far from society, with just his servants for company.

Believing this was the way it would be, until the day he died, Luke resigned himself to his fate. That is, until the arrival at Durra Durra of John Baker. That was the moment Luke knew he was capable of love.

But love from afar. The great man. So strong. Handsome, and

kind, had infatuated Luke. He could admit it now. Just the sight of John, lying naked beside him on the bank of the creek, raising in Luke unlimited passion, that was imperative to restrain.

Suddenly, Luke remembered the story Emma told about Soame, his father, and how, as a schoolboy, he developed feelings for John Baker. And how John spurned his father's advances, causing Soame to reap vengeance on everything John held dear.

It was a strange twist of fate, that God had dealt Luke the same inclination. Was this the only piece of his father's personality Luke had inherited? He truly wished it so.

Then there was Denby. How things changed in the blink of an eye.

'What of my future now?' Luke pondered.

Had he altered since spending last night with Denby? Had the realisation of his true self, and the discovery of what his life could really be, changed him? Was he different in any way, given that he had shown another man his true feelings? He knew his life was transformed; but he was the same person: the pioneer who opened up a savage land; the man who raced a horse, beating them all and winning the Macquarie Cup. Even now, he was still the young master who led his men across the Cataract River, the man who defeated a tribe of warrior natives, and killed the villain Tom Whitton.

There was only one small fundamental aspect about him that was different. Not strange to him, however, but strange for those unlike himself to understand.

The bell for last orders rang, Luke hearing the carousers in the street below his window, begin to wend their way home, still singing, a cacophony of tunes vanishing into the night.

Yet, still wakeful, Luke continued the struggle with his conscience.

"Jesus said, 'Love thy neighbour'," he said aloud, venting his frustration on the blackened beams above him. "Why then am I considered a criminal for loving Denby?"

Luke knew that society regarded him and Denby as sodomites! Fops! Or, as the harlots sneered, queer! But he was honest, brave, and true, with not a wicked bone in his body, and Denby was the same.

Why should he and Denby not have the right to love each other as they pleased? That love shown as a kiss. A warm embrace, or something more. Except, the times were such, that it was crucial they hide their relationship from the world.

If they were to reside together at Thurlow Hall, or Bath, either being Luke's wish, then it must be with careful privacy. Friends can be trusted. Whereas, servants gossip, leading to exposure, ridicule, and possible judicial action.

Perhaps a staff of like minded servants might be a solution, since they would hardly be slighted by Luke and Denby's show of affection, when they held the same feelings themselves.

As The Duke of Thurlow, it was Luke's duty to reside at Thurlow. After all, he had a responsibility to his staff, plus the population of the village. Since folk were unaware of Luke's lineage, if he and Denby intended to live together at Thurlow Hall, in order to curb wagging tongues, it might be necessary to invent a common blood relationship, to explain their intimacy. For example, they might put it about that they were cousins, or even half brothers.

Whatever the outcome, Luke was determined he and Denby find happiness together, enjoying the good times, as well as sharing the bad; a symbol of true love, if only for themselves alone.

At last, Luke smiled to himself in the darkness of the bedroom. He was convinced his love for Denby was natural, as normal as being either right or left handed. Last night had been glorious. Luke suffered no shame for what had passed between them. With Denby, he was himself at last, open, and honest, ready to face a potential hostile world with courage and optimism. There was hope, and he feared for nothing.

***

Early morning traffic on the Edgeware Road woke him, although Luke could see no light peeking around the curtains, just proving to him how early the populous of London began their business.

His new pocket watch lay on the bedside table, and lighting the candle, Luke saw it was barely five o'clock. It would be another hour before sunrise, and he was already wide-awake, the epiphany of the previous night filling his soul with joy. He was ready to face the day, and at sunset, his journey would finally end. He would arrive at his new home. Thurlow Hall.

Therefore, casting aside reflection, caring little for the hour, Luke threw off the blankets, and hastily washed, shaved, and dressed. Then, after re-packing his trunk, went downstairs for breakfast.

***

The inn seemed deserted. Nonetheless, the sound of rattling bottles drew Luke to the taproom, and looking inside, saw Agnes sweeping the floor behind the bar, while a man knelt stacking shelves, replenishing them with full bottles, ready for another day. The man stacking the shelves noticed Luke in the doorway, and stood.

"Morning sir," he said. "Charlie Bloomfield's my name, can I be of service?"

"Good morning, Charlie," Luke said, smiling. "I'd like breakfast, if Mrs Hensy's up and about."

"She is sir," answered Charlie, cheerily. "And by the smell coming from the kitchen, I'd say she's frying sausages."

"Well aren't I lucky."

"Agnes will bring it to you in the dining room, sir. But then again! In there's not a pretty sight. As yet, we've not had time to clean up. Perhaps you'd better eat it here, sir. Take a seat over there, if you may."

Charlie pointed across the bar, to a table under the window.

"Anything to drink sir? Porter? Ale? Rum?"

"No thanks," chuckled Luke. "Tea will be fine."

Minutes later, Mrs Hensy delivered Luke's plate of sausages, remaining beside the table while he took the first mouthful.

"Delicious, Mrs Hensy!" Luke said. "I've never tasted better."

"Thank you, sir," she said. "I gets 'em from the butcher in Church Street. Pork, with a touch of sage and pepper."

"Tell me, Mrs Hensy," Luke said, taking a gulp of tea, "I'm from Australia, and so a stranger to London. How would I find Ludgate Hill?"

"Lorks luva duck! Don't ask me dear!" she exclaimed, smiling.

"I've never been further east than Tottenham Court Road. Charlie's your man. He'll tell you. He was born within the sound of bow bells. He's a proper cockney. Knows everything there is to know about London, and more to boot, I shouldn't wonder."

Mrs Hensy shouted across the bar.

"Ere Charlie! The gent's from the colonies. He's a stranger to London, and wants to know the best way to get to the city."

Charlie stuck his head above the bar.

"Two ways sir," he said. "Both almost the same, although the Holborn way will be your quickest. Then again sir, being a stranger, you'd more than likely wish to see the sights."

"If I've time," said Luke, cutting into his second sausage.

"Where are you going sir, if I may be so bold?"

"Haverhill, Suffolk."

"Then you'll be leaving from the 'Belle'."

"That's right," Luke said. "'The Belle Sauvage'."

"I worked there for two years, sir," said Charlie. "Junior pot man. I remember the Cambridge Coach leaving at noon each day, except Sundays."

Luke laughed.

"Charlie you're a wonder! That'll give me plenty of time. Perhaps I should see the sights."

"Then you'll need to go down Edgeware Road to Oxford Street," Charlie explained. "You'll see Hyde Park opposite. Turn left. Then after a while, right into Park Lane. You won't miss Turnpike. That's where old Tyburn used to be. You've heard of Tyburn, I dare say?"

Luke shook his head.

"Tyburn Tree was the name of the gallows, where they hung the felons. They do say it stood there three hundred years. My grandfather once told me he remembered wagons leaving Newgate, loaded with prisoners, all bound for Tyburn."

"There you are sir!" Mrs Hensy said laughing. "What did I tell you! Didn't I say Charlie knew his onions?"

"Where do they hang people now?" Luke asked, biting into his third sausage.

"Newgate sir," Charlie replied. "Quite close to the Belle. You might be lucky. They hang every day."

Luke shuddered. He cared little about missing a hanging, thinking of far better things to see or do.

"When you get to the end of Park Lane, sir," continued Charlie. Turn left. The mansion you see on your right is the home of the hero of Waterloo, The Duke of Wellington."

"I've heard of him, of course," said Luke, "He was Prime Minister, was he not."

"Indeed sir. And a good one too. He's the leader of the House of Lords these days."

"Where do I go from there?"

"Along Piccadilly, you'll see a load more grand houses to your left and right. Go right into Haymarket, and pass the Theatre Royal on your left."

"Hang on Charlie!" Luke said. "All these left and rights. I'll get lost for sure. Can you write down the directions for me?"

Charlie looked embarrassed.

"Oh I see," said Luke, realising his blunder. "Then once you've finished, if you bring me a piece of paper, and a pencil, and then tell me again, I'll write the directions down."

Charlie continued to describe the remainder of the route, explaining in detail the plans in place to create a new square at the end of the Haymarket, to be called Trafalgar Square, dedicated to, and commemorating the great Lord Horatio Nelson. He then described the Strand; the mansion of Somerset House; the church of St Martins in the Fields, along with other churches along the way.

As Luke enjoyed his sausages, he listened keenly, while the pot man told of the history of the City of London, St Paul's Cathedral, and The Belle Sauvage itself.

"Been on Ludgate Hill for over three hundred years sir."

"Isn't a French name, in the middle of London, a little odd?" Luke said.

"I heard tell sir, the inn was once owned by a family by the name of Sauvage. But then, some say it's named after a book called 'La Belle Sauvage', written around the time of King Louise of France. All about a glamorous French adventuress, they say."

Agnes stopped sweeping, and gazed at Charlie.

"Oh Charlie!" she said, dreamily. "How lovely. Wouldn't I just fancy being La Belle Sauvage? I bet she never swept floors, and scrubbed pots."

"Thanks Charlie," Luke said. "You certainly know London."

"I told you so, sir," said Mrs Hensy. "How do you remember it all Charlie?"

"I hear things, and they stick in my mind," he answered bashfully.

Mrs Hensy picked up Luke's empty plate.

"Well you're lucky, ducks," she said. "I've brains like a sieve."

"You can't miss The Belle, sir," Charlie continued. "As soon as you turn from Fleet Markets into Ludgate Hill, you'll see the sign on the left. A native standing on a bell. An entrance between the houses takes you into Belle Sauvage Yard."

After noting the directions, and thanking Charlie, Luke arranged with him for his trunk to go on to The Belle Sauvage by hansom.

Clarence was saddled and ready when Luke arrived at the stables. So, tipping the groom, he mounted his horse, and rode out of the yard into the Edgeware Road.

It was early. The streets relatively quiet. Therefore, following Charlie's directions, Luke enjoyed a trouble free ride all the way to The Strand.

By then people were about their business, and reaching the Hungerford Markets, Luke found the road completely blocked with hansom cabs, carriages, wagons, and omnibuses. Deciding the noise, dust, and smell was unbearable, plus becoming convinced he had never seen a larger congregation of people, vehicles, and animals, Luke despaired of ever getting through.

Nevertheless, noticing several carriages turning right into a side street, and thinking it might be a short cut; Luke decided to follow. Anything better than being surrounded by such an unhealthy environment as a traffic jam. Thus, tagging on to the line of moving carriages and carts, Luke wound his way along Adelphi Terrace, past York Building Stairs, and the Adelphi Wharfs, where he encountered his first experience of the Thames.

The view of the river was breathtaking, glittering like a sheet of glass in the morning sun, the domes, rooftops, and steeples of the City of London rising majestically above its languid surface.

The sight, and pungent smell of the mighty river, plus the vision of the imposing edifice of Saint Paul's Cathedral, filled Luke with elation. Bath was beautiful, he reflected. Elegant and stylish. London, nonetheless, was magnificent. Beyond doubt, a city proud to be the hub of the world, Luke certain it would remain so forever.

Having negotiated a labyrinth of narrow streets, he eventually emerged into Savoy Street, and was soon back in The Strand, standing before Somerset House. Yet, the traffic was running smoothly, Luke realising the reason for the earlier bottleneck.

A large wagon lay on its side, strewn around it dozens of bales of wool. Luke stared at them, a shudder suddenly overwhelming him, his earlier exhilaration, and excitement melting away.

The sight of these simple bales, tied around with rope, jolted him back to reality. In the previous four months, he had never given his past a thought. The subsequent events had been so exciting, foreign, and strange, he barely gave himself a moment to think of his previous life. But here, in these humble bales, Luke saw comfort and safety. The symbol of his homeland. Was this the beginning of homesickness, he wondered?

Luke forced himself to look away, believing there would come a time to reminisce. There was much to do, and lots to achieve. The road ahead was clear, and digging in his spurs, he galloped on toward the dome of Saint Paul's, and the gradually rising sun.

Charlie was accurate to the last detail, and by following landmarks and street signs, Luke eventually arrived at the archway of La Belle Sauvage Yard, the sign causing him to smile, as it was indeed a naked savage, standing on a large yellow bell.

Taking out his pocket watch, he checked the time. Nine o'clock. And as if on cue, the great bell of Saint Paul's chimed the hour. So, turning Clarence under the arch, he entered the yard.

Chapter Fourteen

Earlier that same morning, at Thurlow, sixty-three miles to the north, Mary Bennet woke to the sound of the cockcrow, and listening to the chorus of birds heralding the beginning of another day, she wiggled her toes. It was impossible to get out of bed she decided, as she relished the soft linen enveloping her. Mary remembered too well the coarse sheets between which she slept, during her years as a servant, being unaware of their roughness until she experienced the quality of Irish linen she was now able to afford, since Her Ladyship's annuity.

"How our lives changed that day," she whispered to herself.

In the stroke of a pen, Mary would never need to work another moment, becoming a lady of leisure, she still finding it hard to believe.

After Lady Soame died, and once a suitable mourning period had elapsed, Perkins, Perkins, and Perkins arranged accounts for each of the servants mentioned in Lady Edwina's will. Considering their age, Mr and Mrs Ives, and Mr and Mrs Denton decided to retire, moving out of Oakwood, into cottages in Twerton, a rapidly growing village beside the River Avon, and south of Bath.

As neighbours, Mr Ives cultivated his vegetable garden, while Mrs Ives crocheted. Next-door, Mrs Denton baked pastries and pies, Mr Denton sometimes frequenting Bath Races whenever they were held. Theirs were carefree lives, and well deserved, after the years of service given to the Soame family.

Before they left Oakwood, however, Henry Waldon, the butler, had the task of recruiting a replacement cook, coachman, gardener and housekeeper, the interviews keeping him occupied for several weeks. Finally, each position was satisfactorily filled, and with everything at the school running smoothly, it was time for Henry to decide his own future.

One morning, a while later, Henry and Mary were sitting at the breakfast table.

"I've not seen Lizzie since she left to look after her father," Henry said. "We've written, but that's all. Neither of us is getting any younger. I'd like to think we'd spend the rest of our lives together."

"By that," Mary said, pouring him another cup of tea, "it sounds as if you want to return to Thurlow."

"Yes. I suppose I do," Henry admitted.

"But who'll take your place?"

It was obvious to Mary, that by Henry's answer, he had given the subject some thought.

"George Jesshope is quite capable of stepping into my shoes. He knows the job backwards. But what will you do Mary? Other than George, you'll be the only one left of the original staff."

Mary shrugged.

"I enjoy working," she said. "I don't know what I'd do if I didn't have sheets to wash, carpets to beat, or fires to make. I'm sure I'd be bored."

Henry laughed.

"I wouldn't. I'd swim, fish, and get a dog. A spaniel. I've always wanted a spaniel."

"Then again," Mary said, "I'd miss everyone terribly. And I'd feel a stranger with the others. I'm hardly close to Emma anymore. I'm sorry. I mean Miss Baker. She doesn't seem to be one of us any longer."

Henry took a while before he spoke what was in his mind.

"Then why not return with me?"

"Henry!" Mary exclaimed. "Should I? It's very tempting."

Therefore, that was how it happened. And Mary never regretted her decision.

Once Mary and Henry made their decision, Susan's future became the next consideration. Since Lady Soame's death, the little girl had become extremely attached to Henry, her grandfather. As a result, he and Emma decided Susan should also leave for Thurlow.

Finally, the day of departure arrived, and after saying goodbye to Emma, and the remaining staff, Mary, Susan, and Henry took the carriage into Bath, to catch the London mail coach from the York Hotel. Recalling the day he said farewell to his dear wife, Lizzie, all those years ago, this time his children, Rebecca, Mary and John James, as well as their respected families, were gathered to say goodbye to their father, with promises to visit, which was now perfectly possible with Mr Brunel's Great Western Railway soon to reach Bath.

With the sad goodbyes over, sitting inside the coach with Mary and Susan, as it rumbled down Walcott Street, Henry experienced mixed emotions. Part of him regretted leaving the city that contained so many fond memories, also still holding his children and grandchildren. Although, he was excited to be going home to Suffolk, Henry knowing in his heart, he wished to be with Lizzie. In addition, with the annuity to live on, they would surely enjoy their remaining years in peace and prosperity.

Back in the present, the memory of that day caused Mary to smile, and in the half-light, she opened her eyes, and gazed around her cosy bedroom at the little bits of furniture she bought once she moved into Sparrow Cottage. Every piece fitted nicely; leaving just enough room for her one and only luxury, a double bed. Stretching her legs to their furthest extent, feeling the soft feather down mattress beneath her, Mary recalled her old bed in the servant's attic at Thurlow Hall. It was the size of a coffin, the sheets, and blankets tucked in tight on either side.

Now she was in her own bed, bought with her own money, her bedroom filled with furniture and pictures, paid for by herself, her cottage rented from Mr Sparrow, the new innkeeper of the Cock Inn, across the street. Yet, before Mary went to sleep each night, she thanked God for her good fortune, and said a prayer of gratitude to her benefactress, Lady Soame.

Seeing the sky brightening through the window, a thought caused Mary some amusement, because, since her arrival in Thurlow, a considerable amount of attention had been paid to her by several members of the opposite sex; two gentlemen, appearing quite smitten. Young Robert French, the schoolmaster's son, for one. Since, despite being half her age, every Sunday, he would turn in his pew, and grin at her, doffing his hat whenever he passed her in the street. Also, the widower, Mr Sheehan, was showing an interest, with his gifts of honey, made by his own bees.

It was curious, she thought, how little attention she received from men when she was young, no doubt caused by the sight of her pock marked face, and thinning hair, both results of the terrible disease that killed others of her family.

Mary hoped Mr French and Mr Sheehan's attention was not due to her being a woman of means. But it mattered little if it was. She was enjoying the courtesy all the same.

"This won't do," she said aloud, throwing back the covers. "Poor Tibi. She'll need to go out."

***

The tiered balconies of the Belle Sauvage Inn reminded Luke of the Royal Hotel, although there was a vast difference between the two establishments, because, when Sydney's Royal Hotel was built, London's Belle Sauvage Inn was already four hundred years old.

An ostler ran across the cobblestones, grasping Clarence's bridle.

"Fine horse, sir!" he exclaimed, squinting in the morning sunshine. "Thoroughbred, ain't he?"

"Indeed young sir!" Luke said proudly. "Racehorse, don't you know. Australian racehorse. Winner of many a cup in his day."

"You're joking, ain't you sir? What's a horse from the colonies doing in London?"

"On his way to his new home, that's what."

Dismounting, Luke handed the lad the reins.

"I'm due to catch the mail to Cambridge at twelve," he said. "Could you look after him until then? There'll be sixpence in it for you."

"Sir! You're a gent," the lad said, laughing. "See it done sir."

He led Clarence away, no doubt eager to tell his fellow ostlers about Clarence's origins and pedigree.

In the meantime, Luke found the front door of the inn, and removing his hat, went inside.

Instantly he was transported to another time and place, as if dispatched to the days of his famous ancestor, Sir Stephen Soame. The man could well have frequented the inn, Luke decided, gazing at the oak beams, and dark studded doors. He may well have feasted on venison, or swan in the dining room, after all, he was the Lord Mayor of London, during Queen Elizabeth's reign, and The Belle Sauvage was famous even then.

The age of everything entranced Luke, since he considered the beams across the ceiling at the White Lion, low. But the ones above him presently, almost brushed his head, and Luke was by no means tall. The Elizabethans must have been very short, he told himself.

Across the hall, was a sideboard, Luke ringing a small bell placed there. While waiting for a response, he smelt an aroma of wood smoke, tobacco, cooked meat, boiled cabbage, and stale ale, deciding it was an agreeable combination of odours.

"Yes sir!"

For a moment, the woman's voice startled Luke.

"Welcome to the Belle Sauvage. I'm Amy Price. My husband, John Price, is the proprietor. Can I help you?"

Turning, Luke saw a comely, middle-aged woman standing in a doorway, a jolly smile on her shining face.

"Good morning, Mrs Price," he said. "My name's Soame. I'm visiting from overseas, and wish to catch the Cambridge coach. Do you think I'll get a seat?"

Mrs Price frowned.

"It is a Monday sir," she said. "It'll be busy. But it starts from here, so you could be lucky."

"Do I pay you," asked Luke, "or someone on the coach?"

"Bless me! Neither sir," Mrs Price exclaimed. "You pay at the office across the street. Can I get you anything? You've a few hours yet?"

"Is there a coffee house nearby?"

"Mrs Miller keeps the best around here. But Farringdon Street is a bit of a walk. If you'd like to try mine. I can't say it'll be up to her standards. But it's a good drop, all the same."

"I'm sure it is, Mrs Price," said Luke, chuckling. "I'd be pleased to."

Mrs Price showed him into the snug, and while she brewed his coffee, Luke sat in a comfortable armchair, taking the opportunity to look around.

Unlike its name implied, the snug was large, the beamed ceiling, twisting and turning, as if the once pliable oak structure had hardened with age. The walls between the criss cross oak supports were once white, Luke presumed, although they were stained yellow by tobacco smoke, having not seen a distemper brush for many years. As at the White Lion, the furniture appeared as ancient as the structure, and likewise, very strong, appearing well able to survive another four hundred years.

A framed picture, hanging over the inglenook fireplace, drew Luke's attention. Therefore, leaving his armchair to take a closer look, he discovered it to be a print, depicting the Belle Sauvage in olden times. Although discoloured and mottled with age, by the ruffs people were wearing around their necks, Luke deduced the era to be that of Queen Elizabeth.

A performance was happening in the yard, actors standing on a makeshift stage, the audience gathered around, some peering down from the balconies above.

It amazed Luke to see the inn in the print, unchanged, showing the identical lead light windows, curved wooden balcony rails, and twisting red brick chimneystacks.

Luke shook his head, the sense of age fascinating him, coming as he did from a country, still scarcely fifty-four years old.

Mrs Price returned, carrying a tray.

"Your coffee, sir," she said, placing it on a table beside his chair. "Ah! You've seen the old picture sir. Interesting isn't it."

"Yes very," Luke agreed. "It seems plays were performed here?"

"Indeed they were, sir. Before they built the playhouse across the river, La Belle Sauvage Yard was used by Mr Shakespeare. You've heard of Mr Shakespeare, sir?"

"Certainly, Mrs Price. Even in the colonies we can see a Shakespeare play."

"From the colonies are you, sir? Gracious me! We are privileged. I hope you enjoy your coffee, sir."

Mrs Price hurried back to the kitchen, leaving Luke alone to drink his coffee, plus smoke one of Mr Wills' splendid cigars.

Refreshed, and realising it was almost eleven o'clock, with just an hour before the coach was due, Luke gathered up his hat and cane, and crossed the street to the booking office.

"You're fortunate, sir!" exclaimed the booking clerk. "One seat remaining on top. Being Monday, we're busy. But you'd have the inside to yourself, if you was to wait until Wednesday."

"No thank you," said Luke. "On top will be fine. The weather's good, and I'll enjoy the view."

The clerk filled in the ticket, handing it to Luke.

"That'll be three florins, sir."

Paying him, Luke returned to The Belle Sauvage.

He began to feel anxious. The last leg of his journey was almost upon him, and he was keen to see it over quickly. He felt as if he had run out of places to see, and things to do. Comparing it to having eaten a delicious meal, but now could eat no more.

Therefore, irritable and edgy, he returned to the snug, and finding a copy of The Times, flicked through it with little interest, habitually checking, and rechecking his watch.

Mrs Price found him there, half an hour later.

"You'll be pleased to hear your trunk arrived a while ago, sir," she said. "Did you manage to get a seat?"

"I did Mrs Price," replied Luke, yawning nervously. "Thank you."

"Would you care for a bite to eat, Mr Soame?"

"I'm not very hungry Mrs Price, thank you all the same."

"You might be later," she continued. "It's seven hours to Cambridge."

"I'm not going all the way. They let me off in a place called Haverhill. I've no idea where it is."

"Even so sir, you should eat something. Would you like me to make you up a box?"

"Thank you, Mrs Price. Although I don't want to be a bother."

"You're not a bother, sir," Mrs Price said laughing. "I'll be back in half a tick."

Glancing at his watch, Luke saw the hands approaching midday, and feeling mounting excitement, decided to wait outside, hoping that in observing the comings and goings, time might pass more quickly.

With sunshine filling the inn yard, the ostlers, grooms, and porters were busy preparing for the Cambridge Mail. So leaning against the wall, Luke watched travellers arriving by foot or carriage, everyone possessing luggage.

The ticket clerk was correct. Monday was an extremely busy day.

Suddenly, with the clarion call of the post horn proclaiming its imminent arrival, a gleaming, black, and red mail coach, drawn by four black horses, rumbled into the yard. A magnificent spectacle to see without a doubt. High in his seat, pulling hard on the reins, sat the driver, appearing splendid, wearing a red triple cloaked riding coat, shining black topper, and a bright yellow neckerchief; beside him the guard, dressed in a grey coat and top hat, and holding a brass post horn.

As soon as the coach came to a halt, four ostlers ran to the horses heads, taking hold of their bridles.

"Good day to one and all!" shouted the coachman. "This 'ere's the Cambridge Mail. All aboard for Hertford. Bishop Stortford. Saffron Waldon. Haverhill and Cambridge. All aboard now!"

Folk gathered around the coach, and waited their turn to climb inside or on top, all the while watching anxiously as porters arranged their luggage in the rack on the roof.

"Here he is sir," a voice called.

Waiting in line, Luke turned to see the ostler, to whom he had given charge of Clarence.

"He's fed and rested," said the young ostler. "Ready for the journey."

"Thanks lad," said Luke. "Here's sixpence. You've done well."

"Ta sir! You're a gent," the lad said, taking the coin, and tugging the curl on his forehead. "You have a good journey."

Luke led Clarence to the back of the coach, and called up to the guard.

"Shall I tie him here?"

"Yes sir!" the guard shouted. "That's right. He's strong, I hope. We've a fresh team up front."

"Don't worry," Luke said. "He'll keep up."

With his horse secured, Luke waited while the six passengers were seated inside. Then, climbing the rungs on the side of the coach, he joined his fellow travellers seated on the roof, everybody shaking hands. The post horn sounded for a second time, and the coachman cracked his whip. At the very moment they were about to move, however, Luke heard a woman shouting.

"Sir! Sir! Your lunch box, sir! Don't forget your lunch!"

Laughing, Luke leaned down to take it.

"Thank you, Mrs Price," he said, but his voice was drowned by another blast of the horn.

Mrs Price watched the coach rumble away under the arch, and out onto Ludgate Hill.

The final stage of Luke's journey had begun at last.

Chapter Fifteen

Each time Lizzie washed the sheets, her hands ached the more, so she was glad she need only wash them once every few months. Ever since her forty-ninth birthday, the pain in her joints plagued her increasingly. However, ignoring the discomfort, Lizzie resolutely refused to allow anyone else to do her washing, even though she certainly could afford to. No one washed as she did, and Lizzie was proud of the results from good hard scrubbing. Anyway, the cottage was too small. There was no room for a servant.

At the cottage beside the river, later that same morning, while pummelling the sheets on the washboard, Lizzie's thoughts dwelt on her son, and two daughters still residing in Bath. Her eldest girl, Rebecca, married to Robert More, already had three children, John, Harriet, and Elijah. Her youngest, Mary, recently married John Bowers, and had a baby on the way.

Poor John James was not so fortunate, however, since his wife seemed unable to give him a child that survived more than a year. Elizabeth Waldon wrote long letters to Lizzie, bemoaning her lot; convinced her husband was about to leave her, should she be unable to produce a healthy child. Of course, Lizzie was unaware of John James' opinion, as he still remained unable to read or write.

With a sheet thoroughly washed and wrung out, Lizzie carried it from the washhouse to the garden, pegging it on the line. Unexpectedly, the wind caught it, causing the sheet to flash in sun, dazzling her for a moment, a picture filling her mind: a little boy lying in the grass, smiling and laughing, his blue eyes dancing as they followed the sheets waving in the wind.

It was too hard to bear. Push the memory away, Lizzie told herself. Do something else. Forget about him.

***

From his lofty position on the mail coach, Luke gazed ahead, as the red sun slowly dipped toward the distant hills. He was hoping it would remain light enough for him to ride the last few miles to Thurlow. Yet, it was necessary to remind himself how protracted the evenings were in England, because where Luke came from, no sooner did the sun set, then it was dark. Though in this part of the world, there might be several hours of dusk before nightfall.

Luke was enjoying the journey more so than the coach ride he made from Plymouth, the previous week. Could it be that he was becoming accustomed to the countryside? Certainly, riding in the open air was a deal more thrilling.

After leaving The Belle Sauvage, the coach turned into Kingsland Road, beginning the slow, north easterly ascent out of the city. Then, leaving the dense metropolis behind, he and his travelling companions were soon bowling along, past flower nurseries, orchards in full bloom, and fields already sprouting spring vegetables. Experiencing the scent of the countryside, and the sweet fragrance of the fruit trees in flower, Luke felt exhilarated.

He particularly enjoyed speeding through the villages, since the approaching mail coach caused quite a stir, children running alongside, poking sticks into the gleaming red wheels, dogs barking, and chickens running for cover.

As soon as they left The Belle Sauvage Inn, the two gentlemen sitting opposite Luke, struck up a conversation. Clearly, they were colleagues, laughing and chatting, enjoying the occasional nip from their brandy flasks, together with a cigar or two.

A lad, dressed in a dark blue, velvet jacket, breeches and cap, was sat beside Luke. But he and Luke remained silent, letting the men do the talking. Nonetheless, after an hour the lad spoke up.

"He's your horse, isn't he sir," he said, looking down at Clarence over the rear of the coach. "I heard you talking to the guard before we left."

Luke nodded.

"He's mighty fine," the boy continued. "I've two horses. One at home, the other at school."

"He's good for his age," Luke said. "He was a present from my father, on my seventeenth birthday. Clarence was a two year old then."

"Really sir! I'm sixteen. The chap I ride at Sandhurst is eighteen. A real old timer. They call him Moses. My colt at home is only a yearling. He'll make a fine charger one of these days."

"Do you hunt?" Luke asked.

"Oh yes sir! We all hunt at Bottisham."

"Where's that?"

"Bottisham Hall. It's in the village of Bottisham. A few miles from Cambridge. Are you going to Cambridge, sir?"

"No," Luke replied. "I'll be getting off at Haverhill. Then I ride to Thurlow."

The boy nodded, although, by his expression, Luke could see he had never heard of Thurlow.

"I raced him in Australia," Luke continued. "We did well! Winning cups and money. He's travelled with me across the sea. We've only been here a week or so."

"Really sir!" the boy exclaimed. "A racehorse. That's why he'd make a good charger. He's well muscled."

"Are you at school in Sandhurst?" Luke asked.

"No sir. I'm at the college. Being you're from Australia, you've perhaps not heard of The Royal Military College. It's where boys like me go to train to be officers."

"What will you do when you pass out?"

"Father wants me to go into the artillery. Although I've a leaning toward the 13th Light Dragoons. They were in the thick of it at Waterloo."

Luke laughed.

"You're keen. I can see that."

"I am sir. If I were two years older, I'd be in Afghanistan. Did you hear about McNaughton, and old Elphinstone? What a fiasco sir! There was an enquiry. But the old boy died."

All of a sudden, the coach driver shouted.

"Duck everyone. Duck as we go under. The silly devils built it too low."

The gentlemen friends, and Luke and the boy, did as ordered, finding it necessary to crouch on the floor in order to miss the arch of a railway bridge, the bricks almost brushing the pile of luggage on the roof. Once the hazard was passed, they resumed their seats, the lad putting on his cap.

"You're from Australia, sir?" he said.

"Yes. That's correct."

"They didn't teach us much about Australian history at school."

Luke laughed.

"There isn't much to teach. It's a very young country. As yet, we've no real history to speak of."

"Are you in England for long?"

"I hope so. I've inherited property in Suffolk."

"Really!" exclaimed the boy. "May I ask from whom? I know most of the connected families in the county?"

"The Soame's."

"How extraordinary," the lad said, laughing. "That's my name. It's not my family name. It's my Christian name. I'm sorry sir. I've been tardy. A gentleman should always introduce himself at the forefront of a conversation. My name is Soame Gambier Jenyns."

In this way, Luke, and young Mr Jenyns continued their journey, laughing, sharing stories, and enjoying moments of silence. Luke thought him a pleasant young fellow, wishing him well in his future career in the thirteenth light dragoons.

***

At Thurlow, earlier that afternoon, Henry and Susan, his granddaughter, were taking their usual walk.

"Come away Jack! Here boy!" Henry shouted. But once the dog was on a scent, he seemed to lose all sense of hearing.

"Go and see what he's found, Susan dear," continued Henry. "If it's a stoat, it'll attack him for sure."

The little girl ran ahead along the path, and grabbed the spaniel's collar.

"He's very strong granddad," she shouted. "He won't let me see."

Finally managing to pull him back from the brambles, she stared into the hedge.

"It's a leveret, granddad."

"Hold him until I get there, Susan, otherwise he'll worry the poor young hare to death."

Restraining the dog until Henry was able to put him on the lead, Susan and her grandfather continued their walk, the spaniel pulling this way and that, following whichever scent he next encountered.

Several months previously, the field beside them was ploughed, drilled, and harrowed, ready for wheat. Now it was sprinkled with a coating of young plants, all reaching toward the spring sunshine. Watching Susan running ahead along the footpath, Henry smiled. In four months, he thought, the corn would be as golden as her hair.

By now, Jack the spaniel was far enough away from the baby hare for Henry to release him. So he unclipped the lead, the dog racing off down the path, his ears flying, his stumpy tail wagging for all it was worth.

"Hey Jack! You'll knock me over," Susan yelled, as he rushed past.

"He wants to be the first to catch a rabbit!" Henry shouted.

A stile was located at the corner of the field, and reaching it, Henry took out his pipe.

"Let's sit for a moment," he said, "so I can have a smoke."

Pulling himself onto the top rail, Henry filled his pipe from his tobacco pouch, while Susan sat below on the step.

"Grandad," she said. "The big house looks sad today."

Susan pointed towards Thurlow Hall on the opposite hill, appearing grey, forlorn and cheerless.

"Yes," Henry said. "Sometimes it does. It depends on the way the sun's shining. Now and then, in the evening, as the last of the sunset clips the woods, it looks magnificent, the windows reflecting the sun. It reminds me of the old days, when they shone, all of the rooms beyond, lit for a grand ball. Your grandmother gave some wonderful parties."

With Jack away chasing rabbits, Susan sat quietly looking at the house, while Henry puffed on his pipe.

"You're my real grandfather, aren't you grandfather." She said suddenly, looking up at him.

Henry smiled. They had the same conversation almost every time they were alone.

"Yes Susan," he answered. "I'm your real grandfather."

"But grandmother from the big house wasn't my real grandmother."

"That's right. Granny Lizzie's your real grandmother."

"But grandmother from the big house loved me."

"She did Susan. That's why she adopted you."

"After my real mother died."

Henry nodded. It was as if the girl needed to hear the story repeatedly to cement it into her mind. Susan looked up at him, her blue eyes shining under a frown.

"Granny Jesshope next door, is my other grandmother, isn't she."

"Yes. She's your mother, Alice's, mother."

"Grandad Jesshope died."

"A long time ago."

"But my father didn't die did he?"

The conversation inevitably arrived at this point, Henry always finding the question difficult to answer.

"No Susan," he said hesitantly. "He didn't die. He went away."

"A big ship took him."

"To a place far away. That's why he never writes."

Henry felt his stomach churn, all the emotions of loss and emptiness returning. In his heart, he wished she would cease asking the questions, although he knew his answers were important to her. They were silent again, while somewhere high above, a skylark sang, its tumbling song filling the blue void.

Susan gazed at the house.

"Will anyone ever live there again, granddad?"

"I hope so dear. I hope you will one day. Lady Edwina would

have wished it. You'll inherit everything on your twenty first birthday."

"I won't live there on my own, will I?" Susan said, suddenly concerned. "I'll be awfully lonely. You'd be there with me grandfather. You, and Granny Waldon and Granny Jesshope."

Henry laughed.

"Well I hope so. But we'll all be eleven years older."

Susan smiled, the frown vanishing.

"I wish we lived there now. We'd have such fun playing hide and seek."

Suddenly Henry realised, that in all his years in service at the hall, the only time he had ever heard the laughter of children, was when it opened its doors to the refugees from the great flood.

"Remembering it as I do," he said. "It would make a splendid place to play hide and seek. But don't you like living in the cottage?"

"I love it. My little room in the roof. My window. The view to the river. And the noise the poplars make, when the wind blows. It's cosy."

She hugged her knees, rocking on the step.

"But I love it most of all because my daddy was born there," Susan continued, "and my mummy lived next door. Granny Jesshope told me they played together, when they were tiny."

"They did. There was never anyone else for either of them. They were sweethearts."

Henry prepared himself for what was coming next.

"Do you think we'll see my daddy one day, Granddad?"

What could he say? If he said yes, he would be building her hopes. If no, she would be disappointed and sad. In the ten years since his son was taken, not a day went by without Henry wondered what happened to him. Was he dead or alive? In addition, what had happened to John Baker? Henry had never heard of his friend again, since the day he rode away from Oakwood. Henry was in doubt, unable to rejoice, or grieve.

Susan was more curious, the older she became, asking more and more questions. However, she was still too young to know the truth, Henry positive she would find it difficult to understand. Accordingly, his answer was always the same.

"Maybe one day. I hope so. I truly do."

Susan smiled, once again satisfied with her grandfather's reply.

"Come on," Henry said, climbing off the style. "Granny Waldon will be wondering where we are. She'll have tea ready by now."

Susan jumped up, shook her dress, tugging at her bonnet.

"Where's that naughty Jack," she said laughing. "Up to mischief, no doubt."

She ran off down the path to find him.

***

Dusk was falling as the coach rolled through the silent streets of Haverhill, the driver pulling up in the yard of The Bell Inn.

"All out for Haverhill!" he shouted, waking Luke's fellow travellers in the process.

Luke said goodbye, wishing the lad Soame Gambier Jenyns the best of fortune. Then climbing to the ground, the guard passed him his trunk, Luke untying Clarence, leading him to the water trough. Subsequently, in the blink of an eye, the coachman cracked his whip, and the coach rattled away into the gloom, leaving Luke and his horse alone in the inn yard.

"Nearly home Clarence, old chap," he said. "Only four miles to go."

A few men were sitting in the taproom, smoking pipes and drinking ale, except, if there had been any previous conversation, it ceased when Luke walked through the door.

"Evening gentlemen," he said. "Is the landlord about?"

"Ring!" someone grunted.

Therefore, walking to the counter, Luke rang a small bell placed there.

"Coming!" someone called from behind a door at the back.

In a moment, it opened, and a young woman appeared.

"Good evening, sir. I'm Mrs Ellis. What'll you be havin'?"

"Good evening, Mrs Ellis," said Luke. "I'm just this minute off the mail. Can I arrange for my trunk to be delivered to Thurlow?"

"Of course, sir. That'll be fine. I'll ask Mr Hagger to take it over on his cart in the morning. Where will you be staying sir? The Cock?"

"Is that the inn at Thurlow?"

"It is sir. Mr Sparrow's establishment."

"Then that's where I'll be. I'm a little uncertain where after that."

Thanking Mrs Ellis, Luke returned to the yard, and Clarence.

"All right boy. Everything's ready," he said, climbing into the saddle. "We're nearly home."

Allowing the horse his head, Luke galloped out of the yard, and into the High Street. Then turning left, spurred him toward the Wratting Road.

It was almost nightfall when Luke arrived at the hamlet of Little Wratting, two miles further north. Nonetheless, with Clarence going well, and the way good, he slowed the pace along the main street, as a caution a person, or animal might be in the road.

Beyond the village, reaching a crossroads, Luke was suddenly uncertain as to which direction to take. Nevertheless, in the gloom, he made out a signpost against a hedge, and after closer inspection, discovered the villages of Great Wratting, and then Thurlow were to the left, and only a few miles further on.

With his excitement mounting, digging his spurs into Clarence's flanks, Luke cantered away, breaking into a gallop, once he was free of habitation.

Reaching the tiny village, just as the last glimmer of dusk vanished from the sky, Luke's journey ended at last. He had finally arrived in Thurlow; his ancestral home, and the community and land around him, which he was soon to inherit. Therefore, wishing to appreciate the moment, Luke stopped and gazed at the scene.

In the remaining light, he saw a cluster of cottages, bordering the lane, their roofs covered in thick thatch, walls of black oak beams, and white daub. Even now, the windows under the thatch, glowed with lamp or candlelight, shimmering behind cotton curtains, concealing the cosy interiors.

Sniffing the rich odour of wood smoke, and cooked food, from somewhere faraway, Luke heard a church clock chime the hour. Counting seven, he imagined what was happening behind the closed curtains. Folk had eaten supper, and were settling down to an evening beside the fire.

Suddenly, with sadness, memories of John Baker flooded Luke's mind, since he would have gazed on the scene many times, and probably sighed, realising he was home. Had it not been for that bastard Tom Whitton, cursed Luke, his mind travelling back to the lonely grave beneath the river gums, John should have been there beside him, to enjoy the moment.

Nonetheless, shaking off his melancholy, Luke rode on, deciding it would be an insult to the peace and tranquillity to canter into the village, instead encouraging Clarence to walk, his hooves on the gravel road, the only sound.

Passing shadowy homes on each side, Luke eventually reached a crossroads, and looking ahead, saw a terrace of ancient dwellings, the doors, and windows facing the street, tall chimneys piercing the darkening sky.

Might these be the Alms-houses built by his ancestor, of which Emma spoke? If so, then the Soame School would be beside them. And sure enough, the dark hulk of a tall building appeared beyond a squat wall.

This is where it all began, thought Luke. Inside the classroom. Where his father subjected John Baker, and his friend, Henry Waldon, to such shame and humiliation.

Riding west, toward the fading sky, a church tower projected between the trees, a flag fluttering in the wind, Luke failing to recognise the emblem, since by now it was almost dark. Then, the lit windows of a large building appeared on his right, a swinging sign over the door. Was this the Cock Inn, he wondered? If so, then the cottage of John Baker's father and mother would be a little way further on.

Before reaching the inn, Luke heard someone calling out of the darkness, seeing a woman silhouetted in an open doorway.

"Tibby! Tibby! Tibby!"

Mary Bennet looked up and down the street, but there was no sign of her cat.

"Excuse me! Is that the Cock Inn?" asked a voice. "If so, I was wondering whether I'm going in the right direction for the blacksmith's shop."

"Oh you startled me!" gasped Mary. "I didn't hear you ride up. I'm calling my silly cat. She won't come in for her dinner. After mice, I'll be bound."

Mary peered into the darkness, searching to see the stranger.

"It's rather late for Mr Baker, sir. He'll have shut down the fire, I shouldn't wonder."

"No sorry," the man said. "I'm not in need of his services. I've information for him."

The stranger came nearer, Mary now able to see his face, lit by the light from her cottage door.

He was young and handsome. Maybe thirty or so. Smartly dressed. Conveying a manner she felt she recognized. Then she glimpsed his eyes. Emerald green. As green as Her Ladyship's jewels. As green as... She stopped, suddenly a memory of that day long ago making her shiver.

"Don't I know you?" she said without thinking.

The man stared at her.

"I beg your pardon?" he said.

"Oh sir! Please forgive me," Mary stuttered. "That was rude."

Astounded by her abruptness, Luke watched as her expression changed, from surprise to suspicion.

"There's something about you," she continued. "Wait. You're to see the Bakers?"

Luke could see her thinking, casting her mind back to some dim memory from long ago.

"You couldn't be," she whispered. "You just couldn't be! But it's remarkable! You so resemble her. But then..."

Mary took a deep breath.

"You're Emma's child aren't you?"

Luke stared at her in astonishment.

"Before I say another word madam, I think I should be acquainted with the person to whom I'm addressing."

"I'm Mary Bennet. I was parlour maid at the hall for many years. I was also Emma Baker's friend for a very long time."

She was looking at him keenly, the light from the doorway, enabling Luke to see her face. A tragic remnant of what was once pretty, but now scarred and pockmarked.

"Very pleased to meet you Mrs Bennet."

"Miss Bennet," said Mary hastily. "Thank you."

"Well, Miss Bennet. Your remarkable observations and assumptions are correct. I am indeed Emma Baker's son, and let me say in all honesty, you're the only person as yet to know. Miss Baker has instructed me that on no account should anyone be told."

Mary was triumphant.

"I knew it!" she exclaimed. "I knew there was something going on. But she wouldn't tell me. So that night, I followed her to the temple. I heard everything. All about the arrangement with Her Ladyship's friends."

"Who, up until a few months ago, I considered as my parents," Luke said. "Lady Soame sent someone to find me, and give me a letter. In it, she told me who I really am. I've travelled all the way from Australia."

"Dear, dear!" Mary said, "But you must be exhausted. You might think me a little forward, but I've just boiled the kettle. Would you care to come inside, and have a cup of tea?"

"Thank you, Miss Bennet. Tea would be most welcome."

Dismounting; then tying Clarence to the fence, Luke followed Mary inside.

"Please sir!" she said, beckoning to an armchair beside the fire. "Sit down. But dearie me, young man! I don't even know your name."

"It's Luke," he said, sitting down wearily.

While he relaxed, Mary bustled about, collecting teacups and saucers from the dresser, arranging them on the table.

"But what puzzles me," she said, "is how Her Ladyship found you."

Although it seemed to Luke that he had told it a dozen times, while Mary brewed the tea, he began to tell the story, Mary standing inside the kitchen door spellbound. In doing so, however, he refrained from revealing who delivered the news, and of John's death, preferring Mr and Mrs Baker to be the first to know of their son's tragic demise.

Mary poured Luke's tea. Nonetheless, she was still inquisitive.

"So you've come all this way to reveal yourself to your real mother."

Luke nodded.

"And now you're going to tell the Bakers they have a grandchild, born out of wedlock. I don't think they'll be very pleased to hear the news, young man. Nevertheless, what intrigues me, is why Her Ladyship should be so involved? It really had very little to do with her. It was Emma's baby, after all. The father obviously wanted nothing to do with her. Her Ladyship simply brought the party's together, and arranged the adoption."

Taking a deep breath, and replacing his cup in the saucer, Luke looked into Mary's eyes.

"Lady Soame had an extremely strong motive, Miss Bennet. You see, I'm her grandson."

Mary gaped, his words reverberating in her mind.

"You're Soames' son!" she said. "So he got what he wanted after all."

"Indeed! It seems so."

"I warned Emma, time and again to avoid him. But in those days, she was flighty, and easily flattered. A fickle piece, she was. Always thinking she could better herself. There you are then! What a thing! You're Soame's son. Of course! I can see it now. You're handsome. Just like your father, when he was young. You've his eyes. But then I see your grandmother there too. Though your face shows me that you're kind, not cruel like him. I'm sorry! I mustn't say such things. He was your father, after all."

"I don't mind, Miss Bennet. Miss Baker told me all about him."

"She did? What everything?"

Luke nodded.

"Well young man," Mary said, handing Luke the sugar bowl. "I'm wondering what Henry and Lizzie Waldon will make of this? Your father caused them terrible hurt."

Luke stared at her in amazement.

"Mr Waldon. Is he here?"

"Of course."

"I must see him."

"It's late sir. I'll take you to the forge in the morning. Then see Mr Waldon afterwards. Now drink your tea, before it gets cold."

At the Cock Inn, Luke was restless. Tomorrow, not only was he to be the bearer of the happiest news Lizzie and Henry Waldon could hear, he would also impart his sad tidings to Mr and Mrs Baker. Therefore, with this knowledge laying heavily on his mind, Luke tossed and turned for most of the night, finding an exhausted form of sleep, a few hours before dawn.

As always, Mary slept well. Although the Waldons entered her mind, as soon as she was conscious. She wondered how they would react on discovering the existence of an offspring of Soame, who was also about to become the Lord of the Manor.

She supposed it would greatly depend on their opinion of Luke. Personally, having only met him once, she considered him a charming young man, appearing entirely unlike his father, and rather akin to his grandmother. Whatever the Waldon's view, the outcome would be the same. Luke Soame was the rightful Duke of Thurlow, and nothing they could say or do would change the fact.

In the cottage beside the river, Henry and Lizzie lay awake listening. At first light, Susan had taken to lying in bed, quietly singing, the tunes mostly hymns she heard in church. She also sang little ditties she learned at school. 'Green Sleeves' and a Handle song beginning, 'Did you not hear my lady go down the garden singing?' her favourites.

Henry and Lizzie agreed; she certainly possessed a pretty voice.

"It's little wonder," Lizzie said, cuddling into Henry side. "Her father sang like an angel. Don't you remember?"

He surely did. How could Henry ever forget the night at the inn?

"What shall we do with the girl?" Lizzie whispered. "It'll be a shame to waste such a lovely voice. After all, we can afford to send her to the best singing teacher."

Lying on his back, staring at the ceiling, Henry allowed the soft voice to lull him.

"But who in the villages teaches singing?" he said. "It would mean her having to go away."

"There are plenty of good singing teachers in Bath," mused Lizzie. "She could board at the school."

"But she'd miss us terribly. And we'd miss her."

Leaving Susan's future singing career in the balance, Henry changed the subject.

"It's been six months since I last checked things up at the hall. How about you come with me. We could take Susan."

"I'd love to," Lizzie said.

"Then I'll get the dogcart ready as soon as we've had breakfast."

***

A knock on the cottage door sent the cat scurrying under the armchair.

"You silly puss!" Mary said, hurrying across the parlour.

"Good morning, Mr Soame," she said, seeing Luke standing on the doorstep. "You're bright and early!"

Luke smiled.

"I'm keen to get on with the day," he said. "But I've decided to meet Mr Waldon first, if that's all right. Is the cottage far?"

"About half a mile."

Mary collected her bonnet and shawl, from the clothes hook in the hall.

"Do you enjoy walking, Mr Soame?"

"Walking!" he laughed. "We'll ride."

"Me sir!" Mary gasped. "Ride! I've never ridden."

"Clarence is steady. All you need do is hold on tight, and no harm will befall you."

Therefore, with the church clock striking eight, and Mary hanging on for her life, she and Luke cantered away toward the river.

Beyond the church, and down the lane, Mary pointed to a gate in the hedge.

"Go down the track." she shouted in Luke's ear. "The cottage is at the end."

Reaching the gate, Luke leant forward, undoing the catch, and swinging it open.

"Leave it," Mary said. "They've no animals; only chickens."

However, Luke turned his horse, and shut the gate behind them.

"I was always taught to close the gate after me," he said, cheerfully.

Soon the cottages came into view, the white weatherboard freshly painted.

Dismounting, leaving Mary in the saddle, Luke walked up to the front doors.

"It's the one on the left!" Mary yelled.

He knocked three times, and then waited for it to open. But nothing happened.

"Perhaps they're out the back," Mary said.

"They've gone up to the hall," she heard a woman say behind her, and turning, saw Mrs Jesshope, a basket of newly trapped fish in her arms.

"Lizzie told me, before they left."

"What time was that, Mrs Jesshope?" Mary asked.

"You've only just missed them. Happen, they took the dogcart up the back lane. Otherwise, you would have seen them."

Thanking Mrs Jesshope, Mary and Luke trotted back up the track.

"Is the lady related to George Jesshope?" Luke asked, shutting the gate once more.

"She's his mother," said Mary, over Luke's shoulder. "Of course. You must have come across our George. How's he doing as butler?"

"Not bad. He takes his job very seriously."

"Oh well! Better than not, I suppose. There's the hall."

Thurlow Hall, standing majestically on high ground, was nothing like Luke had imagined, appearing larger, and even grander than John Baker's description, which secretly, Luke thought his friend had exaggerated. But seeing it now with his own eyes, Luke realised how much John's description had been understated.

Bathed in early morning sunshine, the house appeared serene, its masonry assuming a golden hue, similar to the stone Luke had seen in Bath. Although, nothing had prepared him for the spectacle. Not even Isabella's sketches in her diary, had been close to capturing the scale and grandeur of the six enormous columns, supporting the portico, plus the two wings, stretching east and west, above the elevated terraces.

"What do you think?" Mary said. "Lovely isn't it."

Luke could only nod.

"Carry on up the drive," she continued, "and up to the front door. Henry has a key. More than likely they're inside."

***

"It's stuck," said Henry. "I can't turn it."

Lizzie put her hand over his.

"Come on," she said. "Let's both try."

With their combined strength they succeeded in turning the key, and creaking loudly, the door slowly opened.

"What was that?" Lizzie shrieked, peering inside. "Something moved! It ran across the floor."

Henry laughed.

"A mouse I'd expect. The house is full of them."

"They shouldn't be inside," she continued. "They should be in the fields."

All the windows were shuttered and barred, so it was dark in the marble hall. On his last visit, however, Henry remembered leaving a candle, and a box of matches on a consul table. So, by the light from the open doorway, he crossed the marble floor, only to find them again, the candle having been greatly gnawed by little teeth.

"There we are!" he said, lighting it. "That's better. You can come in now. The mice have gone."

While Lizzie, Susan, and Jack waited below, Henry climbed the grand staircase to the gallery, where he opened the shutters of the oval window.

"Grandfather! Can we explore?" Susan asked, running up the stairs, while Lizzie followed. "I'd like to see grand-mamma's bedroom. She used to tell me how much she loved it."

"There's nothing in there now except the bed," Henry said. "And that's stripped, and covered with dust sheets."

They walked around the gallery, and down the west corridor.

"It was so pretty, Susan dear," Lizzie said. "Great velvet drapes, and golden tassels. Fancy cushions and bolsters scattered across it. Your grandmother spent a lot of time in her bedroom. Especially when she was ill. Her bedroom, and the music room were her favourite places."

Henry opened the bedroom door, and crossing the room, opened the window shutters.

"My word!" he cried, peering through the windowpane. "What on earth's Mary doing? Come and see."

Lizzie joined him at the window, looking around for Susan. But she was gone. No doubt, away chasing Jack.

Staring in amazement, Lizzie and Henry watched a horse and rider, galloping up the drive, Mary holding on to the rider for dear life.

"What's going on?" Lizzie said, as she and Henry hurried out of the bedroom, and along the corridor.

"Henry! Lizzie!" Mary shouted, as Luke helped her from the saddle. "You'll never guess what's happened."

Mary sprinted up the long flight of steps, through the great door, and into the marble hall, Luke running behind her.

"Whatever's the matter? What's happened?" Lizzie called from the gallery.

"Something amazing! That's what!"

Hurrying up the stairs, reaching the oval window, Mary finally stopped for breath.

"Calm down, Mary," Henry said. "You'll do yourself a mischief."

"I want you to meet this young man," gasped Mary, ignoring his concern. "You'll never believe what I'm going to tell you. His name is Soame. Luke Soame."

"But there are no more Soame's, Mary," Henry said. "Sir Humphrey was the last of the line."

"Ah!" Mary said. "That's what you think. And I thought so too. Until I heard his story."

She turned to Luke.

"May I?"

Luke smiled.

"Of course," he said.

"Her Ladyship knew about Luke all along. And you know why? Because he's her grandson."

Henry and Lizzie stared at Luke in astonishment.

"You mean he's Soame's son?" Lizzie said.

Mary was exultant.

"Yes. And guess where he's been all this while?"

Henry and Lizzie shook their heads.

"Australia! And Her Ladyship found him. Well, she sent someone to find him, to tell him who he really was. So here he is."

She made a great gesture of introduction.

"The Ninth Duke of Thurlow."

By their expressions, Mary could see Henry and Lizzie were not impressed.

"Now I know what you're thinking," she continued. "But you'd be wrong. Luke's a very nice young man. I've known him less than a day. But from what I'm able to tell, he's not at all like his father."

With another grand gesture, she let Luke speak for himself.

"Good morning, Mr and Mrs Waldon."

"Good morning," muttered Henry and Lizzie, the lack of enthusiasm plain to hear in their voices.

"I'm sure this has come as a shock to you both," Luke continued. "I must say, when I discovered the truth, a few months ago, I was equally astounded, although, my grandmother explained everything in a letter, which, on my arrival in England, I gave to Mr Perkins, Her Ladyship's solicitor. Of course, you're welcome to see it, should you feel the need. Everything is now official, the title deeds drawn up last week. It was Lady Soame's wish I take the dukedom, and live here at Thurlow Hall. I'm hoping this will not cause too many difficulties, Mr Waldon?"

"No," Henry said. "No difficulties sir. It's been my dream that one day the old place would live again. Although, I never imagined it would happen like this."

Luke smiled, glancing at Mary.

"Nevertheless, there's one more thing I think you should know."

he said. "It'll help clarify the circumstances of my birth. I'm sure the question of my maternal parent will be on your mind. Therefore, to avoid conjecture, as well as placing Miss Bennet in a compromising position, I'll tell you who she is. I'd appreciate it, however, if you keep the knowledge to yourselves, until such time I inform you otherwise."

Henry and Lizzie nodded, too mystified to speak.

"My mother is Miss Baker."

Lizzie gasped.

"Would you believe it, Lizzie!" Mary exclaimed. "Our dear sweet Emma."

"But of course," Lizzie said, turning to Henry. "It all fits. That time she went away, and then came back. Remember?"

Still in a state of complete surprise, Henry could only nod, although Mary was elated.

"I knew something was going on," she said. "I followed her to the temple. I heard Her Ladyship making plans to give Emma's baby away. Though I never thought it was Soame's."

Lizzie shook her head.

"How must Emma have felt," she said. "Giving the little thing away like that, Soame's son, or not."

Suddenly she realised the implication of her statement.

"I'm sorry, Mr Soame. I mean, Your Lordship. Please forgive me."

"Have no fear Mrs Waldon," said Luke. "I'm well aware of my father's failings, and I'm sure I've not heard the last of them. Except, there's one devilish deed for which I wish to make amends."

Henry frowned.

"What could that be, sir?"

Luke took a deep breath.

"You have a son, have you not, Mr Waldon."

"I do sir. John James. He lives in Bath."

"Begging your pardon, Mr Waldon, but I believe you have another son."

"We did sir. But he was lost."

"Lost?"

Henry put his arm around Lizzie.

"Yes sir. Lost to us. His mother, father, brother, and sisters."

"Did he die?"

Henry could hardly string words together, so raw had his emotions become over the subsequent years since James' arrest and transportation.

"No sir," he said slowly. "He was taken from us; and we never saw him again."

By making them unearth bitter memories of long ago, Luke could see the anguish he was causing.

"Mr and Mrs Waldon," he said. "In Australia I was a farmer. As such, it was my entitlement to have assigned convict labour on my land, to assist the everyday working of the property. Ten years ago, I went to Sydney to collect such labour, and was directed to a ship; the Isabella as I recall, from which I took off two convicts."

As they looked at Luke, he could see the anguished expression Lizzie, Mary and Henry wore.

"They were only lads," Luke continued. "Perhaps eighteen or nineteen. My age, at the time. One was George Parry. Well, I think it was Parry. But the other man's name, I'll never fail to recall, as it was quite unusual. It was James Baker Waldon."

With the echo of Luke's voice hovering in the air around them, Henry, Lizzie, and Mary stood dumbfounded.

"Oh sir!" pleaded Lizzie. "Please don't toy with us. Tell us the truth. If you know what became of him, please don't spare us. We've lived in torture since he was taken. But we have to know."

Henry put an arm around Lizzie, and held her close.

"Yes, Mr Soame," he said. "Do you know what happened to him?"

Luke laughed.

"I certainly do. The last I saw of him, which was several months ago, he was fit and well. He had a girl who loved him. Two boys doting on him. Money in his pocket, and was off to make his fortune."

Lizzie clapped her hands, tears of joy running down her face, while Henry beamed with smiles.

"You don't know how happy you've made us," he said, rushing forward and clasping Luke's hand. "His mother and I never speak of him, convinced he was dead."

"Dead! " Luke exclaimed. "James Baker Waldon! No fear. It'll take a lot to finish off old James. He's a man in a million. He and I shared many adventures."

"And you say he's married." Lizzie said through her tears.

"Not quite. Nevertheless, if I know his sweetheart, Cathy, it shouldn't be too long."

"But the boys? You said he has boys."

"They're not James'," explained Luke. "They're her sons. But if I know James, one will be on the way by now for sure."

Everyone laughed, their happiness spilling over, the sound of joy filling the marble hall for the first time in many years.

"But how did Her Ladyship find you?" asked Mary. "You told me she sent someone to Australia."

"It was John Baker, wasn't it Mr Soame," Henry said quietly.

"It was, Mr Waldon."

"Of course," Henry continued. "That's why Her Ladyship sent for him, just before she died. I always thought it odd. Then John saying he was going to the colonies to search for my son. He was looking for you, wasn't he?"

"Indeed he was, Mr Waldon. Lady Soame knew my name. She'd corresponded with my adopted mother and father. She knew I'd been taken to Australia."

Lizzie suddenly spoke.

"Her Ladyship could trust John. He was strong and reliable. The best man for the job."

"But where is he?" Henry asked. "He came back with you, of course. Or perhaps he stayed in Bath, with his sister?"

Being unable to answer, the expression on Luke's face told them everything.

Lizzie gasped.

"I don't believe it, Mr Soame!" she said. "This is a dream. One moment you give us the best news we could ever hear, that our long lost son is alive, and the next you tell us our dearest friend is dead.

Please, Mr Soame, say it isn't true."

"I'm sorry, Mrs Waldon," said Luke. "I wish it wasn't so. He was a dear friend to me also, even more than you could imagine. If it's any consolation, John died in your son's arms. His last words were to tell you he loved you both."

Lizzie wept, burying her head in Henry's shoulder.

"But Mr Soame," Henry said. "How did it happen? John was a tower of a man. How could he possibly have died?"

Luke drew Henry aside, speaking quietly.

"I'm sorry, Mr Waldon," he said. "I feel I should tell you the circumstances of his death at a later date."

"Very well," Henry said. "Do the Bakers know?"

Luke shook his head.

"Emma does. But I've still to break the news to his mother and father."

"They'll be devastated. He was their only son. Would you prefer me to be there when you do?"

"Yes sir. Thank you. That's very kind. I'd be a stranger to them. You being John's greatest friend, having you with me, will be a help."

A barking dog drew their attention to the window, only to see Jack the spaniel, scampering down the steps, Susan chasing him.

"She's my son's daughter, Mr Soame," said Henry.

"Really!" Luke said. "Then John James has children?"

"Not at all. She's James' daughter, Susan. He and his sweetheart Alice had a child. Your grandmother, Lady Soame, adopted her."

Now it was Luke's turn to be amazed.

"She's James' little girl!" he exclaimed. "I remember Emma mentioning Susan. But hadn't put two and two together. How incredible!"

"Yes sir isn't it. Now Susan's your ward, and she'll be next in line to the title."

Luke was staggered. Everything was finishing up so strangely. Here he was, the adopted son of a reverend and his wife, discovering he is the son of a duke, and inheriting the title. Then there is this little girl, the daughter of a scullery maid, and an ironmonger's apprentice, who would eventually inherit everything.

What a pleasing conclusion it was to be sure. Lady Edwina would have adored every minute. Then a thought struck Luke. Had it been her intention that Susan and he would marry? He would need to wait until she came of age, and he would be over forty by then. Was this the reason his grandmother brought about both these extraordinary incidents?

Surely not. Lady Soame had no power bringing about Susan's conception. Nonetheless, she did adopt her, and was aware of Luke's existence. It was too fanciful to imagine.

Except Luke had no wish to marry. He was fully aware of where his emotions lay, and they were not with any woman. He would live his life discreetly, honestly and truthfully, as his grandmother would have wished, hoping to share it with his new companion.

Whether the end was near or far, he would die one day, and if Susan still lived, she would inherit Thurlow. The thought made him happy, as he realised James Baker Waldon, the once wrongly accused convict, would one day become the father of a duchess.

Shaking his head as the idea took hold in his mind, Luke smiled, Henry taking note of his expression.

"Yes sir," he said. "Extraordinary isn't it. What would my son say if he knew his daughter was so fortunate?"

"I think he already knows, Mr Waldon," said Luke. I'm sure John would have told him."

Once Lizzie regained her composure, Mary helped her down the stairs.

"What are your intentions, sir?" Henry asked, as they followed.

"To live here, Mr Waldon, if I may?" answered Luke. "Her Ladyship said in her letter that she wished to see the heart return to her old home, and that's what I propose to do."

The subsequent weeks passed by, as Thurlow Hall began to look its old self again. Henry hired young men from the village, to help unpack the cellar, directing them, as they returned the furniture, carpets, curtains, pictures, and ornaments to the positions they previously occupied, surprising himself as to how much he remembered. Nevertheless, if he met with difficulties, Lizzie and

Mary were always on hand to jog his memory.

Luke left his lodging at the Cock Inn, as soon as the house was habitable; the Waldon's, subsequently, shutting up the cottage beside the river, taking residence in rooms at the top of Thurlow Hall, Luke intending the parents of his friend James, and the grandparents of his ward, should have the most comfortable life possible.

Naturally, a house the size of Thurlow Hall was unable to run itself, and so Luke placed an announcement in the Haverhill, Bury and Cambridge newspapers, advertising for staff, Henry answering the written applications, interviewing prospective candidates.

Therefore, once again, the house was adequately staffed, from the butler, Mr Talbot, and cook, Mrs Webb, to parlour maid, Eliza Halls, scullery maid, Eliza Ward, and footman, coincidently, Steven Ives, who assured Henry that he was no relation of Mr Ives, the coachman. Therefore, in just a month, everything was running as smooth as clockwork.

***

"Luke! You know my real daddy, don't you?"

He and Susan were sitting in the library one evening, a while later, enjoying a quiet moment after supper.

Finally, now the house was in order, Luke was able to sit and write a letter to Denby. Nevertheless, Susan's question took him by surprise, causing him to put down his quill.

"What's he like?" she asked, looking up from her book.

Luke relaxed into his chair.

"He's a fine man," he said. "Tall and strong. He was my blacksmith."

"But why did he go away?"

Susan's blue eyes entreated Luke to tell her the truth. He could see that plainly, but for a moment, he hesitated, wondering what to say. Should he tell her? After all, his father created the dreadful state of affairs in the first place.

"Your grandfather hasn't told you?" Luke said.

"Whenever I ask," Susan said, staring at Luke intensely, "he seems to change the subject."

"Then perhaps I should tell you."

"Please Luke. I'll understand. I'm a big girl you know."

"Well, before you were born," Luke began. "Your father lived at Thurlow Hall. He was a footman to your grandmother. But she grew very sick, and decided to close the house and move to Bath."

"Where I was born."

"That's right. Your grandmother had a son. Unfortunately, he was not a good man, and wished harm on your grandfather. The only way this wicked man could take his vengeance, was to condemn James, your father, to a life of imprisonment and servitude, in a country far away."

"But how did the nasty man do it?"

"By making it appear your father stole a handkerchief. Just a silly handkerchief."

Engrossed in the story, Luke and Susan failed to see Henry standing in the doorway.

"Only a handkerchief," Susan said, incredulously.

"I know," Luke answered. "But it was enough to take him away from everyone he loved. Including your mother."

Luke saw Susan frown suddenly.

"But if he was far away," she said, "how then did I come to be born?"

Henry had silently opened the library door, and was looking into the room. As he listened, he smiled. At last, Susan would know the truth. And seeing the girls face, he realised she was quite old enough to begin to understand.

"Your father and mother loved each other very much," Luke continued. "So you happened along, only weeks before he went away. Then you were born the next Christmas, by which time your mother was all on her own."

"And she died."

"Yes."

Susan's eyes were wide as she listened, Luke noticing they were blue as cornflowers.

"So what happened to daddy?"

"He was taken to Australia, in a big ship, along with lots of other men. When he arrived, I chose him to work on my farm."

Susan smiled, her face shining in the lamplight.

"With all the sheep?" she said.

"Yes. Although he was never a shepherd. He was my blacksmith, because he was strong. He and I were great friends, and shared many adventures. We even went to war with the natives. Remind me to tell you the story one day."

Suddenly, Susan's smile vanished, a frown marring her happiness.

"Do you think he'll ever come home?" she asked.

"Maybe," Luke said, without hesitation.

"But that's what grandfather always says."

"Yes Susan," Luke said. "I really believe he will. My friend John Baker told him about you, and he loves his family. He has a new sweetheart. Her name's Cathy, and she has two boys, William and Richard. They may even be your half brothers, by now. Don't be surprised, Susan, if one day we see them standing on our doorstep."

Hearing Susan laugh, Henry's heart filled with joy.

This man, in telling his granddaughter the truth, something Henry had wanted to do for so long, was the son of Sir Humphrey Soame. But unlike his malevolent father, Luke held the same qualities of kindness and purity of heart, Henry's mistress, Lady Soame, had possessed, when she was alive. Therefore, from that moment, Henry became Luke's faithful servant, if not in body, then in soul.

"Sir," Henry said, at the same time startling Luke and Susan. "I'm sorry to interrupt."

Luke suddenly felt anxious, concerned he may have been wrong in telling the girl. However, the smile on Henry's face reassured him.

"May I light the lamp, sir?" continued Henry. "It was always my duty in the old days. It wouldn't seem right to see anyone else do it?"

"Of course, Henry."

"May I go too, Luke?" Susan said, jumping up. "I can light the candles."

"Certainly," Luke said, laughing. "Off you go, both of you."

As they closed the library door, Luke finished writing, and then slowly signed, and sealed his letter to Denby.

453

Sitting at her sewing table, her work illuminated by a circle of lamplight, Mary looked up and gazed out of the window. It was reassuring, she thought, to see the lit windows of Thurlow Hall, shining out the darkness, like an oriental jewel. All of a sudden, however, another light, far brighter than the rest, took its place in the firmament, sending forth a beam, like a beacon into the night, everyone seeing it as a symbol that everything was as it should be, and would be for all eternity.

Epilogue

From the back of his horse, Elliot peered into the mangroves.

Over the past weeks, the water had subsided, revealing the carnage the floods had caused. Corpses of dead sheep and cattle strewn everywhere, flies being the biggest nuisance, as they gorged on the rotting flesh. Was there any point in looking for survivors, Elliot wondered?

By now, Elliot was accustomed to seeing bloated animals entangled in the roots and branches, but suddenly this discovery caused him to search more closely. These bones he saw were different. White, bleached bones; stripped clean of hair, skin, organ, and muscle.

Riding as close as he dared, dismounting, and tethering his horse to a branch, Elliot began to duck and weave his way through the tangle of roots, and tree trunks.

The closer Elliot came, the more the skeleton appeared odd to him. The ribcage was smaller than a cow, but larger than a sheep. The limb bones longer than a sheep, although shorter than a cow. It was then he saw it, lying half-submerged in the caked mud. A human skull, the eye sockets empty, the place where the mouth had been a yawning jawbone, the yellow teeth fixed in a ghastly grimace.

So twisted and dry was the skeleton, lying amongst the stark arid roots, it was barely held together by the last sinews of its joints, long turned to leather by the searing sun.

Suddenly something flashing in the harsh light, caught Elliot's eye, since trapped inside the encircling ribcage, hung a gold pocket watch and chain. Curiosity overwhelming him, Elliot struggled on, until he was beside the remains, and summoning the courage, reached inside the ribs, pulling the watch, freeing the chain entangled in the sternum.

The brightness almost blinding him, Elliot studied his find. The watch was solid gold, and engraved with a laurel leaf pattern, forming a continual garland around the back and front. Putting his thumbnail under the lid, Elliot flicked it open.

The hands had stopped at a quarter past three, nevertheless, what he saw inside the lid, intrigued him more, Elliot reading what was engraved there.

'To my son, Luke William Reddall, on reaching twenty. Your loving father, Thomas Reddall, Clergyman, Campbelltown, sixth April, Eighteen Hundred and Thirty Two'.

"Mr Reddall!" Elliot whispered. "Is this you? We've been looking for you for months. You just disappeared one day. You and Mr Waldon. It's so long ago now, we gave up searching. Mr Poney always said you were dead. He reckoned you would never have stayed away from the farm, unless you were."

Elliot gazed through the tangle of dead trees.

"Is Mr Waldon here too?"

Maybe they drowned together, Elliot thought.

He could see nothing, however, only the gruesome twisted trunks of the mangroves.

"But what will I do with you, Mr Reddall? I can't leave you here?"

Elliot suddenly remembered the sack he carried in his saddlebag, in case he found a lamb. It was easier to put a lamb in a sack, and carry it home, than hold it in his arms all the way.

"That's what I'll do, Mr Reddall," he said. "I'll put you in the sack. I hope you don't mind."

Reaching out, taking hold of the shoulder blades, Elliot lifted the bones clear of the roots, the leathery sinews holding well, enabling him to pick up the entire skeleton, the weight surprising him, being light enough to carry under one arm.

Once back at his horse, Elliot laid the bones on the ground, and delving inside the saddlebag, retrieved the sack. But as he fed the feet and legs inside, he realised it would be impossible to insert the whole body without bending it.

"I'm sorry, Mr Reddall," he said, staring at the lifeless skull. "I hope this isn't going to hurt."

Prising the lower leg bones and the feet against the thick single femur bones, Elliot bent the legs double, and thus was able to put half the skeleton inside. Then, pulling the remaining sack up over the arm bones, the ribcage and shoulders, he finally, covered the bleached dome of the skull. Once all was firmly tucked away, Elliot tied the neck with twine, laying the sack across his horse' withers.

"Well at least we've found you." Elliot said. "Now we can relax."

He said this with a sense of relief, because, once it seemed clear Mr Reddall was dead, he and Poney decided to buy Durra Durra. But Elliot worried a day might come when Luke might return to claim it. Now he knew that day would never happen.

Elliot found the skeleton beside the Hume River, and half a day's ride to Durra Durra, consequently, night was falling when he reached the yard.

Bill Poney must have heard him arrive, as he was waiting on the veranda.

"Mr Poney!" Elliot shouted, climbing off his horse. "I've found him!"

"Who?" Bill Poney asked, staring into the darkness.

"Mr Reddall."

Poney spat a chore of tobacco into the dust.

"Where?"

"Beside the river; in the swamps. Dead of course."

"I told you. I said someone would find him someplace."

Elliot walked into the light from the house, a million crickets sounding from the grass in the paddocks around him.

"His bones are all that's left," he said. "They're in the sack."

"Then how do we know it's him?"

"Well it's lucky really," chuckled Elliot. "If it hadn't been hanging inside his ribs, the Currawongs would have made off with it long ago."

Elliot took the watch from his pocket.

"It's inscribed."

"Waldon anywhere?" Poney asked.

"No."

"Then Whitton must have murdered them both. The bastard."

Elliot joined Bill Poney on the veranda, taking out his tobacco pouch.

"It's odd we've not seen hide nor hair of Whitton either," he said, beginning to fill his pipe.

"Laying low I shouldn't wonder. He's four murders on his head now."

"What shall we do with Mr Reddall?" Elliot asked. "Shouldn't we bury him with his friend, Mr Baker?"

"I think he'd want to be with his family." Poney said. "Would you like a ride to Campbelltown, Elliot?"

"I'm not crazy about the idea," answered Elliot. "But I suppose I must."

Therefore, the following morning Elliot prepared for the long ride north.

Unfortunately, there was little else in which to put the bones, so he decided it was best they remained inside the sack, and by midday, he was ready for the journey.

"When you get there, old Mr Hurley will be the man to see," Poney said, as Elliot mounted his horse. "He was close to Luke and the family. He'll know what to do."

As a result, six days later Elliot was back in Campbelltown, at The Kings Head, Patrick Hurley's hotel, and the place where Elliot's adventure had begun, four years earlier.

Mr Hurley, aware of Luke's disappearance, reverently carried the sack and its contents to Mr Owen, the town undertaker, who laid the bones in a lead lined, cedar coffin, with solid brass handles, paid for by Mr Hurley. Then, the following day, a shining black hearse, pulled by two black horses, ostrich plumes fluttering from their bridles, conveyed the coffin and remains, on their final journey to St Peter's

Churchyard.

While the sexton, and gravedigger opened the Reddall family vault, rain drizzling from a steely sky, the service was said over the coffin. The last words having been spoken, the two men carried the coffin down the steps, laying it on a shelf, below the one containing Julia Reddall, and opposite her mother, Isabella and father, Thomas.

Once more, the stone slab was laid over the steps, and with the last sod of earth piled upon it, the vault was plunged yet again into the dark endless night of infinity.

THE END

Find out more

VISIT J.A.Wells Author Website

LIKE J.A.Wells on Facebook

FOLLOW @jawells6661 on Twitter

FOLLOW john.wells6661 on Instagram

As an independent author, I rely on the generosity of my readers. If you enjoyed this story, please consider placing a comment on your favourite social media site. Thank you, *J.A. Wells*

Books by J.A. Wells

Thurlow
Book One of The Durra Durra Trilogy

Mutt Mutt Billy
Book Two of The Durra Durra Trilogy

Durra Durra
Book Three of The Durra Durra Trilogy

Books by J.A. Wells
The Merry Millionaire
Book One of The Merry Millionaire Duology
Entering into the spirit of the Jazz Age with gay abandon;
a story based on true events

The Thirties, a decade of decadence and depression, ending in war. This hardly has an effect on Ron and Mervyn, our intrepid pleasure seekers. Disregarding the rumblings of war in Europe, and dancing to a dying tune, they join the waning fast-set, cruising the Norwegian fjords on luxury ocean liners and sailing up the Nile on serene feluccas.

Explore the bygone age of first class sea travel and luxury oriental hotels, summer on the glaciers, and the heat of Cairo's social season: all seen through the eyes of Ron and Mervyn, the gayest pair of lotus-eaters you will ever encounter.

J.A.Wells has succeeded in painting a dense, yet frivolous view, of a time now lost to the journals of debutants and dowager duchesses. In the first of his duology, J.A.Wells uses his rich imagination, creating a colourful cast of living and breathing characters.

We will wonder what may become of the pairing of Ron and Mervyn, poles apart in age and class, yet similar in inclination.

BUY AT AMAZON

Books by J.A. Wells
Pomp and Circumstance
Book Two of The Merry Millionaire Duology
Further adventures with The Merry Millionaire
Entering into the spirit of the Jazz Age with gay abandon;
a story based on true events

In this second book of his duology, J.A.Wells utilises his finely tuned sense of period and historical fact to transport us to a world of caleches, feluccas, mummies and mosques, through which his masterfully drawn characters cavort with gay abandon, caring little for what might be around the corner and naively ignorant of the catastrophe which would end a decade of decadence and depression.

Played against a backdrop of spy-ridden Egypt, pre war England, abdicating Kings and unexpected coronations, we continue to share further travel adventures with our intrepid explorers, Ron and Mervyn, as they discover far more than simply the mysteries of the orient.

After a venturesome jaunt up the Nile, back in Cairo we find Ron and Mervyn at Shepheard's Hotel, where the fascinating Lee Miller has invaded the Long Bar. A flamboyant party at Baron Empain's Palais Hindou serves to whet their appetites for the supernatural. Then joining the luxury ship that will take them home, they rub shoulders with Egyptian royalty, learning more than they should regarding the secrets of the palace. Using his newly found entrepreneurial skills, Ron organises an on board concert, Mervyn's angelic voice and good looks stealing the show. Ghosts are on the agenda once more at an overnight stay at London's Great Western Hotel.

What may become of the pairing of Ron and Mervyn, poles apart in age and class, yet similar in inclination?

BUY AT AMAZON

Printed in Great Britain
by Amazon